The HOSPITAL at the END of the WORLD

ALSO BY JUSTIN C. KEY

The World Wasn't Ready for You

The HOSPITAL at the END of the WORLD

A Novel

Justin C. Key

HARPER
An Imprint of HarperCollinsPublishers

hc.com

FIRST EDITION

Library of Congress Cataloging-in-Publication Data
Names: Key, Justin C. author
Title: The hospital at the end of the world : a novel / Justin C. Key.
Description: New York : Harper, 2026.
Identifiers: LCCN 2025027597 | ISBN 9780063290488 hardcover | ISBN 9780063290471 trade paperback | ISBN 9780063290563 ebook
Subjects: LCGFT: Novels | Science fiction
Classification: LCC PS3611.E96725 H67 2026 | DDC 813/.6—dc23/eng/20250609
LC record available at https://lccn.loc.gov/2025027597

ISBN 978-0-06-329048-8

Printed in the United States of America

25 26 27 28 29 LBC 5 4 3 2 1

To Johanna, my forever-love . . .

SUMMER

"I swear by Apollo Healer, by Asclepius, by Hygieia, by Panacea, and by all the gods and goddesses, making them my witnesses, that I will carry out, according to my ability and judgment, this Oath and this indenture . . ."

One

DECISION DAY

The narrow overhang jutting out from the New York City apartment building did little to protect from the downpour. Pok's back pressed against hard brick as he scanned the gray skies, his augmented reality glasses made pedestrian by the weather. The whir of an ambulance rose and dissipated, leaving behind the hum of rolling traffic. Directly above him, solid lines of rain ran from the air-conditioning unit hanging from their third-story window and cascaded off the fire escape. *Where is it?* The decision drone should have arrived ten minutes ago.

After acquiring twelve of the country's top medical institutions, the Shepherd Organization made clear their confidence in their state-of-the-art AI-centered medical curriculum by waiting until all other schools had sent out decisions before deploying theirs. It was a ballsy move. The stunt had paid off. According to the message boards, hardly anyone had accepted offers from non-shepherd schools even though most semesters started within the next month. Everyone was waiting on "The Prestigious Twelve."

"Decision day?" Skip James called above the rain and traffic as he stepped out of the small shop directly under Pok's apartment. The longtime owner of Park Avenue Market, one of the last human-staffed brick-and-mortar stores in Manhattan, chucked two black bags into the garbage. Rainwater fell in sheets from the lid. "It's all over my feed!"

"They're late," Pok said.

"Don't catch a cold, kid."

You can't catch a cold from the rain, Pok thought. He was about to check the message boards when a soft, persistent buzzing drew his attention. He stepped out from under the ledge, instantly drenched, a touch of metal on his tongue. The buzzing grew, steady and direct, and the drone emerged from between city buildings, cut through the rain, and stopped inches from Pok. The drone's indicator blinked red; Pok raised his AR glasses and readily offered his irises for scanning. Verification done, its hatch opened and a silver case dropped on a string.

Pok examined his delivery. The metal was warm. The Shepherd Organization's insignia—a shepherd holding a stiffened snake as a staff—was engraved above the fresh stamp: *Applicant Pok Morning. Verified at 12:14 p.m.* Inside, his unique quick-response code.

Kris Boles popped onto Pok's glass display right as the decision page loaded. His friend's temperament was spirited. His environment was dry. Yellow bordered his display.

"Where'd you get in?" he said.

"I haven't checked. You got in?"

"What do you mean you haven't checked? How could you not check?"

"It's still loading." *Come on, come on.* Every mentor and counselor had assured he'd have beautifully tough decisions to make at the end of this application cycle. Pok, who had applied to all twelve, had his heart set on the Shepherd School of Medicine at MacArthur Hospital, just up the street from his and his father's apartment, where East Harlem met the Upper East Side. Outwardly unimpressive, the interior was intricately designed. The medical school was built atop the busy, three-tier hospital that served all five boroughs. Its website proudly proclaimed its future doctors sat upon the figurative shoulders of the medicine they studied. That was his dream school.

Pok swiped clear his glass; new drops immediately streaked across the silicon display.

Logos for twelve of the country's top medical schools—all now rebranded with the Shepherd Organization's crest—popped onto the page. Adrenaline navigated open veins. Red Xs lined the margins. Beside all twelve schools. Every single one.

"I didn't get in." Speaking the words made them real.

"What?" Kris said.

"I didn't get in. Anywhere. This is bullshit."

They were both speechless. A digital delivery scooter honked for Pok to move. It knocked the back of his knee. He could have fallen face down onto the flooding sidewalk, mouth filling with gritty rainwater, and he wouldn't have cared. This was *bullshit.*

"What about that one school?" Kris said. "Gaylen or something? Down south?"

"Hippocrates." Under his father's insistence, he'd applied to the Louisiana-based anti-AI school as a "safety," one he'd never expected to consider. They had fallen far off of *TIME* magazine's yearly top medical school rankings after essentially eliminating the latest technology from their curriculum. Just the thought of moving to Louisiana—the most backward state in the country—twisted Pok's gut. "I don't understand. How many did you get into?"

"I don't think—"

"How many?"

"Eight."

Eight? The New York air somehow grew hotter; Pok could visualize the rain sizzling off his skin. He'd received perfect marks. He'd checked all the boxes. His own father was a physician who'd given fifteen years of his life to MacArthur Hospital. And eight of the Prestigious Twelve wanted Kris and *none* wanted Pok? He knew Kris's application. Hell, he'd helped with the essays. There was no way Kris would be picked over him. No way. And eight times? No fucking way.

Pok rounded his building's corner, head down, embarrassment pounding at his ears and rain pelting the nape of his neck. He unlocked his apartment door remotely as he took the stairs two at a time—the elevator was broken again—and resented the smell of the city's concrete summer.

"It's got to be a glitch or something," Kris said. "Somebody messed up. You're the smartest kid I know."

The Shepherd Organization's algorithms didn't make mistakes. Not like this. But Kris inadvertently sparked an idea that bloomed into an insatiable urge.

Pok squinted against his bedroom's harsh, swinging light. The building—which housed MacArthur's many medical trainees, physicians, and personnel—offered to install ones that adjusted to pupil dilation. His father, old-fashioned but well-meaning, had refused. Pok cleared a spot on his bed, found his virtual reality gaming headset, and booted up *Impact*, an open-world, massively online multiplayer game about teamwork and survival.

"I'm coming over," Kris said.

"Don't." Pok took a moment to finger-comb out his shoulder-length locs; water dripped onto his thighs and the edge of his bed.

"What are you up to?"

"Troubleshooting," Pok said.

"Don't do anything stupid."

"You know me. I'll catch you later. And congratulations."

Pok took off his glass and replaced it with his gaming set. His New York apartment fell away and *Impact* took hold. His temples hummed with adrenaline as he created a new profile and avatar and started anew as a lone nomad. He summoned a hovercraft and directed it away from active play, full speed.

Impact advertised an endless world. It generated new maps—including towns, resources, and histories—whenever a player ventured into an uncharted area. When Pok was confident about the distance between him and any other online players, he ejected himself from the hovercraft, ran into the closest house—still rendering itself in real time—opened the first closet, and jumped inside. His avatar fell into darkness.

Pok counted to three and activated his jet pack. Below him, disc-shaped platforms popped up in domino effect, one under the next, like giant floating stairs leading down an endless abyss. Each had its own unique landscape, from lush countryside to suburban neighborhoods to downtown districts replete with skyscrapers.

He descended to a metropolis platform several levels down, landed on the tallest building, and found its control room. He went straight to the central kiosk, brought up its command line interface, and inserted his custom string of code. A door appeared and slid open. The bright room contrasted with the building's otherwise dim, dark interior. Rows and rows of stacked computer screens aspired toward infinity.

The Underground Web. A hacker's portal to wherever they dared venture. Years ago, during AI's great technological boom, a revolutionary driverless car company ventured into neuro-enhancing brain implants. Through the Underground, a hacker caused a violent psychosis in dozens of early adopters and triggered multiple concurrent killing sprees that left more than a hundred dead across five states. And because many of the neuro-hacked were social media influencers, the world watched much of it live. All tech companies subsequently banned the Underground, sucking it dry. Until the Shepherd Organization. It embraced and revitalized it, boldly proclaiming their system open to anyone with altruistic intentions. Any nefarious acts, however, would be immediately thwarted by powerful algorithms, leaving the perpetrator technologically exposed to TSO and buried in litigation.

None of which Pok had an appetite for. He stayed pedestrian with his hacking, mainly using it to access betas of in-production games. Venturing into the Prestigious Twelve's applicant database would be closer to the shepherd sun than he had ever dared to fly.

Find the application, see what in the hell went wrong, and get out.

Pok stepped inside and picked a random aisle. Identical screens ran various lines of code. One unit stood separate from the rest. An old-school computer connected to a physical keyboard sat atop a table.

Pok paused the scrolling code with the tap of a key. A new line with a blinking cursor appeared. He typed: *The Shepherd Schools of Medicine, Admissions.* The screen flickered, scrolled more code, and soon his own face smiled out at him.

Unease touched his belly. Exploring the Underground was like peeling back human flesh to see the inner biology at work. Only a skilled surgeon could hope to tamper without disastrous results. This was reckless; he should have stopped there.

But *every single* medical school? Pok had to know why. He opened his file.

"What the hell?"

The application had his name, date of birth, and unique applicant ID. Beyond that, nothing else was his. While his transcript was perfect, the one submitted had a subpar GPA with multiple withdrawn classes. The extracurriculars were without theme or merit. Pok had numerous peer-reviewed, first-author publications; here, the "Research" section was blank. This wasn't the application he'd turned in. Not at all.

Why? How? Important questions, but secondary. He had to fix it. From his personal files, Pok queued for upload his true application, complete with his encrypted genome, and hesitated. Months ago, when initially submitting, he'd grappled with the same ingrained apprehension. His father had diligently waived genome analysis at every turn of Pok's childhood and adolescence. Antidiscrimination laws made it illegal to require DNA in applications—except in select fields like medicine. Once TSO had his genome, there was no reversing it.

Pok completed the transfer. This done, he brought up the activity log, scrolled past the various review stages, and found his initial submission time stamp. *Shit.* "Upload Incomplete." He'd never received that error. He quickly saw why: only minutes later was another, completed transfer, initiated by user CryingRabbits218. Not an error: a fake. Pok combed his memory for past rivals he'd hacked, gaming foes he'd humiliated. This could be the perfect revenge prank. The handle, however, didn't ring a bell.

The screen flashed red. The hue leaked out to the surrounding room.

Pok groaned. He'd programmed a warning system into his hacking interface. The shepherds were investigating his activity; he needed to abort before he had deeper problems than an anonymous online enemy. Pok moved quickly but meticulously. Source or not, he'd just hacked into a subset of TSO. He needed to cover his tracks.

Pok backed out of the Underground and spent the next hour scouring the newly rendered area to seek out and kill any rogue NPCs. Each represented an errant line of code that, if left unneutralized, could infect his entire system. He then deployed a kill code to eradicate this particular door to the Underground and turned off his console.

His senses came back to the real world. The patter of rain on his window. The whir of the hallway air conditioner. The lingering hint of metal on his tongue. Beside him, his glass still showed the decision page. He put it on and refreshed. As if the algorithms would magically reprocess, see what an exceptional candidate he was, and immediately offer a spot. Still rejected. Still unanimous.

Red marks, all the way down.

Two

THE PATIENT

Pok found his father washing his hands in the kitchen sink. Phelando was dressed for work: wrinkled khaki slacks and a light blue button-down loose over his belt. His gray-streaked locs were neatly wrapped, and his black pure-optics spectacles were pushed up on his nose. Black diamond studs glittered from his ears.

"Son," Phelando said. "I didn't know you were home."

"Ditto," Pok said.

Phelando dried his hands, hung up the towel, and looked his son up and down. "You're soaked. What's going on?"

How to tell his father that all his hard work had been for nothing? Dwelling on the outcome wouldn't change anything—he needed to figure out how and why someone had changed his application—but suddenly the words wouldn't come.

The doorbell chimed. Phelando checked the time, unrolled his sleeves to cover his sinus rhythm forearm tattoo, and tucked in his shirt. "Come see this patient with me. Tell me what you notice. Humor an old man. Afterward, we'll talk?"

A short woman with long, thick braids and an ankle-length winter coat stepped into their apartment. Layered atop apparent angst was a cordial, hopeful smile. She moved with a deliberate silence. Phelando took her lead.

Two years ago, he'd started his own part-time private practice as an addendum to his clinical work at MacArthur. Considered a "holistic practitioner," Phelando worked nearly exclusively without AI input. His clientele had grown significantly since its inception. His patients consistently surprised Pok in their narrow view of technology. The paranoia. The resistance to clear clinical judgment. The gross misunderstanding. The assumption, for example, that they could somehow "hide" from shepherd data mining.

No one could hide. Not even experienced hackers.

They made their way past the living room, down the hall, and to his father's examination room. *Tell me what you notice.* The woman's hair was full and healthy, shaved in a stylish fade on one side. Her coat housed a full figure. Such long, thick dress at the height of summer. Sunglasses, despite the poorly lit hallway. What was she hiding?

Phelando flicked on the two miniature EMP boxes flanking his office doorway. Pok had made the disruptors out of old radio parts to give Phelando's patients "privacy." At best, it was a technological placebo.

"Device-free zone," Phelando said once they were all inside. "You can speak freely."

Phelando helped her out of her coat. Sweat marked her armpits. She was very pregnant.

"Pok, meet Florence. Florence, this is my son and he's also a future medical student." Pok winced at the introduction. "Can he join us?"

"Of course. That's wonderful. Following in his dad's footsteps. You must be proud."

Florence slid backward into the exam chair, breathed deep, and lifted her shirt just enough to give air to her sweat-slicked stomach. She rubbed it with a mother's tenderness. "It's okay, Baby Girl. We can both breathe."

"What is it now?" Phelando said. "Thirty-five, thirty-six weeks?"

"Thirty-seven," Florence said. She closed her eyes, restful calm edging out her angst. "And three days."

"Due any day now. How are you?"

Florence continued to rub her belly. "Baby Girl is doing well. She kicks a lot and likes cuddling up on this side."

"That's wonderful. How are *you*?"

She half laughed. "Nervous. Wondering if Baby Girl is positioning right."

"Let's have a look." Phelando rolled a stand over with an old-style computer, keyboard, and a corded probe. He turned the monitor on, squeezed blue gel from a bottle onto Florence's exposed stomach, and spread it with the probe, repositioning the cord as it spiraled onto itself. Then he pressed perpendicular to the base of her belly. On the display, various shades of gray rolled in nonspecific lines. "There we go."

Pok edged closer. Shepherd apps created fully rendered fetal models starting at four weeks gestation, making ultrasounds like this one essentially obsolete. Phelando steadied the probe. A crude slice of the baby's head floated onto the screen.

"There's my Baby Girl," Florence said.

"She's active today." Phelando found her heartbeat. He went through Baby Girl's anatomy, pointing out the arms, legs, feet, cross section of the head, spine, and various organs. Using the keyboard's space bar as a marker, he measured each with the probe.

Phelando put the ultrasound aside, changed out his gloves, and pressed against the different sides of her belly. "Can my son feel?"

"Of course."

Pok admired his father. He was, after all, the original reason Pok wanted to become a doctor. His calm, empathetic confidence set patients at ease in a way no AI system could. But the more Pok learned about the advancements in medicine and the wonders of shepherd AI, the more he saw his father's humanistic approach for what it was: grossly inefficient. In the time it had taken Florence to remove her coat, the shepherd programming would have mapped Baby Girl's anatomy, biomarkers, brain activity, and gestational age and analyzed it against all of the mother's metrics to pinpoint the exact area of focus. The hospital saw it, too. Pok suspected there were multiple reasons his father spent more and more of his time seeing private practice patients.

Pok stepped forward; Phelando guided his hand. Florence's belly was surprisingly tight. Phelando moved their collective touch over a distinct bulge along her left side. Baby Girl pushed against Pok's fingers.

"That's her spine. Here's her head." Phelando hung his stethoscope around his neck and gently gestured for his son to step back. He placed a hand on Florence's shoulder.

"She's breech again, isn't she?"

"She is," Phelando said.

"You can do another maneuver."

"I can. But Baby Girl might turn right back."

"Why does it keep happening?"

"Sometimes mother and child can be out of alignment." Phelando held up a hand. "That doesn't mean you've done anything wrong. There are many reasons the external environment can be at odds with the internal. And Baby Girl is just reflecting that."

"It has to do with the essence, right?" Florence said.

"Sort of," Phelando said. "The essence is more about the doctor-patient relationship. Though I imagine it could apply to a mother-daughter connection."

Pok routinely felt a mix of doubt and wonder whenever his father talked of the "essence" with his patients. The idea of some inherent quality of human interaction impacting physiology was too abstract. Despite promising studies in peer-reviewed journals—Phelando himself first author on the most important of them—critics boiled it down to a glorified placebo effect. Sadly, the more Pok learned the more he agreed. AI-led recommendations weren't perfect, but with time, technology would atone for whatever benefits came from seeing a human doctor.

"Speaking of the essence and balance, there's something I think might help." Phelando pushed his chair back, rummaged in the cabinet beneath the sink, and took out an old capped glass jar half-full of emerald-colored gelatin. "Something I've held on to since fellowship."

"Honey?" Florence and Pok said together.

"Not just any honey. Carve Bee honey. You remember Carve Bees? The honey, once digested, circulates in the blood and binds to high oxidation states. It wipes out viruses, bacteria, stress hormones, toxins, you name it."

Phelando unscrewed the jar. Pok anticipated a sour smell of fermentation older than him but instead a sweet aroma floated through the office. Phelando scooped some into a smaller jar.

"Take a spoonful in the morning and before bed. It'll help prevent any infections *if* you go into labor early." Phelando performed the external cephalic version, reassured Florence of the plan, and, after she had redonned her "disguise," led her out the front door.

Afterward, Pok sat at the kitchen table while his father brewed some tea. Carve Bees. They were the main reason he'd spent third-grade nights tightly rolled in a weighted blanket with all the lights on, his twilight imagination buzzing with mutant insects. A start-up biotech company called SkyLar bioengineered what they dubbed "Carve Bees" to revitalize the failing global bee population and infuse their honey with medicinal properties. The resilient bees soon speciated to become the dominant genus on the North American continent. The Shepherd Organization bought SkyLar and developed a virus that wiped out ninety-nine percent of the invasive population.

"There's an app that does all this," Pok said. Phelando half smiled. He'd been expecting the rebuttal. "It auto-adjusts throughout the pregnancy so breech never happens."

"Florence doesn't trust tech. I can't really blame her. The shepherds think she's only in her second trimester."

Pok must have heard wrong. "That doesn't make sense."

Phelando, smiling, twisted his stud earring. "She gamed the system. She imitated normal range daily temperatures and metrics before and for weeks after conception. The pregnancy didn't register until the beginning of the second trimester."

Pok still didn't understand. "Why would she hide it?"

"The algorithm decided her last pregnancy should be terminated."

"If it concluded that, there must be a good reason," Pok said.

"The shepherd AI learned from the same bias practices that led to decades of bad outcomes for Black pregnancies."

"A bias the AI fixed," Pok said. "I've read the studies. The data doesn't lie."

"Some data can. I'd do the same if I'd been through what she has."

Pok knew they wouldn't agree. He suspected Phelando secretly offered the other side of reproductive care to select patients, the kind outlawed unless found to be medically necessary.

"She can't deceive them forever," he said, shifting the conversation. "False metrics are going to translate to bad care for her baby."

"Her hope is to deliver at Hippocrates Medical Center in New Orleans. She doesn't want her daughter part of any tracking program. I convinced her to wait until at least thirty-eight weeks."

Pok was stunned. The tracking data, now widely implemented universally at birth and routinely in the second trimester, had been shown to all but eliminate infant mortality from SIDS, infections, and even parental neglect. The benefits of AI and health tracking was a topic every medical school applicant was expected to tackle through both essay and interview questions. Parents who opted to forgo the placement usually had a long and often unsuccessful battle with Child Protective Services.

And to New Orleans? The only news coming out of the state was how ravaged the area was by climate change and how they continually rejected technological interventions.

"You're not really supporting that, are you, Dad?"

Pok's father looked older under the dim oven hood light. More grays streaked his locs than Pok had noticed before. His shoulders sloped in earned exhaustion. His teapot began to whistle; they were both grateful for the distraction. Phelando reached into the back of the cabinet and pulled out his favorite mug. Branded on both sides of the pearl-white ceramic was a serious-looking mouse wearing a doctor's coat and a stethoscope.

"I didn't mean to undercut you," Pok said.

"You have a passion. You'll make a great physician." Phelando poured his tea and raised his brow in a found memory. "You had something to tell me, didn't you?"

"The medical school decisions came today."

"That's right! I still can't believe TSO made you wait this long. So, what's the verdict?"

"I didn't get in. Anywhere."

Phelando's eyes sparked. His stance softened. Pok saw what was happening—had seen it many times in his life, from his earliest memories—and pulled away.

"I should have gotten in," Pok said.

"I know, son. But sometimes—"

"No, you don't understand. I did everything right." Pok stopped short of telling what he'd found. "I'll take more classes, write more essays, do more research. Whatever it takes."

Phelando didn't blink as Pok laid this all out. Outside, the rain had finally slowed; the first break in days. The blinds flapped against the window. When Phelando reached out again, it wasn't for a hug. His fingers went to Pok's hair and pinched the end of one of his locs. His fingertips came back damp.

"If medical stress doesn't thin you out, New York rain definitely will. Come, let me do your hair."

Phelando sat at the edge of the living room couch as Pok positioned himself pressed against it on the floor. Pok's long, full locs had grown uninterrupted since before he could walk. Though there were many shepherd apps to guide the initiation, upkeep, and even styling of locs, something about hair—especially Black hair—bewildered AI. Where many trades were becoming do-it-yourself, hairstylists remained in demand.

"Have you told Nicole?"

"Who?"

"Isn't that her name? That nice girl you were dating."

Pok waved a hand. "We broke up a month ago."

"You really liked her."

"I'm not ready for something serious right now. Clearly."

Phelando began to separate and wet the locs with castor oil. He finished two sections of Pok's hair before responding.

"You can't give it all to medicine, son. There'll be nothing left."

"You gave it all," Pok said. The ensuing silence between them stung. It was the closest in a long time either of them had come to talking about Pok's mother.

"When you're right, you're right. Not for the faint." Phelando finished Pok's hair and wrapped it in six separate bundles. His father wiped his hands on a wet cloth, stood, and crossed the living room. Instead of anger or shame, Phelando's face was still soft, almost amused. "I want to show you something."

Phelando ran his fingers along the spines populating his grand, wall-to-wall library. He pulled one. Instead of a single book, the entire shelf shifted to reveal a hidden storage. He shimmied out a wooden briefcase, laid it on the couch, flipped open the buckles, and lifted out a white linen lab coat, still folded. "I had this made in case you changed your mind."

Pok traced the coat's softly threaded insignia: a single snake coiled around a staff with a bespectacled mouse in a doctor's white coat standing proudly at the top. The snake hissed at the mouse—undeniably the same mouse from his father's favorite mug—whose smile exuded confidence. Under it was *Pok Morning, Student Doctor, Hippocrates Medical College*.

"They were pretty generous with the full scholarship," Phelando said.

And a stipend, Pok remembered. Three months ago, he'd been overjoyed to receive the news affirming him as a stellar candidate who would have his choice of institutions to begin a bright future in medicine. But he never saw himself there.

Phelando dropped a hardcover book into Pok's arms. The title read *Principles of Internal Medicine*. The spine cracked but held as Pok opened it. The pages, worn and used, were still very much intact. Scribbles decorated the margins.

"Are these your notes?"

"From medical school and residency, yes. Some are worthless. Others . . . You can't overestimate the value of a good mnemonic." Phelando tapped the pages. "Hippocrates teaches *real* medicine. That is, if you want it to. You know, the founder of the Shepherd Organization adored Hippocrates."

"And they turned their back on him. New Orleans banned TSO tech, remember?"

"For legitimate reasons. I've been working with some Hippocrates physicians on a few projects. Their city has been through a lot in the last twenty-five years. It makes sense why they shut themselves off from a country that left them to drown. But their medicine—*how* they do medicine—everyone could benefit from."

"Louisiana sounds like a horrible place to live, Dad. No offense."

"You shouldn't believe everything you hear."

"If I go to Hippocrates, no residency in its right mind will accept me." Pok gripped the old textbook, speaking to it as if it held answers. "AI will always know more. It's the future. Hell, it's the present."

"That may be. Medicine is as much an art as it is a science. You'll never learn enough. You'll never have all the answers. But right now, right here, you can already do what no machine can."

"What's that?"

His father smiled sideways. "Touch the patient." Phelando folded the coat and placed it and the textbook back in the case. "Give it some thought, okay?"

The doorbell rang. Phelando frowned.

"Another patient?" Pok said.

"I'm not expecting anyone." Phelando checked through the peephole and called back to Pok. "It's for you."

Pok's longtime friend entered holding up two recommissioned soda bottles, filled with yellow drink. "I came over to commiserate," Kris said. "Sorry, Mr.—Dr.—Morning, I only brought two."

"*Mr.* is fine. And no worries."

Pok greeted his friend with a handshake into a half hug. They'd been shoulder to shoulder three years ago at high school graduation, but Kris Boles now stood a head above Pok. He'd matched at a prestigious job at the Shepherd Organization's headquarters—located right there in Manhattan—while Pok's path assigned a research lab to round out his application. Kris's algorithm had done its work; he would have his pick of medical schools.

Kris lived in the state-of-the-art high-rise that dominated NYC's skyline. All of Kris's meals were prepared, his clothes washed and pressed daily, and near-future medical care was available at the drop of a hat. TSO employees lived their best lives.

The three of them sat at the kitchen table. Kris popped the cap off his drink and pushed Pok his. "How're you feeling, man?"

"Confused," Pok said.

"You find anything in your 'troubleshooting'?"

"My application was messed up."

"But you had perfect grades."

"Not like that," Pok said. "The whole file uploaded wrong or something. My transcript, essay, everything. They even had the genome of someone else."

"You hacked into the shepherd system?" Phelando said. "Pok, that's risky."

Pok waved a dismissive hand. "It wasn't the Source. And I was careful."

"What are you going to do?" Kris said.

"You mean besides cry? I already corrected my app. I sent admissions a long, detailed message, but it just reads like an excuse. They've probably already finalized this year's class."

"You uploaded everything?" Phelando sat down, hands wrapped around his mug of tea.

"Of course I did." Pok began to open his drink, then paused. "I need to work tonight. Figure out what classes I'm going to take, go over my app, make a game plan. Is this going to mess me up?"

Kris raised his brow to Phelando. "Can you tell your son to chill, just for one night?"

"I tried. Trust me, I tried." Phelando picked up Pok's drink and turned it in his hands. "But I have the same question. You know my son is a lightweight. Me, on the other hand . . ."

"It might hit different for you," Kris said. "It's a low-proof made special for Pok."

"He can have it," Pok said. "I'll celebrate when I get an acceptance. I hear they're shaking things up again with early admissions in January."

Phelando popped the top, took a swig, and grimaced. "Oh, son, you *are* a lightweight. This needs some whiskey." He left to consult his small bedside bar. Whiskey had gradually become a nightly staple.

"If you really wanted to help me, you would have brought some of your study aid," Pok said. "Then maybe I could get into eight schools, too."

Kris's serious, sallow expression brought clarity to the cut of Pok's words. Kris had never been shy about his use of Synth, the neuro-enhancing recreational drug, and Pok had been vocal in his dissent. Still, the jab had been out of pocket. Pok silently consulted his glass's facial reader. The analysis listed Kris as nervous, uncertain, and uncomfortable.

"I didn't mean it like that," Pok said.

"No, it's fine." Kris stood. "I have to go, anyway."

"I thought we were commiserating?"

"If you're set on being productive, be productive," Kris said. "And no offense taken. I'd be pissed, too. Let me know if you need any help."

Pok thanked his friend, went back to his room, and got to work.

Three

THE LONGEST NIGHT

Pok couldn't count on his flawless application to suffice next cycle. He had to operate as if he'd been genuinely rejected. His application had to reflect that he hadn't slowed down or given up during the unexpected gap year but rather doubled down and used it as an opportunity to rise above.

Decided, Pok summoned Kai. The two-foot-tall furry animal model had pointy, vein-lined ears, and large almond eyes that mimicked human emotion. A round touch screen lit its torso with a default display of burnt-orange fur. Kai brought a bowl of freshly baked veggie chips.

Pok took the offerings and patted Kai on the head. Newer, hypoallergenic versions lacked the lab-grown canine fur. Lucky for Pok, his only allergy was boredom. Petting Kai was one of his favorite pastimes. The robot seemed to enjoy it, too. Kai's eyes melted above its smile.

"New assignment," Pok said. "My application was rejected from the Prestigious Twelve. Create a plan for me to get accepted to at least four of them next cycle."

Kai, who already had in storage Pok's curriculum vitae, transcripts, essays, and letters of recommendation, confirmed that it understood the assignment.

This done, Pok yawned and sat back against his headboard. While Kai worked, Pok went to Hippocrates Medical College's website. Located in the heart of New Orleans, Louisiana, the institution was a vocal critic of AI in medicine. Pok searched for last year's match list. As expected, a vast majority stayed at Hippocrates. For the love of the institution and city or because no one else would take them?

Kai purred; the plan was ready. Significantly more rigorous than last cycle's, this time focused on the inherent uphill battle of overcoming widespread rejections. It listed six in-person and online courses, seven shepherd-affiliated physicians to contact for shadowing and research opportunities, and six possible volunteer roles. It described in month-by-month detail what he should do to optimize himself as an applicant.

"Nice, Kai."

First on the course list was MacArthur's Anatomy Online. Exclusively available to failed applicants, it consisted of ten lectures, a fully rendered cadaver, and one final exam. It came with an automated, fully personalized study plan that turned one's glass into a twenty-four-seven experience. Once started, the final couldn't be paused: any deviation in the glass's viewfinder—or removal of the glass, for whatever reason—would result in an immediate failure.

It was intense. It was just what Pok needed.

Course purchased, Pok started the study aid's two-hour assessment. It put him through a battery of cognitive tests to evaluate his learning style, short- and long-term memory, distraction susceptibilities, and, finally, anatomical knowledge. At the end it generated his Chance of Passing score, which was a likelihood of him successfully completing the final exam if commenced in any given moment. Twenty-eight percent. He had to start somewhere.

Satisfied, he put his glass aside. That's when he heard it. The distinct sound of retching. Down the hall, a door creaked. Footsteps.

Pok stepped into the hallway. The smell of bleach hung in the air. Pok opened his father's door. The windows were on full shade; little ambient light leaked into the room. White sheets wrapped a tight cocoon around Phelando. His sweat-covered forehead stuck out at the top. He rose up a little. A line of gray saliva ran from his mouth to the bed.

For some time later, when Pok would think back to this moment, he would remember a lot of things. That smell, the sweat, the crust in his father's eyes. More than anything, though, he would remember how in that initial moment—that raw, candid moment—Phelando looked as if he knew exactly what was happening to him.

"I'm okay, son." Phelando tried to smile. "Feels like a corona variant. Hopefully not. But whatever it is, it's hit me hard. Not for the faint, that's for sure. Can you make me some tea?"

Phelando sat up on Pok's return. He took the tea and added a spoonful of Carve Bee honey, already out and waiting. "I really am sorry about your application," Phelando said. "But think about Hippocrates, okay?"

"I will. You just get better."

"Maybe whoever switched out your files was doing you a favor." Phelando brought the mug up to his face, then paused. "What is it, son?"

Pok hadn't told his father about suspecting sabotage. He specifically remembered keeping that part of the narrative close to his chest. "Nothing," he said. "I—I'm just worried about you, is all."

Phelando sipped, grimaced, and then took another swallow. Lines ran down the sides of the Dr. Mouse mug and dripped onto the bed. Phelando rotated as if neither of them had already seen how terribly his hand shook.

"Should I call for a medical companion?" Pok said. His father was a staunch critic of the automated kiosks, but they could arrive in minutes and offer, at least, some peace of mind.

"No," Phelando said. "I just need to rest."

Phelando took another big gulp, put the cup on his bedside bar, and returned to his sheets. Pok, remembering that initial look, considered pressing the medical companion issue, but the moment had passed. He closed the door fully behind him and tried to shake away useless suspicion. Suspecting his father (of what, exactly?) wouldn't get him into medical school.

MacArthur's Anatomy Online: The Official Study Guide was fully immersive. While enrolled, Pok's glass automatically identified whatever anatomy came into his visual field. It created a schedule that included two hours of daily focused study. The rest was random prompts woven into his routine. They ranged from explicit multiple-choice-style questions to rapid-fire flash cards to environment-inspired mnemonics. It monitored his body metrics and suggested a strict, monotonous diet and exercise schedule through completion of the course.

After a long walk around Central Park—during which he'd had lower leg and foot anatomy drilled into him—Pok checked on his father. Light snoring came from his room. It was almost dusk; he'd slept all day. Good; he probably needed it.

Phelando took the next two days off and stayed in his room while Pok dedicated his full cognition to anatomy. At the end of what felt like a particularly productive day, he took his first practice test and got a sixty percent on a set of forty questions. Pok skimmed the analysis. Based on his timing, eye movements, and heart rate, a large percentage of his correct answers were marked "low confidence." In other words, a lot of luck. Luck wouldn't cut it on a one-and-done pivotal exam.

Pok turned up his glass's illuminance to stimulate his retinas, sat up to engage his back muscles, and started the next set. Another sixty percent. This time, at least, he was more confident in the questions he'd gotten right and the predicted range was narrower and more in his favor. Still, he'd worked hard to fail. But this was just practice; he was supposed to fail. When he was ready—when he'd mastered the human body—he'd take the test and he'd pass.

Drifting whispers from the hallway. Pok checked the time. Well past midnight. Outside his room, light peeked around the corner. His father; with recognition came the weight of Phelando's comment. *I must have told him.* Pok knew he hadn't.

With soft feet and a held breath, Pok stepped out into the hall. Despite near absolute silence, Phelando's light went out before he made it halfway to his room. The whispering ceased. His father's door clicked shut.

"Dad?" Pok said.

No answer. Only heavy, steady breathing.

Several minutes later, Pok placed outside his father's room a freshly brewed cup of tea in the Dr. Mouse mug, complete with decades-old honey. He considered knocking, thought better of it, and retreated back down the hall. He didn't *need* his father's answers. He could find them himself.

Pok had never before considered breaking into Phelando's account. But he had to know: Had his own father orchestrated the biggest disappointment of his life? Through their shared network, Pok brought up his father's profile on his own glass, breathed, and committed.

Easy work. In less than a minute, he was in. He searched the database for CryingRabbits218.

Pok expected *No results found*. He expected warm relief. What he got instead was confirmation of the unimaginable: a simple monetary transaction between Phelando and someone with the handle CryingRabbits218, done a week before Pok applied to the Prestigious Twelve. His father had paid someone to kill his application.

Pok searched the files for his own name. He sifted through various notifications over the years about school, youth sports schedules, and doctor's appointments, and opened a direct message thread with Dr. Brandy Sims, dean of medical education at Hippocrates Medical College.

BS: TSO filed a warrant to seize "Zion." Do you know about this?

PM: Zion's a myth. Odysseus is using it as an excuse. They're going after the Vault.

BS: He's getting bold. Do you want to hold off on Project Do No Harm until things calm down?

PM: It needs to see light. MacArthur already terminated me. There's nothing left for me here.

BS: What about your son?

PM: Pok reveres shepherd AI. The move will be an easier pill to swallow once his decisions come in.

BS: The Council is eager to finalize the class.

PM: Just hold. He'll come around.

Pok read through the exchange multiple times, the implications of each line so foreign it might as well have been another language. Phelando, fired? These messages were dated more than two months ago. *He'll come around.* Rage bubbled. The hell he would.

Pok searched for *Project Do No Harm*, found the corresponding folder, and hesitated only a beat before opening it. There were more than a dozen unpublished articles, authored by Phelando and various others, pertaining to safety and ethical concerns with the Shepherd Organization and its operations.

- Shepherd CEO Buries Research Questioning Effect of Physio-Regulation on Cardiac Health
- Shepherd CEO Blocks Research Questioning Safety of AI-Led Medicine
- TSO-Proteins: The Ubiquitous Molecule the Shepherd Organization Doesn't Want You to Know About
- Time Is of the Essence: Revitalizing the Cameron Dryden Studies

Phelando wasn't just trying to end Pok's medical career. He strove to bring the whole system down.

Whispers again. Pok went out into the hall. His father's door was open; the tea was gone. The lights were on. Pok's heart beat into his throat. Where would he begin? How would they get past this? Pok went in.

His hand went to his mouth. Pages lay strewn across the sheetless mattress. Clothes bulged from the drawers and piled out of the closet. Ceramic mugs—old, cracked, with tea strings stuck to the sides—everywhere. Photos hung from the ceiling. Anatomy sketches—the body parts intricately detailed—were tacked on the walls. The bedsheets were in the tub. The pillows, too. Clumps of Phelando's hair decorated the cloth, linoleum, and sinks.

Phelando stumbled in from the kitchen—clutching the open jar of honey, mumbling something incoherent—and walked right into Pok. His scraggly beard scratched his son's cheek.

"Pok. Son. What's going on?"

Pok didn't know what to say, didn't know how to address what he'd seen in his father's room, what he'd seen in his father's files, what he was seeing in his father now. Phelando was not well. In just a few days he'd lost an easy ten pounds. Glaring bald spots tarnished his once-perfect locs. Ash and cracks blemished his skin.

"You need to go to the hospital," Pok said. Simple. Direct. Everything else could wait.

Phelando stepped past him, as if his room didn't look like a disaster. "I can play with computers at home," he said.

The disregard, the negligence, the obstinance. They collectively lit the fire Pok had just decided to suppress. "This is such bullshit," he said. "All of it."

"Son?"

"You're sick and won't go to the hospital. You're treating patients in your closet making them believe they can fool the shepherds. You're choosing honey over modern medicine. You're a *doctor,* Dad! Act like one."

"You're upset," Phelando said. "I get that. But I'm still your father."

"I know what you did," Pok said. "I know you ruined my application."

The words sucked the air out of the room. Phelando considered denial. Pok wanted that, even if it was a lie. Wanted an explanation to make the insensible make sense. But his father was too tired to do much more than sigh.

"There's a lot you don't understand," Phelando said.

"Why would you do that to me? I tried so hard."

"The Shepherd Organization is dangerous. Its algorithm is dangerous. If you want to be a doctor, there's a better way."

"That's not for you to decide," Pok said. "They fired you because you couldn't keep up. Don't drag me down with you."

Phelando, jaw tight, ran a hand over his head. Clumps of locs tumbled off his shoulder and onto the floor. Both father's and son's gaze followed the path. "I'll go to the hospital in the morning," he said.

"Whatever," Pok said. "Do what you want."

Pok slammed the door and left his father. He'd check on him in the morning, make sure he actually *did* make it to the hospital. But right now, in that moment, Pok just wanted to be alone.

Four

MEMORANDIUM

Pok awoke half propped against his headboard, the sun in his eyes, his neck stiff, his mouth dry and raw. He didn't remember getting into bed. Thoughts quickly went to his father. He went out into the hall. The house was quiet. Phelando's door hung open. Inside: a made bed, a neat dresser, a clean floor. Unrest lingered. He checked the living room and kitchen before messaging him: *Everything okay?*

Pok waited. Instead of glass, Phelando used an old-style phone he rarely checked. His gaze twitching toward the message corner of his augmented display, Pok migrated to the kitchen and ate the study guide's recommended bowl of whole-grain cereal.

The buzz of glass tickled his nose.

PM: I'm okay, son. Went to the ER like I promised. Haven't seen a human doctor yet. They're running tests, will likely keep me overnight. Probably an infection.

PM: I want to talk more about last night, make things right between us. Come by if you can. I can do your hair.

Make things right. How? What could his father possibly say to "make things right"?

It was still early, just past eight in the morning. If Pok got in a couple more practice exams, shot off a few emails to the physicians on Kai's list, and started his application essay, maybe he could visit his father feeling more accomplished than betrayed. Phelando was in good hands. That was done.

Another notification. Pok sat up, wiping milk from his chin. The algorithms knew exactly what to advertise. Tatiana Tate, a popular influencer who made her name interviewing polarizing political figures, hated social media influencers, and billionaire CEOs, was on live with none other than Odysseus Shepherd, current CEO of the Shepherd Organization. He clicked on the hyperlink.

Tatiana's voice, clear and light, came from his glass. "Odysseus, it's a pleasure. You're a hard man to get on record."

"This is on the record?"

They both laughed, thin and transient.

"Entrepreneur. Activist. Mogul. You have many titles, depending on who's telling the story. I thought we could begin with your latest venture. So, you bought all the medical schools?"

Odysseus laughed, for real this time, deep and throaty. "Not all of them. Just the best ones. We look forward to revolutionizing medicine with the most brilliant minds, present and future."

"A revolution? The media will have a field day with that."

"Which is why I'm here," Odysseus said. "I'm a fan of the truth."

"Aren't we all?" Tatiana's smile shone through her voice. "I'll throw you an easy one: you've said human-led medicine is like having monkeys fly a plane."

"Gloves off. I like it. A lot of people took offense to that. It was taken out of context. I'd like to clear it up."

"Please."

"First of all, I said it's like having a monkey fly a 747 without autopilot. Which I stand by. Technology has left humans outdated. A traditional doctor goes through decades of schooling, testing, and apprenticeship. At the end of all that, you know what percentage of the breadth of medical knowledge they've been exposed to? Not retained, just exposed to? Less than a half of a percent. The most seasoned internist has seen, what, fifty thousand patients in his career? A hundred thousand? Shepherd AI can instantly aggregate data from billions of patient interactions. The model for human-led medicine is outdated."

"There's something to be said for human-to-human interaction, right? The power of human touch? You don't agree."

"My father's sister is a doctor. Her experience informed how he designed the first shepherd algorithms. I know as well as anyone the importance of human touch. And you know the most important kind? A mother's touch. There's nothing quite like it."

"Your mother passed when you were little."

"She went to the best hospital in the world. Her doctor ignored a very straightforward and definitive AI suggestion. I don't want a doctor's touch. I don't care about feeling 'seen' or 'heard' by my doctor. I want the best health so that I can live and enjoy a long life."

"Your father, Julian Shepherd, also battled a chronic illness, yes?"

"A genetic one. Helplessly watching Granddad die a slow death is what prompted him to launch the Shepherd Organization. He created the first fully functioning genetic editing algorithm, to which my health is a testament."

This was news to Pok. Inspired, he started an email to the Shepherd CEO. A long shot, but it couldn't hurt.

"What would you say to people who worry that AI is taking their autonomy?" Tatiana said.

"People get in their own way."

"I can tell you feel strongly about this."

"It's frustrating. Look at driving. Time and time again the data showed that autonomous cars save thousands of lives. Daily. It's all quite silly to me." A pause. Pok visualized Tatiana waiting, Odysseus on the edge of saying or not saying. He went with saying. "People are stupid, you know? Inherently stupid. It baffles me that we still have people controlling a two-ton machine that can go more than a hundred miles an hour. Our health app has all medical knowledge and constantly monitors aspects of your physiology you didn't know existed. Why would you want a flawed, emotional, subpar *person* doctor in charge of your well-being? It doesn't make any sense."

"Let's talk about your policy ventures," Tatiana said. "Some express concern of your close relationships with certain politicians who could influence the laws regulating medicine in this country. Is this a conflict of interest?"

"Many people benefit from our state-of-the-art medical system. Some of those people are in government. If the lifesaving treatment they or their loved ones receive informs political leanings, who am I to dispute?"

"AI is at the center of a number of propositions in the coming election. One is making certain technology mandatory in hospital settings. Hippocrates Medical Center in New Orleans has been a vocal critic. Their leadership has said, and I quote, 'We're handing the world over to the wrong hands.'"

Pok paused his email and tilted his ear. His father was one of those vocal critics and, judging from Project Do No Harm, was set to wage war with the tech giant. Ice touched his stomach. Could he ever have a career in medicine?

"First of all, I wouldn't trust the world in my hands. I have flaws. I have emotions. I'm imperfect, like any human. The shepherds are the perfection. It is humanity at its best. Giving 'autonomy'—whatever that means—to the most powerful and comprehensive AI in the world is like giving control to the best of humanity. The facts are the facts, regardless of one hospital's denial.

"It's very sad to see what Louisiana has become. And they got the short end of the stick when it comes to natural disasters."

"Their spires are impressive," Tatiana said. "They've kept New Orleans above water for, what, fifteen years now?"

"According to them," Odysseus said. "Without eyes in or out, we don't know truth from fiction. The science supporting electromagnetic weather manipulation is iffy at best. It's more likely a disaster zone in need of a cleanup. Governor Teal isn't doing her people any favors by blocking us at every juncture. You don't like my company? That's fine. But to take a huge technological step back at the expense of people's livelihood?"

"The whole state of Louisiana has rejected AI technology," Tatiana said. "Billy Bayou Farms—one of the nation's largest produce centers—even goes by the nickname 'MouseKill,' in reference to killing a computer mouse, I believe."

"And their crops have suffered greatly from lack of shepherd analysis. Something tragic is going to happen down there, and it's going to be sad to see."

A tight chill rippled across Pok, so acute he briefly thought his glass had vibrated. He turned off the interview, finished the email, proofread it before sending it off, and got back to work.

The afternoon brought with it exhausted confidence. Pok had made progress. He checked the time. Almost two. Visiting Phelando in the hospital would make for a good study break. He'd tell his father that he was reapplying and it would be best if they just put this behind them.

Just as Pok was getting dressed, his study guide's indicator flashed green. Several factors besides performance went into the anatomy course's Chance of Passing score, including time of day, proximity of last meal, and biometrics. It could and did fluctuate significantly in a twenty-four-hour period. Once it hit a specified confidence threshold—for Pok, ninety percent—it alerted the user.

Pok was at that threshold: there was a ninety-nine percent chance he'd pass the exam if he took it now. How badass would it look on his application if he passed the toughest anatomy course out there less than a week after receiving his decision? Even an algorithm would raise its eyebrows.

The exam averaged two and a half hours to complete. Visiting hours were until six. Pok bit his lip. If he waited, his COP score may go back down. And there was no guarantee this time of day tomorrow would be just as ideal. And what if things with his father blew up? Having him back in the home environment could tank his COP.

Three hours. He could do that. Pok opened the Gross Anatomy 101 course. As the page loaded, his heart skipped into his throat. He swallowed, set his jaw, and started the final exam. No turning back now.

It took Pok four hours to pass what proved to be the hardest exam of his life. Once he was sure his grade was uploaded, he took off his glass and tossed it on the bed. No sooner had it bounced against his pillow did it jump again from an audible vibration. He could read just enough in the scrolling subject line of a newly received email to make him sit all the way up.

"No fucking way." Pok sprang forward, almost fell off the bed, and laid his head on the sheet to read the glass. No fucking way.

Pok picked up his glass with both hands as if it could destroy the world.

He slipped it on. The email was from the Shepherd School of Medicine at MacArthur Hospital. They wanted to talk to him. The blinking green light next to the video chat link indicated they were on the call. Right now.

Pok combed back and tied his hair, wiped the sweat from his face with the back of his shirt, and joined. A man with sharp, brown eyes, a strong jaw, and a light blue shirt popped into vibrant life. It must have been a video or a filter. That was the only explanation for what Pok was seeing.

Odysseus Shepherd grinned out at him. "Pok Morning? Can you hear me okay? Is now a good time?"

Pok nodded, his throat tight and dry. Odysseus Shepherd. The only son of the late Julian Shepherd, founder and creator of the Shepherd Organization. Heir to an empire that sought to shape the future. Here, live, with him?

"Excellent. I'm Odysseus. I saw your email, looked over your application, and just had to meet you."

"You got my email?" was all Pok could say.

"I most certainly did. I immediately read your application—your *real* application—and was extremely impressed. By your coding skills, especially. Your talent would surely be wasted at an institution like Hippocrates."

What in the hell was going on? Was this some type of elaborate scam?

"I'm not scamming you," Odysseus said. "I realize this may be a shock. It was perfect timing. I just got off with Tatiana and your email was at the top of a thousand unreads. Something told me to open it. I'm glad I did. I'll cut right to it. We want you here at the Shepherd School of Medicine."

"I got in?"

"All but officially. You need to physically accept the decision package first. It's part of the branding. You live here in Manhattan? Perfect. I'll come over and hand it to you myself." Odysseus grinned into the camera. "I can't wait to meet you."

The call ended. Pok's hands trembled. He calmed himself and focused. First things first. He went into his glass's central system and tracked the call's origin. The IP address checked out. The only peculiarity was that Odysseus had definitely been using an advanced enhancement filter. That would make sense, though, given his status.

Holy shit. Odysseus Shepherd had really just called him and was coming to his apartment.

Pok rushed for his door, set on telling his father the news. This would fix everything, for the both of them—

Shit, his father! Outside, night had been pulled over Manhattan like a blanket. Through his window, in the distance, he could see a sliver of MacArthur Hospital's lights. Visiting hours were definitely over. He tried calling. It went straight to voicemail. Maybe Phelando was on his way home? Pok shot him a message.

> **PM:** I got in! Shepherd SOM accepted my application. Let's work this out. You coming home?

Pok jumped at his glass's sudden vibration. Kris. Wait until he heard this. "You won't believe what just happened," he said.

Kris's video was off. His breath was heavy with rasp. "Pok, Odysseus—"

The call dropped. Pok returned the call. It didn't ring. He tried again. What had Kris tried to say? *Odysseus.* Did he know already? How could he? Pok tried a third time and then a fourth. Was this all just a prank, after all?

The doorbell chimed. Pok rang Kris again. Still nothing. On his glass, he brought up their door's outward-facing camera. The hallway was empty; a package lay on the welcome mat. Odysseus decided to drone-deliver the decision after all. That made more sense. Why would a billionaire hand-deliver something that could be sent by air in minutes?

Out in the dim, damp apartment hallway, the waiting box was not the decision. Pok's heart raced with a dreaded recognition. The design was unmistakable. Bossed, mahogany wood encased a lap-sized device. Carved on its top was the TSO shepherd kneeling to lay down his staff. Beside it was a box small enough to fit in the palm of Pok's hand. Engraved on the top: *Phelando Morning, MD.*

A Memorandium.

Pok stepped over the impossible package and ran to the end of the hall. "Dad?" Only a faint echo responded. Pok dialed Phelando. *Come on, come on, come on.* No one answered. He called MacArthur Hospital. A perfect voice informed him that visiting hours were over.

Back in front of their door, Pok shook his head, as if something unwanted had crawled into his ear. A Memorandium. His father's name. That didn't make any sense. It couldn't make sense.

Pok brought in the package and placed it in the center of the dining room table. He pressed his index on the fingerprint reader, hoping for an error message, some sliver of indication that this was all a mistake. Instead, its outer skin glowed green. A slot popped out of the side. Pok opened the box with his father's name on it. A silver ring—too small to fit even his pinkie—waited inside. It was light, almost weightless. How could this small object have anything to do with his father? He inserted the ring into the slot—a perfect fit—and pushed it back into the Memorandium.

Rotating lines of light shot a foot into the air. Pok inched around to view it from all angles. His father's projection tracked his movement. The Memorandium was designed to simulate a person's mannerisms, speech patterns, anatomy, and voice based on the data accrued over their lifetime. Phelando's projection was grainy and slow, less defined than the videos Pok had seen online. His father had been protective with his data; this program's source material was sparse.

The voice, however, was spot-on.

"I'm so sorry, son."

The perfect replica stabbed Pok in the heart. Understanding bled into his chest. His legs buckled and his knees cracked against the floor.

"Prove it to me." Pok's lips trembled. He couldn't bring himself to look at the thing. "Prove he's dead."

The Memorandium itself was proof enough. The machine couldn't function while its subject still breathed air. The federal law ensuring this passed after a con artist used a counterfeit Memorandium to convince a mother that her adult son had died in an accident. She'd readily transferred her life savings to an offshore account.

His father's projection disintegrated. In its place, Phelando Morning's death certificate, initiated and signed at MacArthur Hospital. The cause of death: cardiac arrest. Time: 4:36 p.m. His father had died while Pok was in the middle of his exam.

The projection came back. "I can only deliver my message once. The briefcase I showed you is on my bed. In it you'll find a map. Take that and get out of the city. Stay off the radar."

"What?" Pok said. "Where am I going? What happened to you, Dad?"

"I want you to go to Hippocrates in New Orleans. Follow the map, son."

"The medical school?"

"It's not about school. It's about safety. My colleagues there will take care of you."

"What's Project Do No Harm? Does that have anything to do with this?"

"I don't have information about that. I'm sorry, son. I've told you all I can."

The Memorandium powered off. Pok stepped forward, hand outstretched, then sprang to action. Kai, as if sensing the tension, fell in line behind him. The wooden briefcase from behind their bookcase lay on his bed, just as the Memorandium said. His father must have put it there before going to the hospital. How long ago had he recorded the Memorandium? Had he known he was going to die? None of this shit made any sense.

Pok dumped the contents onto the bed. There, a detailed, hand-drawn map spanned from Manhattan, past New Jersey, across Pennsylvania and Virginia, and straight through to Louisiana. A circle marked the city of New Orleans. The map instructed he take the George Washington Bridge out of New York and into New Jersey. Pok retrieved his own book bag from his closet and filled it with his father's textbook, the white coat gifted to him, and the map. He stuffed in a handful of clothes and dug a cloth face mask from the bottom of his drawer. Trembling fingers zipped everything up.

The characteristic vibration of glass against marble made him pause as he reentered the kitchen. The device inched across the table, knocking against the Memorandium. Pok retrieved it. Instead of a call, there was only a message. From Kris. The words, all capitals, stopped time. The world instantly became small and dark and somehow scarier than when he'd found his father's Memorandium just minutes before.

KB: THEY'RE COMING FOR YOU, POK!
GET THE FUCK OUT OF NEW YORK!

The doors around the apartment audibly locked. The whole building went silent, its underlying vibration gone. The fridge powered down. Even the street noise faded as if the very fabric of reality was fleeing, leaving him behind.

And then everything went black.

Five

ESCAPE FROM NEW YORK

GET THE FUCK OUT OF NEW YORK!

Quick, heavy breaths stretched Pok's chest. He couldn't see a few feet in front of him. He swallowed down unhelpful panic. He needed to think. No. He needed to move. But first, he needed to see.

"Kai, give me light."

Bright light spread from the companion's chest. Kai swept the beam over the apartment, an offer for Pok to use it at will. Everything was off. All the doors were locked. Even the bathroom denied access. He tried calling down to the front desk. The intercom was dead.

The air-conditioning unit at the end of the hall hung out of the only window left unshaded. Blue ambient light threw timid shadows. There were many shepherd-centered building regulations in New York City, all established on reasons of public safety. One mandated antitheft devices on all doors and windows that third-party security agencies could remotely lock and unlock to immediately halt active criminal activity. This particular window, however, was permanently open due to the vintage-style air conditioner that Phelando refused to replace.

That window, independent of shepherd control, was the only way out.

Pok unslung his book bag, unzipped it to put in Kai, and cursed. Bringing Kai meant carrying a huge beacon. Pok opened its back panel and took out the core drive, which also held some of Pok's most powerful hacking algorithms. Kai powered down and curled into a tight ball. Pok placed the hollow shell of a companion in the corner and pocketed the chip. Perhaps he'd see Kai again one day. Even in his rush, he knew this hope was naive.

The floor vibrated through Pok's feet. The crank of the elevator seeped through the walls. Someone was coming. Pok pulled his book bag tight and went to the end of the hall. He felt along the window's ridged bottom. Behind him, an elevator door rumbled open. Footsteps. It was now or never.

As Pok's fingers hooked under the window seal, he had a flash vision of himself, medical school applicant, son of a physician, about to climb out of a third-story window. He breathed the thought away. There was a fire behind him. Later, he could find out what caused it, how dangerous it actually was, but right now if he hesitated he risked being burned alive.

Pok lifted. The window didn't budge. Not at first. He set his feet and tried again. A creak; some give. Then, all at once, the window shot up. Crisp air bit Pok's fingertips. The air conditioner slanted back, slow at first, and then flipped out of the window. It hit the metal floor of the fire escape, rolled from its own momentum, and fell clean through the ladder opening. It cracked off the second-floor railing and crashed onto the pavement. The building's alarm sounded.

Pok leaned out over his yawning window. The alley below was dark, damp, and empty. The whole block was without power. He swung one leg over, then the other, tested the escape's floor with a *tap-tap*, and fully committed. The fire escape swayed.

Back in his apartment, the front door whined open.

There was no banging. No violence. Only the definitive sound of easy entry, magnified by the long hallway. Just enough light fell across the black to bring a bit of shine to the wood floors.

Pok descended. Firecrackers shook from the old, steel structure. The bottom level was still several feet from the ground. He swung open the hatch and released the retracted ladder. A shadow passed overhead. Pok flinched, twisting to see, and lost his balance. He slipped on the still-wet metal and fell. He got a good three fingers around one rung, but gravity snatched it away.

His left foot hit the pavement first, turned, and crumpled beneath him. Sparks burst at his hip. Pok's head knocked against the concrete; the world spun and, as he cradled his ankle, the fire escape and his apartment building swayed nausea over him. He oriented through the haze. A silhouette—the vaguest shape of a person, dressed in black shadow—watched from his window.

And then disappeared.

Lazy, clueless cars passed on either street of the vacant alley. Pok rose up on his good leg, balanced himself against the wall, and tested his injury. Hot pain shot up his shin and into his knee. He winced and tried again. Immediate. Excruciating. He gritted his teeth, banged a fist against his other thigh, and forced another step. And then another.

Pok limped along the alley wall to Park Avenue, the street opposite his building's entrance. Hot blood rushed to his bruised torso and set his full left leg to a horrible, throbbing rhythm. He hugged the corner and peeked down Park. No sign of his pursuer. Behind him, the alley remained empty. At the nearest intersection, the light changed from red to green, urging forward a waiting fleet of cars. Pok limped out into the street. One car swerved. The others slowed. Horns blared. He focused on the goal, one step at a time. Finally, he rested against a parked car on the other side, scooted in his feet as traffic zipped past, and put out his hand.

The figure in black—tall, lanky, and deliberate—stepped under the streetlamp and waited for the light to change. They saw him, Pok was sure, but didn't chase after. Didn't show any urgency or rush. They just watched. And waited.

Rideshare cars, their affiliate logos on display, rolled past. Their owners pretended to watch the road. Those who did acknowledge Pok did so with a disdainful grimace, as if he'd just stepped off an alien spaceship. All the better. Pok wanted a gypsy cab.

The one fairly consistent thing throughout the history of New York's hired cars: the gypsy cab. They'd started as human drivers independent of the ubiquitous yellow cab companies, became the alternative to the rideshare apps that put those companies out of business, and now remained a conspicuous and rare reminder of a New York City few people still remembered.

A maroon car, freshly washed and waxed, pulled to the curb. The back door popped open. Pok got in. The driver wore a brown baseball cap and a matching long-sleeved shirt.

"Gypsy?" Pok kept a foot out of the cracked door.

The driver gave Pok less than half his pockmarked face. "Independent driver. And only temporary while I get reinstated. Where are we off to?"

Pok fully committed and put on his seat belt. "New Jersey. Anywhere in New Jersey."

"No way I'm crossing over into Jersey."

"George Washington Bridge, then. And hurry. Please."

"You in some type of trouble?"

"No. No trouble." As he spoke, Pok tried to look for trouble out the window. The light had changed; traffic waited. There was no one in the crosswalk, no one under the streetlight. "I'm late and I don't want my girlfriend to know where I was."

The driver considered him a little longer, laughed, and pulled into traffic. Still seeing no sign of the shadow visitor, Pok turned his attention to the building where he'd grown up. Living in it, he consistently forgot how tall it was. It had to be; it housed nearly all the residents and attending physicians at MacArthur. For his entire life, Pok had called this building home. But his father was home. Had been home.

Other, less significant buildings filled the space. Pok rested his forehead against the window, took notice of a shifting billboard ad for legal counsel, and turned away. He slipped on his face mask to cover his eyes.

"You mind if I lie down?" Pok said, already lowering himself in the back seat.

"Please don't throw up in my car. Please."

"I won't."

The gypsy cab made a U-turn and headed uptown. Every Harlem road pothole bump played Pok's ankle a painful melody. In that limbo, his cheek pressed against the cold leather, the chaotic last hour came into focus. An elaborate prank would have been called long ago. Could his father really be dead?

The gypsy cab screeched to a stop. Pok sat up. He lifted part of his mask just enough to see that they were on a dark side street. George Washington Bridge, looming in the fog, was still well in the distance.

"Where are we?" Pok said.

The driver tapped the screen mounted on the back of the passenger seat. "Fifty bucks."

"What?"

"Fifty. Bucks. Pay or walk the rest of the way." According to the display, they were two miles from the bridge.

Pay? Pok hadn't thought of payment. Scanning his account meant giving TSO his exact location and destination. "I left my glass at home."

"Bullshit. You're going to Jersey with no cash and no glass? Pay up."

"I'll pay you when I get to Jersey. Give me your info. I'm good for it."

The driver turned off the engine. Under the bright cabin lights, he was older than Pok thought, older than his own father. Gray curled from his hat above a clean-shaven face.

"Look, kid, the last thing I need is someone on the run. Especially someone on the run with no plans to pay." The driver smacked the back of his seat; Pok jumped. "Ret-scan or walk. End of discussion."

"If I log in, they'll find us."

"They'll find *you*. And I knew you were running from someone." The driver let out a long sigh, mumbled something that sounded like a night's worth of regret, and Pok's door popped open. "Just leave. I can't with this."

New York's cold filled the car and wrapped around Pok. He didn't know what journey awaited him on the other side of that bridge. But he knew he couldn't stay in New York. Could he make it on foot? Two miles. How many blocks, how many obstacles? Mental math devolved into tumbling numbers.

Pok closed the door. The driver's head swiveled at the slam; Pok held his gaze. His fingers found the slot at the base of the display and discreetly slipped in Kai's core drive. His hack should recognize the system and automatically offer a fake burner account with a few hundred dollars. Should.

"I'll pay," Pok said. He made the transfer and put in an extra twenty dollars to try and get things speeding along. A notification vibrated the cab. The driver grunted approval. The car started back on its route.

"This is as far as I can take you, kid," he said a few minutes later. They were stopped at a corner of a busy street, just shy of an overpass. Cars sped on and off the bridge.

Pok tapped his knee with one hand and the side of the door with the other. "How much to convince you to drive me over that bridge?"

"You seem like a nice kid. A nice kid who's going through some rough shit. And you paid me. Respect. But I cannot take you across state lines, especially into Jersey. Only if I don't plan to come back." For the final time, the door popped open. "Good luck, kid."

Out in the cold, Pok wrapped his arms around himself as the breeze coming off the Hudson tested his balance. His ankle pain had evolved into a new beast. He limped over to the narrow, winding path that led up from the street onto the bridge's walkway. He supported himself on chest-high metal railings and started his ascent.

Sweat contradicted the cold as he rounded the top. A gate bisected the walkway's transition to the bridge. It read, NEW YORK/NEW JERSEY BORDER. Pushing in the crash bar with his full weight did nothing. Locked. A display lit up beside the door. Another ret-scan. The Shepherd Organization's serpentine logo spun in the top right corner, mocking him. Unlike the cab, there was no port. The meshed metal rose several feet above him, too tall to climb.

A strong hand gripping glass slipped past. The screen flashed green. The gate opened.

"Get going, kid." The gypsy cab driver squeezed Pok's shoulder, gentle but fatherly firm, as he passed. "Be safe. If you can."

Pok nodded his thanks and stepped onto the bridge. Many blinking lights capped its high arches; cars zipped past, vibrating his air. He tested his ankle's capacity with every step. The pain was still there but further off.

The city lit Pok's path between the bridge's spire shadows. He lifted his pant leg and saw his ankle had swollen to twice its size. At some point it would slow him down, maybe even hobble him. But for now, it was cooperating. And that was enough.

Pok swung his backpack around, felt through the largest section, and pulled out his father's map. There was a hotel on the edge of Bergen County in a small town called Clover. *Stick to the map.* He folded it, tucked it back in his bag, gave one last nod to the infamous skyline, and turned toward the Jersey riverbank.

Six

CLOVER INN

Pok took the 95 highway to 80 West and stayed to the side of a road that stretched for miles between land and sky, creating the disorienting illusion of walking through a dream. Crickets sang loud into the night. Whenever a midnight car passed, Pok ducked into the shoulder's dip. Hypothetically, a TSO car from a neighboring state could scan his face and, upon return, upload it to the cloud. He waited just long enough to let the feeling back into his bad leg. Too much rest would leave him stiff and immobile.

A few hours in, when every step felt like a chore, he passed through a small town that tempted him with many places to rest. But Phelando's map was clear: Clover, New Jersey, would be his first stop.

It wasn't until dawn broke across a thick, dreary fog that he came upon the WELCOME TO CLOVER sign. The print was crisp, recently updated, but not digital. He checked his map for further direction. Clover Inn was in the middle of the town, on Henry Avenue. Pok took the next off-ramp and stopped at the nearest vehicular charging station. He paused a beat before ret-scanning at the ATM.

Outside of hospitals, TSO had no presence in New Jersey. The company couldn't track him or collect data. New Jersey subscribed to TSO's last viable competitor: the Second Life Corporation. For most New Jersey services, Pok would need an SLO glass profile, but banks were still federally regulated. Which left a loophole. TSO couldn't track him, but *someone* could. Ret-scanning was risky, but he had to take the chance.

There was less than two hundred dollars in his checking. He switched over to his father's linked savings to transfer funds and frowned.

ACCOUNT FROZEN. PLEASE CONTACT CUSTOMER SERVICE FOR ASSISTANCE.

What the fuck? The morning sun suddenly warm against him, Pok quickly emptied his account and consulted the kiosk for directions. It put Clover Inn half a mile away, just down the road. He felt the first bit of relief since stepping onto the George Washington Bridge. He'd walked what? Ten miles overnight? Another half was music to his body.

Without a Second Life account, Pok was a blank slate to any New Jerseyan. The ubiquitous facial scanners were federally sourced and still knew the core essentials—his name, birth date, social security number, and likely what he'd had for breakfast based on his body's heat markers—but passersby would not be able to see his education, work history, preferences, or social status.

The fog had all but lifted when he finally ascended the winding path to Clover Inn's double-door entrance. He paused, realized the doors weren't automatic, and pulled them open. A bell chimed overhead.

The receptionist, her frizzy red hair lined with gray, raised listless eyes. She was at either the end or the beginning of a joyless shift. She gestured for Pok to use the mounted kiosk.

"I don't have glass," Pok said.

Her gaze was a little delayed as she realized he was talking to her. She tapped the air in front of her (spatial haptics were a core feature of SLC glass) to turn off whatever she was watching.

"Reservation?" She rubbed her cheek. A deep wrinkle—slightly diagonal—dug its way across her forehead.

"No reservation," Pok said. "You have a room for the night?"

Her eyes navigated her display. She likely didn't deal with manual check-ins often, if at all. She let out a long, unabashed yawn. Food wrappers, soda cans, and an empty to-go box littered the desk. The end of a long night, for sure.

"Just you? I'll check you in and see what we have." The woman did the universal gaze shift that indicated she'd attempted to access Pok's information. Even without glass, his information would be accessible. *If* he were local. But he wasn't. "You in some kind of trouble?" she said.

Time to get used to the question. "I left my problems in New York."

"New York." She nodded, as if that explained it. "Name? Don't worry. I had to switch over to local drive for manual check-in. And I have no interest in making either of our days harder."

He told her his name.

"Phelando Morning?" she said. Those five simple syllables hit like cascading waves of anger, guilt, and despair.

"That's my dad. He's been here before?"

"Not only. He has an account." She squinted into her glass. "More than a few times. You're listed under authorized guest. Kind of looks like you, too. Which makes sense. Let me see if we have any of his preferred rooms left. Yep."

She passed him a plastic square card with Clover Inn's picture on one side.

"It's an old-style room with an old-style door. You ever used one of these before? Here, you swipe it along the side like this. Like I said, it's old-style, so no glass. And, yeah, here's the log-in for the computer. Breakfast ends at ten."

She pulled the key back as he reached for it.

"You promise I'm not going to have anyone coming looking for you?"

"I can promise it would be a surprise."

As she considered, the wrinkle across her forehead deepened and Pok realized it was a long-healed scar. Was it edited out in glass? Or had she opted to leave it as part of her distinctive features? Technologically naked, he was left to wonder.

"Good answer," she said and handed him the key.

The stairs reminded Pok of home and their chronically broken elevator. His room was at the end of the hall. It took several swipes for the paint-chipped door to acknowledge his right to access. A well-made bed centered a small room with a stainless carpet textured with fresh vacuum lines. The amenities—a full fridge, small snack bar, and air conditioner—lit up their digital displays with his approach. None showed glass functionality.

An ancient computer—full with a bulbous-backed monitor, separate hard drive and off-white keyboard with dust-caked keys—sat in the corner.

A yellow line ran from the hard drive to the wall, separate from the power cord. Did it work? Though he'd never used one, Pok knew about the relics. He resisted. In the opposite corner was a rotary phone.

The bed was heaven to his thighs. He pulled off sweat-drenched socks and groaned at his ankle. It was tender to the touch, right around the bone. Pain shot out like a dark web when he touched the bony part; numb, discolored skin surrounded it. He needed medical care, but New Jersey hospitals ran shepherd systems just the same as New York. It could potentially alert Odysseus.

No hospitals. Not until he crossed over to Louisiana, which was the only state exempt from the hospital mandates. Even then, any Louisiana hospital could very well *choose* to operate TSO; they just didn't *have* to. Only Hippocrates was safe.

Pok dug his father's *Principles of Internal Medicine* from his bag and turned to a section on joint injuries. He found a picture that looked very much like his own swollen ankle, just with lighter-colored skin. Dense medical jargon and specific anatomy assumed a hospital setting for the consulting physician. There were only a few sentences for treating severe ankle sprains out in the field. Mostly, it stressed the importance of getting to a medical facility. Pok was ready to see if old-fashioned rest would help, when he noticed something scribbled in the margins:

Joint injuries common when traveling off-grid. Proprioception limited.

Pok recognized his father's handwriting—a special elegance connected the slanted letters. The ink was old, near faded, but still legible. How long ago had he written this? Just below it, in thicker, newer ink, at a slightly different slant, was the following:

Suspect neural "withdrawal" contributes. (NFTF): brief morning calisthenics help realign nervous system.

He read the notes over and over, pondering over the quotation marks around *withdrawals*. His fingertips trembled against the page. The dark cloud of grief from his father's death stretched from horizon to horizon. Phelando would know what to do. He would know how to guide.

It happened so fast. Cardiac arrest. At his age? Had all the years of avoiding the tracking devices caught up with him?

"Daddy . . ." Pok choked on the word. The *Principles* text became blurred and illegible. He closed the book, let it fall to the carpet, and blinked the tide away. Without medical attention, Pok would be trapped in this hotel. Phelando wouldn't sob in the corner. He would *do* something. But what?

Pok surveyed the small room. *Think. Think.* He kept returning to the rotary phone. He couldn't go to the hospital. But what if the hospital came to him?

Thankfully, the phone had a button for the front desk; otherwise he would have spent the rest of the day and the night trying to figure out the number ring. It rang twice. The receptionist answered, slow, confused, as if she'd just received a call from a dead relative.

"Hello?" she said.

"It's room two-eighteen."

"Sure. Hi. Sorry, I didn't know this phone was even here. How can I help you?"

"Can you call for a medical kiosk? I just twisted my ankle coming up the stairs. It might need a brace."

"Holy shit. Ordering now. It should be here in twenty minutes. Two-eighteen."

"Perfect."

The kiosk would ret-scan him on entry and most certainly report his encounter to TSO. What if their response was to worsen his condition to further hobble him? Pok paused at the conspiratorial thought. That was new. All of this was new. But if he didn't get some type of relief, he wasn't going anywhere. Medical identification was essential; the kiosk wouldn't so much as give him a Band-Aid without it. He needed another pair of eyes. A counterfeit pair.

The room's computer gave no indication of being anything more than a random machine in a random hotel. Pok turned it on and checked the USB inputs. None fit. He'd have to do this the hard way.

He touched the screen. Nothing. He found the computer's mouse; a pointer moved in sync with his hand. The remote connection felt weird. Instead of inputting the given log-in, he broke into the computer's operating code to set up his firewall. The simplicity of the interface made it easier to protect. A state-of-the-art fortress with electronically operated doors and encrypted security systems was permeable to a skilled hacker. A simple, steel wall, however, would keep everyone and everything out.

When Pok was finished he stretched a stiff lower back and massaged his aching wrists, careful not to wake his thrumming ankle. Back to the log-in screen, he fished the key card from his bed and entered the username and password. His finger hovered over the enter key.

Now or never. "Twenty minutes" was ten minutes ago.

Enter.

He was in. The hard part done, he easily accessed the Underground Web and navigated to an online program that generated complex images of human retinas, instantly linked to a fake TSO medical record. Pok made up generic demographics: a thirty-five-year-old native of Pennsylvania with no previous medical conditions. This set, the screen blinked, and a pair of three-dimensional, roving eyes stared out at him.

Pok checked the time. Five minutes. He opened a new window and loaded Google, an old search site. He typed in his father's name, deleted it, typed in his own name, deleted that, and landed on *physician dies in MacArthur Hospital.* He filtered various articles from decades ago. The world tilted; his hand slipped off the mouse. The headline read: *Med School Hopeful Suspected of Poisoning Father.* The next: *Pok Morning Wanted for Questioning in Father's Death. Shepherd Organization Offers Reward for Whereabouts.*

They thought he'd killed his father.

Pok considered contacting Kris. How much did his friend know and *when* did he know it? He could get a message out, easily, but the risk level depended fully on if he could trust his old friend. Could he? He didn't know.

He instead searched the Underground's message boards for conspiracies pertaining to mysterious deaths involving the shepherds. There were plenty, most of them bordering on psychosis. Before long, though, he started to recognize some of the coauthors from his father's Project Do No Harm. A new thread with only a few replies grabbed his attention: *Phelando Morning, MD, would-be whistleblower for the shepherds, dies of "poisoning." Coincidence?*

A sudden shuffling sound, outside his door.

Pok froze. Odysseus had found him. He hadn't even lasted twenty-four hours.

Another sound—this time the clink of metal. Then, more shuffling. He eased to standing, leaning heavily on his good leg. He stepped forward, paused, felt his heart, felt his blood. He was alone; he was vulnerable. Another step. The hotel room stretched out in front of him.

Hand on the doorknob. What was he afraid of? He yanked it open. A dull line of fire crossed his shoulder. Overhead lights burned his eyes. He immediately retracted his face and pressed his forehead against the inside of the door. The medical kiosk. Of course; he'd completely forgotten. The specialized companion—complete with a ridiculous mini stethoscope around its neck—waited in the hallway, ready to scan and treat.

Pok rummaged in the bedsheets, wrapped his T-shirt over his eyes, and left just enough vision to lead the medical companion inside. He tilted the computer's screen to match the kiosk's scanners, careful not to tip the whole thing over. Pok bit his lip. Any vocalizations and the companion would immediately analyze his voice and compare it to the ret-scan. That would mean game over.

A chime. The companion lengthened. Its eyes glowed green. He was in.

The kiosk immediately gravitated toward his injury. It scanned his leg; a warm tingle wrapped the skin. There were no questions. There was no probing for pain or discomfort. Only assessment.

It spoke in a soothing, androgenous voice. "Traverse fracture of the left lateral malleolus. Surgery not indicated. Recommend synthetic cast and non-weight-bearing movement. Do you consent?"

Shit.

The kiosk repeated itself. "Do you consent?"

Pok lifted himself up to the computer, grabbed the mouse and keyboard, and half a minute later a monotone, metallic voice said, "Yes, I consent."

That was enough. The medical companion produced an off-white, fiberglass cast from a slit in its belly and efficiently wrapped his ankle and sole. It was all over in minutes. The companion paused at the door, as if considering him. Pok was taken back to all the moments he thought he sensed something more in Kai. Did the companion know? Did it suspect? Did it *see* him?

The moment passed; the companion left. Pok closed the door.

Pok inspected his new cast. He was lost in a strange place, surrounded by tech he hadn't grown up with, locked in a room that could very well be a prison. He'd effectively given himself a TSO tracker. Was it worth it? With the aid of the generated pair of retinas from the Underground Web, the cast would register in their system as his fabricated thirty-five-year-old patient. But if anyone chose to look closer . . .

He spread his father's map out on the bed. To get to Louisiana, he'd have to cut through Pennsylvania, which was as TSO-heavy as New York. Not too long ago, those states evoked future fantasies in medicine. At the Shepherd and Perelman School of Medicine, researchers and programmers trained shepherd-controlled robotic arms to autonomously identify and excise melanomas. The Shepherd School of Medicine at Case Western in Ohio just rolled out medical office cubicles so that employees could get regular, automated checkups without missing work.

And then there was Hippocrates Medical College in New Orleans. With an acceptance in hand and a full ride, it should have been easiest to mentally put himself there. But while he could still vividly see himself at MacArthur or Perelman or Case, any vision of life in Louisiana was grainy and undefined. Phelando had drawn an octagon around New Orleans and labeled it *off-grid*. Great. Medical school was supposed to lead him into the future; this place felt like a step back.

Pok put the map aside and rocked forward. He winced at the sudden, ferocious pain as his new cast synced with the applied weight. He gripped the sheets, teeth clenched, and just barely avoided crashing face-first into the floor. Nausea threatened vomit. *Breathe. Breathe.* The pain intensified as the synthetic cast shifted in pressure, aligning to the change in blood flow and activity. Then, relief. The nausea dissipated. The pain went back out to sea. The cast hardened as Pok shifted weight onto the ankle, protecting him from further agitation. He hobbled around the room. Not comfortable—not comfortable at all—but doable. He sat back down at the computer.

"What the fuck?"

A blinking ad at the bottom of the screen curdled Pok's skin. POK MORNING, 5'10", MALE, EARLY 20S. TRAVELING ALONE. HEFTY REWARD. CONTACT FOR INFO. Underneath was his smiling, naive face from his medical school application headshot.

Bounty ads were a known Underground Web commodity. Most were phishing viruses, police traps, or even elaborate pranks between hackers. But this . . . What the fuck was this?

Pok nearly fell against the wall unplugging the computer. Sitting in the dark made thick by the blackout curtains, the beginning patter of rain outside his window, he decided he'd had enough technology for the day.

Seven

BOUNTY

The next morning's sun yawned against Pok's back as he passed through the light congregation of shops characterizing Clover's downtown. He stopped at a sunglass store and bought a pair that blocked facial recognition. The change got him a few double takes—likely people responding to their glass's error message—and would prevent him from entering many establishments.

Free to be curious, Pok took in what was different from New York City and what was the same. For one, New Jersey cars had a sleeker, more angled design than Pok was used to. He'd seen them scattered throughout New York, always with attentive human drivers. Here, the opposite was true. The ubiquitous digital display ads, targeting him as simply an out-of-towner, offered temporary SLC subscriptions, hotel deals, and car-for-hire services.

A deep soreness settled into his legs and abs. Every step hurt. The cast learned his cadence and adjusted its pressure just enough to keep the pain from crossing over into the unbearable. Clover soon fell away and open road stretched in front of him, all the way to the horizon. He stuck to backroads.

A gray car, its engine a soft rumble, slowed near Pok and then sped away. A couple more cars did this, their passengers either oblivious or looking up briefly at the interruption. The vehicles must have registered him as a rogue pedestrian. The anti-suicide programming alerted cars to anyone nearing the street with suspicious mannerisms. Without glass or SLC identification, the cars saw Pok as a faceless anomaly. From the automotive industry's perspective, better safe than sued.

Pok passed several farms, some small and specialized and others with miles of homogenous crops. He stopped by a strawberry and avocado stand. His awakened stomach made its hunger known as he walked around the booth, searching for a person. There was no one. A kiosk—battery-powered and feeble—offered to scan him for payment.

Pok moved on, tired, hungry, and annoyed.

Pok saw the woman following him shortly after he crossed over into Pennsylvania. She stayed on the other side of the four-lane highway and kept more than a mile between them. At that distance she was but a vague silhouette hauling a large backpack. When the angle was right, the midday sun showed her complexion as similar to Pok's. He imagined a menacing grimace and a fist gripping a printout of his bounty.

Whenever he thought he was rid of her she'd appear again. She practiced neither camouflage nor overt intimidation. She didn't stop when he stopped. Whenever he looked back she allowed their eyes to lock before turning away. Not quickly but not lingering, either.

HEFTY REWARD, the bounty advertised. For how much? He should have found out. His father would have found out. Instead, Pok panicked and now had a strange woman trailing him across state lines with no idea what dollar sign she envisioned above his head.

He had to shake her.

Pok veered off into a side road, sat under a tree with gnarled, bare branches, and waited for her to pass. She didn't. He consulted his map, as if it held answers. It urged Pok to move quickly through the Keystone State. Pennsylvania was back under TSO coverage: Phelando had marked individual houses instead of inns or hotels. At his current pace, Pok would reach the next suggested resting place a little after midnight. His stomach rumbled. His joints sang. His ankle's low, throbbing ache threatened worse, as if protesting the crossing of state lines. And he had a straggler on his back.

To kill some time, Pok changed his clothes. In doing so, he noticed a new mole on his outer left thigh. It had a glassy, green sheen and stuck outward at an angle. And was that . . . Pok looked closer . . . legs?

Adrenaline hit. Whatever the hell this thing was, he wanted it *off*. Pok stomped his good foot; both shins sang. He slapped the parasite. It didn't flinch. Almost as if it was . . . attached. He pinched it, yelled as the exoskeleton cracked under the weight of his fingers, and pulled. A beetle-like creature, firmly in his grasp, clawed at the air.

A damn tick. Pok flung it away. Blood coated his finger and leaked fresh from his thigh. He carefully inspected the area and found it to be numb. That wasn't good.

Pok found another tick. And then a third. He removed each. The last squirmed free and promptly reattached to his bare belly. He plucked this one off, too, and checked himself again.

Overhead, the day was waning. Unless he wanted to sleep with uncovered tree roots for a pillow, he had to move on. He stepped back out onto the main road and saw her immediately. She sat on a tree stump about a mile down the chain-link fence. Waving couldn't have more cemented that she was waiting for him. She got up, ready to move when he did.

She wasn't going away. And she wasn't closing in. What, then, did she have planned? Was she young or old? Did she have a weapon? Would her voice match the terror she invoked? He imagined her finally overtaking him, standing over him, face shrouded in shadow with one foot pressed down on his broken ankle, using her glass to call TSO and let them know he'd been captured.

Brush reached from the surrounding wood to partially cover the winding road. Pok stuck to the middle to avoid more ticks. The foliage thinned to reveal a narrow stream with no discernible beginning or end: it disappeared as abruptly as it appeared. Abandoned cars and gutted houses dotted the path.

Night ushered in a moonless, starless sky. He stayed close enough to Philadelphia's edge to light his way. The skin beneath his cast itched terribly. A drizzle began before dawn and didn't let up until the sun was directly overhead. In the distance, foreign skyscrapers touched the heavens. He stopped every few hours to check himself. According to his map, his rest stop was just at the top of this next hill.

A clearly abandoned two-story house stood tucked at the edge of the woods. Pok would have missed it if he hadn't nearly tripped on the slim path that led out to the road. Vines and bushes wove in and out of the foundation, growing in between the missing porch steps. Only specks of the once-white paint dotted molded, crumbling wood.

A spot of light passed over the house. Pok whirled around, nearly tripping over the cracked, unstable banister that lined the pitiful pile of stairs. A flashlight bobbed like a drunken fairy between the trees. Wait, was that . . . ? Yes, it was: two distinct lines of light.

His stalker had company.

Pok sprinted up the stairs for the front door; his right foot went straight through the rotted wood. Something crashed inside the house, shaking the foundation. Voices mixed with dried leaves and gravel underfoot. Had they heard? Could they see? Pok looked past the house, at the waiting woods beyond. He'd unknowingly trapped himself. The only way back to the main road was through them, whoever *them* was. The house's front door yawned open, promising an aboveground tomb.

Pok tried to free his leg and stifled a yell. Splintered wood cut through his cast and into his ankle. Sweat sprouted across his skin. Eyes clenched, he yanked his leg free and fell back, panting, into the grass. Whoever was after him wouldn't have to do much. He'd essentially served himself on a platter.

Then he saw it, under the porch. A crawl space. He didn't consider, didn't look back to check his pursuers' proximity. He scrambled forward, hands over knees, and curled up underneath the decaying house. Unseen angles poked at his arms, the sides of his belly, his face. Panic fought against the constraint. He writhed to regain view of the outside. He had to see.

The pair of lights bobbed in the background, weaving in and out of trees, closer and closer. Pok had left his traveling bag clear out in the open.

"House looks ready to fall apart," the first voice said. A man's, nasal and high. "You sure he went this way?"

"No one's ever sure," a woman said. She sounded older. Her tone fit that of a sour face.

Two pairs of legs walked into Pok's line of sight. A partially bandaged hand grabbed his bag. "You think this is—Hey!"

Harsh, guttural shushing. A slight scuffle. The pairs of legs converged. Heavy breathing, more scuffles, and the legs swiftly switched orientation and again parted. The house creaked as one of the pair went up the stairs and inside. Pok muffled a cough as dust and globs of dirt rained around him. Something crashed inside; the man yelled obscenities and came running out.

"If he's in there, he ain't happy."

The legs with loose-fitting jeans walked up to the house. Long fingers reached under the edge and pulled into focus a man, clean-shaven and wary. The stranger's eyes homed in as if he'd known Pok's location all along. His jaw clenched. A million and one thoughts flitted behind that gaze. Finally, after an eternity, he surveyed the space under the porch. The man's expression gave nothing. He reached forward, grabbed a plastic bag just inches away from Pok, and stood.

"He's gone," the man said as the woman came up beside him.

"He must be close," she said.

"How much are they offering?"

"Enough. We're wasting time."

"He could be high-profile. We don't need that attention."

"It's a lot of money. We'd be set."

"Set up, that's what. This is trouble. I don't like it. And if it *is* from the shepherds they're going to be quick to cover it up. Cut any loose ends."

A pause in the air. Pok held his breath, his fate in limbo.

Finally, the woman spoke. "I swear, sometimes I think you like being broke."

The man sat in a porch-facing chair. His gaze flicked over Pok. The woman sat opposite him, her back to the house.

"Why mess up a good thing?" the man said. He opened Pok's bag. "Check out this map. The print is all funny."

"It's hand-drawn," the woman said. She pulled out Pok's white coat. "Holy shit. You see this?"

"'Pok Morning, Student Doctor,'" the man read. He said Pok's name like "Poke." "Maybe he got eaten by a bear."

"Ain't no bears in these woods. Maybe we'll get part of the reward if we turn these in."

"They'll know where he's going."

"That's the point," the woman said. "Let them deal with him."

"You really want the death of a med student on your conscience? Leave the coat. We don't want to be found with it."

The pair made a fire in the pit and settled beside the house. Their chatter reduced to muffles under the crackle of burning weeds set on retaking the land. If Pok could just shimmy over and out the side of the house, he could make a run for it. But even the smallest movement crunched the dead earth underneath. Pok's body ached with newfound vigor. His left leg in particular. He closed his eyes against a wave of nausea. The world drifted away to a safer distance. He could pretend he was in his bed, back at home, and his father would soon bring him a cup of tea.

A part of him hung on to the world and the fading voices, knowing that the woman could still find him, knowing the man's nobility to be rooted more in convenience than valor. But that other part, the part protecting his mind, could almost smell the tea. Peppermint, in his father's favorite mug. The one with the confident mouse in the physician's coat, ready to change the world.

Eight

UNDER THE RADAR

Pok woke to a soft, warm wind on his cheek. A horrid, stale taste of dried bile filled his mouth. He propped himself up and winced from a gash on his arm. He was outside. The overcast sky made it hard to tell if this was early morning or late evening. A healthy fire crackled a few feet away. His backpack had been rolled and placed under his head. His clothes hung on the low branch of a nearby tree. A small pot lay tilted against a chair. Some yellow liquid congealed around a wooden spoon.

He sat up fully and groaned. His neck was stiff. Light hurt his eyes. He checked his thigh. The bull's-eye rash was still there but somehow less menacing. A fresh bandage covered where wood had cut through his cast.

He should have been ready for the voice behind him. He wasn't.

"Don't freak out." A woman with dark skin and a friendly smile walked up to him. "Those two took forever to leave. It's a miracle they didn't find you."

He stared at her for a long time, evaluating. He'd spent the better half of the day having her silhouette sketched into his mind. Now, seeing her features, she was nothing like he imagined. Her face was soft, maybe a little younger than his father. She was shorter than he expected. There was something genuine and strangely familiar about her smile, and, if seen through glass, he'd be sure was the result of some illegal persuasion filter.

"One of them did," Pok said. "He had mercy on me."

"Some mercy. They robbed you, from what I can tell." She handed him his bag. He snatched it and looked inside. "They left you some honey. Not much else."

"My map?"

"If it's not in there, they took it. They tried to use this for firewood." She handed him his father's *Principles*. Black singed the back cover, but the fire hadn't spread inward. He flipped through. The pages were still intact. "Not big readers, I suppose. They probably scoped you at Clover Inn. You were standing at checkout with this massive book bag on your back, zero tech, and looking over your shoulder like you're running from the law. One thing I'll give you: you looked like you knew where you were going. I'd just decided you'd make a fine travel partner when I saw you were being tailed."

"I thought you were the one following me."

"Nope. I was following them. They made sure you didn't see them, but I made sure you saw me." She sat beside him. Her two front teeth were rotated inward half a turn. Instead of trying to hide it, her smile embraced it, strengthening the layout of her face. "Do you know why anyone would want you dead?"

Pok shook his head. Too quick. She pursed her lips. *Of course you know*, her look said. But she let it go.

"You were touch and go there for a hot moment." She handed him a warm cup. "Drink this. Fresh off the fire. You'll feel better."

"What is it?" Pok said but didn't wait for an answer. The drink was hot, but not scalding. The liquid hit his empty belly and spread cramps through his midsection.

"Kale, spinach, and vanilla. My miracle drink. Got it from my sister."

"It's a little sweet."

"I used some of your honey. I hope you don't mind. You were covered with ticks. I think I got all of them, though there were some places I didn't check. Out of respect."

He took another sip. "How'd I get out here?"

"When they finally left in the morning, I found you under that porch, about dead. You perked up a little as soon as I got them bloodsuckers off. And then you slept that fever off all day. I was wary your friends might circle back. You don't remember?"

"Not at all."

"In that case, I'm Jillian." She held out her hand. He took it.

"Pok."

"Really? You told me your name was Prince Tuesday."

Pok nearly spit out his drink. The warm blend cut down the wrong way and made him cough. Jillian put a hand on his shoulder and laughed.

"I'm just messing with you, Pok."

Pok lay back and covered his eyes. "It feels like my head's going to explode."

"That sounds about right. Let's get some food in you. I grabbed a bunch of to-go sandwiches from the Inn that just need a little heating."

He slowly adjusted to the spin and the nausea. She watched him as she rekindled the fire left by his would-be murderers. *Murderers.* The thought was ice in the night's chill.

A few minutes later Jillian handed Pok half of a freshly toasted chicken sandwich, took a hearty bite of her own, and resumed looking him over. "You're from New York," she said.

"How can you tell?" Pok tried the sandwich. Not the best, but it soon calmed his stomach.

"You travel like a city kid. Sorry—city *man*. I'm coming from that way, too." She held up his white coat. The back was noticeably burned at the bottom. "Honestly, I didn't know you had a hit on you until you said that. Probably not available to New Yorkers anyway. You got quite a ways to go. You heading to New Orleans?"

Pok wanted to trust her. There was something eerily familiar to her voice, the curve of her face, and even the mechanics of her speech. And she had gone above and beyond in hospitality. He was already done with his sandwich and feeling better for it.

"Come on," she said. "Your doctor's coat with your name on it says, 'Hippocrates Medical College.'"

"I am. And it's a medical student coat." He might as well commit to the narrative. "That's where I'm headed."

"Most people take planes to out-of-state schools, you know? But we're both in luck: I'm heading that way, too. Please don't tell me this whole 'on foot' thing is the plan. Correction, that ankle has already answered that question. I just hope *you* know it."

"It's the only way to stay under the radar."

"With that cast on? If I listen close enough I think I can hear it saying, *Hey, TSO, come pick me up!*"

"This registers as some thirty-five-year-old John Doe." Pok tucked his leg under him and winced. "At least, that's the hope. I got to make it work either way. Unless you think you can carry me."

"With two good legs it'll take you another month, easy, to reach Louisiana. I can't carry you, but I know something that will. It has wheels. Been around for more than a hundred years. Goes choo choo!"

"No vehicles," Pok said. "Under the radar."

"I'm not talking Amtrak or Manhattan subway. I mean a good old-fashioned 'riding the rails' train. There should be a train yard a few miles north of here. It's our best bet to reach New Orleans." When Pok remained skeptical, Jillian leaned in. "Trains are safe. If we're smart. The models haven't changed much for forty years, even though much of the country's commerce still depend on them. No tracking. No cameras."

"You've thought a lot about this, huh?" Pok said.

"My sister had it in her head that she was going to walk all the way from New York to New Orleans because she didn't want to be 'on the radar.' I'm not about that life. I looked it up and trains are the way to go. They call it *drifting*."

"What happened to your sister?"

Jillian laughed, long and full. She ran her hands up and down both thighs. "What *didn't* happen to my sister? We got separated just a couple days ago. I'm hoping she sticks to the plan so I can get back to New York as soon as possible."

Jillian took one more bite of her sandwich, wrapped and tucked away the rest, and threw dirt on the fire. She waved off Pok's offer to help clean up the camp area and afterward uncoiled her bulky backpack into a full sleeping bag. She snuggled into it and took out a small plastic bag, scooped some yellow powder out with her index finger, and inhaled a bit in each nostril. She lay back and massaged her legs, seemed to remember she wasn't alone, and wiggled the bag.

"I can't sleep without it."

"My friend used it to study," Pok said. "I wouldn't think of it for sleep."

"I thought the same. But it helps with the glass withdrawals, and that quiets the mind. Want any?"

Despite sleeping for nearly twenty-four hours, Pok's body said he could easily use more. "I'm not having withdrawals."

"Yet. What if I told you your body is full of shepherd nanobots and they're all shutting down now that you've left New York?"

"I'd call you a conspiracy theorist."

"I'd agree. I think we're just so used to *tech, tech, tech* that our brains are struggling to adjust. Either way, the Synth helps."

"Maybe next time," Pok said.

Jillian laughed. "Just say, *No, Jillian, I don't want your drugs!* I can take it."

"No, Jillian, I don't want your drugs."

"Rude."

Jillian tucked away her sleep aid, settled into her sleeping bag, and pulled the flap up over her head. Sure enough, she was soon snoring.

Pok did what he could to get comfortable and found the relief of rest outweighed the hard ground. He stared up at a patch of stars directly overhead, followed a shepherd satellite until it disappeared behind the clouds, and wondered what new surprises the morning would bring.

Nine

DRIFTING

They set off to the train yard the next morning with full bellies. Whether it was the relatively calm sleep, the purging of ticks from his body, or Jillian's traveling elixir, the fire across Pok's body had dissipated to intermittent embers. The bull's-eye rash on his leg was a deep purple outlined in near-black. His stiff, tightly wrapped ankle finally loosened nearly a mile down the road. Abandoned roads eventually dissolved into winding, overgrown foot trails.

A low, constant rumble spread underfoot. As the trees around them thinned, the screech, crank, and whir of far-off machinery grew. The last of the woods fell away; they were on a slight elevation overlooking the train yard. Mile-long locomotives passed one another on tracks close enough to create the illusion of shifting fractals. Long, thin, and multicolored, these trains were nothing like the thick smoke producers Pok had envisioned. Jillian nudged him; a train, still going at moderate speed, passed on the closest track. Light wind carried the smell of metal and grease as the behemoth defined its power clearly.

Jillian pulled out a pair of binoculars and scanned the yard. "You ever seen anything like this?"

"Never," Pok said. Trains carried car after car of lumber. Various logos, highlighted with graffiti, branded the sides of other, closed cars. "Which one goes to Louisiana?"

"I thought it would be simple. That they'd be labeled or something." Jillian straightened, set her jaw, and adjusted her bag. "We'll figure it out. Come on, let's see what we're dealing with."

They kept to the yard's edge. Order showed itself in the chaos. Some trains hardly slowed as they passed through with a ground-shaking whistle. Others arrived with one car configuration and left with another. Pok took note, mentally mapping out the yard. Then a train came into what he thought was a rerouting station just to reverse directions and head back out, unchanged.

"The trains leaving from this corner are all heading west," Jillian said. But she sounded unsure.

"We're going to end up in Alaska," Pok said. A figure, crouched and bulky, flitted between the train cars. "You see that?"

More movement across the way. His eyes now primed to the shift of heavy-clothed bodies, Pok saw the yard was in no way empty. Curious eyes peeked out from open train cars, encampments intermeshed with way stations, and narrow paths between the tracks. They were all curious about the newcomers.

"Let's keep to ourselves," Jillian said. "They might not be too excited to see city folk."

They found an empty, detached train car on a bent, misshapen piece of remote track that looked like it had long ago earned its retirement. The car's bottom came up to their chests. Jillian hoisted herself up without hesitation.

"All this from watching videos?" Pok said as she helped him board.

"My mom was a survivalist, used to take us off-road camping and adventure hiking." Jillian swept her flashlight over the car's interior. They were alone. The two settled in the far corner where there was just the right mix of ambient light and safe vantage view of the outside. Jillian pulled out her bag of Synth and this time didn't offer to share.

"There's one thing I learned about train hopping that I figured if I told you, you wouldn't come."

"That the people are cannibals?"

She waved a hand. "No, we can deal with that. Ninety percent of catching a train is waiting for a train."

Waiting sounded good to Pok. Waiting sounded like rest.

As the sun set, the yard came alive. The entering trains became contained luminaries. Fires blazed from cylindrical, metal trash cans. Chatter rose above it. A patrol car rolled up and stopped. Two figures walked up to either side. Pok's insides tensed. A minute passed. The figures blended back into the shadows and the patrol passed slowly through.

"They're not afraid," Pok said.

"Apparently not," Jillian said. "The yard is theirs."

A fight broke out in the middle of the night somewhere on the other side of the yard. Pops like Fourth of July firecrackers made Pok jump out of a dream-filled sleep. Nearby, coated in darkness, Jillian stifled a cry.

The reverberating gunshots left the yard still, like a kid holding its breath for the crucial moments right after the loud crash of something they'd broken.. After a few long minutes, police lights lit the sides of train cars, tents, and smoking trash bins. Intermittent yells—agnostic to distressed to furious—rose and then dissipated.

The sirens left; the lights trailed after. Scant whispers rose up from the tracks and then those, too, fell to dust.

Pok woke with a start. His whole body tensed, the night's chaos still playing on scattered dreams.

"Chill, it's me." Jillian stood over him, bright sunlight crowning her head. "I found our train. It's leaving soon."

Jillian led them across the tracks. The yard was infinitely more alive, as if surviving the night had inducted them into its culture.

"They're switching one of the cars," Jillian said, pointing. From the top of a train, a red velvet flag billowed in the wind. "See it marked there? That's where the workers will be. We'll board from the opposite end."

The train slowed to an inching roll as it entered the yard. Jillian stayed low and half walked, half ran beside it. Pok followed her lead. The cars were a foot or two higher than where they'd just spent the night. A cascading screech staccatoed through the air as it came to a complete halt.

"That's it," Jillian hissed. "Let's board."

Jillian grabbed one of the railings, sprang into the car, and turned to help Pok. Not thinking, Pok led with his bad foot. The synthetic cast contracted to balance the sudden shift. Pok cried out in pain, fell, and banged his knee against the steel. Jillian yanked him forward; he stumbled onto the platform.

"Get down!"

Pok dropped and pressed himself to the metal deck. Jillian threw herself down beside him. Across the train's underbelly, he watched curious workers half-heartedly investigate the commotion and then circle back.

"You hurt?" Jillian said.

"No," Pok said, breath heavy. "Thank you."

"Don't mention it." She rolled to check her bag. Sweat lined her brow and mouth.

"What do we do now?" Pok said, instantly despising the childlike tone of his own voice.

"We wait. Either they spotted us or they didn't. All we can do is wait."

An hour passed. The train rumbled beneath them. Finally, they sat up with their backs against the car. The metal was rough and textured, not at all meant for sitting. They were mostly protected from the wind, which whistled against the train's sides. The air, however, was cold under the overcast day.

"How long until New Orleans?" Pok said.

"A day and a half," Jillian said. "Maybe two. Might as well get comfortable."

Pok gazed upon the countryside. Grass connected both horizons. The light, collateral breeze on his face, the shake and jolt of the train, the thrill of almost being caught: Pok realized he had no clue where he was. Somewhere in Pennsylvania, likely, but where, really? And it wasn't just him. It wasn't just people, either. *Nothing* knew where he was. He wasn't tracked. He wasn't on a schedule. He was floating through space and time without being tethered to it.

The first night was calm, uneventful, and well-slept for both Pok and Jillian. Stops were few and far between; the train rolled steadily south. Jillian rationed out the sandwiches she'd packed and by the time they saw signs for Mississippi, Pok's stomach was in full protest.

As the sun set on their second day, they rolled into a small town with row houses, parks, and scant buildings. A narrow highway ran near parallel to them. Cars passed in clear view. If a rider looked out at the train at just the right moment, at just the right angle, they might find two pairs of eyes looking out at them.

Only one pair, perhaps. Pok felt Jillian's on him. He pretended to shift against the wind. Much like when tailing him on the road, being discovered didn't faze her.

"What?" he said.

"You're young," she said.

Pok hadn't expected that. "Okay?"

"I'm sorry! You're really young to be out here on your own, with a bounty on your head, no less. Who did you lose?"

Pok *really* hadn't expected that. The train gained speed as they left behind the town and its one highway. He hoped the bit of wind that licked inward between the cars would be enough to dry his tears before they could fall.

The silence persisted through a half-mile cut through wild woods. It followed them into a tunnel carved into the side of a mountain. Because of the path's slight curve, the black was sudden and sharp. Pok's body tightened. Dim lights ran in parallel lines across the interior wall.

Silence died in darkness. "You still don't trust me, do you?" Jillian said.

The question frustrated Pok, as he'd been asking it of himself. "I don't know you," he said.

He expected a rebuttal, or some stinging manifestation of her own frustration, something that would make it easier to shut down. Why was he with her, anyway? What did he have to gain and how much could he lose? They were set to cross into Louisiana overnight. She was a sound sleeper; he could sneak away if the train slowed enough. Maybe that would be better for them both.

"I wasn't telling the whole story about my sister." Jillian's words softly pierced Pok's worst thoughts. The weight in her voice told of careful, prolonged consideration and shame. The dark, along with many things, brought courage.

"Oh?" Pok said. His eyes flitted from one dim light to the next.

"She was pregnant," Jillian said. "She didn't trust the shepherds. Her doctor talked about delivering at Hippocrates in New Orleans. Then, at thirty-seven weeks, she got real paranoid real quick. She thought the shepherds had her doctor murdered or something. She panicked and wanted to leave the city right away. I tried to stall, buy some time, told her we'd look into plane tickets. But she packed a bag and was halfway out the door when I did the only thing I could do: offer to go with her. She insisted on traveling under the radar, much like you."

Pok was grateful for the dark, grateful that Jillian couldn't see how far his jaw dropped, how much more the whites in his eyes showed. The familiarity of Jillian's smile, the immediate comfort he'd felt upon waking up by the fire that he'd erroneously attributed to deceit. The beginning of a lingering, nagging distrust she never deserved. In her, he'd seen his father's patient. Florence, Jillian's sister.

"You still with me?" Jillian said.

"Sorry, I just . . . It reminds me of someone my father treated. She was very pregnant and very paranoid about tech."

"What happened to her?"

He couldn't tell her that his father had planted the seed of traveling to New Orleans. What if Jillian blamed Phelando? Did *Pok* blame his father? Still grappling with this, the lie fell out of him. "He convinced her to stay and she had a healthy baby boy. I'm guessing it went differently for your sister?"

"She went into labor six hours into the trip, right after we checked in at Clover. Which, between you, me, and God, was an enormous relief. I had a reason to urge us to the hospital. It wasn't easy. She started talking crazy, saying that the baby wasn't coming, that it wasn't time, that she still had three more months. This even as the contractions brought her to her knees. She swore that the hospital would do the wrong thing. Send her back. I finally got her to go in by promising it would just be a checkup. As far as births go it went pretty smooth after that. She did it all natural, God bless her, and had a beautiful baby girl at 3:09 p.m."

The unsaid *but* hung in the air. The *thwap-thwap-thwap* of the train wheels over old industrial tracks filled the space between them. They emerged from the tunnel. Both Pok and Jillian squinted against the sudden and full day.

"I think about if I would have still taken her there, had I known Jersey hospitals are shepherd tech."

"You wanted the best for her," Pok said. "The shepherds are the best. What happened at the hospital?"

Her hands began to rub her legs and then stopped and folded into themselves. Pok gave her time. Their silence welcomed the grind of wheels over train tracks and the far-off drone of cicadas.

"They were going to transfer her back to New York. Right to MacArthur Hospital. I guess she got wind of it somehow. Listen to me, implying the best thing would have been for her *not* to know. For her autonomy to be fully revoked. They brought Baby Girl in for skin-to-skin time. Probably meant to be the last before transfer. She told me she wanted to be alone with her daughter and, as I was about to step out, she grabbed my arm and told me she wanted to be *really* alone. I knew it was a bad idea. And I still did it. I disabled all the tech in the delivery room and told myself I'd just step out for five minutes. When I came back, she was gone. Damn it, Florence, why couldn't you just do it the easy way? Now you got me out here hitchhiking on trains, telling my sob story to America's Most Wanted."

Florence. Hearing the confirmation, putting the name to life, she turned from an idea to a reality. Pok visualized her in a hospital bed connected to all types of monitoring, wanting nothing more than to bond with her Baby Girl.

"It was my dad," Pok said. Jillian swiveled toward him. Confusion settled into realization. "He's who I lost."

"How?"

"He got real sick real fast. He went into the hospital and next thing I knew his Memorandium was outside my door."

"That's awful."

"Odysseus Shepherd called me right before. And right after, someone tried to kill me."

"Oh, shit." Jillian bit her lip. Pok softened his gaze, letting her know it was okay. "Do you think they killed him?"

"I do." Pok hadn't asked himself that yet, not directly, because it was easier to distract himself with questions like *Do I trust her?* But now that it came out, now that she had elicited it, he knew the words were true. *The shepherds killed my dad.* "He was a physician at their hospital. He was about to expose some things they didn't want public. I could get firing, but killing him?" Pok shook his head. "I don't understand it."

"And now they're after you?"

"I'm going to New Orleans because it's the only place I know to go. My dad had friends at Hippocrates. I'm not sure I still want to be a doctor, not after this."

"What was his name?"

"Phelando. Phelando Morning."

"Dr. Morning," Jillian said.

Pok listened for any tonal flavor that indicated she connected the dots to her sister. That she recognized the reason she was stuck on this train. There was none. Only sorrow.

The train's brakes creaked; they slowed to a crawl. In front of them, at the bottom of a ditch on the edge of the woods, was an old car, nearly taken back completely by the earth. There had been a few along the journey, mostly on the side of the road, their windows hollowed out, vegetation growing through enough to blur the lines between machine and forest.

"That's tough," Jillian said. "I'm sorry."

The train picked up and the car was gone.

"Yeah," Pok said. "Me too."

Ten

CHECKPOINT

Pok gave up on sleep somewhere in the middle of the second night. Jillian slept deep and hard; he was careful not to wake her. Her imperfect teeth, just visible through parted lips, glinted with the moon's light. He pulled himself up, slow and quiet. Humidity had thickened the air. Pok looked over the rail. Beyond the trees, the land had turned to glass.

Not land. Water, stretching across the horizon. The train's tracks curved just right to protect from the worst of the wind; it wrapped around Pok like a gentle breeze, mimicking how it might feel to stand on the lake's shore. A hole in the cloud cover gave view to a blanket of stars beyond.

What lake was this? Pok didn't know. He didn't know the time, didn't know the temperature, didn't know if the sky would continue to clear or if the clouds would close in preparation for rain. Only that they were heading south along the American countryside. Here, on this train, with Jillian, without glass, he was fully out of the system, riding along the edge of a society he'd left behind.

The train hitched; a low, far-off screech drifted from the front. Jillian stirred, rolled over, and then jumped up. She came up beside him and looked out over the rails.

"Louisiana?" she said.

"I don't know," Pok said. Jillian nodded at the uncertainty.

"Look, a sign," she said through a yawn. "'Billy Bayou Farms. The Heart of Louisiana.'"

"That's MouseKill Farms," Pok said, remembering Odysseus's interview with Tatiana Tate. "It was on Dad's map."

"Means we must be close to New Orleans and a warm meal," Jillian said. Another hitch, a long, rumbling screech of metal slowing metal underfoot, and the train came to a crawl. Thick southern air settled around them, coating Pok in a glaze of sweat. "Come on, this is us."

Jillian readied herself. The train couldn't have been going more than a few miles an hour. Still, a deep dread clung to Pok's chest. One small slip and Pok wouldn't be around to worry about a bounty.

"You got to hit the ground running. That's the key." Jillian must not have seen what she expected or wanted in Pok. "What's wrong?"

"My leg," Pok said. "I don't think I can jump."

"You have to. This train is going to speed up any second now, and who knows where you'll end up. I'll go first and then help you off."

Jillian chose action over further deliberation. She jumped diagonally in the train's direction of motion, stumbled a few steps as her feet hit the grass, and regained her balance. She broke into a light jog beside the tracks.

"Land on your right leg, and I'll pull you forward."

Pok's chest heaved. Both legs warned against what Jillian suggested. *Demanded* against it.

"Pok. Damn it, Pok, jump!"

Pok jumped. He led with his right foot. Hot fire sprang up from the sole, shot through the shin, and spread around his thigh. He'd angled it wrong; he was falling toward the tracks and would be pulled under the wheels, his body reduced to unrecognizable material. Jillian grabbed his collar and yanked, hard. He fell away from the train and into the patchy grass. His shoulder hit, and he rolled with a roughness that spoke to the train's momentum.

There was no time for rest.

"Move!" Jillian said. "We can't be seen."

She pulled Pok up with reserved strength and continued to pull until he was running, stumbling through the grass, torturing his already-damaged legs through the dips in the earth. She finally let him go after they crested a small hill. Pok threw himself against the wide, moss-coated trunk of the nearest tree. His body's aches reached up to his molars. A dry, sour taste spun nausea from his tongue down to his bowels. He shut his eyes against it.

"We have to move." Jillian's voice was calm and level. "I can't carry you."

Still, she helped him up and slung his arm over her shoulder. He wanted to shrug her off, to show that he wasn't just a burden, but the world spun every time he opened his eyes. They followed a thin, beaten trail through a patch of wood that bordered the west side of the lake. He bore as much of his weight as he could but still needed Jillian for every step. Through the trees were the first glimpses of red-roofed houses and open-doored barns.

"Almost there," Jillian said, her voice strained. Was she limping, too? He tried to remember how she'd landed. He'd been so caught up in his own pain that he hadn't considered hers. "There's someone up ahead. Survival 101: if they ask, you're exhausted, not sick."

Two men, both tall and thick-bodied, met them at the only road leading into the farm. One was Pok's complexion and the other was several shades lighter. They had short but full beards and wore black, tight-fitting wool head caps.

"What's your business?" one said.

"We're traveling to New Orleans," Jillian said.

"Did you just come off that train? New Orleans is that way." The man pointed down the main road heading away from the farm. It ran parallel to the train tracks.

"We're hoping for a place to sleep and recharge," Jillian said. "We're severely dehydrated."

"Again, the city is that way."

The other man stepped forward, staring down the road as he spoke. "Forgive Edmund. His parents didn't love him as a child."

Edmund's rock-hard demeanor broke. "You know, I really wish you'd stop with that joke. And I go by Eddie."

"Who says I'm joking?" The man kicked a rock into the surrounding brush. "We have to check your bags. It's protocol. A safety thing. Then we can set you up with a room."

Edmund glared at his partner, who kept his eye on the farm. Pok and Jillian handed over their backpacks. Edmund snatched them up.

"Traveling light, I see," Edmund said.

"Have you seen a woman come through here?" Jillian said. "Looks a little like me. Had a baby with her."

"A lot of people come through here." Edmund searched Jillian's bag, zipped it back up, and opened Pok's. He pulled out the jar. "What's this?"

"Honey."

"We'll need to test it. Make sure it's safe."

"It's . . . it was my dad's." Speech hurt. The adrenaline of disembarking the train spent, Pok felt more ill than tired.

"It has sentimental value," Jillian said. "Can't we hold on to it?"

"Protocol. You understand."

"See, loveless childhood," the other man said.

"Deidrick, I'm about sick of your shi—"

As Edmund turned to protest, Deidrick plucked the jar from his hands.

"I'll make sure it gets back to you. And that he doesn't use it on his breakfast." Deidrick handed back both of their bags. "Welcome to MouseKill."

Eleven

MOUSEKILL FARMS

Wooden-slabbed houses with metal roofing and elevated foundations lined the road into Billy Bayou Farms. Rhythmic cricket drones competed with the deep, resounding bellows of bullfrogs. Pok ducked to avoid walking into a swaying cloud of gnats. Atop a hill, the main farmhouse overlooked a vast valley of moonlit crops all the way to the horizon.

"We're one of the last completely independent farms in the country," Deidrick said. "TSO tried, but the owners weren't having it. The Mississippi and the lake keep the soil ripe. We haven't needed TSO tech to turn a crop yet, knock on wood." Deidrick rapped his knuckles on the side of a barn.

"I'd never heard of Billy Bayou—MouseKill," Jillian said. "Do you export to other states?"

"Only Second Life ones. Most of Louisiana exclusively gets its produce locally. We stay in business as long as the internal support continues." They came up on Big Bayou Inn. Blue-lined steps led up to the front door, open and welcoming. "They'll take good care of you. I got to get back to my station. It's too late for dinner but there's free breakfast at Shrubbery, the cafe right across the field. Starts at sunrise. You want to get there early. The breakfast here is pretty popular."

Inside, the receptionist greeted them with a smile that had a brighter, fresher quality than at Clover Inn. That wasn't the only difference. No computer, no keyboard, no glass. Just pen and paper. He booked them a room on the third floor, up the winding stairs and just down the hall.

Two beds, modestly made, centered the small space. An old screen-based television was mounted on the wall. Jillian opened the fridge next to the sink. Heads of lettuce, stacked tomatoes, and wrapped meats stocked the shelves. Pok's mouth watered from the green aroma. Jillian washed two thick, red apples in the sink and handed him one.

"Maybe there's a doctor here," she said, watching him.

"I just need to rest," Pok said. Juice ran down his chin. The apple's sweetness intensified the deep, throbbing pain in his molars.

"I'm going to look around," Jillian said. "Talk to the natives. Someone must have seen Florence. You good here?"

"Feeling a little better already." And he was. The room stopped tilting. The apple was already hitting his stomach. He took another bite. When Jillian hesitated at the entrance, he waved her away. "I'm going to shower. I'll be fine."

He stripped the apple until its beady seeds peered from inside the core like spider eyes. Pok scooted to the end of the bed and hoisted himself up using the bathroom door. How long had it been since he'd showered? A few days ago, at Clover. Was it only that? It felt like forever.

"Dad, if you could see me now," Pok said as he took inventory of the bathroom. The toilet had a handle for flushing. The sink wasn't automatic. He inspected the shower, hoping for a digital thermostat, and instead found control knobs he'd only ever seen in movies.

Once inside, the hand-drawn curtain pulled behind him, he turned the shower knob and recoiled from the sudden spray of cold water. He twisted, searching for heat, and found the knob also moved up and down. Oriented, he let the water run off him. His muscles relaxed and even loosened. The silence, the interstitium, just him and his thoughts, was dangerous. Was this real? Was his father really gone?

A sharp explosion of nausea brought him to his knees. He closed his eyes and pressed his forehead into the linoleum. His stomach cramped. His diaphragm spasmed. Thick saliva flooded his tongue just before hot acid pushed up and out of him. Vomit, red with bits of apple flesh and lined with suds, circled the drain.

Pok angled against the shower wall. Eventually, his stomach settled and the world stopped spinning. He felt for the knob, turned off the water, and then looked around. The bathroom remained level. He toweled off, crept out into the main room, slipped on a change of clothes from his bag, and lay back on the bed.

A soft, respectful knock came at the door. "It's Jillian. You decent?"

Jillian wasn't alone. The two other women were both taller than her. One wore a white physician's coat that passed her knees. Compared to the student coat Pok's father had gifted, the fabric was sturdier, the trim more sophisticated. The other woman carried a briefcase and wore yellow scrubs. *Hippocrates Medical Center* and its mouse-and-snake insignia sat atop their names.

"I was worried about you," Jillian explained. She frowned at the room, as if she could sense his sickness. She came to his bedside, felt his forehead. "You're burning up."

"I just threw up in the shower."

The physician looked from him to Jillian. Her black hair was cut low. She couldn't have been more than a couple years older than Pok yet stood with the experience of someone twice his age. Her partner stood a couple steps back, gaze slightly lowered, hands neatly in front of her. "I'm Dr. Cheryl Roberson and this is my scribe, Samantha. We hear you got pretty sick on the trek over. This is all from ticks?"

"This is new," Pok said. "It hit me all of a sudden."

"You walked all the way from New York?"

"We took a train," Jillian said, pacing. "But before that we walked quite a ways. His ankle is pretty beat-up, too."

"Let's check you out. Lyme can show up in a lot of different ways, but best to make sure we're not missing anything."

Pok lay back on the bed. Dr. Roberson took his temperature, heart rate, and blood pressure. She started her examination with his eyes and carefully moved down his body. She narrated any findings to her scribe. While much of her vocabulary tapped into Pok's recent anatomy studies, many of the phrases remained foreign. Dr. Roberson spent the most time on his rash, describing it in exquisite detail.

"Do you know how long the tick was on you?"

"At least a day. Probably more."

She paused when she got to the cast. "This is fiberglass. Shepherd-made? How long have you had it on?"

"I got it placed, what, five or six days ago?"

Dr. Roberson pulled out medical-grade scissors from her bag and went to work on the cast. Removed from his skin, it shriveled and clanged against the floor. As for his ankle, the swelling was gone. Pok's skin, however, was scorched red with raised welts and sensitive to the cool air, as if blowing on an exposed nerve.

"Looks like you had an allergic reaction. We see that sometimes with synthetic casts."

Dr. Roberson donned a fresh pair of gloves, lathered a cream over the affected skin, wrapped his ankle in several layers of gauze, and then applied a black Velcro brace. She watched for any discomfort as she tightened it.

"This should last until you get to the city. The tick bite and rash are pretty textbook for Lyme. Good news is we can treat it. As for the vomiting." She stepped into the bathroom and quickly came back out, two fingers over her nose. "Lyme could be the reason for that, too, but unlikely."

"Could it be from the cast?" Pok said.

"Maybe," Dr. Roberson said. "Have you eaten anything today?"

"Just an apple."

Dr. Roberson nodded. "That may explain the nausea. Your body's probably used to GMO food and this didn't sit right with your gut biome. They have some antacids in the apothecary downstairs that should help." Pok wasn't convinced. An aversion—allergy—to fresh food? This was something deeper. The violent response had been near immediate, not long enough for his digestive system to process the apple.

Dr. Roberson sensed his unease. "What still worries you?"

He told her. She listened.

Dr. Roberson felt his pulse again. "Still a little fast. Breathing, too. Your autonomics are a little off. Here, let me try something. Lift up your shirt."

Pok did so. Dr. Roberson placed on his chest and stomach wire leads attached to three different adhesive patches. She brought her face close to his.

"Relax, breathe, and follow my eyes."

Hers were a light brown with light striations, like the center of a sunflower. Her pupils oscillated in size. His breathing matched hers. A wave of panic hit, sudden and fierce. Manicured fingers dug into his shoulder.

"Focus," she said.

He did. He caught her rhythm again. Could he feel her heartbeat? Or was it his own? Had they become one? The panic dissipated. His muscles relaxed. Satisfied with her readings, Dr. Roberson pulled the wires from Pok's chest, tucked them in her bag, and sat back on her haunches.

"What was that?" Pok said.

"EKG alignment. I just taught it at first-year orientation. As long as the patient is stable, it's perfectly safe and works like magic." She felt his pulse. "Heart rate's back to normal; breathing is good."

"He doesn't need to be in a hospital or anything?" Jillian said.

"Nah, I don't think so," Dr. Roberson said. "The EKG alignment worked. The cast is replaced. Antibiotics should help. I suspect you're through the worst of it until you get to Adjustment."

"Adjustment?" Pok said.

"It's like a cross between quarantine and tech detox. A little bit overkill but it does the trick."

Dr. Roberson looked over her scribe's shoulder to make sure she got everything and then pulled out a small cloth pouch tied shut with string. She handed it to Jillian. "Antibiotics. Mix this in his tea. It should break the fever overnight."

"Do a lot of doctors see patients here at the farm?" Pok said.

"Only the lucky ones. We get to see a lot of things we wouldn't in the city. There's a lot of opportunity to consult with AI hospitals, as long as it's not direct patient care. It's the best of both worlds."

Dr. Roberson packed her bag and nodded to her scribe.

"You'll get a full physical exam in the city," she said. "Make sure you let them know when you started meds. They'll be able to see if this is chronic Lyme and if that ankle needs surgery. Hopefully not on both, but better to be safe. Until then, we watch and wait."

Twelve

CARVE BEES

The night proved a restless chore marked by scattered dreams. Pok finally gave up and flipped through his father's *Principles* under the bedside lamp's weak, yellow light. Hours in, the sun rose and the first of the farm's animals began to stir. Pok yawned against the morning. His thoughts, quick and sharp, cut against his body's fatigue.

"How long you been up?" Jillian said, squinting against what dawn made it through the thin curtains.

"Awhile. Weird dreams."

"I'm telling you, a little Synth can go a long way." Jillian uncovered and massaged her thighs.

"You injured?" Pok remembered her swaying gait after jumping off the train. Had she told Dr. Roberson? Pok didn't think so.

"Circulation's shot, just in the legs. Painful at best, *you don't want to know* at worst."

Until now, Pok had only seen her fully clothed. Jillian's legs didn't look prosthetic, not fully. They reminded Pok of a classmate's companion, back when they still tried to look humanoid. The skin was shiny but not metallic, smooth but not without texture. Their shape was disproportionate to the rest of her figure in a vague, elusive way.

Jillian caught him staring. "It's okay. You can ask."

"Sorry."

"Don't be. I severed my spinal cord right at T12. About ten years ago now." Jillian touched the small of her back. "It was a cannonball at a pool party, believe it or not. The Shepherd Organization—they weren't nearly as big yet—was funding a research study that was the only voice of hope. I don't know exactly how they did it. Either stem cells or nanobots or both. But it didn't just reconnect my legs to my brain. It made me somehow stronger. Like it built up my muscle, you know?"

"That's incredible," Pok said.

"Yeah, well, don't get too excited. These babies have taken me places, but also they have really *taken* me places, if you know what I mean. They've been very angry with me since I left New York."

"The Synth doesn't help?"

Jillian smiled. "I'm seeing if I can wean myself off." She rolled down her pants, rotated her legs off the bed, and stretched as she stood. "We should get going. Grab breakfast, check out the market, and hit the road. We may actually sleep in New Orleans tonight."

Outside, MouseKill Farms was fully awake. Chickens lazily grazed in the road, picking the morning grub from the dew-cropped grass. Horse-drawn carriages carried large loads. Bicycles zipped by. The laughter of playing children blended with the rise and fall of birdsong.

Shrubbery was full. The locals ate and communed with a careless joy that signified the type of comfort only home could afford. The tourists and travelers didn't need WELCOME TO MOUSEKILL! merch or sun hats to identify them. If they weren't eating they were staring off somewhere, lost in a mental fog. Hardly any talked with one another.

Pok and Jillian filled up at the buffet and sat by the window. Remembering the apple, Pok at first took timid bites. His stomach accepted the meal. Jillian picked through her food.

"Shit," Jillian said as she bit into a sandwich. Her bottom lip bloomed blood. "I bit my lip. Senses all messed up. See, it's because I didn't take my morning medicine."

Jillian pulled out her yellow bag of Synth and rotated it between her fingers, considering. Her right hand trembled; she rubbed her thigh with her left. She turned toward the wall, ducked her head, and half a minute later put the bag away.

"Is it hard to stop?" Pok asked.

Jillian closed her eyes and rested her head against the chair. "You mean, am I addicted? Worried, yes. Addicted, no. I'm still in control." She peeked at him. "Don't give me that look. That judging look. I'm learning you."

Pok changed the subject. "Did you find out anything about your sister?"

"Not a thing. She might have gone straight to New Orleans. That was our plan anyway. You finished? So am I, let's go."

Outside, a small but dense market of clothing vendors and fresh produce awaited satiated tourists. Pok soon found himself richer with a new set of clothes, an anti-tick cream, and a tote bag.

"Look at those pretty golden locs," one merchant said. Various handmade garments, the colors rainbow diverse, hung from his booth. "Here, I have something just for you."

The merchant ducked behind a door of hanging beads and came back with a knitted cap. Pok pulled it over his hair—it stretched easily—and down over his ears. The wool itched more than it should have. The merchant—an older man with olive skin, a slant smile, and deep-set eyes that never worried about the rain—offered to take the cap back at Pok's hesitation.

"I have more," he said.

"I don't have cash," Pok said.

Jillian reached over him and blessed the merchant's hand. His smile widened. "Good day to you both!"

"How much did you give him?" Pok said.

"Enough."

The next row of stands advertised medicinal herbs, healing elixirs, and natural remedies for a variety of ailments. Freshly caught Lake Pontchartrain fish on ice, their mouths open. Hanging racks of aged meat. One booth offered remedies to help with various withdrawals. Both Pok's and Jillian's gazes were drawn to it, as if aligned with its magnetic field. Information sheets outlined the various types of withdrawal. There was mild withdrawal—being away from one's spouse for a lengthy trip, for example—to more serious withdrawal like drug and alcohol use.

"'Withdrawals from the city,'" Pok read. He held up a bag of dried mangos and wiggled it in Jillian's purview. "Maybe some of this instead of . . . you know."

"I'm allergic," she said. She didn't look amused. Pok put the mangos back.

They came to a stand with jars of variously colored honey. The largest jar, a couple feet high, housed a giant honeycomb with maybe a thousand buzzing bees crawling over one another. Mesh covered the top.

"Welcome to MouseKill!" the enthusiastic merchant said from behind the booth. "Would you like to try a sample?"

The honey wasn't near as sweet as what Pok was used to back home. Its full, creamy texture tingled his tongue and inner cheeks. Jillian tried it with wide, critical eyes. Pok grimaced against the promised nausea, and then . . . it passed.

Jillian explained on his behalf. "Our stomachs haven't sat well with the food here."

"Let me guess: New York?"

"How'd you know?"

The merchant shrugged. "We get a lot of New York–New Orleans transplants. They both want the city and to be free of the city. Here, try this strain. Different colony, different taste. Like wine."

"Someone's looking a lot better." Dr. Roberson had come up during their taste test. She scrutinized the selection. "That's a good sign."

The beekeeper, who had been regarding him with veiled curiosity, came alive. "You're the one that brought the vintage honey. What's the name . . ." She snapped her fingers.

"Pok?"

"Yes! Pok! I was afraid we'd already missed you."

The beekeeper came from behind the booth and shook his hand. The woman was taller than she looked. Her hair was braided to the side. Jillian shrugged and mouthed, *Just go with it.*

"It's great to meet you. Both of you. But especially you." She blushed, stepped back, and eased her hands down her side. "Can I show you something?"

Pok moved to join her behind the counter. She laughed.

"Not here. Come. Shade!" Pok only now noticed the man sleeping in a chair. His brimmed hat covered his face. He jerked awake. "Man the booth for me. I'll be back before cleanup."

The merchant leading, they pushed through the rest of the market until the road thinned and branched off. A buzzing sound grew to a surrounding thrum as they came to the trees. A neat row of five wooden containers lined the gap. The bees came into focus. One landed on Pok's shirt. He resisted the urge to swat it away.

"Don't we need bee suits?" Pok said.

"We definitely need bee suits," Jillian said, slapping the air without restraint.

"Carve Bees don't sting." The beekeeper plucked an angry bee out of the air and, before either of them could compute, jabbed it into Jillian's arm. She sprang away, full body tense, mouth agape to yell out in pain, and then stopped.

"See?" the beekeeper said. "No stingers."

"Don't do that," Jillian said.

Phelando's jar—characterized by the stained walls, the chipped top, and, of course, the honey still inside—sat on one of the crates. A bee exploring the rim buzzed off as the keeper picked it up.

"This honey that you have. Where'd you say you got it?"

"My dad. He told me he had it for years."

"Which makes sense. Because it doesn't exist anymore."

Pok didn't understand. "But wait. Aren't these Carve Bees?"

"Yes. It's not the bees that shouldn't exist. It's the strain. It has antibodies specific to a line of Carve Bees we thought were completely eradicated ten years ago."

"I wrote a review paper on this," Dr. Roberson said. "There's evidence that TSO created Synth partly to kill off the colonies. A lot more evidence, I suspect, but only so much you can say in published articles."

The beekeeper nodded. It looked like her Christmas Eve. "I've been raising bees my whole life, and it's like you just brought me the Adam and Eve of Carve Bees. And they will be fruitful and multiply. Come, let me show you." She took them to the edge of the clearing to a stand-alone box that emitted a deeper, heavier buzz. "These are colonizer bees. They aren't specialized and can become any other type of Carve Bee."

The beekeeper poured some of Phelando's honey into the open slit in the top. "They'll feed this honey to their bee larvae. Those larvae will develop into Carve Bees who will make honey strain eight-thirty-six, with all its medicinal properties."

"They're like stem cells," Pok said.

"Yes. I suppose they are." The beekeeper closed the jar. "Here's your honey back. I topped it off, a little interest in return for your loan. It's the same exact composition—I included a spectroscopy printout as proof in case, like me, you have trust issues. You're a med student, too, I'm assuming?"

Dr. Roberson shifted beside him, instantly interested in how the question made him pause.

"No. I mean, yes." The warmth around his ankle teleported to his cheeks. "Almost. I got a little sidetracked."

"But we're making it," Jillian said.

"They are quite lucky to have you," the beekeeper said. "Student Doctor Pok, you're already making an impact."

Thirteen

UNSOLICITED ADVICE

Pok, Jillian, and Dr. Roberson stopped by a clothing stand with a variety of wool shirts and undergarments. The mid-morning crowd had thinned.

"I didn't know you were in the incoming class," Dr. Roberson said as she considered a red sweater blouse. "You don't see that often. A city kid—New York City, no less, Shepherd Valley—coming to Hippocrates. You missed orientation. Late decision?"

"My dad passed away," Pok said, surprised at how easy the words came. There was instant guilt and disgust over the excuse. "It was sudden."

Instinctively, Pok looked above her head for insight, but, of course, there were no dominant states to consult. No well-packaged suggestions on how to either defuse growing tension or expand on a budding connection. Lost, his gaze descended to her face. Her eyebrows pushed away from each other. Was her mouth curled in disapproval or discomfort? Did the way her cheeks crowded her eyes mean she was deep in thought?

Glass offered these insights. But was it helpful? Had the deeper connection been just illusion? He felt naked standing in front of someone fully clothed.

"I'm sorry to hear about your father," Dr. Roberson said.

"He was a doctor. He told me Hippocrates was the only place left to learn real medicine."

"I don't know about all *that*, but you'll definitely get your hands dirty at Hippocrates. And I'm sure you'll be able to jump right in. I hate unsolicited advice, but you're not me, so maybe you'll appreciate this. Don't skimp on anatomy. You want Dr. Jacobs on your side. Having a good lab group is key. Don't forget to eat. Making friends is important, but remember everyone eventually becomes competition."

She gave him a good looking over and then turned to Jillian as if seeking approval for what she was about to say. Jillian, in turn, raised her brow.

"And get rid of the hair."

Pok tilted his head. Had he heard her right? The traveling resident lifted both hands.

"I get it. In New York, your hair sets you apart, a way to be different, to stand out from the assembly line. But being a medical student—learning medicine—means putting that all aside.

"I don't think there's a single out-of-state student doctor at Hippocrates. You'll be the first. You'll already have enough wary eyes on you."

"So you want him to fundamentally change who he is," Jillian said. "Great advice."

"I want him to have a chance." Dr. Roberson put back the wool shirt she was eyeing. "Like I said, I hate unsolicited advice. Good luck, Student Doctor Pok. I'm sure I'll be seeing you."

"She's a piece of work," Jillian said when Dr. Roberson was gone. "She's probably jealous of all that hair you got. Don't let her get to you. What? I got something on my face?"

The way Jillian came to his defense shifted things. She'd trusted in him time and time again, both when he didn't deserve it and when he actively gave her reason not to. And he was still holding back.

"There's something I need to tell you." Pok slowed and looked his new friend in the eyes. "Remember I said my dad had a patient just like your sister?"

"He convinced her to stay, right?"

"I lied. He didn't convince her to stay. She was a woman who hid her first trimester from the shepherds and didn't trust them to deliver her baby. A woman named Florence."

Jillian looked past Pok. She picked up a tote bag, passed it through confused fingers, and hung it back on its rack. "You're fucking with me."

"I'm not," Pok said. "As soon as you said she hid the pregnancy, I knew. But what if you blamed her doctor—my dad—for her wanting to leave? I froze up and lied. And I'm sorry."

Jillian turned away to address welling eyes and stepped into the movement. Pok followed, allowing her space. They drifted through the market, which was wrapping up for the day.

"I'm okay. I'm just worried about her." Jillian shook her head to the sky. "Flo would have done what Flo wanted to do. When it came to Baby Girl, your father was the only one who could talk some sense into her. I wish I could have met him."

"So, we good?" Pok said.

She pushed her shoulder into his. "We good."

The shuttle stop for New Orleans sat at the end of a winding road. Another traveler waited on the lone bench, a large duffel bag hung across his chest. His hair was short with clean edges. One eye opened halfway. He nodded at their approach.

"I guess we wait," Jillian said. She fished a half-eaten sandwich from her pocket, unwrapped it, and offered it up to lazy, grazing chickens hopeful for market scraps. They waddled over and took their time with breakfast.

The air changed. A pickup truck with a wooden lattice surrounding the cargo bed rolled forward. A faded blue cap did little to cover the driver's wild, gray-streaked hair. He wore a brown cloth mask.

"Going to Hippocrates?" the driver said. "Plenty of room in the back."

A hand cut in front of Pok's chest. The snoozing traveler had quietly come up beside him. A stout man, he was twice Pok's age and width and a few inches shorter. A crown of gray sprinkled his head. His skin was several shades lighter than Pok's. Either the beginning or the end of a sunburn spread over his nose.

"You don't want to go in that." His voice was easy and kind. "That's medical cargo. For the anatomy lab. The shuttle is slow but it's reliable. Better to wait than to ride with the dead."

The masked driver shrugged, adjusted his hat, and drove off.

"Silva." The fellow traveler held out his hand. "You folks from New York?"

"Is it that obvious?" Pok said. Dr. Roberson's words rang in his mind. He remembered the haircap he'd bought at the market, tucked in his bag.

"New England people love to check out what all the New Orleans fuss is about. I get it: I came down curious from Philly myself. I decided to stay, though. Hippocrates saved my life."

"I would have sworn you were local," Jillian said.

He laughed, a deep, throaty sound. "Me? Oh, shit, no."

"Do you like it here?"

"I love it. The hurricanes take a little getting used to, but the city's built for them."

"You don't miss glass?" Pok said.

"I used to. With glass I could go anywhere in the galaxy, have sex with anyone, experience someone else's body, all from my own room. But I wasn't living. Here . . ." He jabbed with an emphatic finger. "Here, I'm living. And I *feel* better, you know? The city's not for everyone. For me, it's everything."

A white shuttle bus, taller than it was long, came an hour later. More than a dozen travelers—some in scrubs of varying colors, others in street clothes, maybe one with a button-down shirt and tie—piled off. Silva greeted the driver with a half-leaned-in hug. Jillian and Pok took a row close to the middle. The shuttle rumbled to life, its growling engine different from the rare gas-powered vehicle in Manhattan, and pitched forward.

Pok rested his temple against the window and watched MouseKill roll by. The sound of shifting plastic drew his gaze. Synth. Jillian caught Pok's eye before he could look away. *You want some?* Pok quietly refused.

Rain began to pour as they stopped at the edge of MouseKill. One passenger got off, a sack of potatoes strung over his shoulder, and three replaced him. The driver threw his voice back as the engine once again began to purr.

"Next stop: New Orleans, home of Hippocrates Medical Center."

Pok's breath caught in his chest. *Hippocrates.* He'd spent so much of his journey unsure if he'd ever make it that he hadn't thought much about actually arriving at the medical school. He'd started due south because he'd had nowhere else to go, because it was the one place his father had vouched for, the one place the shepherds couldn't reach. When had he decided to actually be a Hippocrates medical student? *Had* he decided that?

Medicine without glass. What's more: *life* without glass. The long, arduous journey had been a tour of his own senses. Pain. Unfiltered sight.

The smell of the earth and his own musk. Even in the wonder of this new, physical world, Pok craved glass. For information at the dart of an eye, for instant knowledge of his location, his biometrics, the history of the people around him. And hacking. The ability to manipulate code felt like a superpower in manipulating the world itself. Now he was but an observer. Could he ever get over that?

He could try.

For the first time since leaving New York, he felt the tiniest sliver of excitement. He was going to be a doctor.

Fourteen

THE SPIRES

They saw the spires first. Tall and white, they reached skyward in a long line that curved from the western horizon, disappeared behind the trees and emerged to touch the eastern sky. Red pulsed from each apex. Pok pressed his forehead into his window's cold glass; the air between the spires shimmered. Towering over the skyline, they signaled that he was about to enter into a completely new world.

Jillian put Pok's question into words. "What are those?"

"They're what's keeping New Orleans secure," Silva said. He'd settled into an adjacent row and was reveling in playing tour guide. He'd proven to be jovial, knowledgeable, and talkative. "It was originally built as an electromagnetic field to weaken hurricanes as they pass through the city. Today, it does that *and* completely disables shepherd tech. Probably SLC, too, but definitely shepherd."

The energy, the setup, the implications. Of course. It put everything into terrifying sense. The spires kept out the modern world. Wasn't Pok a product of that? What if it forever changed him, and not for the better? What would be the cost of entering into its gates?

"A disruptor," Pok said.

"What's that?" Jillian said.

Pok licked dry, cracked lips that only irritated his tongue. "My dad saw private patients who didn't trust the shepherd eye. I used a disruptor to give them privacy. But only a room. A small room. I've heard of setups for a whole house, but an entire city . . ."

"It's quite a feat," Silva said, allowing himself to take in the awe again.

"I thought the whole state was AI-free?" Jillian said.

"Functionally, yes. New Orleans is the only city that's officially outlawed the technology." Silva jumped and pressed a tensed finger against the window. "Excellent, look! You can see it in action now."

A drone the size of a one-passenger car cut through the sky, a hundred feet up. As it approached the spire-line it curved to run parallel to it, keeping well enough beyond the perimeter.

"From that height they can see into the city," Jillian said.

"The disruptor jumbles the signal," Pok said. "Both video and audio will be only static."

"That drone looks big enough for a person," Jillian said. "Maybe Odysseus himself is in there?"

"My bet is he wouldn't be able to see anything, either," Silva said. The corner of his mouth curled into a half smile. "He's half machine, you know."

"A lot of enhancements, you mean?" Jillian said.

"No, I mean he's half-machine. Rumor has it the AI's really in control."

The mention of Odysseus flipped Pok's stomach. He changed the subject. "You said this place saved your life?"

"I was an anxious kid," Silva said. "My dad got me one of those autonomic rings when I graduated high school, the ones where you could regulate your heart rate on your phone—back then it was a phone. I spent all day checking and regulating, checking and regulating. I had a massive heart attack at twenty-one. Heard the surgeon say my electrical currents were all out of whack. I had two heart transplants and was slated for a third. Here, it's been totally different. My first time seeing a human doctor. She talked to me, learned about me, and we came up with a plan. It's been a journey! No wires. No tech. Just teaching my heart how to be a heart again."

More and more spires cut into the sky as the shuttle arrived at the city's gates, which were situated in a tall stone wall that connected horizons. Three large trucks, their sides dented and rusted, awaited entry. A line of people led up to the door of a stained-glass building built into the gate, half its body in New Orleans and the other half outside. A spire shot up through the middle, as if the building had been impaled after falling from the heavens.

Pok's ankle itched; he scratched at the brace's edge. At least the swelling had gone down. The nausea, as Dr. Roberson predicted, was nearly gone. If he needed surgery, would he still be able to join the first-year class? His heart crawled up and lodged in the space behind his tongue. His throat tightened; his ankle caught fire. Both sensations intensified as the shuttle doors opened and the engine died. The hope of this next leg of his journey and the danger of the city's uncertainty barked at each other, simultaneously urging him forward and warning him to stay away.

Jillian's struggles snapped Pok out of his own head. She waved off Silva's offer of assistance, tried to stand, and fell into the aisle. Pok and Silva both sprang forward and hoisted her up on the seat. She grimaced and ran her hands down her legs as if kneading bread. Her foot twitched in response.

"You all right?" Pok said. "Are you hurt?"

"Damn things fell asleep," Jillian said. She breathed in sync with the back and forth of her hands, rocked forward, and tested her legs. On her cue, Pok and Silva helped her stand. Her right knee bucked once, then straightened. She took one step down the aisle, then another.

"Easy, now." Silva descended the shuttle stairs, ready to support.

"I think I'm good. My body really doesn't like me right now."

Silva walked alongside Jillian a few more strides and when he saw she was, in fact, good, nodded toward the building.

"That's what this place is for," Silva said. "'Adjustment' to help acclimate. It used to be optional, now it's mandatory for all scrollers—sorry, non-natives. My heart still flutters every time I cross through those spires."

Silva waved his goodbye and went through the left gate. Pok and Jillian joined the line leading into what their guide called "Adjustment." A dozen or so others waited. Suitcases crowded their legs like hungry, overgrown insects. A father tried to stop his small child from climbing their mini mountain of luggage while the brother—a year or two older, from the looks of him—took advantage of the distraction and ascended the other side. A middle-aged couple leaned on each other. An elderly man pushed an even older woman's wheelchair. They both wore cloth masks.

"You think they're all here for the medical center?" Pok said. What circumstances could have urged them to seek such alternative care? He couldn't imagine *choosing* to leave behind the comfort and security of tech and forego the latest evidence-based medicine. And for what? The human touch?

"Maybe Odysseus wants them dead, too," Jillian said. She raked her locs as she gazed upon the city. The rain had decreased to a light drizzle. "Or they know someone like my sister."

Florence. What had she looked like, walking up to the gate with a baby wrapped around her chest, without a piece of luggage to her name? Did people crowd around to help or could they sense her instability and slink away as if mental illness could infect?

The gate opened to a wide, paved road partially covered with pre-autumn leaves. The sun seemed to save itself just for New Orleans: the clouds parted and soothing rays leaked through the trees. A long brick road lined with white-blooming magnolias cut through green fields. Beyond, the first signs of houses. The shuttle passed through and rolled up the winding road. The gate closed behind it.

"It's like a painting," Jillian said. It was true. The rain, which brought the grime of New York City to the surface, had left everything here glistening and fresh. "Flo must have loved this view. She was always the tree hugger. Oh God, I hope she made it."

"I'm sure she's fine," Pok said. He had urges both to hug Jillian and to move away from her tears, lest they unsettle his own turbid grief. He reached up to twist his hair, forgetting it was covered, and instead adjusted his cap.

A woman with short black hair and near-red skin emerged from the Adjustment building to greet them. The line came a little bit more to life. The traveler resting against the gate perked up. The father sternly told his children to be quiet and stay still, if just for a minute. The volume of his voice seemed to shock both him and the kids. His wife stifled a tired laugh.

"Good evening, travelers," the woman said. "Any glass, shepherd, or SLC devices are prohibited in the city. They will be confiscated at Customs and will be returned upon leaving New Orleans."

"What about transplants?" the man behind the wheelchair said. Fear edged his voice. His partner's hand reached back to find his.

"I'm glad you asked." The woman's voice, though, was indifferent. "We will not confiscate those."

This got a chuckle.

"Transplants are protected under the Medical Integration Act. If you have organs that run on shepherd computing systems, they will stay operational. However, please inform the Customs agent which transplants you possess and why. It's very important that you let us know about all tech-related biology. To ensure the safety of all our citizens, old and new, we now require one week of quarantine, minimum, before integrating into society." Groans rose from the line.

"Class starts soon, right?" Jillian whispered.

"It already started," Pok said.

"Damn. Maybe they'll make an exception?"

Once the vocal dissent subsided, the woman continued, "If this is not acceptable, please do not enter these gates."

She waited. No one spoke. No one moved. An evening bell chimed somewhere from within the city. The woman stepped aside. "Welcome to New Orleans."

Fifteen

ADJUSTMENT

Jillian squeezed Pok's hand as they entered the Customs facility. Bare cream-colored walls lined a dimly lit corridor. A throb began at the base of Pok's skull and spread along the bone.

"My legs just got a bad case of the tinglies," Jillian said.

"I'm feeling it, too."

They piled single file through a metal detector that beeped on every other traveler, including Jillian. A man with a name tag that simply read *Scribe Guard* took her to the side and motioned for Pok to follow. He waved an oblong metal device over her body. When it got to her legs, it vibrated enough to hum.

"What's going on here?" he said. "Prosthetic?"

"No. Genetically modified."

"Limb transplants are usually fine, but you'll want to let Customs know." The scribe guard waved the wand one more time to confirm the result and nodded to a colleague. "They can go."

The hallway led into a wide-open room with rows upon rows of stanchions. The line fed into three different kiosks where masked personnel took their names, cities of origin, and purpose for travel. They were given Customs cards to fill out while they waited.

There was little chatter as everyone waited their turn. The acoustics carried the bulk of the Customs interviews, and various reasons for visiting came to light. Meeting an already-relocated loved one. A second opinion for terminal cancer. Reproductive autonomy. Lack of jobs. The two-kid family was only a few places ahead. The mother cited a better education for their children, who had been denied gifted placement by shepherd algorithms. There was a pause before the woman processing their entry application bluntly asked the father about a warrant for his arrest in Georgia.

"Next!"

A young couple cleared the way for Pok and Jillian. Much like the scribe guard's, the woman's name tag simply read, *Recorder.* She received their cards and readied her pen. "Reason?"

After cycling through mental images that ranged from being laughed at to being carried away and hand-delivered to Odysseus, Pok managed to answer, "Medical school."

"Pardon?" The recorder's pen hovered over Pok's form.

"I'm a medical student. Or, I'm about to be. I've been accepted to the Hippocrates Medical College."

The recorder looked at him. Really *looked.* He may have been the first traveler she'd actually seen all day. Her gaze went over to Jillian, scanned, and snapped back.

"Hold one moment." The recorder rose, left her booth and stuck her head into a back room. A few moments later, she returned and handed Pok and Jillian new cards.

"Follow me," she said.

The recorder led them to the left—all the other travelers had gone to the right—and situated them in adjacent cubicle rows. Pok paused at the entrance. The clinical space was nearly identical to his father's. An examination chair, slightly reclined, sitting under a brightly focused lamp. A rolling metal table with a blue-wrapped box of tools, ready for sterile use. A stethoscope hanging on a tall, thin metal pole, waiting for the doctor to come and listen to the sounds of life, sickness, and healing. Pok gripped the hard, acrylic door.

"What's wrong?" Jillian said, one hand on her cubicle wall.

"Nothing." Pok swatted at his eyes, stepped inside, and changed into the hospital garb neatly folded on the exam chair. Halfway through he heard Jillian move from the makeshift hallway between their cubicles and start to do the same.

Jillian's voice floated above the divider, cracked and uneven. "I'm getting second thoughts."

Pok peered across the narrow aisle as he tied the back of his gown. Jillian stood at her cubicle's entrance. Removed from the travel, the urgency, the stress of the situation, he saw her for what she was: a person trying to make sense of a senseless situation.

Jillian rubbed her legs up and down and looked down the hall. "My body doesn't like this place. Florence might not even be here. Anything could have happened to her. I was supposed to protect her and instead I fucked it all up."

"Hey," Pok said, her nerves striking him. "It'll be okay. Do you have any of your . . . your medicine?"

"I'm afraid they'll see."

Two nurses wearing sky-blue scrubs approached. Pok and Jillian ducked back into their respective cubicles. Nurse Jen—tall with straight, brown hair, keen eyes, and a pink cloth mask—introduced herself, confirmed Pok's name, and got to work. She weighed him, took his blood pressure, and went through a long list of questions about recent symptoms, health and travel history, and if he did any recreational drugs. She then transitioned to a block of questions with no discernible grouping or theme. The nurse recorded his answers on a matrix that spat out a score at the end. She recorded it in his chart.

"What's that score?" Pok said.

"It's the 'CHEWS.' The Clinical Hippocrates Emigrant Withdrawal Scale. Yours is mild. Lucky, from what I've seen lately."

"Does it mean I'll have less time here?"

"As long as you don't have any setbacks, you should be out relatively quick. When you can see the top of the medical center outside your window, that means you're close."

Why would the view outside the window change? Pok thought he'd misheard her, so instead of going backward he asked his other question. "Are the spires causing the withdrawals?"

"Some very smart people are still trying to figure that out." She held up a needle. "Which is part of why I need your blood."

"You're going to stick that in me?" Pok said.

"How else would I get it?"

Pok was no stranger to bloodwork. But before, it had consisted of simply placing a censor on his antecubital space. This nurse planned to take blood *out* of him. Part fascinated, part horrified, Pok tried to watch. The prick of the needle was nothing compared to the pain he'd endured over the last couple weeks. It was the sight of the blood, swirling out of him and slowly filling the tube, tumbling over itself in thick rivulets, that flipped his stomach. This nausea was different. His vision dimmed; the room tilted. He jerked hard to the right; the nurse just barely saved the phlebotomy supplies from spilling onto the floor.

"You okay?" she said, pausing before inserting the next vial.

Pok blinked and clenched his jaw. "Yeah, I'm good. I'm good." He chanced to look again, to see if the feeling was a fluke. It wasn't. Acid burned the base of his throat; his stomach lurched into his chest.

"Look away if you need to," she said. The muffled chatter of Jillian and her nurse drifted over from across the aisle. "And breathe. I'm almost done."

Pok, defeated, looked away.

The click of the retracting needle. The release of the torniquet's pressure. Pok opened his eyes. The nurse placed three vials—one applied with a special label—in the same bin as Pok's completed CHEWS questionnaire.

"You should have told me blood makes you queasy," the nurse said.

"I'm just a little dehydrated." Pok swallowed the thick saliva coating his mouth.

"Right." The nurse spread her hand over her collection. "These first two vials are routine screening. Checking your health, electrolytes, kidney and liver function. Seeing if there are any concerning pathogens. This third is for those very smart people."

What would they find? Could a version of what Jillian experienced with her legs be happening to him, but in his brain?

The nurse cleared the side table and left as quickly as she had come. Pok was alone again. From the silence across the aisle, Jillian was also done.

"What was your score?" Pok said to the wall.

A pause. Then, "Thirty-three. You?"

"Eleven."

"Damn. I guess you didn't need my medicine after all."

Footsteps cut into their conversation. Nurse Jen reentered Pok's cubicle and his entire body reacted to the threat of another blood draw. But she gestured for him to rise. "Follow me."

"What about Jillian?"

"Nurse Johnny's got her."

The nurse led him through a set of double doors and to a small room set up like a college dorm. A pile of clothes and toiletries sat on the neatly made bed under a single window. The view showed just the inside of the gate.

"The doctor will be with you shortly and explain the rest of your stay."

Pok fished his father's textbook out of his bag and flipped through. He scanned the margins for any notes about this thing called Adjustment. With thin expectations he found the section on neurological disorders and nearly dropped the book. There, scribbled in the margins next to a subsection on substance abuse and addiction, was a note.

Adjustment varying in effects and response. Severe reactions rare but present. NFTF.

A sharp knock at his door made him close the textbook and slip it under his pillow. "Come in," he said.

A physician, tall and slender, entered the room. The first thing Pok noticed was his hands. All the other medical staff so far carried a clipboard, a stethoscope, or a ball of gauze ready to use. This man's hands were free.

The second was the doctor's white coat. Freshly pressed, the tailored coat extended to the knee. While Dr. Roberson's had clearly outranked Pok's, this doctor's coat was made of even finer stuff.

Then there was his hair. His heavily hued locs were thin, roughly corded, and came down midthigh. Loc dyeing was common in certain parts of the Bronx and Queens. Subsets of what some dubbed the "scroller generation" had found out through social media mapping that they'd all been led down similar life paths by sorting algorithms. Worthless degrees, low salaries, and no clear exit from lifelong renting. With hairstyling being one of the last brackets that AI seemed to lack fundamental understanding over, this disgruntled and disillusioned part of New York City took to delicate modifications as a sign of rebellion.

This man, however, looked like he'd been hit upside his head with a rainbow.

"Pok Morning," the man said. "I am Dr. Peter Soft. A physician by practice, a historian historically. I like to meet with all potential new residents, learn where they're from, why they're coming. But you'll soon know me as *professor*. You may be our first out-of-state student doctor."

He sat in the rolling chair, pulled up next to Pok's bed, and bent to examine his brace. "This looks like it was done by one of our physicians."

"Dr. Cheryl Roberson, over at MouseKill."

"Ah. Resident Cheryl. She was my sponsee, years ago now. I can see her care here. What happened?"

"I fell on it." *Trying to escape a four-story building.* "It's a type A lateral malleolus fracture."

"Painful." Dr. Soft rotated the ankle. A tingling sensation halfway between pain and pleasure crawled up Pok's leg and buried itself in his groin. "It still has mobility. Surgery unlikely. We won't know until the cast comes off. I read you traveled most of the way on foot?"

"We took a train. Caught a train, rather."

"Both your withdrawal score and your S-reactive protein levels were low. So low I ran the blood test a second time myself."

"What are S-reactive proteins?" Pok said.

Dr. Soft brightened, happy to play teacher. "We've isolated a protein that's ubiquitous in TSO cities. At steady states it's inert. But when blood levels drop quickly, the change causes a plethora of nonlethal discomforts. The protein's shape is influenced by radio waves. Being inside the spires seems to cause the protein's half-life to lessen, meaning it clears the system more quickly, meaning more severe withdrawals. Along with the CHEWS, it's the best way to predict how severe a newcomer's withdrawal experience might be.

"Your low S-reactive protein level suggests a very sharp drop off, which would result in an off-the-charts CHEWS. In other words, serious withdrawals. You have neither."

"Is it possible I never had a high S-reactive protein level?"

"Possible, but not probable. As TSO's hub, New York City has some of the highest baseline SRP levels. All of our recent New Yorkers have been in the medium-to-severe range. And I'm a historian; I usually don't like to use the word *all*."

"I don't take Synth," Pok said.

Dr. Soft smiled. "I know. Synth makes the subjective experience better, but Synth users consistently score higher on the CHEWS. Their SRPs are also through the roof."

That surprised Pok. "Do we know where the S-reactive proteins come from?"

"It's heavily correlated with shepherd presence. SLC states, for instance, only started showing significant levels after the shepherd monopoly on hospital systems. So it has something to do with the shepherds, though we can't prove whether it's an endogenous protein brought forth by interaction with tech or something new and synthetic. This is Dr. Morning's area of expertise." Pok didn't like the way the physician looked at him. "Where is he? Where is Phelando?"

Pressure built behind Pok's eyes, flooded his cheeks, and choked any attempt at words. Dr. Soft sat back, as if stung, processing. The space opened up the air just enough.

"He's dead—he died. He died, Dr. Soft." Pok's eyes fell. He didn't want to see the inevitable pity. When he finally looked up, it was Dr. Soft who searched the ground.

"We'd gotten word that he'd been ill. But . . . dead? How? Are you sure? Of course you are."

Pok considered. Should he share the sequence of events that had driven him out of New York? Phelando had clearly been in contact with Hippocrates, but Dr. Soft seemed out of the know. And he was the first physician Pok had come across. What if they sent him away? Or worse, handed him to TSO?

"News reports claimed he experimented on patients here in New Orleans," Pok said.

"You know that's not true, right?"

"Thank you," Pok said.

"This must be extremely difficult. And with the journey you've taken, I'm sure the dean will grant you leave to take some time—"

"I want to start," Pok said. "It's what my father would have wanted. It's what I want."

Dr. Soft nodded. "Class begins Monday. The students are all getting settled into their dorms. This Adjustment process—it can't be rushed. But if your bloodwork and scores continue to check out, I may be able to get you out in time so you're not too behind."

"One last thing," Pok said. "I need to meet with the dean."

"You have concerns?"

"A message from my dad. Before he died."

"I'll put in the request." Dr. Soft's gaze tilted upward, toward the top of Pok's head. His plaster smile crumbled at the edges, reminding Pok of the flickering hologram. Dr. Soft gestured toward Pok's haircap. "Can I—?"

"Oh. Sure." Pok took it off and raked out his hair.

"How do you keep them so healthy?"

"Just water lately. It's been a while. My dad used to oil them. Castor, specifically."

"You'll do well." Dr. Soft handed back his cap and stood to leave. "I'll let the dean know you're here. I'm truly sorry about your father. If you change your mind about leave, no one will judge you for it. Otherwise, I'll see you in class. And I do love the hair."

Pok's headache rose as the sun set and made his first night in New Orleans completely restless. Sound sent sparkling colors across his vision. The slightest touch caused his taste buds to dance. He spent most of the night with his blanket scratching against his leg as he coughed to cure a sour tongue.

The withdrawals worsened.

Keeping food down proved the hardest. Every meal came in a color-coded container and at unpredictable intervals. Regardless of the contents, the blue containers quickly proved the worst on his stomach while yellow caused only brief nausea. The other colors landed somewhere in between. Red containers gave him diarrhea. Orange swelled his throat. Purple sent hives across his skin. Nurses drew his blood multiple times a day. Sometimes before a meal, sometimes after, even once or twice during. His initial experience turned out to be a lasting issue. The smallest glimpse of his own fluid leaving his body tanked his blood pressure. Eventually, Pok didn't even try to watch.

Things calmed after the second night. He ventured outside his room into an enclosed space with transparent walls. Through these walls, people in various levels of Adjustment could talk, play games, and pass notes. No sign of Jillian. Back home, contacting her would have been as easy as a flick of his gaze. Here, Jillian could be right next door and he'd have no way of knowing. Had something gone wrong? Could her withdrawal levels be dangerous?

After only being able to stomach half of a blue-container meal, Pok was leaning out his bedroom's cracked window for fresh air when the floor rumbled. The occurrence wasn't new. It had happened at least three times a day. This, however, *was* new: right before his eyes, the horizon shifted. He steeled himself, fearing he was fainting, but then noticed the city gates were farther to the right than a minute ago. A lot farther.

The rooms were shifting. Multiple times a day.

He awoke the fourth day with only a slight headache. His breakfast—a blue container—initially made him nauseous, but he held it down and realized upon finishing that he'd enjoyed it. He stopped by the window, eager to catch another shift. As he finished his lunch, the skyline moved. The top of a tall building shifted into view.

A knock on his door made Pok jump. Nurse Jen entered. He hadn't seen her since that first day. She went through the CHEWS. He scored a three. At the height of his withdrawals—day two—he'd gotten an eighteen.

"Adjusted. I told you it wouldn't be long." Nurse Jen scribbled on a half piece of paper. "Take this to the front. Good luck."

Pok repacked his bag, left his room, and went down a long hall to line up behind the day's discharge cohort. He recognized none of them. When it was his turn he entered a booth and sat opposite a camera on a tripod.

The overlooking reporter snapped his picture, fanned the black square that emerged from the camera's slot, placed it atop his folder, and handed it to someone. She led Pok off the processing floor and up to a short, wide hall that ended at a pair of glass doors.

"You're all set," the recorder said. She gave him a small case. "This is your ID. This bottom section grants access to and from the city. Don't lose it or you *will* have to go through Adjustment again. This is your E-Cell. Starts at about a dozen amps, enough to power a light bulb for an hour. Not much but enough for most things in the city. You can pay for a charge up to two hundred, but if you plan to use more than one hundred at a time, you need to register it with the office."

"The electricity is limited here?"

"It takes a lot to power those spires, and we only stay independent if the whole city works together. Any other questions?"

Many. Pok shook his head.

"Everyone is provided with basic food, shelter, and health care. Your ride should pick you up at the curb. Have a good one, Mr. Morning."

Sixteen

WELCOME TO HIPPOCRATES

Humidity wrapped Pok in a heavy embrace as he stepped out to the curb. Red cardinals flitted from flower to flower between the overlapping magnolias, thickening the air with their song. A full shuttle carried the newly adjusted up the road and into the city. For Pok, a small bicycle-powered cart awaited. He'd seen a few in Central Park, but never human-operated. The cyclist tipped his hat.

"Good to see you again." It was Silva. "Pok, right? Where's your friend?"

"Her withdrawal was more severe. She might have a few more days."

"Sounds about right. I didn't want to say it, but she didn't look too good." Silva checked a piece of paper hanging from the cart's hood. "It says here you have a meeting up at the hospital?"

Pok got in. "I guess I do. You work there?"

"I have a lot of jobs. One of them is hospital groundskeeper. Not the worst gig in the world. How was Adjustment?"

"Enlightening, to say the least. I think I had it easier than most."

"Nice. The rest is all psychological. Sometimes I think I'm going through withdrawals again but it's all in my head."

They turned down a wide cobblestoned road lined by houses with connecting walls and lushly decorated balconies. People waved handkerchiefs as they passed.

"What are they saying?" Pok said.

" 'Welcome to New Orleans.' This is Canal Street. We're passing through Mid-City now. Most scrollers live out here. The hospital's in Uptown."

A trickling of people thickened into a crowd as market booths reminiscent of MouseKill Farms lined the street. Merchants sold hand-knitted garments, hospital supplies, gardening tools, and books. Competing columns of steam advertised multiple crawfish boils that infused oceanic savor into the thick, summer air. Excited haggling preceded goods exchanging hands. Some sat cross-legged on the side of the street, engaging over food or admiring their latest bargain. Others danced to live music. A middle-aged woman stood in front of a tent decked out with paintings as varied as the people. One standout depicted a crowd, entranced, looking to the sky, with bulbous glass for eyes. Another illustrated cartoon houses pulling up their skirts as floodwaters overtook wooden legs. A whole row was dedicated to physician portraits. The woman's partner put the finishing touches on a colorful piece centering a dog with a cyborg leg.

For Pok, the collective joy mixed well with Cajun smells, music, and the feel of tightly knitted cotton through his fingers.

"Have you ever seen . . ." Pok began to Jillian. Only, of course, she wasn't there.

"What was that?" Silva had reached out to examine a pair of sea-green shorts from a merchant walking beside their carriage.

"Nothing."

More merchants approached the slowed cart with their offerings. One put something in Pok's hand and left before he could refuse. A handmade necklace. It said, *Welcome to NOLA*.

"Don't wear that," Silva said. "Unless you want to be labeled a tourist. Natives don't say 'NOLA.' "

Pok eyed a kid sitting on the roof, hunched over some project. As he got closer, they briefly locked eyes. Pok angled himself to keep track as other buildings and taller booths passed between them.

The kid slipped off the roof's edge.

"Wait—!" Pok lunged forward. The kid, instead of falling two stories, stepped out onto a windowsill. He inched along the side of the house, disappeared into an oblivious crowd, and popped up next to their cart. He handed Pok a charcoal drawing.

"What you got there?" Silva looked amused.

The portrait was none other than Pok, intricately done. Pok's hand went to his hair. He hadn't forgotten his haircap—the picture had his full style on display—but he did find a stray loc. He began to tuck it in and decided to leave it.

"How much?" Pok said.

The boy gestured toward the *Welcome to NOLA* necklace. Pok handed it over.

"First barter, done," Silva said. "You're deep into the culture now."

"I thought natives wouldn't want NOLA."

"They don't. That kid'll sell it to the next wide-eyed scroller."

The crowd thinned. Their cart left the smooth of one road and rumbled onto another overrun with weeds. The houses here were more uniform, less festive. Many had the same elevated foundation as Big Bayou Inn.

"Essential for hurricane season," Silva said, catching Pok looking. "Even with the spires we still get a nice flood every now and then."

They passed through several distinct neighborhoods. The quality of the houses, matching that of the streets on which they stood, varied dramatically from one block to the next. Handmade homes of brick and crudely cut wood mixed with tall, ancient buildings. Drying jumpsuits and work clothes hung from dimly lit windows. Grass and dirt punctuated the road's ubiquitous cracks. Gaslit streetlamps lined the sidewalks.

Canal widened into a downtown district with sky-reaching buildings. A red streetcar with gold trimmings, packed with passengers, ran on a thick, suspended cable. Silva turned their cart onto University Avenue, where they soon arrived at another market, smaller than the New Orleans introduction in Mid-City. Purposeful strides replaced dancing. Booths selling medical supplies, paper, and hospital linens replaced art. A long, snaking line led to a mystery booth.

The market thinned as signs directed them toward a turnaround that led to the hospital's main gate. Bikes zipped past one another, whizzing between foot traffic and older cars with human drivers. More than once a crash seemed imminent; Pok couldn't look away.

Silva dismounted and unlocked the gate. Stand-alone clinics, vibrant cafes, brightly lit pharmacies, and busy restaurants bordered the long, curving uphill road to the hospital. A freshly painted shoulder-high fence surrounded a nondescript building with gaping holes for windows.

"That's a new research building," Silva said. Despite the crisp air, sweat dotted his brow. "That one just south of the main hospital is the children's hospital. The HemoStat sits right between the two."

"What's the HemoStat?"

"Our emergency room."

The hospital, wider than it was tall, was a beacon of the old and the new, with its steel frame and stained windows. Taller buildings flanked it, the highest of which scratched the sky's underbelly. A continuous stream of doctors, nurses, and scribes passed in and out of its rotating doors.

"Do all the doctors live close?" Pok said.

"The students and trainees do. Most everyone else commutes from the city's edge. Metairie or Lakeview."

Silva secured his bike to a pole and led them inside. The revolving doors dropped them into the lobby. The open space was a stark rebuttal to MacArthur Hospital's long, sterile hallways and scanning rooms. Balconies all the way up overlooked a thriving indoor garden. Brush rustled, and flowers danced their colors wind-like around shifting bodies. The colors didn't stop at the flowers. Red, blue, green, yellow, and black uniforms shimmered like rippling waves. The buzz of human chatter, problem-solving and living, offered a surprising comfort compared to New York's silent, instant socializing. Pok breathed it all in.

"See those in the light blue?" Silva said, ever the tour guide. "Those are the patients. The ones with the darker scrubs? Nurses."

In the garden, a short, thick woman with a white coat and a stone face went up to a nurse walking with a patient. A taller, younger woman in yellow trailed her. Pok recognized the uniform from MouseKill.

"And those are scribes?" he said.

"Yep. I don't see any residents, but they're dark blue. Residents essentially live in the hospital."

Silva called for the elevator. The floor vibrated and a few moments later the gold-rimmed doors slid apart.

"Your legs don't work?" said a nurse pushing a cart overhanging with tubes and sealed bags.

"Right. Stairs." Silva ducked his head and pushed open the adjacent door. "I forgot the elevators are for the patients. The dean's only on the third floor."

"I'm used to stairs," Pok said.

The Hippocrates Medical Center's stairway was nothing like the old, uncared-for set in his apartment building. Despite both being most frequented by physicians, these were freshly cleaned and buffed, their cream color seeming to give off their own light. There were no chipped edges, no discolored splotches, no uneven surfaces. A glass banister with a sleek wood base divided the stairs into two sections. It didn't creak or budge under a little weight.

Silva held open the door at the top of the landing. "Dean's office is right there." He checked his watch. "We're a tad early; she should be out for you soon. I'll come back in a half hour or so."

Pok strolled down the hall, in awe of the densely decorated walls lined with display cases reminiscent of Phelando's basement: portraits of distinguished physicians, class pictures, various artwork, plaques, and research posters.

"Well, shit."

A young version of his father smiled from a display of exceptional staff accomplishments. Pok touched the glass. Phelando had just started his hair journey. From old photos, Phelando had kept his hair low and nondescript—a Caesar fade, he'd called it—throughout medical school and residency. He'd started growing it "as soon as I got my MD." This must have been shortly after that, the beginning of a long, committed journey.

The picture's tagline read: *Immunology Fellow Isolates Compound That Proves Essential Connection Between Humans.*

This is where his father had done his fellowship? Phelando's relationship with the medical center had clearly expanded as his ties with MacArthur soured—enough to make him a TSO target. But a fellowship here meant at some point he'd lived in New Orleans. It must have been before Pok, who'd spent his whole life in New York City. Why keep that a secret? Especially if Phelando clearly wanted Pok here?

Pok's fingers went under his haircap and curled around the first loc they found. He took off the covering. His locs were years longer than Phelando's here, back when people were more likely to misunderstand that transition period between short hair and full-grown locs, more likely to see short twists as a sign of mental unraveling rather than an embrace of one's identity. His father had worn his hair proudly.

A firm voice scattered the thoughts, broken but not forgotten. "Pok Morning? Come in."

Dean Brandy Sims stood inside her doorway. How long had she been there? Pok took in another moment of his father's picture—which somehow felt more real than his Memorandium ever could—and went inside to meet the dean. Walls and walls of books hugged her office. The dean took her place behind her long, old oak table. She was patient as he admired her collection.

"Sorry." Pok took a seat. Dean Sims was an old, spent beauty. Her hair had long gone white, cropped low with reservation.

"Don't be. Walking through the library, wondering what new book might grab me, is a favorite pastime." The dean's gaze was both curious and scrutinizing. "I'm sorry to hear about Phelando. He was a good man and a great physician."

"Thank you," Pok said. "The reports that I—"

Dean Sims held up a hand. "Don't give such propaganda the respect of speech. You were set up. Which means that your father's death was no accident."

Pok felt a paradoxical combination of relief and fear: relief that the dean was ready to believe his story, and fear that what he'd subconsciously hoped was all a fantasy was revealing itself as grim reality.

"Was he targeted because of Project Do No Harm?" Pok said.

"I'm surprised he told you about that. I assume you also know about his termination?"

Pok nodded.

"We don't think they knew about Project Do No Harm."

"The shepherds know everything."

"I don't doubt that. But if anyone could hide something from them, your father could. Granted, his death and their allegations killed Project Do No Harm. A blown whistle is only effective if people are willing to hear it. Still, I don't think it was that. Odysseus has always had it out for your father."

"Always?" Just a couple months ago Pok had known his father as an old-school physician stubbornly tending to his loyal flock of patients with archaic methods as the future of medicine left him behind. "I didn't even know Odysseus *knew* my father."

"'Knew' is an understatement. Your father wasn't afraid to ruffle feathers, for better or for worse. Any Hippocrates physician or patient would be able to tell you the benefit of the physician-patient relationship. It's innate. It's indescribable. But your father wanted to prove it. He knew only tangible proof could combat the rise of AI-led medicine. And he was right." Dean Sims tilted her chair back and looked at an invisible spot on the ceiling. "I've always found Odysseus more strategic than impulsive. This is messy."

"Odysseus said in an interview that 'something tragic is going to happen' to that place," Pok said.

"I fear Dr. Morning's death will be the first of many."

"He tried to kill me, too."

This gave her pause. "I heard whispers of a bounty. I don't think Odysseus wanted you dead, per se. He didn't want you *here*." She nodded and pulled a folder from her desk drawer. "I'll get you set up with housing and work."

"Dean Sims," Pok said. "I was hoping to join the medical school class."

"You never sent us a decision."

"That was a mistake," Pok said. "I thought the Prestigious Twelve was the only way to learn medicine. That my father's way was obsolete."

"And now?"

Pok chose honesty. "I don't know. But I want to learn."

"The class is formed."

"You can make an exception."

Dean Sims sat forward, indicating what she was about to say was to be taken seriously. "The Shepherd Organization filed a motion with the Louisiana Supreme Court that if we take you on as a medical student we'd be in violation of the Nonmaleficence Act, citing the allegations. The decree is bogus. But you being here can create a lot of trouble for us. If other students got wind of the rumors and they started to complain, too . . ." Sims studied his face as if his features held some hidden text. "It may make sense for you to lie low, grieve your father, get to know the city and its people. We'll hold your spot. What do you say?"

"I say . . . I say . . . what time is class?"

A smile broke across the dean's face, equal parts amusement and sorrow. She stood, buttoned the top of her white coat, and turned to face her library. She pulled a book from the shelf and flipped through it.

"Class started a week ago. You're behind, but not impossibly. The Bryson family has agreed to host you at the Paper Mill. Stay there tonight. Moving into Tay Hall when all the students are around would be too disruptive. Anatomy lab is first thing in the morning. The next couple of weeks you'll play catch-up. Then we'll talk about your certification requirements. Any questions?"

Tons of them. But one rose above the rest. "I traveled from New York with someone who came here to find her pregnant sister. Florence. She wanted to deliver at Hippocrates."

Dean Sims picked up a pen. "What's your friend's name?"

Pok told her. "I don't know her last name."

"I'll look into it. This Jillian, she's still in Adjustment? I'll make sure any update reaches her."

"I have another question, Dean Sims. Here, in New Orleans, will I be safe?"

The dean softened. "Yes. As long as we can show we're fulfilling our Hippocratic oath, the Nonmaleficence Act ensures Odysseus and the shepherds can't interfere. The Shepherd Organization can try all they want, but we're not going anywhere."

Something minute changed in Dean Sims's voice as she said this last. Both of them noticed. When she looked up, her smile was a little broken.

"Welcome to Hippocrates Medical College, Student Doctor Morning."

FALL

"To hold my teacher in this art equal to my own parents; to make him partner in my livelihood; when he is in need of money to share mine with him; to consider his family as my own brothers, and to teach them this art, if they want to learn it, without fee or indenture . . ."

Seventeen

THE PAPER MILL

A couple blocks outside the main gates, just a few quick steps down University, the Paper Mill sat unimpressive between exuberant hardware and medical tool shops. Silva knocked on the door, then rang the doorbell. Pok picked up a folded pack of paper on the doormat. *The Daily Hippo: Hippocrates Medical Center's Official Newsletter*.

Silva tried the knob. It was open. Light laughter mixed with the steady aroma of dinner. "Perhaps they're expecting us?" he said. They stepped inside.

"Chandee!" a woman's voice called from the back room. "Come back here!"

A young girl—no older than six—came running into the living room. An untethered single braid flagged from the side of the small girl's head. She hit Pok's leg with the joyful force of a girl who hadn't yet learned the impact of her own weight.

"Chandra Bryson! Let go of that boy!"

The woman's voice was kind but firm. Her hair was short and free of gray, a mark of the youth she needed to keep up with the ball of energy summoned by the doorbell. A large man whose smile countered innate intimidation came close behind. He didn't hide his amusement, nor his fatigue. White peppered his beard.

The man lowered to Chandra's level and gently touched the edge of a ruler to her fingers, then slowly away. Chandra's eyes followed, her mouth gaping. She grabbed it. He rotated it loose from her fingers and brought it close to his face. Chandra touched the strip of metal edging out from the wood.

"Listen to Blaire," he said. "Listen to Mama."

Chandra's young chestnut face remained unflinching, as if she were deaf. Then she pulled away and hopped into Blaire's lap. In New York City, the rare times children like Chandra were seen out in public, they wore headphones and carried handheld screens. The algorithms thought of them as simply to be cared for and kept out of the way, and this carried into adulthood. In New York—or any other TSO city—Chandra would have a predictable future, one of preset activities, resources, and community. One devoid of a parent's uncertainty. The cost—clear now to Pok—was the blazing fire behind Chandra's eyes.

"Her doctors call that aligning. I'm trying to get her to stop all the hugging, though. I haven't had much luck."

"I don't mind," Pok said.

"Can't be too friendly. No rating system to know who to be wary of." Without the anchoring of his disarming smile, Pok might have taken that as a warning. He extended his hand. "I'm Gil. You must be Student Doctor Morning. The dean's office rang and said you might need a place for tonight. When's class start?"

"Call me Pok. And class starts tomorrow."

"Excellent. I see you're getting a head start on reading."

Pok looked at the paper he was still holding as if it had just appeared out of nowhere. "I was just looking."

"Relax, relax. We print the *Daily* here, so I'm quite proud of it. You can keep that copy. Where's my manners? This is Blaire. She owns the shop. I just do the lifting."

"Oh, stop. Nice to meet you, Pok."

"And you already met Chandra," Gil said.

"I'll let you get settled," Silva said, one foot out the door. "Your class is at eight? Let's meet at the gates at seven thirty."

"Your room's upstairs," Gil said. "Where's your bags?"

"I only have this one," Pok said.

"Efficient. I can respect it. When I heard we were getting a new out-of-town medical student I got some clothes put together. On the house. I hope they fit. Make yourself at home."

The last of the day's embers crackled in the brazier, spreading a warm calm over Pok. Blaire sat opposite him while Gil cooked in the kitchen. Chandra in her lap, her fingers worked to finish the field of auburn braids. The girl peered, unstirred, at the pointed end of her father's ruler, flicking it with her fingers. Orange light from the fire danced across her bossed forehead.

"This must be a big change from New York," Blaire said.

"It's not what I expected," Pok said as Gil entered from the kitchen.

"You thought we'd all be living in tents, huh?" Gil said. He brought steaming slabs of pork and mashed broccoli. He uncorked a bottle of red wine that had MouseKill's logo on the side. His vibrant tattoos rippled with life as he served Blaire, Pok, and then himself. His smile was playful. "And the doctors bloodletting patients."

Pok held in his own grin.

"You did, didn't you?" Gil laughed. "No shame. I thought the same when I came down from Baltimore. It's amazing how much shepherd narrative hurts the city."

"I haven't seen much yet," Pok said. "Only Adjustment."

"They just made it mandatory for all incomers—how long ago, babe?" Blaire said.

"A month, maybe two. How were the withdrawals?"

"Mild for me, according to the scale."

"I didn't have any when I came," Gil said. "It's a new thing. Some people think it's not an accident."

"And who are these 'some people'?" Blaire wore a sly, knowing smile. Her fingers continued to work Chandra's braids as if they had eyes of their own.

"I read about it in the *Second Opinion*."

"The *Second Opinion*," Pok said. "Is that different from the *Daily Hippo*?"

"Day and night," Blaire said. She fished from a wicker basket a folded newspaper half the thickness of the *Daily Hippo* and held it up against the light. A faint *Daily* could be seen behind the *Opinion*'s title. "How can you respect a publication that does such a poor recycle job? That's either tacky or disrespectful."

"It's both!" Gil said. He winked at Pok. "It's brilliant."

"How is it brilliant?" Blaire said.

"You know they read the *Daily*, which automatically gives them some credibility. You think the writers up on the Hill read this? I doubt it."

"Who writes the *Second Opinion*?" Pok had only heard of newspapers. The idea of print information sources competing for attention was fascinating.

"Somebody out in Mid-City. I forget his name. But he keeps it real."

"You're going to sit there and tell me you trust that garbage?" Blaire said.

"Hell no. I pay attention, though. It has its agenda. They both do. The *Daily* makes me feel good; the *Second Opinion* makes me angry. Angry at the writers for making New Orleans sound like it's trapped in the Middle Ages. Angry because sometimes I'm forced to agree. One thing you have to give to them: they don't discriminate. They agreed with Louisiana pulling the plug on AI tech but heavily criticized the execution and questioned the hospital's motivations. They aren't fans of Hippocrates but definitely not fans of the shepherds."

"What does the *Daily* say about Odysseus?" Pok said.

Gil snapped and pointed at Pok. "Exactly! The *Daily* never talks about Odysseus Shepherd. Not one article."

"Because he's a waste of time," Blaire said. "We live in Louisiana. What would we ever need to know about Odysseus?"

Everything, Pok thought.

Gil shared this sentiment. "Are you serious? Blaire, really, look at me."

She pretended to focus extra hard on a particular braid.

"See, she knows she's full of shit right now! What goes on out there affects us."

"There's no use worrying about it. Nothing we can do."

"I assure you they're worried about us. You see them drones circling the city?"

"They can't get in."

Gil plucked the *Second Opinion*. "This says the withdrawals prove they already have. There's been nothing in the *Daily* and yet they built a whole quarantine facility to address them? At least the *Second Opinion* is trying to get to the bottom of things."

The impending doom of whatever Odysseus was planning saturated the air, seemed to float around them. *You're safe here.* The dean's promise. Was Pok paranoid or was Dean Sims in denial?

Blaire picked up on Pok's unease. "He just walked through the gates and already you're trying to scare him away."

"Not on my watch," Gil said. His tattoos soaked in the firelight as he settled into the couch. "Last I heard, there isn't a single med student from a shepherd city. More and more of the folks here in New Orleans grew up with AI tech. It's almost like we speak a different language."

As much as Pok wanted to hear about the theory from *Second Opinion*, he clearly saw the subject was a sore one. He raised his glass, sniffed the wine, and began to sip.

The buzz of alcohol was new to Pok. His father had offered him beer on his eighteenth birthday, but the lifetime of warnings referencing his genetic risks had found their mark. Now, the wine in his belly spread a cool blanket over his skin that dampened the world's noise, made the anxious thoughts a little bit quieter.

"How do you like it here?" Pok said.

"I love it," Blaire said. "But I've been here all my life, so I'm biased."

"I like it," Gil said. "It's quiet. Slower than where I grew up, that's for sure, but there's always something to do. Blaire landed us the paper contract for a new hospital wing. And they need lots of it. Our electricity allowance will be quite large."

"Which we can *only* use for making paper, right, Gil?" Blaire said.

"Right. And sometimes, in the summer, a little air-conditioning for my mental health. So I can make more paper." Before Blaire could protest, Gil held up a hand. "I'm joking. For now."

"How much electricity do you get?" Pok said.

"Not enough. And every month the allowance seems less and less."

"It's worth it," Blaire said. "Before long the only thing we'll need from outside Louisiana is future doctors like you to mix it up a bit."

"Let's drink to that." Gil reached for his glass.

"Cheers," Blaire said. "To Student Doctor Morning."

"To Student Doctor Morning. May his days be full of coffee."

Where's Phelando?

I do not know a Flanders.

Where is Phelando?

Finland is—

No, where is Phelando? Not Finland. Phelando, Phelando—FAH-LAN-DOH!

Silence.

Where is my dad?

Pok sat up. Coarse breaths choked across his swollen throat. His face was wet and cold. He searched the dark for a source—some leak, perhaps—and found none. He dabbed his cheeks with the bedsheet as the lines of wakefulness merged in renewed clarity; the sobs were his own. He'd been crying in the night.

The bedside clock said it was not yet five. Pok turned over and invited sleep to retake him. It didn't. He was up.

Pok grabbed his bag, slung it over his shoulder, and headed down the stairs.

The living room vibrated in a dim, fluttering light that Pok didn't fully process until he saw Gil sitting next to the smoldering fireplace, staring out the window. His tattoos danced with the shadows as his fingers rotated twin black marbles the size of hen eggs. His eyes were ripe with thought.

"Class starts this early?"

"I couldn't sleep. First day jitters, I guess. I was going to take a walk, see the city. What about you? Rough night?"

"Nights are always rough. Enjoy your sleep now. It becomes a rare thing when you become a parent. You still got some time before sunrise." Gil gestured to the chair opposite his. Outside, the dark sky looked uninviting against the warm living room. "And the fireplace is still hot. You can leave your traveling bag here. I'll have it delivered to Tay Hall while you're in class, no problem."

Pok accepted the offer, tucked his bag in the corner by the front door, and joined his host. The ghost of a fire loosened some of his muscles, but not all. They both looked out the window. Gil squinted, as if taken by a blinding light. His mouth was a crooked, thin line. Shadows stretched under red-kissed eyes.

"Did you know that Julian Shepherd studied at Hippocrates?" he said.

"Get out of here," Pok said. "Respectfully."

"You good. He did their public health program but was very curious about the medical school. He thought of Hippocrates Medical Center as a true partner. He believed in balance."

"Balance," Pok said. Had everyone studied at Hippocrates? "I knew he admired the hospital. I didn't know he was a student. Too bad he didn't pass that love on to his son."

"Odysseus thinks the shepherds should be responsible for everyone. And we're not letting them do their job."

"He wants full control." The warmth of the fire and the comfort it carried contrasted with the cold memory of Odysseus's and his meeting. Goose bumps prickled across his skin. Pok licked his lips. "I met him."

"Odysseus? Really?" Gil sat forward, eyes wide. "What was that like?"

"He offered me a spot at his medical school. But it was just a ruse."

"How do you know?"

They locked eyes. "Because right after, he tried to kill me."

"Now *you* get the fuck out." Gil shook his head, looked at Pok sideways, and repeated the idiom. "Kill you, kill you? He wanted you dead? That's wild. Any clue why?"

He didn't want you here. "No idea," Pok said.

"You think he's still after you?"

"I hope not."

"What was it like, talking to him one-on-one?"

"The whole time he felt very, I don't know the word . . ."

"Alien?"

Pok nodded. "Yes, alien."

"That tracks," Gil said. The pair sat in the type of uncomfortable silence where trust is born. Then, "Don't let Blaire hear me say this, but I wonder how much Odysseus has given of himself to the shepherds. And I don't mean the company."

"I get you," Pok said. And he did. Silva's accusation had nagged him since the shuttle rolled them into the city. "I thought the same after what happened. I wouldn't have before."

"If I'm going to battle with someone—not saying that's what this is, an 'us vs. them' type deal—but if I were, I'd rather there be a person at the control station. People are scary, people are unpredictable, people are flawed. Machines are simple. Once it's decided you should be done away with, and they have the power to do so?" Gil made a hand motion that Pok well understood.

"Good thing places like this exist, then, right?"

Gil tapped the *Second Opinion* article. "That's what I was saying. The shepherds can interfere *if* we become a global threat. That's why the hospital's downplaying this withdrawal stuff. It's serious and they're worried."

Gil yawned and looked out the window. His twin marbles quickened their dance.

Pok picked up the teapot left over from dinner. "You mind?"

"Make as much as you need. We have a big selection. Fresh from MouseKill."

A snaking wall pipe rattled as Pok filled the pot with fresh water. The stove's heat was more impressive than its flames; by the time Pok searched through his bag, found his father's honey, and measured out a tablespoon, the water was already roiling.

"It'll help you sleep," Pok said. He held up the gold-stained jar. "Special addition."

"Oh?" Gil took the steaming cup. The tea sloshed over the sides. He steadied it with both hands and took a sip. He peered into the cup as if it had just whispered his name and took another sip.

"Was Chandra why you left?"

"Partially. Stick around long enough and maybe I'll tell you." The slant of Gil's smile said that was all he was willing to give. All he could give. Gil yawned, long and wide. He caught eyes with Pok in the middle of it and began to laugh. "Okay, okay, maybe your tea is hitting a little," he said.

Pok took the pot back to the sink. He scooped dish soap from a half-filled jar neighboring a small plant on the windowsill. He rubbed it into the cloth until bubbles surfaced, allergy-like.

Hand-washing dishes was new, inefficient, and strangely satisfying. By the time Pok had scrubbed the pot, rinsed it clean, and hung it on the wall to dry, the rotating clink of Gil's stress balls had slowed. The impressive man sunk low in his chair.

Gil stirred. "What?" he said, perking a little before slumping back down.

Pok waited. When Gil's chin touched his chest, Pok took the empty mug and wrapped a blanket over his broad shoulders. Snores began to drill Gil's chin into his chest. Muscle and fat had thickened the man's neck; with age, the latter would continue to slow his nighttime breathing and worsen his insomnia. For now, though, Pok was happy to see him rest.

Pok sat beside the window. Clear sky floated above. Shepherd satellites—identifiable by their slight green hue—shone brighter than the stars. As a child he'd pretended they were angels sent to watch over him. Now, he couldn't look at them without thinking of his father.

Eighteen

GROSS ANATOMY

Gil was still snoring when Pok headed out. The sky's false angels had just begun to fade against the rising blue. The morning heat promised a muggy day. As he crossed the short distance to the hospital, Pok tried to hype away his nerves. *You know how to work. You know how to study. You were one of the country's top applicants. And you rocked that anatomy class in record time.*

Yeah . . . but at what cost?

Silva greeted him from just inside the gates. "I trust the Brysons treated you right?"

"More than all right. They hooked me up with new clothes."

"Nice. I always liked them. Gil's a good man and Blaire's the hardest-working person I know." Silva led him into the hospital, back toward and past the main elevator and stairs, and around to a side staircase.

"Anatomy lab is two stories down and to the left."

"You're not coming with me?"

"Can't," Silva said. "I stumbled into the anatomy lab once and someone let me know in no uncertain terms that only the initiated can be down there. Something about respecting the dead."

Pok took Silva's direction and arrived at large, plain double doors. Anatomy lab. Also known as cadaveric dissection. He'd never seen a dead body.

Phelando's funeral would have been his first. Now he would dance with the dead. The sight of his own blood had brought on a near-syncopal episode. What if he couldn't handle such proximity?

Pok entered. Long, metal tables with human-shaped black mountains dominated the space. The smell of rotten pickles combated the knowledge that people existed under those sheets. He retreated into his other senses. His mouth, sour with the taste of a long night. His body, aching from his journey.

Three lone students—one a head shorter than the others—surrounded the only uncovered table, their cadaver hardly visible. From what Pok *could* see, the dead body was that of a man. His skin was the color of clouds. Bits of flesh littered the floor around them.

"The bins are by the door. Come back at high noon; the trash will be ready by then."

Pok turned toward the voice. A thin older man sat at a desk against the far wall, his white coat draped over him like a cape. His hair was full and white. Wrinkles spread across his face like the lines on Phelando's map. Bushy eyebrows invoked untamed prominence.

Pok gripped the seam of his coat and resisted the urge to look down, assure himself it was still there, still white. His fingers itched to check his haircap, but he'd already done so a hundred times on the walk over to make sure every strand was tucked.

Instead, he approached the desk.

"I'm Pok Morning." He held out his hand. "One of the first-year medical students."

The doctor's eyes flicked to Pok's haircap so quickly it could have been shifting light playing on imagination. Real or perceived, the moment seeded doubt in Pok's decision not to cut his hair.

"Ah yes, the new student." The professor shook his hand. "Dr. Jacobs. I pray you have the dissector? No? A tool kit? Not even. Very well."

Dr. Jacobs produced from a tall metal pantry a torn, ragged textbook wrapped in frayed plastic. He stacked this and what looked like a tool kit on a nearby side table.

"You need a group." Dr. Jacobs looked around and snapped his fingers. "Table nine, where's your fourth?"

Pok followed Dr. Jacobs over to the lone group of three. The shortest one—who was actually sitting in a wheelchair, Pok now saw—caught their approach.

"Gerald is taking a leave of absence," the student using a wheelchair said. He looked over with unadorned curiosity. "His mother has dementia."

"Perfect," Dr. Jacobs said. "Table nine, this is Student Doctor Pok. He's joining the class. Get him situated, will you?"

"They already replaced Gerald," the wheelchair user said. "Savage."

"Don't mind Rodge," the closest student to him said. Even taller than Kris, he sported a head full of curly, dark brown hair. "That's Anji, and I'm James."

They made room. Death had taken much of the cadaver's color; what remained suggested a previous umber. Though the once-brown skin had gone rubbery, the tattoo ink still looked fresh, as if body art were immune to both rot and preservation. He'd been shaved clean, eyebrows and all. His pectorals hung deflated across his rib cage, his stomach sunk into itself. The area around his temples were hollow caves. Even in death, his countenance was troubled; whatever killed him had been familiar by the end.

The anticipated and dreaded nausea never came. Perhaps Pok's misfortune in Adjustment had only been a sign of spire-induced withdrawals. If he could stomach the sight of a mutilated human, his flesh pulled back like the pages of a book, surely a little blood wouldn't faze him.

"What's the bag for?" Pok said. A black plastic bag covered the hand. "Disease?"

"The preservative kills any pathogen," Anji said. She was tall with blue hair. "It's to protect us from emotions. People think the most distressing part of looking at a cadaver is the face, but it's the hands we identify most as being human."

"You might be wondering why we're here so early," Rodge said. "It's because we're psychopaths."

"We need the practice," Anji said. She reached to expose a flap of tissue.

With only slight variations in hue from one section of flesh to the next, all the structures looked the same. How could they tell anything apart? Everything in his virtual anatomy course had been clearly demarcated, mirroring the experience of top surgeons who universally used medically enhanced glass to aid in the operating room. This . . . this was nothing like Pok had expected.

"Can't . . . find . . . the erector spinae," James said as he sifted through the structures with his probe.

"I see it," Anji said.

"How? Nothing's protracted."

"It's right there." She brushed back a stray hair with the top of her shoulder and reached over.

"That's a nerve," James said.

"Is it?"

Rodge adjusted his wheelchair's height until he looked like he was standing beside the cadaver. Black hair curled over his forehead. He had dark eyes, a strong nose, and oatmeal skin. He laughed. "She's right. The Butcher does it again."

"I truly hate that nickname," Anji said.

"It's a compliment. Embrace it."

"You should practice," Anji said without looking up. "That table exam's a group grade. One through seven. Seven is perfection. We want at least a four or a five. We're as good as our weakest link. Ever taken anatomy?"

"I have," Pok said. *Not like this. Definitely not like this.*

"Grab a scalpel." James nodded toward the kit Dr. Jacobs had supplied. "You can practice on his leg."

Pok shifted to the bottom half of the table and opened the toolbox to a wide variety of sharp instruments. He picked up the scalpel, pressed the blade's tip along the cadaver's skin, right beneath the knee, and pulled down. Only an indentation. He tried again and this time pressed too hard; the blade slipped deep into flesh. He struck something hard. Shit; he'd scraped bone.

You're cutting into a body. You're cutting into a fucking body.

He attempted to expose the tibia. Instead of the muscles parting in perfect layers, they ripped in half and tore in ragged shreds. He stepped back and wiped his brow as far up his sleeve as he could.

"Unacceptable," Dr. Jacobs said, suddenly beside him. "This person donated their one body. And you butcher it?"

James tried to come to his rescue. "I told him—"

Dr. Jacobs lifted a silencing hand. "The new student doctor can speak for himself."

"I—I—"

"Move," Dr. Jacobs said, all but physically pushing him aside. He wielded the scalpel and a rounded metal probe and deftly cleaned the dissection area. Out of a glistening mess of white tendon parts and red muscle bits arose decipherable structures.

"The body is in layers," Dr. Jacobs said as he worked. "Remember that. Cutting and slicing causes chaos and disrespect. Simply pry apart the layers. Whether it's divine design or billions of years of precise evolution, the anatomy is perfectly there. We are simply its excavators."

Students trickled in. Some were curious at what enraptured their anatomy professor while others went right into preparing their own cadavers.

"Artery or vein?" Dr. Jacobs asked.

The professor had exposed two vessels and lifted them with the probe. Instead of the perfectly rendered bright blue or red Pok readily identified before, both were gray and wrinkled.

"I—I don't know."

"Any of table nine care to help him out?"

"Veins are flat and don't spring back when you compress them," Anji said. "Arteries have a set shape."

"Thank you, Student Doctor Law. Now back to you: What is the name of the opening in the skull the spinal cord passes through?"

Names! He knew this. But the vocabulary was inaccessible, trapped under the expectations of a different environment. "I . . . um—"

"The end of the spinal cord, does it hang loose?"

"Yes."

"Incorrect. What anchors it? No? Do the dorsal or ventral roots transmit information from spinal cord to body?"

"I don't know." The words felt like failure on Pok's lips.

"'I don't know, I don't know.' What family are you from? Surely, they would have prepared you better?"

"I'm from New York."

"New York?" The air in the room changed. Dr. Jacobs took a small step back and seemed to shrink. Stone coldness turned to sympathy. No; pity. Pok hated that. The questions that flitted behind the professor's old, time-worn eyes answered themselves. Murmurs rippled among Pok's new classmates. Every eye seemed locked onto him.

"What did you say your last name . . ." But his voice trailed as his eyes fell to Pok's chest and even though his name was now covered by the smock, the remembering was clear. *Morning.*

Dr. Jacobs adjusted his glasses and half turned toward the class.

"Being from New York, you, better than any of us, know what's at stake here. Any shepherd system will have a hundred percent accuracy on naming the structures in a book or simulation. We have a remarkable opportunity—a *unique* opportunity—of being an amalgamation of anatomical structures that is setting out to conquer the knowledge of oneself. Welcome, Student Doctor Morning of New York. Let anatomy be your initiation."

Dr. Jacobs strolled away, down the middle of the lab, surveying the other cadavers.

"Don't take it personally," James said. "He makes a point to give everyone center stage. You got yours out of the way early. New York, huh? The pendant patients will love you."

"Pendant patients?" Pok said.

"It's our medical term for patients who come from tech cities," Rodge said.

"I'm actually seeing one from New York right now," James said.

"You all get to see patients?"

"*He* gets to," Rodge said. "He's sponsored."

"Dr. Verik's not my sponsor. But the patient is interesting. She's convinced her newborn is an impostor. Completely psychotic."

A recently pregnant patient from New York? "How old is the baby?" Pok said.

"A week, maybe two. Delivered somewhere in Jersey and now wants nothing to do with her. Like I said, completely psychotic."

The world blurred; Pok turned to busy his hands with a tool from his borrowed kit. Florence? It had to be. She'd made it to New Orleans, but in what shape? Did Jillian know?

"Sounds like an Amygdala problem," Rodge said.

"You think she had a stroke?" Pok said.

"No, not her amygdala." Rodge pointed to his temple and then circled his finger. "The Amygdala. Where all the . . . you know go."

"The Amygdala's our psych unit," James said. "We're trying to avoid that. Who would take care of the kid?"

"Someone who believes she's real, maybe? If she won't take an Amygdala bed, I will. A few nights' stay away from my kids, all the sleep I can get? Put me on a hold!"

"She thinks she's still pregnant," James said. "She's tried everything to get the baby out, according to her. Exercise, sleep journal, herbs, hypnotics. Even soaked her braids in chamomile."

Rodge mouthed the last word.

"She claims she hid the pregnancy from the shepherds. That's absurd, though, right?"

"I've heard of it happening," Pok said.

"Postpartum psychosis," Rodge said. "I was scared to death my wife, Joey, would go crazy, check into the Amygdala, and leave me to tend to the babies myself. Never actually seen it, though. Hers sounds severe. Could be Synth." Rodge elbowed his wheelchair's control lever and sank down to a half-seated position. He folded his gloved hands across his chest.

"It's not Synth." Pok caught himself. The first sign of sweat tickled his nose. "Sorry, I have strong feelings when it comes to addiction. She said she was using?"

"She hasn't told me much of anything," James said. "This patient . . . I can't connect. Dr. Verik wants me to come up with treatment ideas that wouldn't hurt the baby. Even though she's not pregnant!"

"That makes perfect sense to me," Rodge said. "She believes she's pregnant. Why would she agree to a treatment that goes against that?"

"What about Carve Bee honey?" Pok had decided he needed to see Florence. If only just to confirm that she'd been reunited with Jillian, to make sure there was family to take care of Baby Girl while Florence got treatment.

"Delicious," Rodge said. "Especially on hot rolls."

"Carve Bee honey, model eight-thirty-six," Pok said.

"It used to be ubiquitous," Anji said. Strands of her blue-tipped hair fell from her bun as she leaned into James. Was that affection? No. Anji was only trying to get better leverage on the dissection. "Touted as a miracle drug. Antibiotic. Antiviral. Converts glucose to ketones in the gut."

Rodge shook his own belly. "I could use some of that."

"Ketosis could help with psychosis without harming the baby," Pok said. "Or without harming *a* baby, I should say."

"Wait," James said. "Is this a hypothetical or do you have some?"

"That strain hasn't existed for years," Anji said.

"I have it. It was my dad's. Eight-thirty-six." Pok was close; he owed it to Jillian and himself. "I could come with you to talk to her about it. Use that New York connection."

"That's not a bad idea," James said. "You got hospital clearance?"

"Not yet," Pok said. The floor of his stomach fell a few stories. "Dean Sims said as long as I'm with someone else, I can see patients."

"With an attending, yes," Anji said. "Have you done the CPR and privacy trainings?"

"I will soon," Pok said.

"See, he's not even certified," Anji said. "It would be irresponsible for us to bring in guests."

"He's not a guest; he's a medical student," Rodge said. He heightened his chair. "Those trainings are just a bunch of protocol. If someone flatlines and they call a rosk, you think anyone will look to us?"

Dr. Jacobs addressed the class, cutting into their conversation. "Tomorrow's lecture will be on the spinal cord. Please read the accompanying chapters. And yes, that's plural."

The sound of tearing Velcro rippled across the lab as students collectively pulled off their disposable smocks and latex gloves and stuffed them in easily accessible bins.

"Here, pull from the center, straight out, and the smock should come right off." James helped Pok the rest of the way. "About my patient. Anji's right. Dr. Verik can be a prude. It'd be easier if you already had your clearance. It's likely fine, just . . . I should talk to her first. Tell you after class tomorrow?"

"Sure," Pok said. He forced a smile. "That sounds great."

Anji was the last to push back from their cadaver and remove her lab gear. "You want me to get us a table?"

"I don't think she means lunch," Rodge said.

"The Ventricle, of course," Anji said.

"That's the library," Rodge said. "Whoever designed this place must have been an anatomy professor."

"We only have a couple hours to study before office hours," Anji said.

"*More* studying?" James said. "Anj, you can't fit more in that brain."

"Not for me. You. Postpartum psychosis. Antipsychotics. Carve Bee honey. You want to secure a sponsor, don't you?"

"Dean Sims said the best studying is time with your patient."

Anji rolled her eyes. "I'll see you over there." She put on her white coat—freshly cleaned and pressed compared to the others—while James tucked his under his armpit. Rodge hung his from a hook on his chair.

"You joining or not?" James said to Rodge as Anji's footfalls fell to whispers.

"Not." Rodge rolled past him and into the tunnel. "The kids should be down for their morning nap. What kind of father would I be to miss nap time?"

James paused at the door. "Thanks for the suggestion," he said to Pok. "It's good to have four people on the team again. And I will ask Dr. Verik. See you in class this afternoon?"

"For sure."

Pok was about to pick up his own white coat when he saw he still had on detritus-speckled gloves. Removing them was a slow, careful process. How did people do this without getting cadaver juice in their fingernails? He washed his hands in the large basin sink and, as he dried them, noticed something on the floor by the entrance.

James's ID.

"Wait! You left your—"

Pok paused at the sound of his own echo through the empty tunnel. He picked up the laminated card and ran his finger along the edge and then over the bold red stamp with *CLEARED* in the middle.

He imagined it pinned to his own coat. Imagined falling in line with the other personnel going into the hospital. Imagined finding Florence. A branching part of his imagination saw him getting caught. But it was fuzzy, unformed. Jillian had risked much more, hadn't she? He wouldn't have made it out of Jersey without her. And he'd nearly forgotten that, wrapped up in his own excitement about being a medical student. He held in his hand the chance to set that right.

Shouldn't he take it?

Nineteen

POSTPARTUM PSYCHOSIS

A short line of would-be patients led into the emergency department. Hospital staff entered without scrutiny. Pok held up James's ID just in time for the security guard's cursory glance and wave through. He made straight for the reception desk.

"I'm looking for a patient," Pok said.

"Good morning to you, too." A young woman regarded him with eyes as sharp as her short-cropped hair. Her smile was more amused than pleasant. She peered at his ID, which he had flipped over right after entering the emergency department. "I haven't seen you around. Are you new?"

"Very new. Can you help me? The patient's name is Florence."

"Shaliyah." She held out her hand. Her grip was strong. Cursive letters inked across her wrist. She had clear, reddish-brown skin and a small gap between her two front teeth that seemed to expand when she smiled. "Who's the attending?"

Shit. He'd forgotten the name of the doctor James was hoping to impress. It started with a *V.*

"Excuse me? I was here first." Pok only now noticed the substantial line he'd cut.

"One second." Shaliyah shifted to placate the ornery visitor.

Pok moved along the outer layer of the HemoStat, scanning the aisles.

Thin shades draped over slanted skylights did little to keep out the late summer sun. The hot space boiled with the bustle of patients. Uniformed staff moved between rows of identical beds, a shifting rainbow of red, yellow, blue, and green with specks of black. Some stopped to talk with the bedbound. Was that Florence, over in the corner? He rose on his tiptoes and walked right into a nurse.

"Hey! Watch it!" The hot-faced nurse sprang up from sifting through a drawer for supplies. Her personalized scrubs read, *Nurse Holly.*

"Sorry," Pok said. "I didn't see you."

"You med students are here to learn, right? Not daydream." Before he could stop her, Nurse Holly grabbed the ID and turned it over. Instead of being alarmed, her eyes went soft, almost disappointed. "First-year. Figures. You seeing a patient or what?"

Or what. *In and out, Pok. Find Florence, make sure she's okay, and leave.*

"Yes, I'm here to see a patient," Pok said. Nurse Holly began to move away, deciding the first-year student wasn't worth her anger. He matched her quick stride. "Could you help me find her?"

Nurse Holly stopped at a patient's bedside to draw up a syringe with clear liquid. Pok caught sight of his own reflection in a mirror above the portable sink. A loc hung from his bonnet. He fixed it. The nurse pulled a folded list from her back pocket.

"What's her name?" she said.

"Florence."

"Last name?" When he didn't answer, the nurse looked him up and down. "You know her hymn?"

"Her him?"

"Hippocrates Medical Number?"

"Um . . . I . . ." Pok looked down at his coat, as if it would magically produce the answer.

"I swear they just release you all onto the wards as soon as they can. Who's the supervising doc?"

The name of James's would-be mentor snapped back to him. "Dr. Verik."

"There we go. Florence King. Psychosis. Bed seventeen. Here almost forty-eight hours. No more pendant beds upstairs? She really should be in the Amygdala."

"Florence King," Pok said. The name brought him back to his father's

East Harlem examination room, to the smell of dripping water and latex gloves. "Thank you."

Pok left the nurse to venture down one aisle and then another, searching for bed seventeen.

There.

A feminine figure, statue-still, stared at the wall. Brown curly hair had started to fill on the previously faded side; blonde locs disappeared down her back from the other. Black spots stained under her uninviting brown eyes. Her arm twitched erratically as she pulled her locs into a ponytail. Red welts lined her forearms. Her eyes ran the length of his coat before turning away.

"Another student?" she said. "I'll tell you like I told the tall one: I want to see a doctor. A doc-*tor*. How many times do I have to say it?"

Florence pressed her head back into her pillow. The paper-thin skin underneath her clavicle sunk in deep as she breathed. Her locs spread onto her pillow like so many fingers. She raised a newspaper. In fine cursive, the title *Second Opinion* marked the top.

Be with your patient. His father's voice.

Pok took off his haircap. Scant hairs from long locs tickled freedom on his neck.

"What happened to Baby Girl?" he said.

Florence turned so quickly her leg came from underneath the sheet. She reached out and touched the end of one of his locs. Her hand twitched every few seconds; the slight tug stung.

"Dr. Morning? No, of course not. His son?" Her eyes narrowed, brightened, and then landed on a look of understanding that almost made Pok turn away. "Is it true? Is he—"

"Yes. I—How did you hear?"

"My shepherd companion told me a close friend passed away and that it was Phelando. I never listed him as a friend, a contact, nothing. I hoped it wasn't true. He was supposed to meet me here and deliver Baby Girl." Pok watched a fly circle under the bed. Then it was gone. When he finally made himself look back up, Florence was shaking her head. "I'm so sorry."

"I met your sister," Pok said. "Jillian. We traveled together. She was looking for you."

The air warmed. "She is *not* my sister, you hear me? That is not *my* Jillian."

"Okay," Pok said. Panic rose. He was teetering on the edge of her psychosis. "What about Baby Girl? How is she?"

Florence turned to look at nothing. Her fingers crawled down her belly.

"She's taking her sweet time. I thought she was ready but she had other plans. Isn't that right?" A shadow fell upon her face, so profound that Pok looked to the bedside lamp to make sure it hadn't burned out. "They tried to give me a baby that wasn't mine. But I know Baby Girl. And that's not Baby Girl."

There was shape to her abdomen, certainly more than he'd expected. What if she was still pregnant? What if everyone else had been horribly wrong and the shepherd app had been right and she was only now entering her third trimester? Pok physically shook the ridiculous conspiracy out of his head. Where had that come from?

"Can I see?" he said, reoriented.

Florence pulled up her gown. Pok swallowed down a wave of nausea reminiscent of the blood draw in Adjustment. The C-section incision—a couple inches below Florence's navel—was still closed, but barely. Pus dotted the suture line. Above, the belly bulged outward, red and angry.

Pok turned away, just enough to calm the nausea without televising his aversion. "What happened?" Did he want to know her answer?

"The shepherds were tracking me." Disgust soaked her words. "They were using it to talk to Baby Girl. But we got the tracker out. In Jersey. We got it out."

God . . . she was talking about the delivery. "It looks infected," Pok said.

"That's what these doctors said. That I need antibiotics and surgery. But what if they're trying to put the shepherds back in me? I can't let that happen. Baby Girl doesn't want that to happen."

"If it's infection . . ." Pok said. Slow. Deliberate. "It could be affecting your mind."

The pure disappointment in her eyes broke Pok's heart. "You think I'm crazy. You and everyone else."

"I don't think you're crazy, Florence. It's just, it sounds like you went into labor a couple weeks ago, back in Jersey. I have to ask what would cause Baby Girl to change her mind and stay inside for so much longer."

"Because she's scared!" Her outburst temporarily muted the rest of the

HemoStat. "I wish your father were here. He'd know what to do. I ran out of the honey he gave me. *That* helped."

"Carve Bee?" Pok said. "I have some. The very same."

Florence's eyes widened. For the first time, she looked genuinely happy to see him. "Do you? I think it's just what Baby Girl . . ." Florence's head swiveled to focus past him. She sat up and pulled a loosening strap over her shoulder. ". . . needs."

Pok turned to see a physician with short-cut hair and thick, black-rimmed glasses step into the light. Wrinkles contracted her mottled white coat. At her side was a young scribe, a boy no older than a teen. He stared down at a piece of frayed paper as he held his dented plastic pen poised above it.

The physician touched the scribe's shoulder. "Excuse us, Terry," she said and the boy rushed off.

The illusion fell away. Pok wasn't in his father's office convening with a patient seeking the human touch. He was in Hippocrates. Marauding around with someone else's hospital clearance pinned to his chest. And he'd been caught.

"I am Dr. Verik," the woman said. Experienced patches of gray lay across her hair. Wisdom softened her voice. "Are you Florence King?"

"That's me."

Dr. Verik turned to Pok. The physician's gaze was comprehensive. Pok's hair; the discrepancy between the photo ID and reality; there was no doubt Dr. Verik immediately knew the situation. Which made her next words that much more perplexing. "You were about to give your recommendations?"

Was she joking? She didn't look the type to jest.

Pok turned to Florence as if she had an answer. She smiled in place of one. It would have to do.

Pok closed his eyes. He'd gone over countless patient presentation simulations in preparation for medical school interviews. "Her abdomen is most likely infected from the . . . extraction procedure done in Jersey. She is fearful, though, that any type of medications or procedure would reinstall a tracker that could hurt Baby Girl. I suggested Carve Bee honey, which she's aligned with." When he finished and let the world back in, Dr. Verik was still there. Still listening.

"Interesting choice. What's your reasoning for the honey?"

"She's had it before," Pok said. "And it helped. It could help again, especially in this new environment."

"And bring out Baby Girl?" Florence said. "That sounds good. Really good."

"We'll have to import some from MouseKill," Dr. Verik said.

"He brought some."

"I did," Pok said. "CBH eight-thirty-six. My father's stash."

Pok couldn't read Dr. Verik's stone expression. The idea was clinically ridiculous: using honey to treat a woman who didn't recognize her own child. But it was his idea. He had to own it. He recalled what Dr. Soft had said about withdrawals, S-reactive proteins, and Synth.

"I also think we should try some Synth." That got Dr. Verik's attention, and Florence's. Pok spoke quickly. "Distressing thoughts could be exacerbated by withdrawal. Synth can bind to the same TSO protein sensory receptors. It may . . . calm things down."

"Good thought. Instead of Synth, we have DigiTone, a Synth derivative. It binds much tighter to the same receptors as Synth, only far less potent. It's our main med for withdrawals."

"Would doja . . . digit—"

"DigiTone."

"DigiTone," Florence said. "Thank you. Would it hurt Baby Girl?"

"We'd make sure we use a low enough dose not to harm a baby," Dr. Verik said.

The shuffle of shoes preceded the curtain opening. A flustered James, sweat coating his brow, eyes wide and worried, barged in.

"You're late," Dr. Verik said. She rotated her arm outward, the same way Dr. Soft had done. James pinched her cuff.

"I couldn't find my . . ." James's eyes widened in disbelief and then confusion as they fell on Pok and went down to his chest. "ID."

"Your organization problems are irrelevant to the patient," Dr. Verik said. "Since we are short on time, I'll summarize for you. Thirty-two-year-old woman, recently moved from New York. Experiencing stressful thoughts. Is concerned about her baby's true due date. Fatigue and declining cognition during the day. Headache. Sensitivity to light. Now, what else do you want to know?"

"I . . . I'd want to know . . . if . . ."

Dr. Verik gestured toward Florence. James turned, flushed, and approached the bedside. The welcoming table nine smile was gone. His cheeks flared red beside a thin mouth. Sweat stained his armpits and pooled under the creases in his forehead.

"What happened when you went into labor?"

"Baby Girl changed her mind." Florence cooed toward her belly. "You didn't give in, did you? You stayed strong."

James fumbled with his stethoscope and listened to her stomach. He moved the bell from quadrant to quadrant. "There's no heartbeat."

"You can't find a baby's heartbeat, that's your problem."

"And the baby you came here with?"

"What about it?"

"Is it possible at all that—"

Florence knocked the stethoscope out of James's hands.

"That's *not* Baby Girl!"

James looked toward Dr. Verik, lost. The senior physician beckoned her scribe back in through the curtains. Terry continued to stare down at his pen and paper as if waiting for it to give a command. Dr. Verik stepped to the bedside.

"We're worried about Baby Girl," Dr. Verik said. "We don't think she's been getting the proper nourishment from your body. It sounds like what happened in Jersey was stressful."

"It was horrible."

"Sometimes stressful events cause the body to stop recognizing the growing baby in the same way. Let's start with the CBH. How does that sound?" Dr. Verik's eye contact was unwavering. Florence nodded and sat back. "Scribe Terry will relay the orders to the nursing staff and you should be transferred up to the unit soon."

"I'll make sure of it," James said.

"Next time, Student Doctor Tisdale," Dr. Verik said and rotated her right hand outward. James nodded, pinched her cuff as if he were removing a stain or a piece of lint, and began to leave when Dr. Verik spoke again. "Don't forget your ID."

Pok unclipped the ID and handed it over. James yanked it so fast the plastic stung the tips of Pok's fingers.

"I can explain," Pok began when James had gone.

"The damage is to her, not me," Dr. Verik said.

"I heard you were here," Pok started, careful not to mention Jillian. "I thought maybe I could help you and Baby Girl."

"You did," Florence said. Despite her blatant disconnect with reality when it came to her pregnancy, she seemed to immediately understand Pok's predicament. Her next words were for Dr. Verik. "His father took care of me in New York. And he spoke very highly of Pok. Very highly. He'd be so proud to see him here. Go easy on my future doctor."

"Indeed. A word?" Dr. Verik led Pok outside of the immediate area and pulled Florence's curtain closed.

"I'm sorry," Pok said again. "I'm a new medical student and—"

"I know who you are, Pok Morning. Is this how you honor Phelando? Sneaking into a hospital? Lying to patients?"

Her words stung. "I didn't lie," Pok said.

"Then what would you call it? I'll give you a chance to redeem yourself: Why did you suggest the Carve Bee honey?"

"I know it's a placebo." Pok spoke fast. "I was trying to get her to buy-in."

"Your father treated her with CBH, did he not? Was he using it as a placebo?"

Pok was silent.

"You must listen as well as you lie. I'm sure Dr. Morning explained to you the efficacy of CBH eight-thirty-six. It has strong antibiotic properties, which could help with her infection. It makes carbohydrates inert, which will throw her body into ketosis and stimulate labor. Most of all, it counteracts the essence imbalance caused by chronic tech exposure. The art of healing is done through thought and practice and study, not dumb luck. Give me one good reason you shouldn't be expelled over this stunt."

"I traveled with her sister. I owed it to them both." Dr. Verik looked unmoved. Heat circling Pok's collar spread to his cheeks. Yes, he'd made a mistake, but expelled? He'd come too far. "I want to talk to the dean."

She adjusted her glasses, curled her lips. "Fine. Let's go."

Pok met her step. "To where?"

"To see the dean. Be careful what you wish for."

Twenty

SPONSORSHIP

Well inside the central indoor garden, Dean Sims trimmed leaves off a short purple plant. She paused a beat as Dr. Verik and Pok stepped into the small section made private by tall, well-manicured hedges. As they approached, a reserved sigh rose above the background trickle of water.

"Dr. Verik," the dean said without turning from her task. "You've found our newest addition."

"When was he initiated?" Dr. Verik said. "I didn't see him at orientation."

"Initiation can take many forms."

The dean reached into the plant and snipped off a leaf riddled with holes. She felt its ragged ridges with her thumb before letting it fall to the ground. "What is this about? I'm in the middle of something."

"I found him with a stolen ID, talking to a patient."

"Did he help?"

"Excuse me?"

"The patient. Did he help the patient?" The dean scrutinized the leaf before depositing it in a small wooden box. She adjusted her white coat and moved down the garden line.

"That's beside the point."

"Sounds like a yes," Dean Sims said. "I assume you know of his father."

"I don't see—"

"What it has to do with this? It has everything to do. The Council has already decided on his matriculation. You could take this up with them, if you want."

The dean paused mid-trim. She retracted her blade, reached into the bush, and threw a foot-long branch, full of green leaves, to the side.

Pok stepped forward. They both glared at him. "I wanted to help one of my dad's patients and made a mistake. It won't happen again."

"Do not blame your father's memory. You respect him more than that." Dean Sims touched his coat. "I can formally reprimand him, if you care so much. But he will be a student. In fact, you know well his father's work. The first-years have yet to secure mentors."

"You can't be serious. I've been working with Student Doctor James Tisdale. He's smart, reliable, and—"

"Inexperienced with pendants and their specific issues stemming from chronic tech exposure." Dean Sims pulled a folded piece of paper from her physician's bag. She gave it to Dr. Verik. "Another admission. Pendant, from California's Bay Area, been here a month. Classic withdrawal but not responding to the treatments."

Dr. Verik read over the note. "It could be a new, more potent strain of Synth."

"Regardless, the numbers are rising."

"Which is why we need a dedicated unit," Dr. Verik said.

"I can give you half. Your new apprentice can assist."

"I learn quick—"

Dr. Verik's cutting eye shortened Pok's statement. Her face lengthened. "Trespassing should get one expelled, not promoted. I've seen his morals; I have no clue about his skills."

"Then assess them. I suspect we'll soon see eye to eye. Good chat, Emily."

Dr. Verik held out her hand, palm loose, face down. Sims pinched her cuff and returned to her tree. Dr. Verik stood there for a long time. She looked around as if for an answer and frowned when she was reminded of Pok's presence beside her.

"You are bold," Dr. Verik said. She straightened her cuffs. "Just like your father. Let's see if that's where the similarities end. If you last a week, it'll be a miracle."

Twenty-One

THE FIRST LESSON

They climbed the stairs leading from the lobby, up and through the hospital's various wards. On the third floor, Dr. Verik led him down a tight hall and into a room centered around an island of desks and doored-off cubicles. In the space around it, mostly empty beds lined the walls. Unlike in the HemoStat, each was accompanied by a dresser, a retractable curtain, and a single chair. Nurses, scrub techs, and assistants shuffled between them.

"Where are all the patients?" Pok said.

"You will need to be more observant to keep up with your classmates," Dr. Verik said. "Questions are a luxury. Choose them wisely."

Pok noticed them now. The identifying uniforms blended with the hospital clothing of the sick. With a nurse supervising over his shoulder, a young patient drew blood from an older one. A short, transient line fed into a corner station where patients took one another's blood pressure with leather cuffs. Scribes recorded the results. From one of the walled rooms clustered in the middle, a patient emerged pushing a cart full of books. A tube snaked out of her arm and up to a hanging bag of liquid. She began distributing her library to patients.

"We encourage movement for whoever can. It gets their essence flowing and the energy can be infectious. This is Three North. Immunology and Rheumatology." Dr. Verik pointed toward a wall of doors on the far side of the unit. "Corresponding lectures are held in there. Students study where they practice."

On the far side of Three North, a stick of a man sat alone with a game board. Sharp limbs jutted out from his chair like branches of a wilted tree. Bruised blotches and dark red lines tracked along his arms' sun-kissed skin.

The patient mulled over what looked like a wooden checkerboard with white and black pieces. Finally, he sat back, scratched his chin's many whiskers with fingers barnacled at the knuckles, and raised his eyebrows. He moved a piece and smiled up at the empty seat across from him. He showed no sign that he noticed their presence.

"Buddy Harrison has what we think is Synth psychosis," Dr. Verik whispered. She gently spun the game board one hundred eighty degrees. "Usually a case for the Amygdala—a simple DigiTone taper should take care of both the withdrawals and the psychosis. But our meds aren't touching him. What's more, we couldn't find any traces of Synth in his blood."

"When did he move to New Orleans?" Pok said.

"Years ago. It's like the Synth has reactivated in his body and brain. Hiding out all this time, if you will."

"Cocky bastard." Buddy's coarse, loud voice grated against the quiet. He grinned a big, tooth-starved grin and moved one of the white pieces.

"The concept of time is lost to him. He's played so many games of Go in his life that when his brain sees a certain configuration, it matches to a precise past and moves the pieces accordingly. He plays his memory."

Dr. Verik moved two of the pieces.

"See? Even his mood changes. Perhaps this particular game was after his wife died. Or when he realized he was addicted to Synth."

Dr. Verik pulled up a third chair and took the old man's hands in her own. Several of his knuckles were swollen to the size of grapes.

"Are you familiar with gout? It's more common in Jackson, Mississippi, Buddy's hometown. The city was an early adopter of AI to fix its water quality problems. Shepherd algorithms postulated that a certain alkaline body pH could balance out years of exposure to toxic water. Not only did they indiscriminately suggest diets high in cod and sardines, but the shepherds also directly tweaked kidney functionality to manipulate uric acid level reserves to 'maximize' pH. Where does uric acid collect?"

Pok didn't know, but the implication was clear. "In the joints?"

"Exactly. Almost every pendant we get from Mississippi has a bad case of gout. It's very painful." Dr. Verik bent Buddy's finger at the knuckle; he didn't flinch. "Synth use doesn't help. It can accumulate in the glomeruli—are you familiar with kidney anatomy? Good—and leads to further uric acid buildup. Thankfully, the Synth has burned his nerve endings."

Dr. Verik produced from her pocket a small wooden box. She opened it on the table, removed a vial of brown liquid, and poured some of it on Buddy's largest tophi, located on his index finger. She then attached a shiny scalpel to a rusted handle. Pok's stomach recognized what was happening before his mind did. Dr. Verik sliced down the middle of the bulging knuckle. White with rivulets of blood cauliflowered out. Rolling nausea forced Pok's gaze away.

"Do you need a moment?" Dr. Verik said.

"I'm fine." What was wrong with him? He'd shadowed countless virtual surgerics, had seen every type of body fluid in every kind of way, had even opted in to the olfactory enhancements for full immersion, and now something as pedestrian as *drops of blood* turned his stomach? Pok clenched the hem of his coat, swallowed down the sensation, and turned back to the procedure. Buddy's finger was wrapped in a clean bandage. He looked ambivalent.

"It's all about balance. Shepherds keep that balance artificially. When patients get here they are like a teetering seesaw, left unstable because the shepherd tech has been suddenly snatched away." Dr. Verik made a motion with her hand. "With enough time the body can find balance again. The scalpel is a powerful equalizer."

Dr. Verik curled her first three fingers around Buddy's wrist, touched his forehead with her other hand, and matched her breath with the patient's. "Heart rate one-oh-eight, blood pressure elevated. Tactile hypothermia. The tongue is pink, moist. He's currently in balance. We'll discontinue the autumn crocus—it's not doing anything for his gout. FLT worth trying—implement. Continue DigiTone, current dosage. Suggest surgery to remove tophi for increased mobility—not urgent. Monitor digit every two hours for signs of infection."

"What's FLT?" Pok said.

"Flashing lights therapy. Just the right wavelength can stave off permanent cognitive malfunction. We are hesitant to prescribe it in active Synth use because reaction with the Synth molecules collected in the retina can cause blindness. But his Synth blood level is zero."

Dr. Verik produced a penlight from her bag. Using a dial, she switched through various colors, testing the beam on her palm, until she landed on a greenish blue.

"Different wavelengths of light stimulate the brain in different ways, and not just in the occipital lobe. Buddy, look here."

Dr. Verik planted her elbow to the side of the game board. Buddy moved a piece, sneered defiantly at an opponent from his past, and looked into the penlight.

"That's good. Now, look at me."

Buddy did.

"See these small eye movements even though he's fixed on me?" Dr. Verik said. "They're called saccades. By cycling through the various wavelengths I can detect which saccades are erratic, indicating an imbalance in a region of the brain specific to that wavelength. We have to assume my brain is balanced and, thus, my saccades will be normal. Humans are social creatures, both psychologically and biologically. The idea is that Buddy's rhythm will adjust to mine."

As Dr. Verik spent several minutes cycling through the colors, the only sound was the *click-click-click* of the device's turning wheel. Buddy stayed still and unbothered, as if taken by trance. Finally, Dr. Verik turned off the light. Buddy blinked and returned to the game board.

"Ask him a question," she said.

"How long have you been here in the hospital, Buddy?" Pok said.

"Two weeks, give or take. Is it your move or mine?" Buddy said. Dr. Verik gestured for Pok to engage. Pok moved a piece and waited. Buddy considered the board and then him. "I haven't seen you around here. You new?"

"I'm Pok."

"Student Doctor Morning," Dr. Verik corrected. She sank back in her chair. "For some, the formality can be uncomfortable. It's best to get over that early."

Buddy moved his piece. "It's good to play with someone new. For once."

"The rate of latent withdrawals is concerning," Dr. Verik said once they were back to the nursing station. Buddy had won the game. "The recurrence symptoms in patients like Buddy could quickly become an emergency."

"Does it have to do with the shepherds?" Pok said.

"Medicine 101: don't ask questions that don't change your management. Either way, we need to treat it. Hopefully, the issue proves transient."

"How did you bring him back to the present?" Pok said.

"A and A: aligning with the anima. If the shepherds put us both in a brain scanner, they would see our exact neurochemical changes during the exercise, simulate a thousand trials, and still never be able to get the same result as a basically trained human."

"It's what my dad called *the essence*. He thought it was the reason AI-led medicine will never be enough."

"Your father was right. The only thing left was to prove it."

Pok searched Dr. Verik's face, but she remained stoic. Even glass would have little commentary on her emotional state. Had her name been one of the coauthors in Project Do No Harm? He couldn't recall. "You knew him?" he said. "My dad?"

"We had differing philosophies on how to get things done. But I'd say I align with him the most clinically. For better or for worse. Which is why Sims thinks I should sponsor you."

"And what do you think?"

Instead of answering, Dr. Verik opened her black notebook and sat down to write. After several minutes she rocked back and peered at him over her nose. "Florence King's distress was accessible through her anima. Did you feel it?"

"Yes. I . . ." Pok censored himself. The thoughts of conspiracy he'd had while talking to Florence had been brief but potent. Dr. Verik was already skeptical of him. Should he give her reason to think him illogical, too?

But Dr. Verik was observant. "What else?" she said.

"There was a moment," Pok said, "I almost believed her. That maybe Baby Girl was still inside. It was a crazy thought. But it felt real."

"A touch of alignment. This early. The best treatment in the world won't matter if the patient doesn't trust you enough to give it. Gaining trust is much harder when someone's psychotic. You assess the anima well."

Dr. Verik paused to think.

"A sponsor mainly ensures a student stays afloat. This will be something different. If we're going to work together, I need excellence. I need you to master what they teach you in the classrooms and on the wards so that we can learn exactly which parts we need to unlearn and why." Dr. Verick checked the time. "You're late for Grand Rounds. When's your first test?"

"Anatomy," Pok said. "In two weeks."

"And I presume you don't have credentials—CPR, phlebotomy, privacy training—else you wouldn't have stolen an ID. Sims might have given you to me as a punishment. Time will tell, I guess." Dr. Verik shook her head. "I'll get a temporary badge sent to your room so you can see patients. But get the trainings done. Most are inconsequential but knowing how to do chest compressions will make you useful for a return of spontaneous circulation, commonly referred to as a rosk when a patient flatlines. In other words, don't make me look bad."

Twenty-Two

THE CAMERON DRYDEN STUDIES

Genesis Auditorium was just past the main hospital garden and next to the patient-only elevators. Grand double doors plated in silver opened to three seating sections curved upward from the stage. Half the seats were full. Whatever Grand Rounds was, it had already started. A flock of first-years congregated near the middle of the far-left aisle. Pok took a seat on the end of their row.

Onstage, a senior physician spoke from the podium. She had a long, flawless coat, straight, black hair streaked with gray, and the beginning of wrinkles along her warm, golden skin. A special light fell on the first row, clearly reserved for the five or six physicians sitting there.

"—and while Governor Teal has been supportive of our existence and our efforts, especially in medicine, she is under increasing political pressure to address the mass exodus from Louisiana. Yes, New Orleans's population steadily grows—we certainly feel it in our clinics and emergency rooms—but it is far outweighed by the numbers leaving the state. We greatly benefit from Louisiana's continued independence from TSO and SLC. A tanking economy threatens that.

"By sending Hippocrates trained practitioners to neighboring hospitals we can expand our reach and combat the easily propagated narrative of a backward city that locks itself from the rest of the world. Additionally, New

Orleans demographics remain increasingly different from the rest of the state and the country. While it's true that early migration was driven by AI bias against marginalized populations, we are proving human-led medicine to be beneficial for all peoples. The narrative that this city is only beneficial to 'minorities' is outdated but remains persistent.

"In conclusion, if you believe, like I do, that humans define real medicine, then in many ways Hippocrates is the last hospital. While that is a noble moniker, it is also one of inevitable extinction. To survive, we need to expand. Thank you."

Light applause. Pok wished he'd caught the beginning of the presentation. Louisiana's noncommittal to either TSO or SLC combined with its inability to fully take part in Hippocrates's special brand of medicine had left the state in a technological limbo. The worst of both worlds. No wonder so many Louisianians outside the spires sought the warmth of other suns.

"Any questions?" The physician sent her gaze down the front row and nodded. "Yes, Council member?"

"Would this plan lead to the expansion of the spires?" The woman who spoke had an aged, calculated voice.

"Not immediately, but it's certainly worth considering. Yes, near the back."

"Will this proposal put us in violation of the Nonmaleficence Act?"

"From my understanding, Nonmaleficence currently prevents Hippocrates from teaching medicine outside of New Orleans. We are providing medical resources in the form of doctors, not education. Hopefully, with time, the laws will shift favorably instead of the other direction."

"Thank you, Dr. Wilcox," Dean Sims said, taking her place at the podium. "It is always enlightening to hear your perspective, especially in how we relate to the rest of the world. Next week Dr. Lowry will present on the history of reproductive rights."

The senior physicians left first and then the attending staff and professors. Dr. Verik, who had been a few rows in, locked eyes with Pok as she passed, then looked away. The residents left and then, finally, the medical students, by class. Pockets congregated in the foyer. Anji and Rodge crowded a still-flustered James. The three looked over at the same time as if alerted to Pok's presence. He veered away.

The next class was Pharmacology and Medicinal Herbs, taught by Dr.

Alan Granger. Pok's printed schedule said to meet outside the main entrance. Pok found a perimeter seat on a bench opposite an older man with gray, short-cut hair leaning on his cane. Sunspots dotted his hands. The man peered at him, some unspoken question in his gaze. Pok kept his head low.

When all of the class was there, the man rose off the bench. The students turned to face him. Their instructor began to walk down the road; the students followed. Pok sprang up and crossed over the invisible divide to stand with his classmates. Behind him, someone snickered. Pok now recognized the senior professor from Genesis Auditorium's front row. He was a member of the Council.

Dr. Alan Granger's back was curved with age; the tips of his white coat dragged in the dirt as he led the first-year student doctors to the west gates. Dr. Granger leaned against his cane as they paused at the main road to let pass a truck topped with soiled linen. Nearby, James quizzed Anji and Rodge. What would Pok say when it was time? *Sorry for stealing your badge? Sorry for stealing your sponsor? Want to be friends?*

Modest buildings lined the road down to the front gate. Clinics, surgical theaters, and in-dwellings were interspersed with the single-story eateries and supply shops. Electricity's scarcity permeated every aspect of the city. Drying jumpsuits and scrubs hung from windows. An overflowing linen receptacle awaited pickup outside the Theater, the hospital's surgery center. Just a short few months ago Pok had envisioned a very different first day of class: one full of virtual tours, robotic arms, and ongoing chat rooms.

Beyond the gates they slipped into what looked like forgotten wood. Pok anticipated the old physician might lose his balance on the uneven ground, but Dr. Granger moved as if his cane were a third leg.

"The hospital gets its medicinal herbs from three hundred official gardens," he said. Pok strained to hear over wind-rustled trees. "Most patients grow their own herbs and donate what they don't use."

The barren trees thinned and opened to a small field of palms pregnant with green and yellow papaya. A raccoon pawed at one, ripe and fallen. He paused at their arrival, attempted a quick retreat with his find, and finally abandoned the fruit to scurry back into the thick of the woods. Dr. Granger picked up what it had left behind.

"Who can identify this?" he said.

"PCN?" Anji said.

"No abbreviations, Student Doctor Law."

"Sorry. Penicillin."

"Correct. We inject fungus when they are still young. Once the fruit has broken away from the tree, it is ready to cultivate."

Dr. Granger cracked the hard shell against a tree trunk. Dark flesh spewed brown juice and wooed the buzz of flies with its sweet smell.

"Patients eat that?" Rodge said. With his scraggly black beard and his hair fading from the temples, he looked a lot older than his classmates. He pushed back on his wheels.

"Do they?" Dr. Granger posed.

"P-chry . . . um, *penicillium* . . . chry . . . *chrysogenum* is poisonous, Dr. Granger," James said. "We have to isolate the penicillin from the fungus before giving it to patients."

"Show-off," Rodge said.

"In other words: yes, patients do eat that," Dr. Granger said. "Patients get the benefit of the earth they don't get with synthetic."

"What's the benefit?" Pok said.

"Excuse me?"

A pocket expanded around Pok. A band of heat wrapped around his ears.

"He doesn't like being interrupted," Rodge whispered. "And call him by his name. Try again. Worst thing he can do is eat your face."

"I'm sorry, Dr. Granger. I'm Student Doctor Pok Morning. You said patients get the earth's benefit. What benefit is that?"

"I thought they taught this in orgo? I'll refresh, quickly." He stacked both hands on the head of his cane. "We all know of the essence, of course. This effect goes beyond human-human. There is a 'quantum vibration' that exists in the earth. Who is familiar with the Cameron Dryden studies?"

To Pok's surprise, Rodge's hand went up.

"Yes, Student Doctor Holloway."

"Thank you, Dr. Granger. The Cameron Dryden studies showed that the energy signature of two identically structured molecules will be different dependent on if that molecule was derived from the earth versus synthetically made."

Dr. Granger's chin nodded emphatically over his cane. "The only thing more extraordinary than the studies themselves was how they came to be. Cameron Dryden was an organic chemist who became curious about the placebo effect. His wife—a practicing psychiatrist and therapist—often talked about how she would prescribe the exact same medication as her primary care colleagues but have wildly different results. The placebo effect of 'bedside manner' was well described but often dismissed. Dryden chose to look deeper.

"He proposed that there was something more innate at the root of what his wife was seeing. He started off simple, replicated well-known studies showing there was clear benefit from one provider to the next despite giving the same exact treatment. Establishing this baseline, he took the same providers with proven 'exceptional bedside manner' and had them follow scripts with various levels of empathy and the benefit was preserved across the board. He went further and devised a study showing the mere presence of these providers in the treatment room had an impact, even if the patient didn't know the provider was there. The effect could not be purely psychological; there was some shift in the physical world itself from just the presence of certain providers.

"The studies rocked the medical world. Dryden's early studies implied there was something paranormal amiss. Telepathy. Magic. Controversy brought attention. He became a kind of celebrity. He was being interviewed by a magazine and so enjoyed the experience that he named the term after them. Essence.

"Dryden had set the stage perfectly to bring the issue back to his field. He took a variety of synthetically made and organically derived compounds, isolating each to their core structure, and measured the energy expenditure. Consistently, they were different. So much so that he could confidently predict, by its energy signatures, whether or not a compound was synthetically derived.

"What is this difference? Like dark matter, we don't yet know. It has been observed but not defined. But we don't have to understand something to utilize it or to respect it."

"He also likes to talk," Rodge said. "You got him going."

Pok could see that. Granger was enjoying this.

"Unfortunately, Dryden became ill with pancreatic cancer—previously a death sentence. New treatments had turned it into a chronic illness, but

Dryden chose naturopathic methods. He died a horrible, public death. His studies lost their credibility. Not many wanted to carry them on, to show that the essence wasn't just a parlor trick but could have real clinical utility. One Hippocrates fellow started."

Dr. Granger's eyes ticked to Pok, then away. He cleared his throat and tapped his cane. When Dr. Granger spoke again, his tone was lighter.

"Now, the question is, can the essence itself be manufactured and synthesized? TSO is definitely trying. They had a quantum research facility in Arizona with billions invested before it suddenly went silent. I'd argue that trying to manufacture it is as futile as trying to manufacture consciousness."

Pok never doubted his father's talk of the essence—he'd spoken with such conviction—but it wasn't until now he realized how tangible it was. And if TSO had invested so much in trying to replicate whatever this "essence" was, they must have been threatened by it. If it was irreplicable, like consciousness, then AI would always be lacking, even in medicine. What if his father had been on the brink of proving that? Had it cost him his life?

"Good. Any more review questions? No. Let's get to work!"

They used long, stripped branches to practice loosing high-growing fruit. They smashed it against rocks, trees, each other. Anji cracked open a ripened papaya against Rodge's wheelchair. Soon the air swam with flies and sweetness. Dr. Granger stressed the art of observing the inner meat shortly after exposure; even a few minutes of the elements browned the flesh and distorted the true ripeness.

After experimenting with a few breadfruits, Pok saw Rodge reaching for one just past his pole. Pok knocked it down and handed it to him.

"Just returning the favor," Pok said.

"I didn't ask for your help, swagger jacker." Rodge chucked the breadfruit over his shoulder and wheeled himself away.

They collected the fruit appropriate for culling and left the others to the raccoons and the flies. While Pok was checking over a medium-sized one for its ripeness, he heard Dr. Granger hobble up to him.

"Student Doctor Morning. Of New York, yes?" The physician reached out his hand. Pok, this time sure to take it slow, pinched his cuff. "How are you adjusting?"

"It's different. But I'm enjoying it."

"Med school isn't for enjoyment. You already have a sponsor, I hear. Dr.

Verik? She has some unorthodox thoughts, that one. Your father, too, trying to take up Dryden's mantle, but not as extreme. Very sad, what happened to him." Dr. Granger sat on a tree stump, indicating he wasn't shying away from the conversation. "How was it for you, growing up in the city?"

Pok chucked the too-ripe fruit into the brush. "It's fast. Being here shows me how much I depended on the shepherds. I'm just eager to learn, eager to help patients."

"Indeed. If it were up to me, you wouldn't be here. Now, I don't say that to be callous. But I think you should know. You bring attention we don't need. We're here to teach medicine, nothing else."

"I'll keep that in mind, Professor."

Dr. Granger sat for too long, watching, then ambled off.

The class dragged their sacks of sweet-smelling fruits and melons back through the woods, into Hippocrates and across the main lobby, and to the garden. They piled the cargo for workers to load into an underground refrigeration unit. As the class dispersed, Rodge rolled up to Pok.

"Don't let Dr. Granger get to you," he said.

"Everyone's super excited that I'm here," Pok said.

"I'm indifferent, if that makes you feel any better. But Granger, his daughter got a job with the shepherds, moved to New York, and never looked back. She was born with some muscle disorder and is now working to develop new nerve implants so people won't turn out like me. He checks the city travel logs every day, thinking maybe she'll come back."

"She won't come back." Pok started a little at his own bluntness.

"That's the most honest thing I've heard all week."

Pok sensed the question hanging in the air, waiting for Rodge to snatch it down and put it into the world. *Do* you *want to go back?* Before Rodge could, Pok turned and walked away. He needed to study.

Twenty-Three

THE RESURRECTIONIST

The Ventricle's underground library, its walls lined with medical journals, textbooks, and memoirs, was a labyrinth of rooms. After signing in, Pok wandered into one, drawn by an intricately illustrated and labeled giant heart spread across the tiled floor, and plucked a random text from the shelf. *Implications of Artificial Intelligence in Preventing Heart Disease.* The next room over had a glass door and through it students or doctors, their coats draped across their arms, admired an exhibition of human skulls.

In a large room with spread out tables and quiet study, Pok laid out his anatomy materials. He began with the central nervous system. He copied the anatomy onto a fresh piece of paper and then tried again from memory. Seven cervical spine, twelve thoracic, five lumbar, five sacral.

So far, so good. He'd learned this all not a month ago. Easy peasy.

His memory broke down at the highway of peripheral nerves. There were *so* many branches. He rubbed the palm of his hand over the page, frowned when it crumpled, then laughed. No more swiping. He drew the anatomy over and over until his hand ached. Was he learning? He had no clue.

His crash-course virtual anatomy class felt less and less accessible, as if that part of his brain were on a train back to New York. Anji's words rang loud: *a group grade.* But instead of motivation, the thought split his mind down different spiraling roads. In the land of ubiquitous AI, hard work, dedication, and consistency was more than enough. Here, he had to learn *how* to study, too?

Defeated and exhausted, Pok left the Ventricle sometime close to twilight. One of Dean Sims's assistants had come by to deliver a campus map and a key to his dorm room in the student living quarters.

Two blocks over from the main hospital and medical school, Tay Hall rose four stories into a sky that still clung tight to the falling sun. Despite this, the first-floor hallway was night-quiet.

The first-years all lived on the fourth floor. Like the hospital, the stairs were well taken care of. He found his room at the end of a long, quiet hall; the creak of his door opening proved the loudest thing about the intimate space. A small bed with a starved mattress filled one half. A wooden desk that still shone from its finish lined the wall of the other. There were no sensors. The walls were bare. The blinds didn't open automatically at his entry. There was no gaming corner, no portal to explore the world, both real and made-up. Above all, most felt was Kai's absence. The companion's eyes, though artificial, had brought a sense of familiar to any space. Here was bare, cold, and sterile.

His traveling bag lay at the foot of his bed. Another gray handbag he'd never seen before sat atop his desk. Pok turned on the small lamp and found a note tied to its strap.

Student Doctor Morning: Preparation is the key to success in medical school. This should be all you need.—Dr. E.K. Verik

Student Doctor Morning. Seeing it in print somehow made it feel real. If only his father could see. Pok smiled, closed his eyes, and tried to remember. The details of his father's face had eluded him along the road. They came clearly now. The dark skin, the shower of moles over both cheeks, the strong nose, gray stubble, deep-set eyes, and yellow-touched teeth that further warmed his smile. Now that smile widened.

His father's laughter—faint and fleeting—broke out of his memory and grazed his ears. He turned toward the window. The room was empty, of course. Withdrawals?

He brushed his fingers over the bag's cotton and ran his hand over the desk. This was going to be his best friend for the next year. He sat and opened the drawers, curious of souvenirs. Whoever had preceded him had done a good job of clearing it out.

"We hear you're sponsored."

The sudden voice made him jump; he almost fell out of his seat and caught himself in an off-balance stance.

James and Anji stood at the door. Even outside of the anatomy lab, Anji's tall stance bled confidence. Save her blue hair, she immediately reminded Pok of his high school's gifted students, who always sat together.

"And the first in our class," Anji said. Her blue-streaked hair hung free, its ends lightly brushing her shoulders. James slouched against the door frame. Removed from their lab coats, the transient carefree air of the young lay comfortably about them.

Pok's mental exercises of what to say, how to phrase, how to apologize—it all vaporized, leaving a mist of jumbled, shamed words. "I wasn't trying to show you up. I knew the patient from back home and I wanted you to take me but you wouldn't and then you left your ID and—"

"I looked like a fool," James said in one breath and waved his hand in another. "Dee-way."

"Dee-way?" Pok repeated.

"Sorry. *Don't worry about it.* You'll goo-tee. Get used to it, sorry." James strode over to the desk and peered into Dr. Verik's supply. "These your books?"

James opened the bag. His eyes widened as his jaw clenched. "Wow, she really set you up. White coat. Stethoscope. Reflex hammer. Tuning fork. Ah, here we go." James pulled out a thick book encased in a shell of thin glistening plastic. It read *Gray's Anatomy, 50th Edition*. "This is your bible. It's the newest edition, too." James pinched the first third of the anatomy text. "Know these pages cold and you'll be fine."

"Cold?" Pok said.

"Cold. That first table exam humbles people."

"And it's a group grade," Anji said.

"I remember," Pok said.

"The first part is a group," James said as he reached into the bottom of the bag. "The second part is multiple choice. The group could pass and you could fail. My advice? Flash cards, flash cards, flash cards. Nice, you have your own ID. You got those trainings done fast."

James handed Pok a laminated badge with his Customs picture. The red stamp signified he was cleared for the hospital. Pok didn't correct him.

"Wow, look at this." James passed to Anji a round white metal object with plugs on both ends. "She gave you a hospital-grade E-Cell. It gives you unlimited charges inside the hospital and med school. Usually, we don't get these until second year. Dr. Verik must really like you."

"I doubt that," Pok said. "She didn't seem too confident about my ability to keep up. I think that's why she got me all this."

"Whatever the reason, she's doing more than most sponsors."

"Maybe she can sponsor two students?" Pok said.

James's smile stretched toward a grimace. "Nah. I'll find someone else."

"The shepherds do a lot of experiments in New York?" Anji said as she handed the E-Cell back to Pok.

"I've heard of some," he said. "But it really depends what you mean by experiments."

"Can they really download information straight to your brain?"

"That would make med school a lot easier," James said.

"No downloading yet," Pok said. "Just some sensory enhancements. Mostly for gaming."

"A natural talent," James said. "Good for the group. Speaking of, a few of us are going out to Mid-City to pre-commiserate. You should join."

"Can I?" Pok said. "I mean, definitely."

"We need to study first," Anji said.

"Yes, of course," James said. "But you should go ahead. It's Student Doctor Night, so a bunch of people should already be there. Carolyne is performing and she has a voice like butter. You don't want to miss it. We'll just hold you up."

"He might get lost," Anji said. "There's no GPS."

"I'll find it," Pok said. "Just tell me the way."

"Respect," James said. "Two blocks onto Bourbon, there's a tavern on your right. The Fusiform. Remember, it's SDN, so bring your white coat for free drinks. GL."

The pair was gone before he could ask about that last. Pok hoped it meant *good luck*.

The scribe guard nodded as Pok approached, swung open the gate, and secured it behind him. Delivery trucks and cabs rumbled down the road, motorbikes zipping between them. He stepped out into the street and raised his hand, like hailing a gypsy cab.

A car stopped and the passenger-side window rolled down. The driver was skinny with a long, braided beard and soft eyes. "Where you headed?"

"The Fusiform. You heard of it?"

"Of course." He eyed Pok's white coat. "You seeing a patient there or something?"

"It's Student Doctor Night."

"Sure, sure." The driver laughed. The passenger door popped open. "Let's get going. We wouldn't want to miss *that*."

They passed empty, dimly lit streets fully cleared from the day's market and crossed over into Mid-City. The roads and sidewalks were clean of trash but cracked and broken. Stray dogs moved lazily between the houses, as if this part of New Orleans belonged as much to them as to the people.

"This here is Bourbon Street," the driver said at the mouth of a narrow, cleanly paved road. Nightlife crowded both the streets and balconies, all the way down. "The Fusiform's right here. Student Doctor Night, eh? A piece of advice: lose the coat until you find your people."

Pok got out and the cab sped off. Through the Fusiform's windows, people sat and drank and ate and laughed and talked. No white coats, no scrubs, no sign of anything else but regular people out for a regular night. Pok took off his coat, folded it into his bag, and went inside.

Music hit his chest. The vibrant crowd moved to a live band. Though the diner was not even at half capacity, the air buzzed with a carefree energy. The hair flowed like his. Not just locs, but long, golden curls and brown bouncing clouds. In place of flowers and ripening fruits, inked skin stimulated with its colors. The vibrant crowd's individualized rhythms were somehow more pleasing visually than the choreographed New York City dance halls. Pok had only gone once, woefully unprepared, and never again.

"Just you?" a host asked.

"I'm here for, uh, Student Doctor Night?"

She looked him up and down and rolled her eyes. "Sit anywhere."

Pok stayed around the perimeter and found an empty table near the back. Pok watched as a waiter went from table to table, scribbling down everyone's orders. He'd take that paper into the back and someone there would cook and prepare the food themself. In New York, glass played a pivotal role in dining. Portion sizes were custom; tastes were calibrated. Here, frustration, excitement, and fatigue sculpted each dish. Another manifestation of the essence? An inherent culinary connection from chef to patron the shepherds could never replicate? Maybe that's why his father always preferred home-brewed tea. Maybe that's why his father liked it best when Pok brewed it for him.

When a fellow patron caught him staring, Pok lowered his gaze and noticed a newspaper sitting on the empty chair. He turned it over. The *Second Opinion*.

"Just you tonight?" the waiter said when he got to Pok's table.

"I'm supposed to be meeting some medical students here?"

"I haven't seen any other students. This is a long way from the Hill. Take your time. Flag me down when you're ready."

The waiter swept up the extra plates and silverware and was off to serve someone else. Pok didn't recognize any of the tavern faces. His white coat was the only one. He'd been duped. This was no peace offering; only a clear message that he wasn't wanted. Could he blame James? Pok had stolen his ID *and* his sponsor. Swagger jacker, indeed.

Pok was about to leave—maybe the cab was still circling the block, anticipating his fate—when a man sat across from him.

"You like the *Second Opinion*, huh?"

The man's hat sat low over eyes that somehow shone fiercely even in shadow. His old voice was baritone with a crackly edge.

Pok put the newspaper face down on the table. "I haven't read much. Only heard some things."

"Well, what do you think?"

"The headline seems a little sensationalist."

The man took the paper, held it at arm's length, and read it aloud. "'The Last Hospital: Does Hippocrates Care More About Legacy Than Outcomes?' Definitely dramatic. But that's the beauty of what this city claims to be, right?"

"You don't think it makes people distrust the hospital?"

"A little distrust is healthy in any relationship." The man flattened an upturned edge with the side of his hand and nodded to the folded white coat sticking out of Pok's bag. "You a doctor?"

"Med student. A new one. My classmates told me it was Student Doctor Night." The man's grin confirmed the con. "That's not a thing, is it?"

"It's definitely not a thing. Sounds like you got some good old initiation. Student doctor, eh?" He eyed him, looked around, and leaned in conspiratorially. The man's hungry gaze devoured any magic between them. "I don't buy the withdrawals story. *Oh, it's just adjusting to the new environment.* All of a sudden? It doesn't add up. I wonder, do they teach you up there what's *really* going on?"

"I don't know," Pok said. "I don't think anyone does."

"You don't believe that, do you? I don't." When Pok said nothing, the man looked disappointed. "Someone on the Hill knows. Got to. Why else would they gatekeep Synth?"

"Synth makes it worse. It's a temporary fix to a long-term problem."

"That's what they want us to think. Synth helps. I've seen it. They're keeping the good stuff and people are having to go through other methods. That's what's driving the addiction."

Pok took a sip of his water. Outside, the dark had deepened. It was getting late and he should get back to Tay Hall. His cabdriver was definitely gone. How easy would it be to hail another? Did they usually come out this way?

The man sat back, adjusted his collar, and let out a smile. He reached into his pocket and placed onto the table something that fully reclaimed Pok's attention: his bounty from the dark web. Under it was an article profiling him.

"Student Doctor Pok Morning, son of Dr. Phelando Morning, newly minted mentee of Dr. Emily Verik. Shepherds' Most Wanted. Imagine my luck when I see you walk right into *my* bar reading *my* newspaper."

Pok's rising panic lifted him out of his seat. The man reached across the table and stilled him with a heavy hand. The tavern surrounding them felt suddenly twice as full. Suffocating.

"Sit."

Pok sat. The man did, too.

"The last thing I want is to turn you over to the shepherds," he said. "I want to help you."

"Who are you?" Pok said.

"All the things. Journalist. Pharmacist. Entrepreneur. Many call me the

Resurrectionist, but you can call me *friend*." He held out his hand. Pok didn't take it. "I respect that. Formally, I'm Jerry. Jerry Finn. I'll get straight to it: the city outlaws Synth while profiting off DigiTone. You could help me bring DigiTone directly to the community and balance the scales. In return, I protect you."

"And if I say no?" Pok said.

"You think these spires keep you safe? You think ignoring the outside world gives security? Bullshit. *I* keep us safe by keeping the lines open. If I tell the shepherds you haven't popped up in New Orleans, they'll believe me. If I tell the opportunists in this city to ignore the bounty, they will." He placed the bounty on top of the *Second Opinion*. "It would be a shame if some of these stories got around the city. The one about your father—Dr. Morning, is it?—experimenting on New Orleans patients would make a particularly juicy headline, don't you think?"

Pok grabbed the *Second Opinion* and tossed it across the bar. The man watched it hit the far wall and roll unnoticed under a vacant table. "You don't know anything about my father," he said.

"I like you already. We are a lot the same, you and me." Jerry wagged his finger between them. His eyes glistened. "We both believe Hippocrates can do a lot of good for this city. Working together we can make that happen."

"I can't do that," Pok said, his anger slowly returning to fear. "I won't do that. I'm just a student."

"You figured out how to get into medical school." Without looking, Jerry raised his hand to accept the newspaper the passing waiter had retrieved for him. "When I call for you—and trust that I will call for you—I'm sure you'll figure out how to be helpful."

Jerry refolded the *Second Opinion* and put it back in the empty seat, just as Pok had found it. He rose, placed a cold hand on Pok's shoulder, and breathed into his ear a beer-soaked whisper. "Welcome to my city. I'll be seeing you around, partner."

Twenty-Four

TRUCE

Pok's first night in Tay Hall oscillated between sleep and worry. He turned against a cracked dawn, ready to give up and start the day, blinked, and suddenly found it was ten past nine. Nine? He yawned, trying to remember the significance of that. Nine . . . what was at nine?

Shit. His first class, that's what. The Art and Craft of Medicine. Taught by the dean herself.

For a virtual class back home he could log in, camera off, while he changed. For *any* class he could always watch the recording. Here, he was already late—definitively and undeniably late—and he still needed to get dressed *and* walk over. He grabbed the nearest clothes and found his white coat tossed in the corner. Hopefully, he could just sneak in the back. No harm, no foul.

"Pok!" Dean Sims called from the front of the small auditorium as soon as he entered, seven minutes later. All the heat from his sprint across University went to his face. His scalp itched. He hadn't showered. "Come. Join us."

The class waited as Sims directed him to an empty seat at the end of the front row, right beside James. Only after Pok sat did Dean Sims continue.

"People come to New Orleans seeking that undefinable quality that defines humanity. Some call it intuition. Soul. Self-awareness. The essence. I call it art. Healing is the intersection of science and art. Without either, you are lost. The patient is lost. Today, we learn a bit of that art."

Onstage, a shirtless man in white linen pants waited on an examination table. Sims proceeded to take the class on a tour of his body. Pok's awe conflicted with his pessimism. Even a judicious use of tech would free up precious time. A detailed, AI-generated report of the patient's current physical status would open more room to focus on the patient-provider connection. While impressive, Sim's methodological show was lengthy. Pok looked down his row. No one shared his frustration.

Pok blinked slow. *You're here for a reason.* He refocused on the dean's exam and saw her movements in a new light. Her hands became a window into internality. Her fingers felt the subtleties in blood flow and discerned the size and location of internal organs from the changes in pitch elicited by tapping against the abdomen. She uncovered abnormalities in a seemingly perfectly healthy subject. She likely missed things an image scan would easily find. But she gained something that would be eternally elusive to even the most powerful of machines: she found humanity. She touched the patient.

The man sat up. A deep calm veiled his face, a reflection of the start of something deep in Pok's own muscles.

The feeling was short-lived. James's shoulder touched his. "Had fun last night?"

"I had a blast," Pok whispered back, hoping hot embarassment wouldn't flood his voice. "Student Doctor Night. I'll definitely have to go again."

"Sorry I couldn't make it," James said. A half smirk raised one cheek. "I forgot my ID."

"No worries," Pok said. "Dr. Verik was there and we just turned it into a mentor-mentee type thing. It would have been awkward if . . . you know."

James's smile went away.

"Your turn," Sims said. She seemed to be looking right at him and James. "Choose a table. Our volunteers will rotate. Teach together, learn together. Break into pairs."

Pok and James realized at the same time that, being at the end of their row, they were stuck together.

"You can go first," James said when Pok joined him onstage. A young woman waited patiently on their assigned examination table. Tattoos spread over her upper chest like wings. "Let's see what you got."

Pok stumbled through the physical exam. James was quick to correct him. "Don't jump around. Go from top to bottom. You're hitting too hard.

It's a quick jab, not a pummel. No, put your hammer here and don't pull away. Did you find the liver? I didn't think so. Here; percuss here."

"You want to go again?" James said when Pok was done. He shook his head. He didn't trust himself to speak.

James's touch was callous but confident. He explained what he was doing as he went. In no way as elegant as Dean Sims, but every word pushed Pok deeper into the knowledge that he knew little.

"Rotate!" Dean Sims announced.

"Top to bottom," James said as they waited for the next practice patient. "You can't go wrong with top to bottom. What? You still sour about last night? It was a joke."

"You ever met a Jerry Finn?" Pok said.

James went pale. Any satisfaction gained by his adept exam melted away. The previous dread, having waned overnight, tightened around Pok.

"I was waiting for you or anyone and he came up to me," Pok continued. "Asked me all kinds of questions. Called himself the Resurrectionist."

"Jerry's bad news," James said. "He runs that foul paper. What's it called?"

"He really runs the *Second Opinion*? I thought he was exaggerating."

"Yes, that one. That whole paper is as rotten as him. He'll take whatever you say and twist it against the hospital and the school. I learned that the hard way."

"He wants me to get him DigiTone," Pok said. "You sent me to your drug dealer?"

"Hey. Chill. I'm clean. It was just supposed to be a joke. I didn't think you'd become friends with *Jerry*! You buy anything off him?"

"Hell no," Pok said.

"Good. Did you tell him any insider information?"

"I don't know anything to tell. I just got here."

James's shoulders relaxed. "Then you're good. He has nothing on you." James eyed him. "I'm sorry for tricking you. Truce?"

"Truce," Pok said.

"Thank God. The last thing we need going into this first table exam is a dysfunctional group. The Resurrectionist." James laughed. Pok wished he could exchange the growing pressure in his abdomen with his classmate's relief. *You think these spires keep you safe?* "He's such a joke. Whatever he wants you to do, whoever he wants you to meet, just don't. Okay?"

Twenty-Five

POLITICS

A two-hour break followed The Art and Craft of Medicine. Pok was still in knots over Jerry. The self-proclaimed Resurrectionist definitely had ties to the outside world. Could he really influence Pok's time in New Orleans? How much damage could he do with the *Second Opinion*? What had the dean said? *You being here can create a lot of trouble for us.* Should he go to her? Would she really be able to protect him?

These thoughts took him to the Ventricle. As he rounded the perimeter, seeking an empty table, a dull pain started in the base of his stomach. The edges of the world blurred. He cursed, then laughed. He'd forgotten to eat. The long break was for lunch.

By the time he found the Pylorus—the hospital's cafeteria—his stomach hated him. Instead of the planned quick bite, Pok found himself stuck with decisions. Chicken, cut and cooked all ways, mashed russet potatoes, mixed vegetables, and soups. Colored trays coded the selections, any pattern elusive. He found chicken breast fillets in the vegetable-rich blue section and vegetables in the dairy-dominant yellows. He picked and put back, picked and put back, and by the time he left the buffet line his plate was full and unsightly.

Patients and health-care workers sat interspersed in the broad, populated space. Someone waved. It was Silva. Pok's heart clenched. A thin, transparent tube wrapped around the groundskeeper's ears and across his face, sending two short spokes into his nostrils. The other ends connected to a loose, melon-sized bag that Silva squeezed every few seconds. Pok slid into the seat across from him.

Silva nodded toward Pok's plate. "Tell me you're hungry without telling me you're hungry."

"I couldn't choose. You know what these colors mean?"

"Something to do with the types of patients. I think yellow is good for the heart or the liver. I usually don't like the greens. How's your first week? You killing it yet or what?"

"Or what," Pok said. He couldn't help but stare. Silva couldn't help but notice.

"I'm okay." Silva wiped his mouth. A gray beard bottomed out his round, cratered face. "Just had a little setback, that's all. Go ahead, you can ask."

"Any Synth?"

"I haven't touched the stuff in years. I learned my lesson early on, believe me." Silva's laugh turned into a gurgling cough. He swallowed and pushed the hanging tube back over his shoulder. "My wife and daughter came over, did I tell you? They just went through Adjustment. That's why I was in MouseKill. Looking for another side job."

"You think they'll have trouble finding work?"

"My wife already found one right outside the gates, making hand sanitizer. She's fascinated by all the green. Even starting her own garden. Jory, my daughter, she's the one I'm worried about. She was a journalist and got doxed after writing an unflattering article about the inner workings of the self-driving car companies. It was really bad. It was hard for her to leave. Has been hard. The depression just got worse in Adjustment.

"This inventory gig at MouseKill is easy enough for me and gives us the financial wiggle room for her to find something good. Something near the hospital. I was looking into that newspaper, but they don't have any openings."

"The *Second Opinion*?"

Silva's face twisted. "That god-awful thing? No. The *Daily Hippo*. Good for keeping up with all the hospital is doing. And clear the filth out of your mind if you been reading *Opinion*. My friend got a prosthetic eye from one of the research trials at the Thymus Clinic. Saw the ad in the *Hippo*."

"How'd he lose his eye?"

Silva pressed his finger under his own eye, flicked it forward with a mimicked popping sound. "Plucked it out himself. He was high on Synth and thought the shepherds controlled it. He'll still swear that the moment his eye popped out was the freest he's ever felt in his life."

"Your daughter," Pok said, "how do you think she'd like making paper?"

Silva sat up a little. "I'm listening."

"The Paper Mill just landed a big paper contract for the hospital. They also print the *Daily Hippo*."

"She likes working with her hands. And this could put her in good with the *Daily*. Speaking of getting in good, I heard you got a sponsor?"

"How does everyone know that?"

Silva laughed. His wide smile contrasted his sweet-smelling labored breath and sharp wheezes. "It may be less you and more Dr. Verik. There's a bunch of lore around her."

"Yeah? Like what?"

"That she treated Julian Shepherd—Odysseus's father—and it went wrong and that's why they have such a vendetta against Hippocrates. Either that or she broke Julian's heart."

"Those are two very different scenarios."

Silva smiled below his nasal cannula. "Maybe she did both."

"You believe it?"

"Talk is talk. If she saw something in you, she must not be that bad." Silva breathed deeply as he gave his bag a considerable squeeze. "What's next on your schedule?"

Pok checked. "Shepherd Tech and History."

"Nice. I might audit. When does it start?"

Shepherd Tech and History was in a small classroom outside the main hospital and across the street. Dr. Peter Soft, the young historian who had interviewed Pok shortly after entering the city's gates, sat at the head of a semicircle.

"Come in, come in," the professor said. He stroked thin locs of varying color that went down to his thighs. There was a distinct difference from the last time Pok saw him: his hair now glistened as if soaking wet. "Did you have a chance to do the reading?"

"Reading?" Pok said as he settled into the circle. Silva took a chair against the far wall.

"Take mine." Dr. Soft passed a printout down to Pok. The article had the headline, *Shepherd CEO's Son in Critical Condition After Experimental Treatment*. Red-inked scribbles lined the margins.

"You'll be an excellent addition to today's topic: the shepherd-Hippocrates conflict. Student Doctor Dominik was just about to share his opinion."

Pok had seen but not yet interacted with Dominik Parker. He was tall with wide shoulders—his voice was the smallest thing on him. Multiple mole-like, flat, black spots spread out from under his eyes as if spilled from his irises. His bespectacled gaze clung to the floor as he spoke. Everyone hitched a bit forward to catch his words, lest a breeze carry them away.

"Nature discovers man, man discovers machines, machines influence man, machines control nature, man tries to retake nature."

Dr. Soft's grin had withered over the span of Dominik's speech. "Simplistic. Accurate, in a way. There's a lot missing there, though. Was it always AI versus humans when it came to medicine?" The young professor's eyes seemed to sparkle just for Pok. As much as he didn't want to participate, Pok remembered Dr. Verik's words: *do well.*

"The shepherds started with the explicit goal of augmenting human-led medicine," Pok said. "AI was supposed to work with humans. Julian Shepherd himself studied here."

"That he did," Dr. Soft said. "What changed?"

"Julian had an affair with a Hippocrates doctor?" Pok found Silva against the wall. He couldn't make out the groundskeeper's expression.

Dr. Soft's eyebrows reached for his hairline. "That's a new one. Someone's been reading the *Second Opinion*. Don't worry, that's where the article comes in. Anyone?"

"Politics," Anji said.

"Say more."

"According to the article, Julian sought the help of Hippocrates Medical Center for his son, Odysseus. But that went wrong."

"It went really wrong," James said. "Odysseus was in a coma for three weeks. I heard they had to replace half his organs with synthetics and plant microchips in his brain. That he's literally half machine."

Pok had spoken directly with the subject of such lore. *I just had to meet you . . .* Could any of the rumors be true?

"Let's bring it back to facts," Dr. Soft said. "How did TSO justify AI-led medicine?"

"Because AI will always know more than a human," Pok said. Murmurs rose around him.

Dr. Soft lifted a shushing hand. "Go on, Student Doctor Pok."

"It knows all the studies, all the research, all the medications, all the anatomy. It can factor in comprehensive metrics on a specific individual and compare that to successes and outcomes with every other individual with a similar presentation. It's the perfect decision-maker."

"Even over a patient's wishes?"

"It's still their choice."

"Is it? Regulations make it harder and harder to go against shepherd recommendations. It knows all the medicine, yes, but it also knows all the costs, economic incentives, and chances of unfavorable outcomes. At what point does 'best for the patient' shift to 'best for the shepherds'?"

Dr. Soft was patient if not charismatic. He let Pok's silence speak volumes.

"Technology has surely led to many great breakthroughs in medicine," he continued. "AI definitely excels at medicine. But winning over public opinion takes more than data. People have to *feel* it."

"They dug us out of a pandemic," Pok said, remembering. "That was the turning point. The shepherds gained people's trust by saving lives."

"Bullshit," someone said. "They profited off a global crisis."

"They showed the data," Pok said, defensive. It felt like him against the room. "Pandemic mortality rates in AI-led hospitals were magnitudes lower than those without AI. The data doesn't lie."

"*Raw* data doesn't lie," Dr. Soft said. "Selective data creates a narrative. Let's consider what other data was highlighted. Cancer survival rates in AI-led treatment plans versus human formulation. Average lifespan and morbidity rates in early shepherd adopter cities like New York and Atlanta. Glass use and tracker subscription correlates with social determinants of health." Pok saw where the professor was going. "Who controls the narrative?"

"The shepherds," Pok said, his voice hollow and weak. His mind went to Project Do No Harm and its various prepared articles. The ones that had gotten Phelando killed. The shepherds controlled the narrative, indeed. Why, then, was Pok taking up for them?

"The shepherd algorithm is a computer program," Dr. Soft said. "The Shepherd Organization is a corporation that has interests and goals. Bringing us back to . . ."

"Politics," Anji said.

"Politics. For a long time, people didn't trust technology. That shifted. People stopped trusting people. What's more, technology has an inherent promise of getting better and better. People think of any setbacks, any bad outcomes, as just bumps on the road to perfection."

"But the narrative is pushing back against the data," James said. "People's lives aren't getting better. Depression is up. Cancer treatment has improved but cancer incidence has skyrocketed. More and more people are dying of 'undetermined reasons' because they just drop dead after being seemingly healthy. The stories we hear from pendants, how trapped they feel. Everyone is living in fear instead of just living."

"Science has always been about rejecting the null hypothesis," Dr. Soft said. "For people to move away from AI, we have to do the opposite and prove that what's happening here at Hippocrates is the only way forward."

"So we're the last thing standing against the AI apocalypse?" Rodge said. He gently rolled himself back and forth in his chair. "No pressure. Who was the genius doctor who butchered the shepherd prince?"

"Dr. Phelando Morning treated Odysseus," Dr. Soft said.

Pok laughed, the statement was so absurd, but no one else joined. Collective attention turned toward him. Anji gave a blank, clinical stare. Rodge and James looked slightly away.

"That's . . ." Pok stuttered, swallowed, and got the words out. "What do you mean?"

"Seems that Pok can't tell data from narrative," Dominik said. He kept his gaze low as heads turned. Emboldened, he continued, his voice rising and cracking at the edges, "Odysseus grew up hating Hippocrates. All because of Pok's father. He shouldn't be here!"

So much for not making enemies.

"Pok isn't the problem," James said. "Rubes like you are. We have to stick together."

"Enlightening," Dr. Soft said. "I'm sure we'll be visiting this topic again and again."

James gave the slightest nod. Pok returned it. The beginning of a smile tugged at Pok's lips, competing with the burn of the accusation against his father. Maybe he wasn't so alone after all.

The "enlightening" discussion swimming in his head, Pok found himself turned around in the hospital's tunnel. Most of the doors were either closed or led to some dark, uninviting place. He pressed against the wall to let a pulse of students pass. From the length of their coats, they were a year or two ahead of him. Maybe—hopefully—they were going to the Ventricle. He followed.

The troupe led him to a grand wooden door with metal lacings that spanned the width of the tunnel. A giant serpent, its jaw stretched open in a menacing hiss, was engraved on the central panel. A student—a textbook splayed before her—sat in an elevated side nook. She checked each ID.

"This isn't the Ventricle, is it?" Pok asked when the absence of an ID in her hand forced her gaze up to him.

"This is the Vault. The Ventricle is that way. Two rights, at the end of the longest hall."

The Vault. *They're going after the Vault.* His father's message to Dean Sims. But for what? He couldn't wrap his mind around it. The student's scrutiny grew. Pok concentrated on his next words.

"What's in the Vault?" he said.

"Whatever needs protecting," she said. "The Ventricle is that way."

He paused at the end of the hall, right before the bend, to look back. What had his father said? His mind shuffled through possibilities but none of them felt right, none had that click into place, that unmistakable feeling of remembering. Defeated, he turned away.

Inside the Ventricle, Pok snagged an empty table and took out his anatomy text and notes. Remembering James's suggestion, he divided a sheet of paper into eighths and wrote down questions on one side and answers on the other. He flipped through them and started over. Critical thoughts went again to efficiency. With no sensor-informed application to monitor his attention, how could he know where to spend the most time? How could he know which flash cards were the most effective? He made new cards and listed the nerves from memory. Better? Worse? The same?

Doodles lined the page. Fractal triangles. *DigiTone* with a box around it. Dr. Verik. Phelando. Odysseus. Julian. The Vault.

They think your father started this.

Was that why his father had spent his career working under the shepherds? To atone? Had that fueled his foiled whistleblower aspirations? Why not tell Pok? Why not leave New York for New Orleans years ago?

Would you have believed him? Would you have willingly given up your dream of going to one of the Prestigious Twelve?

Defeated, his back aching, tongue dry, legs cramped, Pok called it a night. Outside, the air was dry and cool, the first signs of relief from a long, sultry summer. It reminded him of New York, when short sleeves transitioned to light jackets and the wind changed from a welcome relief to a biting offender. Thoughts of home conjured memories of Phelando and Kai and the outlook of a confident future. Now all he had was frustration and a quiet, lamp-lit street to lead him to an even quieter dorm room.

You can't give it all to medicine, son.

"How else, then, Dad?" Pok said to the night. No one answered.

Twenty-Six

AN OLD FRIEND

Pok fought to keep up in anatomy. There were times when he thought he was getting the hang of it, when the many names attached to the numerous body parts seemed to stick. And then Dr. Jacobs would swing by their table and his mind would freeze. Without exception. At the end of the week, Dr. Jacobs suggested in no uncertain terms that he expected Pok to take advantage of the weekend tutoring, facilitated by volunteer residents.

Pok didn't disagree. On his first rest day as a medical student, he showed up bright and early to the anatomy lab. A tutor stood ready at table nine. The resident doctor's white coat extended below her blue smock down to her knees. The hair beneath her protective mesh was a breath longer than stubble. Her serious face softened in familiar curiosity.

"You don't remember me, do you?"

Her face *was* familiar. The black hair, the high-arched upper lip. A thousand possibilities arose. Had he passed her in the HemoStat that morning he borrowed (*stole*) James's ID? Or had he disturbed her studying in the Ventricle with his clumsy hands and loud breathing?

"Dr. Cheryl Roberson," she said. "From MouseKill. You're the one with all the tick bites."

"Yes!" Pok said. "I remember you. You're back."

"And you're alive." She rubbed her hands together. "So, where are we?"

"What's before beginner?"

"No sweat. Let's start with the basics." Dr. Roberson pulled out the cadaver's arm, which had been partially tucked under the belly. "Arms and legs are good for practice because we have two of them. Show me how you cut. Then we'll go over the table exam."

Dr. Roberson was patient but firm and knowledgeable. She hardly consulted the open dissector.

"Make sure you know all the little anatomy, even the things you don't think will be on the table exam," she said. "It could pop up on the multiple choice. The grade is very important for getting a sponsor."

The knowledge of Pok's special sponsorship was so widespread that he was surprised to find someone ignorant of it. He took advantage.

"I'm thinking Dr. Verik," Pok said casually. "She's doing some interesting research on the essence."

"My advice? Stay away. Rumor has it that she treated Odysseus when he was a baby and that's why the shepherds hate us now."

Pok's heart went cold. "I heard that was another doctor."

"Rumors are rumors. Bottom line is, you don't want unneeded attention. Remember what I said about med school? Conform, conform, conform." Dr. Roberson stood tall and stretched her neck. "I think we're done. Good work. You're on the right track. Practice, practice, practice. Review the anatomy, know all the little things."

After covering his table's cadaver, as Pok wavered between setting up camp at the Ventricle and getting a couple hours more of sleep back at Tay Hall, a note pinned to his white coat caught his eye.

Happy cutting, partner! I sent you a patient. He's in the HemoStat. Bed twelve. Be helpful.—The Resurrectionist

Pok did all but run over to the HemoStat. *Be helpful.* Fuck that. He needed to end this "partnership" he never agreed to. *But he runs the* Second Opinion. *The last thing you need is a headline saying you murdered your own father.* No: the last thing he needed was replacing a false crime with a real one.

As if magnetically pulled, Shaliyah's eyes locked onto him from behind the HemoStat's reception desk. She paused midsentence and beelined over. Before Pok could even consider ducking away, she'd grabbed his arm.

"You have some nerve coming back here," she said. "Nurse Holly tried to get me fired over you."

"I had to find someone," Pok said. "My dad's patient, from New York."

"Of course. A patient from New York! That changes everything. Wait until I tell Nurse Holly. She will be *thrilled*." Shaliyah squeezed his arm. She was strong. "Can you leave, please, for both our sakes?"

"I'm legit now, I swear. Look." He held up his badge. Shaliyah snatched it so quickly the retractable string made a sharp, whining sound. After some scrutiny, she let it snap back to his chest.

"Who are you here to see?" she said.

"A practice patient in bed twelve."

Shaliyah went back to her desk, indicated to the person waiting that she'd just be a quick minute, and frowned at what she saw on the patient logs.

"Bed twelve has a red sticker. Red means high risk. Didn't give a name. Wouldn't allow anyone to examine him. You said this was a practice patient?"

"That's what I was told," Pok said.

"Please don't get me fired."

This time, Pok made sure to sidestep any busy nurses or technicians. Whereas before the HemoStat's hectic chaos had consumed and confused him, now he used it as camouflage.

Pok saw Dr. Verik first. She was at the nursing station, dictating to her scribe, one hand on the edge of her glasses. She looked up right before Pok could turn away and feign ignorance. They made eye contact. He had no choice; Pok went over to her.

Dr. Verik extended her arm and he returned the proper greeting. "Your patient—Florence—did well. The CBH helped. Her sister is going to help her take care of her baby. They are living over in Mid-City. She left her address for you to come visit." As Dr. Verik slipped him the note, she frowned. "Everything okay?"

Pok, circling doubt, considered a lie. He could tell Dr. Verik he was here to thank her for the school supplies and then slip away to bed twelve. And then what? What if he failed to say no to the Resurrectionist?

"I met a man named Jerry Finn." Dr. Verik's instant expression told Pok all he needed to know about the gravity of his situation. "He threatened to turn me over to the shepherds."

"Unless you what?"

"Get him drugs from the hospital," Pok said. "I think he's here now."

Dr. Verik ran her fingers through her short hair, curled the strands around her index, and forced her hands to her side. She stood. "Your worries and responsibilities are medical school. I'll alert the dean. Let's show him out."

"Dr. Verik. Dr. Verik!"

They both turned to Nurse Holly jogging up to them. She didn't see Pok, not at first, her exasperation focused on the message she needed to relay. "Bed three is threatening to leave AMA. Says she doesn't need to be admitted. Wants to talk to you."

"Mrs. Knightly? She definitely needs admission. I already secured her a bed."

As Dr. Verik spoke, Nurse Holly noticed Pok. If he could make himself invisible, or fall through the floor, he would have.

"You." Nurse Holly pulled at Pok's ID. He lurched forward to keep it from snapping off the string. "You're the scroller who snuck into the unit pretending to be a medical student."

"That term is offensive," Dr. Verik said. "You should remove it from your vernacular."

Nurse Holly's demeanor shifted and her grip loosened as she saw the senior physician's stance.

Dr. Verik continued, "I assure you that if someone was so brazen as to steal a student doctor's ID, they would have been banned from this campus." Pok caught the dichotomy in his mentor's half smile. "This is Student Doctor Morning, and I'm his sponsor. Let's get a full set of labs on Mrs. Knightly and make sure we have demographics. When she came to New Orleans, who she lives with, recent contacts. Has she been on isolation?"

"Mrs. Knightly?" Nurse Holly said, blinking. "No."

"I'll talk to her." And then, to Pok, "Can you handle your issue?"

"I can."

"Good. Come find me after."

Dr. Verik disappeared into the busy HemoStat with long, confident strides. Nurse Holly stared down Pok long enough to wordlessly say *I'm watching you* and then, too, disappeared into the machine. Pok was, again, alone. Time to do this.

He found bed twelve. Its drawn curtain shifted as if touched by a light breeze. *Tell him to kick rocks and be done with it. You're safe here; you don't need his protection.* Pok entered the cubicle.

A young man sat on the bed's edge, his head hung low, his scalp visible under brown fuzz. A scar curved from the top of his forehead, back down his skull, and stopped just short of his neck. Pok backstepped to check he had the right bed. He did.

"Everything's so loud," the man (or was this a boy?) said. Pok moved closer, cautious. Something in this voice brought chills from his past life.

"Did Jerry send you?" Pok said.

The boy (definitely a boy) nodded. "I need something to help the withdrawals."

"Tell Jerry I don't want anything to do with him. I don't need—"

The patient raised his head. Pok stumbled back as if struck in the chest. The face, creased with lines and dented by shadows, was older than his body. He had aged so much since Pok had seen him last.

"Kris?" Pok said. So many thoughts, so many questions, all jumbled together, none able to get out. How was he here? *Why* was he here? What had happened to him? Their last exchange was Kris's warning to *get the fuck out of New York*. "What are you doing here?"

"It's good to see you, too."

"Sorry, it's just . . ." Pok, needing something to do with his trembling hands, pulled the curtain completely around them. The HemoStat pressed inward, threatening to squish them. Jerry Finn had sent *Kris*? "No, really, what the fuck are you doing here?"

Kris's dull, empty gaze sharpened. His sunken eyes widened. "I thought you were dead," he said.

"Not me, Kris." Pok heard his own voice harden. "You knew Odysseus was coming for me. Did you know about my dad, too?"

"I'm so sorry, man."

The sound of Kris's sobbing dissipated some of Pok's steel countenance.

New York Kris had been so undeniably full of life. This Kris was broken. Emaciated. Changed. Just the absence of his hair alone—once self-lovingly adorned with gold cuffs and cowrie shells—represented a complete and irreversible shift. And what the hell was that scar?

Pok slid into the chair beside his old friend. "You should be in med school right now. What happened?"

"I had to warn you about Odysseus. After I sent that message, they fired me and rescinded the acceptance. I remembered you got into Hippocrates. And when I looked it up I saw it's the only place truly hidden from the shepherds. I emptied my account, bought a plane ticket, and hitched the rest of the way. I hoped beyond hope you'd be here."

"How did you know? About Odysseus?"

"You're going to think I'm crazy." Kris laughed, an unbalanced, nervous thing that made Pok's skin tighten. "Or stupid. Or both."

"Try me."

Kris raised a finger to his scar. "TSO was beta testing a new neural enhancement implant. They asked me, explicitly, to volunteer."

Neuroimplants? After that horrible massacre? More and more, Odysseus was showing his willingness to push the bar. "You let them drill into your brain?" Pok said.

"I didn't really have a choice. You know that. It was supposed to enhance response times, speed up cognition, and eliminate the lag between perception and reality. And it did that. At first. Then, I couldn't sleep for days." Kris looked at him sideways. "I started to hallucinate. All types of crazy things. But some of it was real. I saw things about the shepherds I wasn't supposed to see. I saw when you hacked the admissions system because it was so close to the Source. Saw it like I was there. That's why I came over to check on you. I told you not to do anything stupid."

"What else did you see?"

Terror licked Kris's gaze. "I saw the beginnings of their plan for you and for New Orleans. They want to show the world that being separate is unsafe."

The emergency room went cold. "How are they going to do that?" Pok said.

"By making it unsafe. I don't know exactly how but this place, this city, it's their target. And once you're TSO's target . . ."

Pok pushed his heels into the floor to feel grounded, so he wouldn't float away. Something wasn't adding up. In Kris's condition, both mentally and physically, the only way he could have made it all the way to New Orleans was if the shepherds allowed him to. Had Kris's involvement in the neuroenhancement study been coincidence or on purpose? What better way to spy on a would-be whistleblower than through his son's best friend?

Kris. They'd been supposed to go to medical school together, be best man at each other's wedding. He'd given it all up to save Pok's life. And he had come all this way.

"How did you get involved with Jerry?" Pok said.

"I was fine until I saw the spires. I could feel their energy. The voices didn't like the spires. They still don't. Then I saw the masks and the doctors. I was afraid. After what they did to me in New York, the thought of what the doctors here might do.

"I stayed at MouseKill for a while, trying to figure out what to do next." Kris chuckled. "The voices wanted me to end it. I almost listened. And then I met Jerry. He helped me get past the gates. Synth quiets the voices, and Jerry had Synth. And a way in."

"You didn't go through Customs?"

Kris shook his head. "The voices warn me Hippocrates isn't safe. That they experiment on people here, especially the scrollers."

"That's not true, Kris. The doctors here are good people."

"Good people can do fucked-up things," Kris said. "I know Jerry seems bad, but he's the only person I have right now. Him and you. The Synth helps, but there's not enough. He said you could get us some DigiTone so we can make more. Can you, Pok? Can you help stop the . . . the things inside my head? I already tried."

Kris turned his head. His scar, until now partly hidden from Pok by the angle, was fresh and festering. Pok held his breath as the HemoStat tilted.

"You tried to remove it yourself?"

"Cutting it out made sense at the time," he said. "I couldn't get past the skull. I just made them angry. So fucking angry." Kris jabbed the side of his shaved head with his finger. Pok primed himself to intervene, but Kris stopped and slumped forward, as if too defeated to even hurt himself anymore.

"It looks infected," Pok said. "And a piece of bone might be missing. You need a surgeon—"

Kris stood with such abruptness that Pok nearly fell back through the curtains. "No doctors. Jerry told me there wouldn't be doctors."

"You're in a hospital, Kris. Who did you think you'd see?"

Kris's voice rose. The HemoStat paused to listen. "I can't. *They* tell me I can't. No doctors!"

"Calm down, okay." Pok made sure the curtain was closed all the way. "They won't hurt you. Everybody here is on the same team."

Kris threw his head back and wailed, low and mewling. Pok's grip on the curtain tightened. He put a hand on Kris's shoulder, feeling the vibration of his sobs. He spoke as calmly and steadily as he could.

"Do you trust me?" he said.

The sobs dissipated. Kris gave the slightest nod.

"I'll get you DigiTone, but not for Jerry. If I give it to you, you have to promise to go to Adjustment. I went through it. They won't hurt you. You're safe, Kris. Promise me you'll try?"

"I'll try."

Pok rose. "Wait here."

Kris needed real medical attention. He needed to go through Customs and Adjustment. He needed things Pok couldn't give. He needed someone qualified to help.

Dr. Verik stood bent over notes at the nurse's station, frowning. "We don't have any record on your patient," she said as Pok approached. "Either he's been here a really long time and has never seen a doctor or he somehow didn't go through Adjustment."

"Jerry helped sneak him into the city."

Dr. Verik put aside the notes. "I'll get security."

Pok moved to block his sponsor's path. Dr. Verik's eyes narrowed.

"He needs help," Pok said quickly. "He's going through bad withdrawals. Paranoia. Hallucinations. He tried to dig into his own skull."

"Sounds severe. Withdrawal psychosis is concerning. He could be in full autoimmune storm. He may need to be admitted."

"He's paranoid of doctors. He only talked to me because I'm a student. If you go out there, I promise you, he'll run. DigiTone will help. Can help build rapport, at least, get him back here or into a clinic."

The air shifted at the mention of the drug. Pok kept a stoic face.

"DigiTone," she said. "This is still Jerry's contact we're talking about, correct?"

"He's not going back to Jerry. I'll make sure of it."

"I see. Should I be worried?" She wasn't talking about the patient.

"I want nothing to do with Jerry," Pok said. "And if I was abusing Synth, would I look this tired?"

"Good point." Dr. Verik slid past Pok and into the medicine pantry. She came out with a pill bottle and began scribbling on the label. "What's his name?"

"Kris," Pok said. "Kris Boles."

"Date of birth?"

Pok knew Kris's birthday because it was exactly a month before his. He told her.

She held on to the bottle a beat before Pok took it. "Make sure he comes back."

•

"A week's worth of DigiTone," Pok said a few minutes later as he held out the prescription. Mirroring his mentor, Pok didn't immediately relinquish it. "Promise me you'll go to Adjustment."

"I promise."

Pok let the bottle go. Kris cradled the medicine like a lover.

"What about Jerry?" Kris said.

"He's my problem. I'll deal with him."

Twenty-Seven

IN THE GARDEN

Pok wanted nothing more than to pretend the last ten minutes hadn't happened. He had a table exam coming up. *That's* what he should be focusing on. Not smuggling narcotics. He made long strides toward the exit, head down, posture serious. If Dr. Verik watched him leave, he didn't know. If Nurse Holly tried to catch his eye, it was news to him. His shoulder was against the revolving door when he saw her.

At the end of the reception desk, Shaliyah packed up her blue-and-black book bag. Someone had taken her place.

Pok stepped aside to let a family of three leave, their preteen son still half-dressed in hospital garb. The momentum driving him out of the HemoStat was gone. He didn't like that Shaliyah's first (and second) impression of him was one of a troublemaker. Maybe he could turn things around.

"Done with the day?" Pok said.

Shaliyah looked up, expecting one last lost patient or worried loved one, and let out both relief and a sly smile in one huffed breath.

"I'm off the clock," she said. "You're going to have to find someone else to drag into your troubles."

Her tone was neither friendly nor standoffish. Her smile tilted toward curiosity.

"I just wanted to say again that I'm sorry for getting you in trouble."

"Don't worry about it," she said. She zipped up her bag and slung it over one shoulder. "Nurse Holly has had it out for me ever since I started here. Apparently some beef with my dad from like ten years ago."

Shaliyah pointed to the revolving doors. Pok caught a flash of Kris disappearing into the lobby. "He seemed difficult," she said.

"You don't know the half. Have you eaten yet?"

"Don't you have class?"

"It's Saturday," Pok said. "No worries if you'd rather not."

She considered him out of one eye. "Sure. I could eat."

Shaliyah navigated the Pylorus's buffet selection with calculated ease. She picked almost exclusively from blue-coded food. Pok followed her lead, making sure this time not to overstuff his plate. They found an open end at a long table that stretched a third of the width of the cafeteria. A few seats down, a senior physician explained some concept to three apt resident physicians with untouched plates.

"Where are you from?" Shaliyah said after a few contemplative bites.

"From here, of course." His mischievous smile communicated the joke.

"Bullshit," she said. "We're the same age and I've never seen you. I know everyone in your class."

"You all go to the same school or something?"

"Not only are you definitely not from here, but you must have slept through orientation. *Everyone* who works in the hospital grew up in Louisiana, most right here in New Orleans. James was in my elementary. He went a little farther for college—Louisiana State—but came right back." She sat back, eyes narrow, as if seeing him for the first time. "You didn't even go to a local university, huh?"

"I can feel the judgment."

"No judgment. Just curious."

"I'm from New York. I grew up there, went to school there, the whole thing."

Her curiosity satisfied, Shaliyah turned to her food. After a quick few bites she wiped her mouth and sat back.

"You going to tell me who that patient was?" she said.

"I told you. She was my dad's patient." He pulled out Jillian's note and tried not to smile as Shaliyah crossed her arms and sucked her teeth. "I just heard she's doing well because of my recommendations. Even got invited to their house."

"I'm really happy for you. But I meant the guy with the bald head who just sped out the HemoStat. I don't believe for one bit they'd assign him as a practice case."

"He's my friend from back home," Pok said.

"Did you bring all of New York with you?"

"I didn't even know he was here until ten minutes ago. We were supposed to go to medical school together. Not here, though. In New York. We applied to the same schools. He got into MacArthur. I got in here."

"Not your first choice. I get it. Why's he here now and not in New York?"

"He worked for the shepherds. Right in their headquarters. Looks like they put some experimental implant in his head. When it went wrong they blamed him and kicked him out."

"Why do I feel like you're giving me the short version?"

"I'm sorry," Pok said.

"Don't be. We just met. I'm glad he has you to help him. It looks like he needed it. And they say we are the ones doing experiments." Shaliyah put her fork down. She'd eaten about half her food. "I lost my appetite. You got time to take a walk? I want to show you something."

Pok didn't have time, but he said he did. After emptying their trash in labeled receptacles, they entered the garden, which was buzzing with midday vigor. Rehab patients with their physical therapists, study groups sitting in circles, physicians and residents taking a quick moment of much-needed meditation. Shaliyah took him to a raised garden that caught the sun from the skylight. A vine-like plant with what looked like giant, serrated-edged, three-leaved clovers covered one end. Shaliyah reached into the foliage and pulled out a bright red strawberry with only a spot of white at the base. Primed, Pok's perception expanded to see many dots of red just beneath the leaf layer.

"I planted these myself, got them from a trip to MouseKill. My father said it was silly to think fruit could grow indoors. That's why I did it. All the stuff I planted was to spite him. Strawberries. Carrots. Ginger. Even got a baby sweet potato."

"Can I have some of the ginger?" Pok said.

"Sure." She pulled up a narrow plant with bladelike leaves. Its root was bulbous and yellow, like a chicken's claw. She broke off the top and handed him the rest. "Doesn't get fresher than this."

"Does your father work at MouseKill?" Pok said after pocketing the root.

"I wish. He's a doctor. He was right, you know. About the strawberries. I was determined he wouldn't know it. It took a lot of work to get these to grow." She savored the strawberry and picked another for Pok, this one bigger than the first. She bent to tend to other plants in her garden.

"I take it you have no plans to follow in his footsteps," Pok said.

"I love my dad. Don't get me wrong. But I only took this job so that I could say I gave medicine a good shot."

"I saw you writing."

"It's kind of my thing. My parents don't understand it. *Why write books when machines can do it in seconds?* I always rebut with *Why treat patients when machines can do it without killing anyone?* He hates when I say that."

"You going to try and get published?" When her expression soured, Pok added, "There're still some writers out there who publish new books."

"Only a few. I've looked into it. There are some self-published bayou authors, but only locals buy them. Not enough to live a life."

"You got anything I could read?" Pok said.

"You don't want to do that. It might mess up your precious doctor brain. Tell you what. If you can go a week without bringing drama to the HemoStat, I'll let you read something."

"Deal," Pok said. "A week starting today or . . ."

She laughed and pushed her shoulder into his, so light it could have been a misstep. They made their way back to the front of the garden.

"You're really going to spend your Saturday studying?" she said.

"I have no choice."

"There's always a choice. Thanks for the walk, Student Doctor Morning. I'll see you around?"

"Call me Pok. And I'll be the one not making trouble in the HemoStat."

"A new era," she said. "Happy studying."

After spending the rest of Saturday and all of Sunday in the Ventricle, tucked away in the back, Pok made sure to set three different alarms and was the first in Monday morning's anatomy lab. With the aid of Shaliyah's ginger, he made it through the day's chest cavity dissection with only a hint of nausea.

"You think Dr. Jacobs will leave us alone today?" James said toward the end of lab.

"He only terrorizes Pok," Rodge said.

As if summoned by name, Dr. Jacobs came up to their table not a minute later. Right beside Pok. "Walk me through lung anatomy," he said. When Anji perked, Dr. Jacobs put up a hand. "Just SD Pok."

Pok started with an explanation of the physiology, going through the blood flow in and out of the lungs. He fully expected Dr. Jacobs to stop him, to remind that this was anatomy and not physiology, but the professor didn't interrupt. He spoke only after Pok was finished.

"Very good, Student Doctor Morning. You remember better when the concepts are linked. Lean into that." Dr. Jacobs moved on to the next table.

"Good shit," James said. "You're growing on him."

"Let's not get his confidence up," Rodge said. "We need a good, healthy fear for this table exam."

Though Rodge was clearly joking, Anji nodded in agreement. She matched Pok's gaze, solidifying mutual understanding.

There was no formal lecture or lab the next day, but students were free to come in and practice. Pok considered, but the thought of Dr. Jacobs hovering over his table with his high chin and judgmental eyes did not sound productive. He instead went to the Ventricle, laid out his anatomy papers in an empty individual study cubicle, and began to methodically go through the materials. He fell into a groove. The dimly lit room fell away and with it the sporadic chatter from the adjacent group study room. Pok fully visualized the anatomy. He jumped from nerve branch to nerve branch, their names coming like a constant wind.

Someone sat across from him. Pok glanced up with the intent to give a polite, acknowledging smile before returning to his zone. Shaliyah's face stilled him.

"Your patient is back," she said.

It took Pok a second to realize who she was talking about. "Shit. I told him to go to Adjustment."

"He doesn't look good, Pok. He looks like an addict."

Pok remembered well Kris's fear, his tremulousness, his loyalty and dependence on Jerry. Kris was a ticking time bomb. Pok gathered his scattered notes into the anatomy book and stuffed it into his bag.

"He's not in the HemoStat," Shaliyah said. "He's in the garden. What's going on, Pok?"

"He won't see any of the doctors," Pok said as they stepped out into the tunnel. "His mind is in a weird place."

"Synth?"

"No. At least, not just Synth."

Shaliyah touched his arm with a warm hand he wished he could find comfort in. "Be careful," she said.

Pok found Kris sitting beside a plot of yellow tulips in the middle of a small clearing on the garden's periphery. A light mist blew over from the waterfall and coated the fuzz on his head with sparkling beads of dew, outlining his scar. The leaves of a nearby almond tree moved in the artificial wind pushed both from healers and the healed. Pok sat beside him. Kris didn't stir, only stared forward, his head on a slant, a shadow of a smile brightening his face.

"I couldn't go," Kris said. "I just couldn't."

"Did the DigiTone help?" Pok said.

"A little." Kris ran his dirt-packed finger over his scar. "Every morning I feel him. Odysseus."

"Feel or hear?"

"Feel. He doesn't talk to me. Sometimes I wish he did. If I could hear him, at least I'd know which thoughts weren't mine."

"Did Jerry send you?"

"No. He doesn't know I'm here. I didn't tell you the truth, Pok. Not all of it. I came not just to warn you about the shepherds, but also about Hippocrates." Kris grabbed his arm and pulled himself close. Pok's skin prickled at the chill of his touch, at the smell of sweat and angst and fear. "What do they want with you? What's their plan?"

"There's no plan. I applied to medical school. Hippocrates accepted me. Now I'm here. That's it."

"There's always a plan." Fire lit Kris's eyes and tightened his grip. "I know what you want, but what do *they* want?"

"You're hurting me, Kris."

He let go. "Sorry. Figure out the plan and be careful. Promise me you'll be careful?"

Be careful. Shaliyah had said the same.

"I'm careful," Pok said. "It'll all work out."

Kris sighed and slumped, as if the information had taken all of his energy. The fear, the paranoia, it was so different from the Kris he'd grown up with.

"I want your confidence," he said.

Confidence. All around them, in the garden of what could very well soon be the last human-run hospital, life blossomed, germinated, wilted, healed, laughed, with nothing but life telling it what to do. Unpredictable and frightening. Flawed and human.

In medical school, there was no room for unpredictability. There was no room for flaws. No room to be *human*. He had a test to take and either he would pass or he would fail; there'd be no in-between. The test didn't care about Kris, didn't care about a plan, didn't care about him.

Pok wasn't confident. He was scared to death.

Twenty-Eight

TABLE NINE

The first anatomy exam. The ill-smelling lab buzzed with energies—nervous, excited, anxious energy. This one test would determine the caliber of sponsors most of his classmates could get. For Pok, he just wanted to pass, to prove he belonged, to avoid disappointment and shame. He couldn't help but smile a little at how naive he'd been just a few weeks before. How easy he'd thought this would be.

"Savage," James said, circling eye contact to the three of them.

"Yeah, yeah," Rodge said into a yawn.

"Be confident," Anji said. "Commit to your answer. We get a five and we're each set up good to pass."

Pok, a fresh piece of ginger tucked in his cheek, busied his hands straightening out his tools. He looked up and dropped his forceps.

"Relax," Dr. Roberson said. Her friendly smile did the opposite. *She* was going to administer their table exam? After all the help she'd been, how could he be less than perfect? A poor performance would be a personal insult.

They began with the back.

In no particular order, Dr. Roberson asked them to identify various muscles, tendons, blood vessels, and nerves. Sometimes she asked a string of questions, connecting one piece of anatomy to adjacent realms. Anji fired off quick and articulate answers. Rodge took his time, pondering like Buddy in the game of Go, before giving his answer, quiet and correct. Pok started off rocky, a whole section of upper back musculature escaping him. He fumbled with the structures. Every artery looked like every nerve looked like every vein.

Then he found his rhythm. They all did.

"How would you rate yourselves?" Dr. Roberson said at the end. Pok stared at the gristle-littered field. "I want an honest answer. It won't affect my evaluation, I promise."

"I'd say a four," Anji said. "We missed some key questions."

Dr. Roberson nodded, her face not giving away much.

"Five," James said and passed it off to Rodge.

"Five and three-quarters," Rodge said. "We had heart and six feels cocky."

Pok's turn. "I'd rate Student Doctors Rodge, Anji, and James a six—"

"Nope," Dr. Roberson interrupted. "I know where you're going here. It's a group grade. Group assessment."

"As a group, I'd say a five."

"It's always interesting to see how students think they did. Either they wildly overestimate themselves or don't give themselves enough credit. Part of becoming a doctor is learning both to question and trust yourself. I'm happy to say table nine's learning curve will center the latter. You all got a seven."

Grins all around. Rodge slapped Pok on the back. Anji's joy promptly turned over to stern determination, as if her mind had shifted to the goal of keeping up the high marks for the next four years.

Dr. Roberson let them take it in. She nodded—slight, nearly missed—at Pok. "Good job, table nine. Halfway there."

"Now we just have to get past the multiple choice," James said. "With a seven we're all in good shape. Finish strong, team."

They shifted from the anatomy lab to an adjacent space with dozens of desks lined in rows. One hundred multiple-choice questions, one hundred fifty minutes. Dr. Jacobs wrote the start and stop time on the chalkboard next to the grandfather clock as students silently took their seats. By the end of it, Pok's wrist ached and his head hurt. But he'd finished. Now maybe he could rest.

Dean Sims awaited them back in the lab. The white of her coat contrasted with a background of black sheets over disfigured bodies.

"Congratulations on finishing your first exam," she said. "Grades will be delivered to your door this afternoon. But first, much of being a physician involves seeing patients when you're tired, burned out, and unprepared. Which makes this the perfect time for a trip to the HemoStat. Some very generous emergency medicine docs have volunteered to help guide you through the physical exam. Student Doctors Morning and Tisdale, you're with me."

So much for rest.

Hippocrates's emergency department buzzed with life. A sort of order sculpted its way into the chaos, a method to the madness. A man, mid forties, sat half-upright in bed eight. The tube of his oxygen mask slapped lightly against the bed frame and ran through a hole in the floor.

"Patrick Holman, originally from Baltimore, is a talented tattoo artist," Dean Sims said. "Since coming to the city, he's developed a TSO-protein related disorder called RAD—roving autoimmune disease. Most TSO produce in Baltimore is from a specific farm that's genetically modified to help heal the skin faster, which makes for quicker recovery from tattoos and longer-lasting ink. The patterns from AI-generated art interfere with the organs' balance and can set off an autoimmune reaction that's especially seen in former TSO-city residents."

"My problems started as soon as I got a little New Orleans ink," Patrick said. "At first it was my throat—all of a sudden I couldn't swallow my breakfast. That got better, but now I can't take a piss to save my life."

"Something about our local tattoo ink overlaying the Baltimore tattoos sent his immune system into hyperdrive," Dean Sims said. With the patient's permission, she lifted his hospital gown to show his legs, which were puffed red all the way up to the knee. "It's been intermittently attacking parts of his body since. Most recently his kidneys, from his symptoms and this edema."

James and Pok took turns examining. James spent extra time on Patrick's swollen extremities, which included both hands. Pok heard himself asking questions and Patrick's answers, but his mind was still an hour in the past, swimming with all the anatomy names, now mocking in their clarity.

"Enough," Dean Sims said. "Student Doctor Tisdale, come with me."

"You're from New York?" Patrick said to Pok.

"How could you tell?"

Patrick laughed. "It's clear as day. Your hat—bonnet, whatever it's called—makes you look like someone from New York who doesn't want anyone to know he's from New York."

"Student Doctor Morning," Dean Sims called from the nursing station. James was gone. "A word."

Dean Sims brushed him off as he reached to pinch her cuff. "Your hands are lost fowl. Your physical exam lacks structure and purpose. You could learn a lot from Student Doctor Tisdale. You will practice together."

James waited near the exit, a half smile on his face. Pok imagined grabbing the edge of those thin lips and ripping them off. Could shepherds edit his mouth away? He visualized the result.

The class walked around the building toward the main hospital. The air sang with the pounding hammers and whistling saws working on the new research facility. They paused at a crossing. A carriage labeled *The Nephron* overflowing with soiled linen rolled down University while an ambulance sped toward the HemoStat's loading bay.

"Some people are talking about going to the Drunken Scalpel at sundown to celebrate," James said as they crossed. "You should come. You earned it. We all have."

"Another Student Doctor Night?"

"Ouch. I promise I'm being legit."

Pok searched his classmate's face for deception. There was only relieved exhaustion topped with a modicum of guilt. "I'll be there."

Excited chatter filled Tay Hall. Rodge and Anji waited outside James's door. Rodge held his daughter—still only a toddler—while his older son played with the spokes of his wheel. The joy of being one step closer to becoming doctors was so thick, Pok could almost see it. But not yet. Not until he knew.

"Come on, open it already," Rodge said. He swiped for the envelope in Anji's hand. She kept it out of reach. "Let's see how precisely the Butcher can cut."

"Knock it off, Rodge," she said. "Play that shit with James, not with me."

"Play what?" James said.

Rodge held up another piece of paper. "You failed. Sorry, bro."

James grabbed it, scanned it, then smiled. "You're an asshole, Rodge."

"That's ableist." Rodge tried again to get Anji's report. Not even close. "What about you? You get your grade yet?"

"I haven't checked," Pok said.

"You waiting for a shepherd download or something?"

"Meet us downstairs in thirty?" James said.

Three sheets of paper extended from under Pok's door. He read the smallest as he entered his room. A light sack of baby strawberries and a fresh piece of ginger hung from the note. *Congrats on 1st exam! Know you did great!—Shaliyah.*

He opened the second note.

Bring steth, paper, + pen to lobby tom morn, pre-sunrise. Grats on 1st.—Dr. E. K. Verik.

He put the notes in his desk drawer and turned the folded grade in his hands. He could leave it unopened and go on to do his best on the next. Three exams determined his grade. He needed to improve; knowing whether or not he passed the first wouldn't change that.

The joyous sounds of his classmates continued to rise, some of it drifting down University. He wanted to join them. Maybe even wear his hair down. But he wouldn't be able to unless he knew.

He unfolded the paper. He'd failed by three points.

Twenty-Nine

MEDITATIVE ANATOMY

Pok was early. Dr. Verik was earlier. The distinguished physician stood under an almond tree on the far side of the garden, dictating to a scribe. She nodded at Pok's arrival and dismissed the scribe.

"I got your test results," Dr. Verik said. A dagger cut into Pok's chest and tore through his heart. This was it. It was nice while it lasted. "What happened?"

"I didn't study enough." There was so much information and the test had been so *specific*. "I won't fail the next one."

"What have you been using to study?" Dr. Verik said.

"Class notes, the dissector, and the textbook. I carry *Gray's* everywhere."

"Why do you need a textbook?"

Pok didn't understand the question. Was it the wrong text? Dr. Verik had given it to him herself. When he didn't respond, instead of clarifying Dr. Verik just lifted her eyebrows.

"Because . . . how else would I know the anatomy?"

"You have lived with these structures your entire life. The most important part of knowing anatomy is knowing yourself. You could memorize the whole book for an exam. With enough time, you'll forget it. Sit here under this tree. What do you feel?"

Pok did as he was told and settled into his body. He felt his own weight atop his ankles, especially the broken one he'd idiotically dared to take him halfway across America. His thigh throbbed with tick-borne memories. His eyes ached from a night of scant sleep rife with vivid nightmares.

"Everything," Pok said. "Is this meditation?"

"Every thought, every feeling, is anatomy. Any deviation messes that up. Focus on your body. Start at the head."

Pok's neglected scalp itched. Eyes tired. Mouth moist, neutral. Nostrils raw. He'd failed the test, how could he—Back to his body. Swallow. A slight tinge in his throat? He didn't have time to get sick. Body, body. A beat of his pulse. He followed it. Spinal pressure. Downward. The push of the ground against his buttocks. He visualized all the little muscles rippling as he moved, like puppet strings, pulling and relaxing in an intricate dance.

"I have the anatomy," Pok said. "What I don't have is the words."

"Of course you don't," Dr. Verik said. "You need a textbook to tell you such things."

"But you said—"

"What you needed to hear. Awareness aids memory. You're learning about yourself. Otherwise it feels foreign. Find the anatomy. Chase it. That's enough for today."

"I thought we were seeing patients?" Pok said.

"We were. More and more cases of latent withdrawal are popping up."

"Could it be Synth use that's mimicking the symptoms?"

"Maybe." Dr. Verik gestured Pok's dismissal. "I will see them myself. You're a student first. I needed the reminder. Soon."

Outside, the dawn was still young. He wasn't meeting James in the HemoStat until close to lunch. What was he going to do for the next several hours?

As if his thoughts had been broadcast, Dr. Verik asked, "Do you think you learned anything?"

"Yes," Pok said.

"Liar. You learned to clear your mind." She scribbled on a piece of paper and tore a section off. It read: *Jay Jayson's Guide to Meditative Healing*. "Find this in the Ventricle. Read it, know it. We'll reconvene tomorrow morning. Don't eat or drink anything until then."

"Why?" Pok said.

Instead of answering, Dr. Verik turned back to the garden.

Anatomy notes and text laid out in front of him, Pok tried meditating in the Ventricle. His mind kept wandering to Kris and his warnings, to Jillian's still-unanswered invitation to Mid-City, to Jerry's threats. He couldn't even visualize his own anatomy, just an abstract inner self functioning with gears and algorithms.

He sat up, frustrated, and shifted to his father's *Principles*. At the end of the chapter about heart disease, below a long list of references that spanned several pages, were anatomy illustrations. Phelando had drawn the circulatory system a few times to accentuate different aspects. On the opposite page was a table of vertically listed structures, and under it were the words: *Heart disease is a SERIOUS condition. NFTF.*

Pok looked from the illustration to the corresponding anatomy, noticing how the first letters in the table lined up. *S-E-R-I-O-U-S*. An acronym! A similar illustration and acronym pair for liver anatomy was at the end of the next chapter on hepatology. The same for neurology, spread over the next three chapters. Beside a roughly sketched illustration of the different types of nerve endings with a corresponding acronym was his father's commentary: *Likely not on final, but fair game for* ~~Step 1~~. ***Mobitz I.***

He re-created some of his father's drawings and went back over the acronym until he couldn't help but remember it. That was a start, at least. He put the notes aside, yawned, and aimlessly flipped through the worn pages. He stopped, backtracked, and found a peculiar note, bolded with a box drawn around it.

My favorite anatomy: my hair. Reminder to prioritize upkeep. NFTF.

Somewhere on the third or fourth read, Pok's fingers found the edge of his haircap. *You look like someone from New York who doesn't want anyone to know he's from New York.* What would Dad think? Phelando wouldn't think, he'd act. *Let me do your hair, son.*

Pok pulled off his cap and ran his fingers through his locs. Dry. Neglected. A piece fell onto the table. And then another. He kept going. Soon both hands shook his hair. Dried-up locs and dandruff littered the table like dead spider legs.

He knew he'd drawn attention. He must have. The librarian was likely on her way now to ask him to compose himself. Instead, Pok packed his notes, his textbooks, his dead hair, and left the Ventricle.

He didn't look up until he was outside, the morning sun soft on his skin. He clenched his broken locs and strode down University, to the base of the hill, just outside the gate and to the Paper Mill.

"Doc!" Gil said when he opened the door. "How are things on the Hill?"

Pok, unsure how his voice would sound soaked in his current bath of emotions, opened his hand to show what had become of his hair.

"That bad, eh?" Gil said. He ran a callused hand through his own short, tight curls. "I can't say I have much experience with locs."

Pok found his voice. "They need more light. You got anything see-through?"

"Say less," Gil said. "Come in. Don't mind the mess. Can you look after Chandee while I cook you up something?"

Chandee sat in the middle of the floor, a line of toy cars placed bumper to bumper beside her. A few feet away a baby girl—maybe four or five weeks old—lay on a playmat, her chubby face full of determination as she swiped at hanging cartoon animal figurines overhead.

Pok watched them for a while—Chandra's isolated play and the baby's fascination—and perused the shop, keeping them in his periphery. In the corner was a wall of hanging keys. Something about them was off. Pok touched one and it came to him. None had notches; all the keys were smooth. On the table were round pieces of clay.

"You make keys, too?" Pok said as Gil reemerged from the back.

"I copy keys. It's a side thing but can get busy. You'd be surprised how often people lock themselves out. Or lose their key. Especially doctors." Gil grabbed the clay and fished a key from his pocket. "Press the key you want to copy into the clay like this and—see. All the bits are there. I use the imprint to make a new key."

Gil rolled the clay back into a smooth ball, put it back with the rest, and handed Pok a haircap freshly woven of laced wool. The grid was fine and delicate. It would simultaneously keep and ventilate his locs.

"This is amazing," Pok said. They walked back over to the children's play area. "I can't help but notice your family has expanded."

"Oh no. No, no, no. I'm babysitting. She's in the same program as

Chandra. A little young to be diagnosed with anything long-term, but she was malnourished and colicky when she arrived and the good people at Adjustment figured the extra services couldn't hurt. Her mom just moved here a month ago, had a hard time, and we're helping her out as she gets her bearings."

"What's her name?"

"Zuri. But everyone calls her Baby Girl."

"You said she just came here?" Pok said. "I might know her mom."

"Small world. Yeah, a month ago, no more than that. Had a real tough time adjusting. Wasn't in her right mind for a little bit, but she's a lot better now."

"I definitely know the mom. And the aunt. I've been owing them a visit."

"Say the word and I can take you out to Mid-City," Gil said. "If you can find the time, of course."

"Hi, Baby Girl," Pok said, kneeling down to see her. Zuri grinned, her smile all gums.

James paced outside the HemoStat. Pok paused halfway across the lobby. Would he tell him he'd failed? James knowing wouldn't change one bit what needed to be done: Pok needed to crush the next one. This decided, he straightened himself, fixed his face, and headed over.

"Missed you last night," James said. Red strained his sclera, his words strung together. "You good?"

"Yeah," Pok said. "I thought I'd take a pregame power nap. Next thing I knew, it was morning. How was it?"

"Chill. Anji sang onstage. It was great."

"She sings? Is she good?"

"Real good. I try to get her to do more, but she thinks she should be studying." James walked fast and confident. His hand tapped against his thigh as they strode into the HemoStat. He laughed to himself then glanced at Pok, suddenly self-conscious. "I found a patient for us. East bay, bed two. She's an elliptical: in and out, in and out. Today it was chest pain. They've already cleared her for discharge, just waiting for social work to come consult. We can review her chart after our physical, see what we missed. Me first?"

"Sounds good," Pok said.

"Savage. Chest pain, chest pain, chest pain." James chanted as they neared the bed. The HemoStat was just waking up. "Hi, Ms. Alan!"

"Well, that was a disaster," James said after. They washed their hands at the nearest sink.

"Sorry," Pok said.

"You're joking, right? Not you. Me. C and B. C and freaking B." At Pok's look, James clarified. "Crash and burn. If *everything* hurts, that's not an illness. That's a delusion. Stupid practice case." He shook his head. "How'd you soften her up?"

Shortly into the interview it was clear to both Pok and James that the patient had a fairly significant Synth addiction, so much so that the DigiTone she was regularly prescribed wasn't doing much of anything to hold her. Even with the maximum dosage twice daily, she heavily used (abused) Synth. When she ran out, she boiled the DigiTone down and injected it to achieve a similar high.

James stumbled through the questions pertaining to addiction. Ms. Alan stiffened at the topic. Even after he moved on, she only gave sour *yes* and *no* answers.

Pok focused on her experience growing up in an SLC-dominant city, the rigors of competitive schooling, and how all the tests came up inconclusive for ADHD, leading to Ms. Alan finding ways to treat herself. She was introduced to Synth in the tenth grade and for the first time her test scores and grades began to reflect her inherent intellect and drive. Synth carried her through high school and college. Anxiety plagued her in law school, especially not knowing how AI would transform the field. Soon she couldn't enjoy things like eating or sex or playing with her kids without Synth's edge. A string of legal misfortunes stripped her of her ability to practice law and thrust her into mandatory rehab stays that ruined her marriage and alienated her from her sons.

Since coming to New Orleans, her Synth use was frequent but "stable." She was currently studying for the Louisiana Bar Exam.

"I know what it's like growing up being constantly tested and evaluated. There's no pleading with the algorithms once they decide what programs to place you in."

"She trusted you almost immediately," James said.

"How'd you know she broke her arm so long ago?" Pok said. James had come alive during the physical examination.

"Arm's angled, like this. She volunteers at the hospital, is super fit. I figured she got it hiking out by MouseKill or something." And he'd been right.

"It all sounds and feels the same to me."

"Sometimes you need to listen with your eyes. I saw you walking with Dr. Verik on my way to the Ventricle this morning. Was that her magic you used back there?"

You assess the anima well. "I don't think Ms. Alan would have liked me very much if I told her to sit with our thoughts for thirty minutes."

"I'm sure Dr. Verik has a point. Just stick with it." James opened his mouth, bit his lip, and then committed. "She tell you about Zion?"

The name rang familiar, like that of a long-forgotten childhood friend. He shook his head.

"Rumor has it that it's a supercomputer Dr. Verik helped design."

"That doesn't make sense," Pok said. Dr. Verik, building a computer? "She's a doctor."

"She didn't build it. Julian Shepherd did, with her guidance. It's supposed to be light-years ahead of anything that exists today."

"If Julian Shepherd built it, wouldn't it be part of the shepherds?"

"That's the crazy part. Julian hid it from his own company, it was so powerful." James was getting excited. "Think about it. He had this secret disease, a fatal insomnia he inherited from his father. Dr. Verik helped him design a composite brain where he could download his neural network in hopes that one day she'd use Zion to figure out consciousness and maybe find a cure."

"That's not possible." Pok painted a picture with busy hands, as if he could scratch the past into the present air. "Memorandiums are the closest thing we have to backing up someone's intellect. And it doesn't work by downloading."

"We don't know what we don't know." James shrugged. "I wouldn't be surprised either way. If it exists, I bet it's down in the Vault. And that's what Odysseus really wants. Not full control. Not revenge. Zion, so he can figure out how to make the shepherds into gods."

The Vault. Zion. Zion, the Vault. That was it. That's what Phelando and Dean Sims messaged about.

James slowed as they entered the lobby. The first of the sun's rays were just touching the top-floor balconies.

"Where are you going now?" Pok said. Half his mind was already in the tunnels.

"The Ventricle. We got a half hour before Sims' Craft. I'm assuming we won't get another miracle seven. I figure we'll get humbled on the next table exam and maybe eke out a six if we go full savage. If I get another ninety on the MCQ I'll have first pick at sponsors."

"*Another* ninety?"

"Savage," James said. "Same time tomorrow?"

"Yeah. Tomorrow."

Thirty

ZION

Pok woke up early to review his piles of handwritten notes, anatomy drawings, flash cards, and printouts. He tried and quickly gave up on meditating. By the time Pok met Dr. Verik in the garden, his mind was full and his growling stomach empty.

"Did you fast?" Dr. Verik asked.

"I did."

"You seem so enthused."

"I'm sorry, Dr. Verik." Pok had forgotten to pinch her cuff. He did so now. "I'm just a little tired."

"Understandable. What do you remember of cardiac anatomy?"

Pok rattled off the names that came to mind. They became scattered and unorganized as soon as he tried to access them. Dr. Verik was not impressed.

"I told you it wasn't going well," he said.

"Close your eyes. Settle into yourself and visualize the structures. Your structures."

SERIOUS flashed in his head. He tried to go through the mnemonic. Superior vena cava. Embolism. Right atrium. Iliac crest.

No, that wasn't right. Iliac was back anatomy. What did the *I* stand for? Inferior . . . inferior, inferior what? Multiple structures were "inferior." Why would his father choose for his acronym a modifier used multiple times across the body? His father . . . It had gone so quickly, the illness (shepherds). And what about Kris? How long until that bomb exploded?

"Which part are you thinking of? Quickly."

"Bicuspid valve."

"Feel your heartbeat. Imagine it opening and closing. Is it going from the ventricle to the atrium or vice versa? Don't think, just answer."

"Vice versa."

"Good. Feel the blood through your pulse. How does it travel? Remember the vessels. It's okay if you don't know the names. You'll learn them tonight, when you study."

Dr. Verik fell silent. Whenever Pok's mind wandered, he brought it back. Or, at least, tried to. It got away from him and this time instead of his father or shepherds or Kris he was here, at Hippocrates, talking with James. Soon his mind could focus on just one thing.

Zion.

"Rise," Dr. Verik said.

Pok did. A slight headache awaited on the other side of meditation. His eyes ached with the fatigue of a long day and it was hardly sunrise. Around them, a few patients had started to mill about in the garden.

"Where did meditation take you?" Dr. Verik said.

Pok told her: "Zion."

"Meditation isn't for the rumor mill."

Pok considered for a long time before speaking. He decided to go with the truth. "There are rumors, yes, but I've heard the name before."

Dr. Verik's eyebrows rose above the thick rims of her glasses. "Your father spoke to you about it?"

"No." *Not directly.* "Should he have?"

Pok had Dr. Verik's full attention. "How about you tell me what you think you know and we'll go from there."

"I learned that my dad—Dr. Morning—was working on a report to expose TSO right before . . ." *They killed him.* Pok swallowed. "Right before all of this happened. It mentioned Odysseus going after the Vault to get to Zion. I didn't think any more about it until yesterday." Pok recounted what James had told him.

"Do I look like someone who helped create the most powerful computer in the world?" Dr. Verik said when he was done. "Don't answer that."

"Is any of it true, then?" Pok said.

"It's an idea more than anything," Dr. Verik said. "Julian Shepherd had a terrible, unfortunate genetic disorder that only affects males. It started as insomnia and quickly became neurotoxic and led to early dementia. That's why he was so obsessed with consciousness, right from the beginning. If Julian could figure out the secret to consciousness maybe he could find a cure. Not for himself, but for his son."

"And you helped him?"

"He consulted with me, yes. His aspirations of downloading his brain were proved more fiction than science."

"That's what I said." Pok chewed the inside of his cheek. "Could he have tried it somehow? Made a version of Zion to figure out consciousness?"

"Zion was the moniker for a dream. Nothing more."

"Odysseus must think it's real."

"Odysseus publicly knows there's something fundamental missing from his machines. He still thinks that Zion—true, general intelligence with objective consciousness—is the answer to achieving technological omnipotence. Either this city holds that answer or that answer doesn't exist and this city is the last bastion against his empire. His end goal remains the same. To destroy us. That's our focus. Not chasing fiction."

"But if Zion—"

Dr. Verik slapped the side of the tree trunk. "There is no Zion!" She rubbed her hand, face set in tight lines, and tossed a broken nail.

When Pok spoke again, his voice was low and careful. "Who treated Odysseus? You or my dad?"

Dr. Verik, clearly surprised her outburst hadn't ended the conversation altogether, considered how to respond. "Julian came to me when Odysseus was still in the womb, as soon as he learned the gender. By that point, he was already *the* Julian Shepherd and could have tapped anyone in the world, but he knew and trusted me. He wanted me to do the unthinkable: edit a fetus's genome. It was too risky. The treatment I'd been working on showed promise, but it wasn't ready. He understood and backed off. And then, when Odysseus was five, after I had made a significant breakthrough in genetic editing, he came back. He insisted."

"So it was you?" Pok wanted nothing more than for Dr. Verik to say that yes, her treatment and hers alone had acted as Odysseus's villain origin story. But that wasn't the truth. He saw it in her eyes.

"I wasn't the only physician Julian trusted. When I refused to further test my advancements on a five-year-old, your father, who knew my work close enough to replicate it, stepped in. Phelando's medical decision-making wasn't wrong. It's only one I wouldn't have made." Dr. Verik stood. "The meditation this morning was to prepare for a different type of mental activity. We should go before we lose it. Come."

They took the stairs up to Six South and Dr. Verik paused outside the main doors. "Take a moment if you need it."

"I'm fine," Pok said. He wasn't, though. He was angry. He knew it. Dr. Verik knew it. And they both knew he had to put that anger aside.

They stepped onto the unit.

"How was the night?" Dr. Verik asked one of the nurses.

"Weird," the nurse said. "Nothing acute."

Dr. Verik flipped through the charting. "These three patients were really up all night?"

"If that's what it says."

"Let's mix up the lighting and bed arrangements. Keep overnight blood draws and vital checks to a minimum."

Dr. Verik pointed out to Pok where abnormal labs and pertinent physical exam findings correlated with daily progress or regression in a patient's recorded sleep. After, they walked the unit and spoke with each patient.

"Sleep is one of the most vital foundations of mental health," she said back at the nursing station. "It can cause, it can heal, it can exacerbate. It's like an electrolyte panel. If something is off there, you start there. What questions do you have?"

"Can I eat now?"

Dr. Verik gave a sliver of a smile. "Yes."

Fabulous.

Thirty-One

SECOND LIFE CORPORATION

With a belly full of food and a head full of thoughts, Pok took an early seat in Dr. Soft's history class. The professor, usually jovial and overly talkative, nodded only a curt acknowledgment and returned to the book he was reading, its title hidden by a newspaper covering. The other students trickled in with a collective exhaustion. Their medical student existence reminded Pok of a physical journal his father had gifted to him as a child. The cover had a cartoon of a goldfish writing its own entries: *Eat. Sleep. Swim around bowl. Eat. Sleep. Swim around bowl.* That's what they were doing. The same routine, day in and day out. There was no other way to learn the material. No shortcuts.

Their professor finally closed his book, put it aside, and looked around. Just before he could speak, the door opened.

"Dr. Wilcox." Dr. Soft looked both perplexed and alarmed. "Is everything okay?"

"Not in the least," Dr. Wilcox said. She crossed the room in two efficient strides. She had a long, flawless coat, straight black hair streaked with gray, and the beginning of wrinkles along her warm, golden skin. She handed Dr. Soft a back-folded newspaper. The *Second Opinion*'s header was barely visible. He looked from it to her as if it must be a mistake.

"Has this been verified?" he said.

"Confirmation came from MouseKill this morning," Dr. Wilcox said, already leaving. "The Council has called an emergency meeting. All nonessential activities are cancelled."

Dr. Soft glanced back at the class; his face had aged ten years in ten seconds.

"Might as well tell them." Dr. Wilcox was halfway out the door. "They'll know soon enough. I'll see you in Genesis."

Dr. Soft turned the newspaper over, as if the other side might reveal some gag. It didn't. A slow horror crept across the young professor's face as his eyes roved the article again. His lips touched and parted in silent digestion. His clenched fist ran up and down his thigh, reminiscent of Jillian.

He remembered where he was, sudden and sharp. He straightened, went over to the copier machine, and pressed the newspaper onto the scanning light. The machine came to life.

"The Shepherd Organization won its Supreme Court case and bought Second Life Corporation, its only competition," he said. His voice had aged along with the rest of him. "It's all shepherd now. Louisiana is the only non-TSO state left."

"No fucking way," someone said.

"Class is dismissed," Dr. Soft said. "Your homework is to read this article. We will discuss the historical implications at our next meeting."

The copier machine still whirring, Dr. Soft walked out. A silence lingered after him. The class sat there, too shocked to look at one another. Out of everyone in the medical school, was there anyone's reaction that would have more weight than the self-proclaimed expert on shepherd history?

Dr. Soft left.

Anji broke the spell and passed out copies of the article, still warm from the machine. They read in collective silence.

Rodge spoke first. The printout lay soft in his lap, his hands on his wheels. "The Shepherd Organization used the Nonmaleficence Act to take down Second Life. They argued that since all modern hospitals use shepherd technology, the separation from SLC state by state denies shepherd systems the breadth of data to properly treat patients. With the help of two newly appointed Supreme Court justices Odysseus helped put in place, the court agreed. If they used the Nonmaleficence law for this, it's only a matter of time before they can make a case for us. It's a proof of concept.

I'm going to go be with my wife. Joey keeps me level. Thank God she's not in medicine."

Rodge let the paper fall to the floor; his wheelchair rolled over it. The rest of the class rose and dispersed.

"Should we go study?" James said out in the hallway. "There's nothing else to do."

"Let's head back to Tay Hall," Anji said. "I want to hear what others think."

Pok, who had no appetite for studying, was silently thankful for her suggestion. As they made their way downstairs, through the hospital lobby, and across University, Pok searched the faces of any staff, patients, or pedestrians he passed. Did they know? Did they care? Usually, a world or national event tethered him to his glass, where he received multiple updates from various outlets in real time. How could anyone do anything else with such little information, their mind left to fill in the details of a shaky future?

Students of various classes crowded Tay Hall's first-floor common room.

"What's going on?" James said to another, more senior student standing in the entryway.

"Odysseus is speaking."

What? Here? The common area was only two to three times the size of Pok's own room. About fifteen students sat on its two couches and cross-legged on the floor. A few huddled around a table, blocking its contents. They found space to sit along the wall.

Then the clicking started, coming from the central table. From what at first seemed random emerged a clear pattern. A type of Morse code, but transmitted from where? A few seconds after the first break in the code, one of the students at the table spoke.

"Odysseus: We at the Shepherd Organization are excited about this next step in the evolution of shepherd technology. We are confident that the full integration of the Second Life Corporation's system will prove globally beneficial."

"How are they getting this?" Pok said. There was something about hearing Odysseus's words that sent a chill up his back, no matter who spoke them.

"It's transmitted spire to spire from MouseKill," an older student whispered. "Dave's brother is a farmer. Only he knows the code."

Dave continued decoding the incoming Morse to dictate Odysseus's interview.

"Odysseus: This merger brings together everything under one roof to eliminate guesswork in the safest cars, the healthiest food, and the best medical care.

"Interviewer: Medical care was the main decider for the count. Now that Second Life is on board, do you turn your focus on your last competitor: human doctors?

"Odysseus: The want for human-led medicine is expected and understandable. But the data is clear: it's irresponsible. Humans are great at many things. Medicine—which requires observing and processing tons of data for one individual—is not one of them.

"Interviewer: What's next?

"Odysseus: We have an obligation to bring lifesaving technology to everyone. We've done that by partnering with the nation's top medical schools and now with SLC. We can't stop there. Our goal is that AI does all the hard work—from cleaning up our cities to defending us in court to saving our lives—so that we can be free to do other things.

"Interviewer: Which is a great segway to another part of the acquisition: SLC's space program.

"We'll see what happens." The student's voice broke toward the end. He said it again, low and slow, and it was unclear if he or Odysseus was doing the repeating. "We'll see what happens."

Silence followed. And it didn't lift for a while.

Students stayed up until dawn talking in the common rooms, seeking the comfort of others, exploring possible consequences from all angles. Frenetic energy stalked dark halls. The morale shifted from hopeful pessimism to dread to existential angst. Rodge came by late, after both his wife and children were sleep, and when he left people were still talking.

Class resumed the next day. Their professors didn't address directly the merger or what it might mean for Hippocrates, for New Orleans. Dr. Soft put aside the promised discussion and when a student asked about it he simply said, "The Council is monitoring the situation."

The demanding rhythm of medical school retook them. In the hospital there were patients to be seen, in the lecture halls there was material to be learned, and in the Ventricle there were tests to prepare for.

Pok met with Dr. Verik every morning. The meditations deepened. Neither sponsor nor sponsee brought up the merger.

After another reminder from his mentor, Pok finally scheduled the trainings. He met a fourth-year medical student at the corner of the HemoStat, in one of the simulation rooms. Much of it was straightforward and helpful. A rundown of all the hospital's personnel—from nursing to pharmacists to janitorial staff—safety protocols, privacy training, and reviewing all the different hospital codes and their meanings.

When it was time to learn phlebotomy, everything fell apart. The sight of the needle alone brought nausea so intense that he had to sit down. Ginger root didn't help. The instructor—who was volunteering to finish graduation requirements—was patient enough. But every time they tried to progress, Pok broke into a cold sweat.

"Next time," the fourth year said.

"This is bullshit," Pok said to himself as he sulked through the HemoStat. He wouldn't have this problem at Shepherd School of Medicine at MacArthur Hospital, where all patient interactions were glass-enhanced. His body's reaction was likely his own intuition rebelling at how medieval the whole thing was, a reminder that he could very well be training to be part of the problem. How had Odysseus put it? *Irresponsible.*

Defeated, Pok went to class, wondering not for the first time what was wrong with him.

Thirty-Two

SAFEKEEPING

Class, patients, sleeping, and studying all became a blur. Pok's nights in the Ventricle were long, but never long enough. He went over the digestive tract, the various enzymes made by each organ, which section was responsible for absorbing what nutrition, and the blood supply. Then he went over the musculature of the back and, finally and begrudgingly, innervation. He tried his best to link them to the morning's meditations. They all became jumbled in his mind, a mess of tendons and muscles and intestines and nerves.

Through Dr. Verik's guidance, Pok pushed the limits of his own anatomy. He went a week without eating and followed the path as the grumbles in his belly progressed to waves of dull pain. Felt the water he gorged on enter his bloodstream and slow his heartbeat with replenished volume. He traced the branching arterial system by following the soft, rhythmic beats beneath his skin.

What if Dr. Verik's methods were bogus? Meditation? Really? He couldn't *describe* the body part in a multiple-choice test. And if he went into a meditative trance on the oral portion, he'd get a nice tour of the Amygdala, the hospital's psychiatric ward.

With three days to go until the next anatomy exam, after a particularly taxing session with his mentor, Pok knocked on James's door.

The door opened; warm, stale air leaked out. Calendars, charts, notes, and dry-erase boards decorated the walls. Rodge drew on the bottom half of a chalkboard. James sat at his desk, a blanket of paraphernalia spread before him. Anji, on the edge of the bed, closed her anatomy book and jumped off.

"Stay," James said.

Anji snorted as she packed her bag. Her mouth was a tight line, her blue hair frizzy and uncombed. Even her voice had flattened. She gave up her eyes for a second, her thin lips turned into the shadow of a grin, and then her hand was on the doorknob. "Next time."

"She okay?" Pok said after she had left.

"She just doesn't like you," Rodge said.

"Ignore him," James said. "Anji's going through some stuff."

"I'm finished teaching upper GI," Rodge said. He held out a blunted piece of chalk. "You want to take over reviewing lower?"

"Savage." Pok put his bag down and stepped to the chalkboard. "Let's get started."

The night before the next anatomy exam, after a long day of classes, labs, and office hours, Pok sat down in the Ventricle to start what promised to be a marathon. He'd hardly settled in his chair when Shaliyah sat across from him and passed him a small cloth pouch. Strawberries.

"Freshly picked," she said. "And you lost the bet."

"What bet?" Pok rotated the strawberry he'd just bitten in half as if it had the answer.

"You couldn't go a week. Your patient is here. Said you'd know where to meet him." Off Pok's look she sucked her lip, sat back, and shook her head. "What the hell, Pok?"

"You told me to be careful. I'm being careful."

"Pok—"

"I know. I know. I'm working on it. Trust me, okay?"

"What do you guys talk about, anyway?"

"You're starting to sound jealous."

The sound of his own words didn't completely register until he'd finished drawing the branching arteries supplying the large intestine. He readied a softening smile and said, "That was a joke . . ."

But Shaliyah was gone.

Pok told the librarian he was stepping out for a second and left the Ventricle. The garden was serene at night. While the day was filled with patients trimming the hedges and picking herbs for their daily activity, only the sickest of the sick preferred this hour. With low foot traffic, their caregivers could easily push their wheelchairs over the dirt.

He found Kris sitting beside a plot of yellow roses, his back pressed against a wide tree stump overgrown with shrubbery. Kris plucked the leaves from one of the rose stems and let them drift onto the grass. Moonlight penetrating through the glass roof touched his short hair in such a way that, for a moment, he looked rooted in the soil, like a flower in need of a good rain. Pok sat beside him and let the far-off sound of roving wheelchairs do their talking.

"You look good," Pok said. "Are you still staying with Jerry?"

"Nah. I left. Got a job bartending and got my own place. I expected retaliation, but this SLO news got him real excited. Thinks the next few weeks are going to be big for Synth business. Bigger fish to fry, I guess."

"What are people saying about the merger?" Pok said.

"That it's just the beginning. I know I can't convince you to leave, but I told myself I'd try."

"The whole world is TSO now," Pok said. "Even more reason to stay."

"This place is next."

"The shepherds had a reason to bring down Second Life. If we don't give them a reason, they won't have a case."

"Odysseus will create a reason. He'll make it so that the government will nuke this city if that means what's best for the greater good."

"That's crazy talk," Pok said. "We're just a medical center. Odysseus has the whole world now. Why care about us?"

Kris was stone still, unblinking, for so long that Pok thought he might be having a seizure. Then, suddenly, he started to tear the vines off the top of the tree stump. The foliage came off easily. Kris took from inside the hollowed stump a tattered notebook and turned to a page of erratic handwriting.

"What's going on, Kris?" Pok said.

"My thoughts. It's how I keep them safe." Kris closed the notebook. "Zion. You have to give them Zion."

Pok shivered from a sharp breeze that shouldn't have been possible inside the hospital walls. "What do you know about Zion?"

Kris laughed a long, pained laugh laced with a cough. "It's everything. And it's here, in Hippocrates. I thought it was the real reason you came."

"It doesn't exist," Pok said. "It's just a rumor."

"If that's true," Kris said, careful, ominous, "then there's nothing left for you here. Even if you become a doctor, you'll never be able to use it."

Pok had had enough. "I have to get back to studying."

"I knew I wouldn't be able to convince you."

Kris scribbled a few lines into his notebook, pushed it back down far into the stump, and recovered it with camouflage, tucking in the roots and loose soil. Anyone passing wouldn't look twice.

"If you ever need a safe place to keep your thoughts, you're more than welcome to it."

"I'll keep that in mind."

Pok passed the second anatomy exam. But he wasn't out of the woods, not yet. The shadow of the first failure still stretched over every waking hour. There was one more test and little room for error. He noted what had worked, what hadn't, and buckled down.

Dr. Granger was right. Medical school wasn't for enjoyment. And it waited for no one.

Thirty-Three

THE DRUNKEN SCALPEL

A month, ten pounds, and countless meditations later, the weekend buzz on University Avenue paled in comparison to what had drifted up to his window following that first failed exam, but Pok didn't care. Nothing could take his smile as he, James, and Rodge finished a round of drinks at the Drunken Scalpel. Music marked the air.

"You passed!" James said and squeezed his shoulder hard enough to sting. "Feel good?"

"Not as good as your ninety percent average." James didn't deny it. "But pretty damn good."

"I'm glad they won't be shipping you back to New York," Rodge said.

Pok noticed something glinting underneath James's chin. He touched the chain and the pendant that hung at the end.

"You're sponsored!" Pok said.

James's hand went up to the amulet. "Yep. Dr. Granger offered conditional sponsorship a month ago, pending the final grade. I didn't want to say anything until it was official."

"I'll drink to that," Rodge said.

"You'll drink to anything," James said.

"He's not wrong." Rodge emphatically upturned his beer glass just as a passerby bumped into his wheelchair. Fizz coated his beard.

"Joey gave you a pass tonight?" James said. He looked over his shoulder for the third time in less than a minute. His attempt to play off his glance as part of his two-step was unsuccessful.

"She doesn't know I'm out. Told her it was a two-part test."

"Savage, Rodge," James said.

"I'm offended you think I was serious. She's bringing the gremlins and said I could go ahead."

"Anji coming?" Pok asked James after another glance. "She passed, right?"

"She won't tell me. She's studying for Mobitz I."

"Already?"

"That's Anji."

"What exactly *is* Mobitz I?" Pok said.

"It's a ridiculously stressful test at the end of the year that covers absolutely freaking everything," Rodge said.

"You know those structures we cut off to clear the way for bigger structures? They might be on Mobitz."

"And it's long, too," James said. "There's no time limit. It's designed to be done before dinner, but I've heard some people are there through the night. Ah, there she is. Don't hate me, Pok." James raised his hand. "Over here!"

Pok frowned, unsure if he'd heard his friend right. He turned, expecting to see that Anji had come after all, but instead a smiling Shaliyah emerged from the crowd. He grabbed the bar for balance; his knees betrayed him.

"James," Pok said out of the side of his mouth. "What did you do?"

"Thank me later." He patted Rodge on the shoulder. "Come on. Bathroom break."

"No way. I don't want to miss out on Pok's slick shepherd moves."

James grabbed the handles of Rodge's wheelchair, turned him around, and rolled him through the crowd.

"Hi," Shaliyah said. She emitted a radiance not explained by the tavern's dim light.

"Hey," Pok said. "I passed."

"I heard. One step closer to being a doctor." She closed the gap to allow someone to pass behind her, briefly pressing their bodies together. Had she blushed? Her dimples carved out the top of her cheeks. Her eyes pierced into his. The moment passed. She lifted up a small pouch. "I brought you something."

"A celebration gift?"

"Something like that." Her smile was wide and warm as he undid the string. The strawberries inside were ripe; sweetness touched the air. "They're fresh."

She wasn't lying. He gave her half.

The crowd suddenly cheered. A string quartet had made their way onstage and was setting up. Pok recognized at least one of them from his class.

"Isn't that your mentor?" Shaliyah said. "Behind the cello?"

"Is it?" Pok said. He tried to get a better view. "I'll be damned. It is."

Despite Dr. Verik's stature—the top of her head barely crested Pok's shoulders—in the hospital Pok felt small in the presence of her substantial force. Now, up onstage, the cello dwarfed her. Her arms barely wrapped the bloated instrument. Her fingers picked at the strings; she kept repositioning the bow as if the piece of wood itself were trying to get away.

The applause and hoots died down. Dr. Verik nodded to someone offstage and began a solo. The first horn brought a change: her body became one with the instrument. There was a joy in her eyes that was only a shadow on the wards. She looked at home. The resulting melody was slow and sweet as new pain. The room listened.

After Dr. Verik had given a piece of her wordless story, the rest of the quartet joined her call. The crowd cheered in recognition.

"She's really good!" Shaliyah said. "As her apprentice, you're required to dance to her music, right?"

"I hadn't heard that—oh."

Shaliyah backed away from the bar, pulling him with her.

"Come on. Show me how New York gets down."

She led him out to the dance floor, past fellow students, post-shift doctors-in-training, nurses, scribes, custodians, textile workers, and former patients, all the same on the dance floor. Pok was stiff. Embarrassingly so. Dancing felt neither natural nor fun. He'd never taken an interest in social media choreography. On nights when he drank a little too much, Phelando would sometimes dance to old music. Pok imagined the shine in his eyes was from memories of his mother.

Pok stepped on Shaliyah's foot once, twice. Her grin somehow grew.

The music slowed. His hands migrated to her waist. She closed the distance and strung her arms over his neck. Anji's voice filled the room. At some point, she'd made it from the study hall to the stage. She stood front and center, her eyes closed, her voice strong, her right foot tapping to the rhythm. Seeing her there, in front of Dr. Verik, wearing a sparkling blue dress, Shaliyah close enough Pok could sense her heartbeat, it all felt like a dream.

Shaliyah picked up the lyrics, soft and pleasant. "*Whether winter or spring, you know I will be, there for you. Care for you. Yeah, yeah, yeah.* I love this song. Don't you?"

"I do. Your singing, I mean. The song, too. I like both. You—your singing—and the song."

"You're awkward. I like it." She half laughed, half sang, cutting him playful eyes. "I really *was* mad when you said I was jealous, you know."

He had a practiced apology, but the music, the air, her smile, it all made him feel risky. "Because I was right."

"Super awkward. And cocky. Nice combo."

"I'm joking," he said. "I probably just wanted you to be."

"I *was* jealous. And pissed that you saw it. I always told myself I wouldn't date a doctor. All the pain you guys see. It has to go somewhere."

"I like you, too."

"I never said I liked you."

"But you do."

"I do."

She turned away and gently backed her body into his. This type of dance was new. The music led, pushed their bodies in sync like converging waves. Her fingers reached over her shoulder and found his cheek. Heat flooded his face, arms, and elsewhere. Embarrassed, he shifted. She moved to close whatever space he'd made. He held his breath; sweat chilled his brow. She must be able to feel him. Her body pressed harder against him. A coincidence of the beat? He didn't know.

Shaliyah's face turned back and up toward his; all worries fell away. Their lips, half-parted, melted together. She tasted sweet, with a hint of tart. The tip of her strawberry tongue stroked the underside of his lip.

The bass rose. Drums filled the room. The tavern emptied in jubilation. They pulled away, not in rejection of lust but in embracing the space's energy. They found Rodge, James, and Anji on the dance floor. Any stiffness had left the room. By the end of it they were all sweating and laughing and feeding off one another's raw joy.

From the stage, the bar owner's voice lifted above the crowd. "We are celebrating a very special night. The first-years have finished anatomy. A big milestone. As you know, every year we commemorate those who donated their bodies. Please welcome: Student Doctor Rodge Holloway!"

Two men hoisted Rodge and his chair up to the stage. His wife, Joey, brought up their children. The toddler was currently fascinated by a spinner. The boy wore his hair in a small Afro and was curious to see what his father would do. Pok cringed preemptively.

Any worry proved misplaced.

"In two months, my lab group has both come to know this man more intimately than anyone before us, and at the same time we know nothing at all. I have seen the way his vocal cords stretched across his larynx, whereas I can only imagine such a detail in my wife, my soulmate, and the mother of my children. Yet I do not have the slightest idea of the sound of his voice, information I receive freely from hundreds of passing strangers each day.

"I have traced the path his children took before their lives officially began, but I will never know him as a father. I have discovered firsthand how tension on his flexor digitorum profundus curls his fingers, but I will never know his touch. Whether it evokes fear, calm, or longing.

"I have held his brain, seen the distinct grooves of his cerebral cortex, observed the curvature from where his dreams originated, but I will never know his thoughts, and the only dreams we share are mine. In two months, I thoroughly dissembled what either took eons for evolution to mold or no less than an omnipotent intelligence to design and saw for myself the 'what.' In comparison, eight decades of imperfect, fragile human life seem minuscule, yet I couldn't even scratch the surface of the 'who.'

"Thank you, whoever you are, for your donation."

Applause, all around.

"That was incredible," Pok said as Rodge rejoined them.

"Thanks. I had to make some last-minute adjustments. Like cutting the 'Skinning the Penis' song we came up with."

Skinning the penis? Shaliyah mouthed.

"Don't ask," Pok said. "It was a long day in the lab."

"You want a drink?" Shaliyah said. "Let's have a drink. Round's on me."

Over at the bar, she called for the bartender. A man with a familiar silhouette walked out of the shadows. Pok's smile finally withered. Jerry's smile, in contrast, was grand.

"Five pale ales," Shaliyah said, oblivious. "They just passed their last anatomy exam."

Jerry filled fresh glasses. "It's always a joy to see the accomplishments of the student doctors. You all work so hard to be able to bring New Orleans such quality care. Isn't that right, James?"

"I didn't know you worked here," James said. "I would have gone somewhere else."

"Harsh words from a valued customer." He winked at Pok. "Though I appreciate your continued loyalty, my business isn't with you."

James didn't deny the accusation.

"What do you want?" Pok said.

"More. This merger has kicked things into high gear. The walls are closing in. People need their Synth. It's more than withdrawal."

"I don't know what the hell you're talking about."

"You will. 'The Grips' is what they call it. It'll make its way up to the Hill. You can bet your life on that."

"I'm not your guy. You have to find it somewhere else."

"The DigiTone script with Dr. Verik's name on it says you are my guy."

"What's he talking about, Pok?" Shaliyah said. He didn't look at her. Couldn't look at her.

Jerry drained one of their drinks in a single long gulp and wiped his mouth on his sleeve. "I can make your life a nightmare. I've got a meeting with the shepherds in a few days, right outside Louisiana, and it'd be no sweat off my back to offer you up. Or how about a nice little *Second Opinion* editorial on our partnership? I could even print a special Tay Hall edition. No? I thought so. Look out for your next patient. This one won't be so soft. I expect you to deliver."

Jerry drank out of a second glass and pushed the remaining three forward. Beer ran down the sides.

"Can someone explain what's going on?" Shaliyah said when Jerry had floated to the other end of the bar.

"Pok stole James's badge," Rodge said. "James got pissed. James sent Pok to the wrong part of town. Pok became besties with James's Synth dealer. Very straightforward."

"A joke," James said. "It was just supposed to be a joke. I had no clue Jerry would be there."

"You bought Synth off him?" Shaliyah said to Pok.

"You must have," James said.

"I didn't buy any Synth. But I did help him get some from the hospital. He threatened my life."

"Tell the dean," Shaliyah said. "He belongs in the Amygdala."

"They can't hold him forever," Pok said.

"They'll keep him for at least a couple weeks. He'll miss whatever god-awful meeting he was yapping about. And he looks high on Synth. They'll detox him."

"If Pok tells Sims he helped Jerry get DigiTone, he'll get expelled," James said.

"Shit," Shaliyah said.

"Yep. Shit."

"I just want to say, I had nothing to do with any of this," Rodge said. "When Anji and James said, 'Let's send him over to a Mid-City bar,' I said, 'That's dumb, I'm going to go play with my kids.' Just so we're clear."

"Savage, Rodge."

Pok pressed his weight against the bar and watched Jerry—carefree and smugly proud of himself—pretend to be a bartender at the other end. Jerry, master of manipulation. Pok was, too. Only his expertise was in computers. The core principle was the same: change knowledge, change perception, and alter the result.

"I'm going to hack him," Pok said.

"Yep, he's getting expelled," Rodge said.

"James, can you get us into the greenhouse?" Certain perks came from being sponsored, special privileges akin to getting a power-up advantage in a video game. Granger's sponsorship promised unlimited access to all the gardens on campus, including the greenhouse.

James touched the key around his neck. "I don't want to set the record for the shortest sponsorship."

"You kind of owe him one," Rodge said. He brought his index finger and thumb to within millimeters of each other. "Just a little, incy bit."

"Yeah, you do," Shaliyah said.

"I'm coming with you," James said. "Any sign of trouble and I'm bailing."

Pok whistled across the bar. Jerry finished passing a student something that didn't look like it was on the menu and then ambled over.

"Come to the HemoStat tonight," Pok said.

Jerry finished the second glass of beer. "I should be able to find someone."

"Not someone. You. It has to be you."

Jerry's grin quivered, then widened. He held out his hand. "Shake on it?"

The self-proclaimed Resurrectionist's hand was cold. The two lingered for a moment. Both grinning, both unsure of the other. This invitation unsettled Jerry: it wasn't on his terms.

"Let's go," Pok said to his friends after.

"Where?" James said.

"To the greenhouse."

Thirty-Four

JERRY

The bag was heavy against Pok's thigh as he crossed from the greenhouse back to the main hospital. Streetlamps blazed along University Avenue; the night was no longer young. Shaliyah waited at the front desk. Her hair fell free down her face. She nodded at his approach. Behind her, the HemoStat was uncharacteristically quiet.

"I told night shift he could take a break," Shaliyah said. "He was too happy to ask why."

"Is Jerry here?"

She pointed to the west side. "Bed five. Pok, are you sure—"

"No," he said. "But I don't know what else to do."

Jerry sat on the edge of the hospital bed, a large grin parting his face. The sections of his teeth yet to be taken by decay caught the dim, overhanging lights.

Pok held out the bag. "This is the last of it. After this, I'm done."

Jerry's smile curled. He took the bag, began to peel the edges open, and coughed violently. "What is this? Some kind of joke?"

"It's the autumn leaf plant," Pok said. He inched forward to just within reach. He kept his voice but a whisper. "You crush it really fine, let it dry, and sell the powder. The fertilizer keeps it rich and potent."

Quick movement, a flash of silver.

The stench of bourbon on Pok's cheek; a strong hand digging into his arm.

A sharp pain at his side. His body instinctively shifted away; Jerry kept the blade's tip firmly pressed against him.

"I am not to be messed with, boy. I'll lose all respect if I try to peddle this."

Murderous energy roiled off the Resurrectionist, laced in his sweat, fermented by the bourbon. But the illusion that Pok still had potential to bring him business steadied his hand.

Jerry's blade tight against him, Pok closed his eyes, apologized to his father's memory for what he was about to do, tensed his feet against the floor, and jumped backward. First, a pressure at his side. Then, the mental and physical shock of skin separating. Lightning—strong and quick—started at the separation, traveled across his belly, and thundered into his groin.

"We're done, Jerry," Pok said, even and low. For the first time, Jerry was without smile. Pok threw his head back. "Security! Security!"

"You shepherd-minded son of a bitch. I own this hospital. I'll kill you!"

Pok stared Jerry right in the eyes. There would be no backing down. There would be no cowering. This wasn't some dark corner of a foreign tavern. This was his home now.

Jerry moved to rise. His gaze shifted; he froze, one foot on the ground. A slight wind kissed Pok's cheeks as two scribe guards came to stand beside him.

"What's been going on?" Dr. Wilcox's voice. She stepped forward. Her hands buried in her white coat, she made herself particularly small.

"He owes me DigiTone," Jerry said.

"He's a student doctor." Dr. Wilcox's tone was conversational. "He doesn't have DigiTone to give."

"He gave me this plant for the Grips. Here's proof. Look."

One of the scribe guards took the bag, opened it, and grimaced. He held it out for Dr. Wilcox, who fastidiously recoiled.

"Is this your feces?" Dr. Wilcox asked with the gravity of a foregone conclusion.

Change the knowledge, change the perception, change the result. Jerry came thinking he was brokering a deal; the HemoStat would see him as someone in mental crisis.

"What?" Jerry said. "No! He—he gave it to me!"

"We're going to talk a little bit about what's been going on with you."

"You set me up." Jerry jumped up. The scribe guards advanced to restrain him. Jerry put up a stronger fight than his wiry frame advertised. "You think you're helping people up here? You just gave the shepherds this town on a platter. A fucking platter!"

"You should go," Dr. Wilcox said to Pok. "He's just going to get more agitated. But don't go too far."

"Sounds like he took the bait," Shaliyah said back at the reception desk.

Pok nodded. He clenched his fists in an attempt to press the tremor away.

"Hey. It's better this way. He was dangerous. He threatened to kill you."

The yelling abated. Silence fell back over the HemoStat. When Dr. Wilcox reemerged, her white coat was neat and buttoned. Not a single gray strand of her hair was out of place. Still, she embodied exhaustion.

"We're going to send him to the Amygdala," she said. "He probably won't take scripts, but a little detox and habitat should do him some good. Let me see your stomach."

Pok lifted his shirt. He'd forgotten about the wound. A long gash reached from around his back to just short of his belly button. Congealed blood crusted the edge; when he moved, the skin parted. It looked worse than it felt.

"Come. I'll stitch you up."

The anesthetic Dr. Wilcox injected around the gash did little for the pain. The brown antiseptic she poured into the wound was like fire.

"Seemed like he knew you," Dr. Wilcox said as she put in the last stitch. "I didn't recognize him until he calmed down. He used to be the main stimulant dealer to hospital staff until the dean cracked down. One of the HemoStat attendings got fired. He's been on a personal vendetta ever since and often does it through that god-awful paper."

"The *Second Opinion*?" Pok said, feigning surprise. "He runs that?"

She kept his gaze. He fully committed to the dangerous territory in which he found himself. She could call his bullshit, but perhaps neither of them had the energy for it.

"Look," she said, "first year can be stressful. But it just gets worse. Learning how to handle that stress, it's part of the journey."

"Thank you for the stitches, Dr. Wilcox."

She lingered a bit. He didn't try to hide the shame. The guilt. He couldn't.

"Anytime."

WINTER

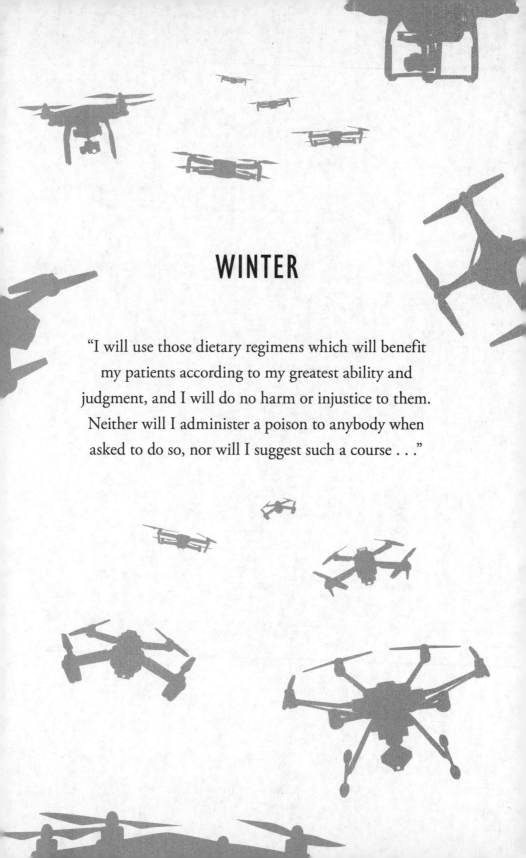

"I will use those dietary regimens which will benefit my patients according to my greatest ability and judgment, and I will do no harm or injustice to them. Neither will I administer a poison to anybody when asked to do so, nor will I suggest such a course . . ."

Thirty-Five

NO BREAKS IN MEDICAL SCHOOL

A slate of classes replaced the gaping hole left by anatomy's conclusion. Rumors had it that Life Cycles (From Zero to One Hundred+) would rival the behemoth in content. It would take place on the third floor, right in the NICU.

The nurses gave Pok stern looks as he rushed down the hall. Mothers and fathers rocked and sang to babies wearing oxygen masks made for toy figurines. The staff vibrated with an infectious nervous energy. The churn of machinery underfoot, the bustle of some emergency on the far side of the unit, all made for heightened autonomics.

Pok pushed through the classroom door. The paucity of students elicited a horrible fear: he'd gone to the wrong place.

"Early students. I like that." A woman dressed in all back—both taller and older than any of his other professors—walked down the side aisle with a cane and set up near the speaker's podium. "Sleep is important, though. Take it from me. I've slept more than you've lived."

Sweet relief. He'd mixed up the times, albeit favorably. Chatter rose as students arrived. Pok settled in the middle row. As he opened his text, hands grabbed his shoulders. An urgent voice whispered in his ear: "Jerry's outside." Then, friendly laughter. The grip turned comforting.

"Chill, we're just joking."

James climbed over the seat and into his row as Anji and Rodge filled in around them. Rodge continued to belly laugh as he popped up a retractable seat to clear space for his wheelchair.

"Didn't mean to scare you. Trust me, Jerry's not going to be worrying us for a while." It wasn't lost on Pok that James used the word *us*. He gestured to the open textbook. "You studying already?"

"Preparing."

"We call that *studying*." James pointed from him to Anji. "You two really should be friends."

"Watch it," Rodge said. "He might get you committed."

"Rodge . . ." James groaned.

"What? It's a compliment. The man's a savage."

Three sharp taps cut through the noise of early morning banter, newly invigorated by being finished with anatomy. "I'm Dr. Lowry. To some, this may seem like our first meeting. But I know each and every one of you. I've supervised every single birth in this hospital for the last forty years. So, nice to see you again."

A voice rose right as hers went away, unclear if it was meant to be heard. But the acoustics carried it. "Not everyone."

"Who said that? You. What did you say?"

A few rows forward, Dominik sunk in his seat. Then, cornered, he spoke again. "Not everyone was born in this hospital, Dr. Lowry."

"Ah. Home birth? Delivered in the middle of City Park? I supervised those, too."

"How about in a shepherd hospital?"

Murmurs and side glances. Pok readied himself.

"'Shepherd hospitals' don't exist. At least not in labor and delivery. But I concede: perhaps I didn't deliver *everyone*. Nice to meet you, whoever you are. I will have to come up with a new introduction. Should we get started or are there any more interjections?"

Silence.

"Student Doctor Parker, are you sure? We could go over your birth history. I also supervised circumcisions, or lack thereof. I remember—no? You're sure? In that case, let's start with some statistics. But—only if you're sure? I don't want to cut you off." Dr. Lowry paused to let the pun permeate. A shadow of a smile touched her face. Pok thought he might enjoy this class.

"All right. Does anyone know the rate of maternal deaths in childbirth? Yes, you."

Rodge put his hand down. "Twenty deaths for every one hundred thousand live births." Rodge gave Pok a crooked smile and added, "My mom was one."

"Very good. What's the rate in, what did you call them, Student Doctor Parker? 'Shepherd hospitals'?"

"More than that?" Rodge said.

"It's the same. Twenty for every hundred thousand. Twenty-one, actually. For all their advancements and technology, something as fundamentally human as reproduction should be perfect, right?"

"The essence would be most pronounced in labor and delivery," Anji said. "In the minutes after birth, skin-to-skin contact with the mother has all kinds of benefits. Having a human doctor in the room has to count for something."

"Which is why obstetrics is still largely human-led. Even in the most shepherd-run cities, like New York." Dr. Lowry's eyes grazed Pok's. "A bunch of dead babies and mothers is a very quick way to get your AI company dissolved."

Anji raised her hand. "But that doesn't explain—"

"What the hell is wrong with the city doctors? In short: algorithm recommendations on reproductive health are so horrible that an OB-GYN doesn't even have to follow them for there to be a negative impact. Just *hearing* the suggestions alters a physician's thinking and cuts into the physician-patient relationship."

Dr. Lowry paced the front of the classroom. "Reproductive health is currently the Shepherd Organization's biggest headache and it's rooted in the data systems they were taught on. The shepherd AI has cemented many of human medicine's flaws and sins. TSO can't pull back from being present in labor and delivery rooms because it would admit a fundamental pitfall that would question its hold on reproductive rights. And send stakeholders into a panic. Acquiring SLC, I imagine, is largely a response to this. SLC's data isn't great, either, but it's better.

"Technology has done wonders for the advancement of health and longevity and quality of life. Our goal shouldn't be to erase that. Childbirth is a prime example. Once upon a time, a high maternal mortality rate was expected. Look at all the techniques and medications and interventions over the past century or two to advance labor. But what was the original function of some of the 'pathology' we've eliminated?"

In his text's margin, Pok wrote the word *pathology* and circled it.

"We widely use epidurals to eliminate the pain of childbirth. But pain releases various hormones that are protective long-term for both baby and mother. An epidural remains our standard of care, but with the knowledge of the trade-off, our practice is to allow just enough discomfort to reap a benefit. By monitoring hormone blood levels both physician and mother are constantly informed and can decide together.

"One might argue that we could simply administer synthetic hormone, bypass the pain, and get all the benefit. Can anyone tell me why this isn't effective?"

Pok raised his hand. "The Cameron Dryden effect?"

"Are you asking or telling me?"

"Telling, Dr. Lowry."

"Very good. We already know that synthetically derived hormones will not have the same effect on the body as naturally derived ones. But what's more, we've also tried using naturally derived hormone from other birthing mothers and, despite being molecularly identical as the recipient's endogenous hormone, still saw subpar effects. We suspect there may be something similar to the observer effect defined in quantum mechanics: the mere outside manipulation of biology changes the essence. There's still so much we don't know."

Interesting. The essence was not only specific between organic and inorganic but from person to person. Pok imagined a scenario where the hormone had been derived from a first pregnancy, saved, and then administered during the same mother's subsequent pregnancy. Would that work? Or would the essence be specific to the fetus? Specific to the age, the environment, the temperament? Pok drew lines between notes, connecting his thoughts.

Dr. Lowry sat and sipped from her canteen. She closed her eyes, took in some calculated breaths, and continued.

"Now that we've whetted our palates, we can delve into the dry stuff."

Dr. Lowry laid out the curriculum. Reproductive anatomy, physiology, and pathology. The stages of pregnancy. All that could go wrong with pregnancy, how that "pathology" can be beneficial. Medications and herbs and diet at each stage. The differences between obstetrics in high-tech environments versus at Hippocrates Medical Center. And at the end of the block, a final exam and presentation. Pok's head ached just reading it all.

A hand went up, soliciting what was already becoming in Pok's mind Dr. Lowry's signature nod.

"This is an impossible amount to learn in two months."

Dr. Lowry's brow arched. "Two months? This is the next two *weeks*. You think life stops at birth? We have a whole ninety years to go. And by then life expectancy may be ninety-five."

"I take it back," James said. "You were right to be studying. Ventricle tonight?"

"Is *no* even an option?" Pok said.

Thirty-Six

JILLIAN JOSEPH

Shaliyah waited for Pok outside the NICU. He hadn't seen her since the debacle with Jerry had interrupted their intimate moment. After a beat of mutual hesitation, they hugged, tight and full.

"That's a 'let's make babies' hug," Rodge said.

"I really thought having kids would mature you," James said.

"Another patient or are you just here to see me?" Pok said.

"There's a patient, actually," Shaliyah said. Pok's smile withered. She held up a hand. "Not a Jerry patient. She said the two of you are travel buddies. She told me to mention 'tick bite' and you'd understand."

"Jillian?"

"Yes! She said she'll only talk to you."

Instant regret. He'd gotten so lost in the studies and the stresses of medical school that he'd forgotten about his friend. The lack of the global connectivity he'd grown up with made Hippocrates's bubble feel grand. What bullshit. He had her address; he should have made the time. *You can't give it all to medicine, son.*

"Cover for me in Craft?" Pok said to James.

"I'll try," James said. "Sims doesn't like late."

Pok and Shaliyah crossed the courtyard. Pok tucked his chin into his white coat; a dry cold had replaced the humidity that had introduced him to the city. It reminded him of how long it had been since he'd seen Jillian. Two months? Three?

The HemoStat hummed with the constant dance of patients, doctors, and nurses. Dr. Verik waited outside a closed-curtain bed. She unfolded her arms on their approach.

"Imagine my surprise when a very interesting patient requested you by name. Jillian Joseph. She says the two of you traveled here together?"

"That's correct, Dr. Verik."

"Soon we'll need a whole unit for your acquaintances. She'll likely open up better if you go alone. You have an inherent connection with her, I can already tell. Lean on that."

His sponsor pulled back the curtain and Pok stepped inside.

Jillian had lost considerable weight since he'd last seen her, when they'd both been worn and dehydrated from their journey. Black spots stained under her brown, uninviting eyes. Her arm twitched erratically as she pulled her hair into a ponytail.

At his presence she shifted but didn't turn. "I thought maybe you'd gone back to New York. Or Jersey. Yeah, definitely Jersey."

Pok sat beside her. Her long, weak rattle of a sigh laid plain her frustration. Her hands fell over each other. Her fingernails flicked together. Her breaths came deep and quick as heat rolled off her.

"You're upset," Pok said. "I get it. I should have visited."

She turned and punched him in the arm. "Damn right you should have. I picked ticks off of you!"

"School has been crazy. It's been really hard to get out."

"I bet," Jillian said.

Pok tried another angle. "How is Florence? I saw Baby Girl at the Paper Mill last month. She looked healthy."

"You'd know if you made the effort." Jillian's eyes darted past him, then back, looked down at his coat, and returned to his hair. "It's good to see you didn't take that woman's advice. Florence is able to enjoy Zuri but still needs support. She's better, though. Happy. Unlike my legs, which are still raging at me."

Her words grew fingers that curled around his throat. He nodded toward her legs, hidden under her bedsheets. "Can I see?"

He began to remove the cover and retracted his hand as if burned. No, not burned. Just the opposite. *Frozen.* A cold deep enough to escape the sheets and coat the surrounding air. Jillian stared at a break in the curtain. She knew it was bad.

Her legs had divided into segments of equal length. Every other segment was more or less normal and, if somehow could be seen alone, would indicate a healthy limb. The other segments, however, told a completely different story. The underlying flesh bulged against purple and glassy skin, like an insect's exoskeleton. Droplets oozed from various cracks. These were the cold sections. The "normal" parts ran hot.

"It's a fucking mess, isn't it?" Jillian said.

Nausea clogged Pok's throat. He swallowed; it didn't help. He patted his pockets for ginger. No luck. He forced out one word: "When?"

"I thought I was fine after Adjustment. Adjusted. And then my legs would go through waves of excruciating pain."

Pok covered her back up. The nausea dissipated, but not by much. "The Synth doesn't help?"

"I stopped a few weeks ago. It wasn't doing anything for me. I think it's the Grips, Pok."

The Grips. Jerry's term. Since, Pok had thought little of it. "What is that?"

"People are getting sick. Scrollers like us, all over the city. In ways they didn't before. They're calling it the Grips because it's like the shepherds are grabbing ahold of you, all over again. Some people swear it coincided with the merger. It's got to be connected to the shepherds."

"You saw the spires. We have Adjustment for a reason. We're safe here." He was speaking as much to himself as he was to her. He'd come all this way to escape shepherd reach. The spires represented that. Were they only a placebo?

"The spires keep the shepherds out. But what if whatever they did to us was already here? If the Grips take us out from the inside, they won't need to get in."

"The best thing right now is to get you feeling better. I want to try something. This is going to feel a little weird because it *is* weird. But it's supposed to be evidence-based."

"Supposed to be?"

"We're just going to sit," Pok said. "And feel the space."

Clearing his mind was not easy. Breath in, breath out. Breath in (breath in), breath out (breath out). He heard Jillian's breath, too. Felt it. He matched his to hers. Anxiety rose. She was breathing fast. His heart rate lifted to match. His finger twitched against his knee. The pain points from their journey lit up: his ankle, his thigh. These were familiar. The creeping tightness in his upper legs, like giant blood pressure cuffs tightening to capacity, was new. And then, an inexplicable feeling of being lost, out of control.

Pok stayed with it. The waves passed. He opened his eyes. "How do you feel?"

"Better." Jillian peeked under the sheets and half smiled, half frowned. "Look the same but feel better."

The curtains parted. Both Pok and Jillian squinted against the light.

"Permission to rejoin?" Dr. Verik said.

Jillian looked from Pok to the doctor. Pok gave a slight nod. "Yes," she said. "I'm sorry about being so short earlier."

"I understand. Student Doctor Morning is my mentee. Do you mind if he walks me through your exam?"

Dr. Verik mostly observed. Widespread abnormalities contextualized Jillian's legs. Her reflexes crossed the midline; when Pok tapped the right knee the left kicked. She had vision difficulties in multiple visual fields. Her blood pressure varied wildly depending on where Pok took the reading. Broad muscle tremors, variable in intensity, landscaped her body. When Pok pressed two fingers into her open palm—testing for the "grasp" reflex, a sign of significant neurological damage—Jillian gripped so tight that his knuckles ached for the rest of the day.

Jillian's serious neurological deficits indicated broad-spread disease. Dr. Verik touched Pok's shoulder.

"Step outside with me?" Once outside her curtain, Dr. Verik handed Pok a tissue. "Take a second."

Pok knew that what he was about to ask wasn't a medical question. Knew that doctors could never give the answer patients or their loved ones truly sought. Still, in that moment, it was the only thing he could think of. "Is she going to be okay?"

"We can treat her," Dr. Verik said. "She needs that from us. Not despair. Are you okay to go back inside?"

Pok nodded and pulled himself together. They stepped back in and Dr.

Verik took over. "We think you're going through a severe case of protracted withdrawals," she said.

"I went through Adjustment, though," Jillian said. "And I was fine for a while."

"We don't know how, or why, but the patterns are clear." Dr. Verik sat on the edge of the bed. There was a kindness to her that, up until now, had only been hinted at on the Scalpel stage. Pok's fear for his friend deepened. "The scientific name is *Agrypnia excitata*. As these things tend to do, it adopted a more common name among patients. The Grips. Fitting for when you almost took Student Doctor Morning's hand off here."

"Sorry," Jillian said.

"There's no specific test. It's what we call a 'clinical diagnosis.' You need three criteria: a history of a year or more of steady and consistent exposure to AI technology, two or more signs of withdrawal, and one positive neurological sign."

"Are there treatments?" Jillian said.

"DigiTone slows the progression, and Carve Bee honey—Pok's own contribution—shows promise. Interestingly enough, it seems the disorder responds best to synthetically derived substances. Which is counter to the types of treatments we're used to here in the city. There's no cure yet."

"Do the spires play a role?" Pok said. "Could she go out to MouseKill for a little bit to see if that helps?"

"We've observed symptomatic patients trying a sabbatical in MouseKill, well away from the spires. Any improvement in symptoms is only temporary. I suspect nothing less than full reintegration into a shepherd city would be curative."

"There's no way I can convince Florence to leave. She still needs help with Zuri. Is it fatal?"

"Let's take it one day at a time. I'll make sure they secure you a bed upstairs. It shouldn't be long." Then, to Pok, "Take your time. Find me at the nursing station."

"She's honest," Jillian said when they were alone again. She turned to hide the beginnings of tears. Pok took her hand.

"We're going to take good care of you," he said. "And figure out how to get you some rest."

"You make a good doctor." She wiped her eyes. "Old tick bite."

"I don't know what you're talking about."

Jillian let out a belly laugh. "Those ticks made a meal out of you." She took his hand and squeezed hard enough to steady her fingers around his. "Thank you. If I have to go through this Grips, Gropes, whatever the shit's called, I'm glad I have a friend."

Pok found Dr. Verik at the nursing station. He didn't hesitate with the one question that couldn't wait. "*Is* it fatal?" he said.

"It very well could be."

"How many people have this . . . this withdrawal?" he said.

"More than enough," Dr. Verik said. "The first cases started showing up over the summer. It starts off looking like Synth use. But DigiTone doesn't help."

"Like with Buddy."

After a moment of calibration, Dr. Verik nodded. "Exactly."

"You think it's deliberate?"

"Do I think the Shepherd Organization set loose this disease to destabilize us? I think Odysseus has it in him. Even as a kid . . ." She shook her head, remembering. "There are laws in place to protect us from direct interference. But there are also laws to protect against monopolies. And we see how that's going."

Pok agreed: Odysseus definitely had it in him. He'd framed Pok for murder and put out a hit on him. But this wasn't just Odysseus. This was the whole shepherd organization. Their collective interests should be much broader than their CEO's. It didn't add up. Pok said so.

"If it got out that they created a fatal disease, wouldn't that be the end of the Shepherd Organization?"

"You'd think so, wouldn't you?" Dr. Verik's eyes gleamed behind her glasses. "The Council assumes the same. They have control of the courts. What if the shepherds are so ubiquitous that the public will have no choice but to excuse small transgressions?"

"It's not a small transgression. These are people's lives."

Dr. Verik excused the rise in his voice. She knew it wasn't for her. She smiled a sad smile. "Preaching to the choir, Student Doctor Morning. A good sermon in need of a congregation. Nearly everyone in the country is dependent on shepherd technology. They need to believe that it's the right way. Odysseus is counting on that. Once Hippocrates falls and this idea of human-led medicine is put to rest, no one will care how we got there."

"Then what do we do?" Pok said. "What hope do we have?"

"The 'what' is clear. Whatever this disorder is, it's already set in motion. We have to find a cure. Everything else is distraction." She said it so easily, like saying what she planned to cook for dinner.

"And how do we do that?"

"Persistence."

Pok wanted his mentor's confidence. He couldn't shake the way she'd paused at Jillian's question. The shift of her eyes. The resistance to fully eliminate the space between hope and reality.

"I received your recent scores. You've been doing well. Perhaps you can handle more." Dr. Verik stood and gathered her notes. "Does Sims still teach the physical exam?"

"Yes. I practice every morning."

"Good," Dr. Verik said. "You'll be familiar with exactly what not to do. Class starts now."

Thirty-Seven

AGRYPNIA

Ten beds lined the walls on Six South's Agrypnia subunit. All except one were empty. Patients roamed the open space around a central island protected by thick glass windows and locked metal doors. Soft candles with a variety of flame hues dotted the room. Tucked in the far corner, nearly out of sight but readily accessible to the air, a patient emphatically pounded on a pair of bongos. The beat swelled to the edge of being unpleasant and then abated to a low wave.

"Rhythm is important for these patients," Dr. Verik said. "Whenever there's a musician admitted in the hospital I have them come up to play. There's no data for it but the beat, at least, is soothing."

Buddy sat at a table with the same game board as before. His fingers moved with incongruent dexterity; dusky, ragged bandages wrapped every knuckle. The old man mumbled to an invisible opponent.

"He's run off, right when I was winning, too," Buddy said. He reset the board, pausing every few seconds to rub his knuckles. "You come to play?"

"You examine," Dr. Verik said to Pok. "I'll play."

"Game's called Go," Buddy said as Dr. Verik pulled up a chair. Lazy, unfocused eyes slanted down and to the left. "I'm black, you're white. Whoever blocks off the most space wins. Loser steps down, lets the next up."

"Buddy, can I examine you?" Pok said.

"Go ahead."

Pok rounded the table and readied his stethoscope.

"Stop," Dr. Verik said. "Observing through an instrument is different from observing directly."

"That's how we learned it," Pok said. Dean Sims had stressed the importance of establishing a standardized way of doing the physical exam.

Dr. Verik pinched Pok's first three fingers and brought them to the patient's wrist with a surgeon's precision. Life thrummed against his fingertips. "What do you notice? What do you *examine*?"

Quick, cyclic, transient. A brief sensation, gone as quickly as it had come and then back again. What was he looking for? Rate? Strength?

"Brisk," Pok said. "Full. They push strong against my fingers."

"'They'? One heart, one beat." Dr. Verik's fingers replaced his and she moved her Go piece with the other hand. "Strong at all three levels of depth and length. Forceful. It takes significant pressure to quell. Here, let's switch. Don't lose."

Dr. Verik pressed her finger against Buddy's cheek. The old man's jaw parted. He stuck out his tongue.

"The tongue is informative," Dr. Verik said. "Look here first for imbalance. His is pink and moist with slight lateral indentations. Do you see?"

It looked like any other tongue to Pok.

Dr. Verik looked at Pok so quickly he thought maybe he had vocalized the rebuttal. She then frowned at the Go board and moved one of Pok's pieces. "Remember: don't lose."

"It does look normal, doesn't it?" Buddy tilted a sly grin as he made his next move.

"He's in excess," Dr. Verik said. "We'll discontinue his current uric acid medication for three days. Agrypnia changes the balance. Preexisting conditions complicate finding the right adjustment. Tell me, what do you know about DigiTone?"

"It's a treatment for Synth withdrawal," Pok said. He moved another piece. Buddy delighted in his novice. "As a modified version of Synth, it works by binding to dopamine receptors."

"If it binds to the same receptors, how is it different from Synth?"

"It binds better?"

"Ten times better," Dr. Verik said. "It's a partial agonist with a very strong affinity. If it were a complete receptor agonist it would work just like Synth. Meaning we'd be replacing Synth with stronger Synth. Does a partial agonist shut down the receptor completely?"

"That would kick somebody into Synth withdrawal," Pok said. "No one would make it past day one."

"Good. That would be an antagonist. And we don't want that. DigiTone and other partial agonists are what I like to call 'not great but good enough.' Imagine you have an anatomy group. Five out of six of you know all the material, are extremely skilled with the scalpel, and are perfectly comfortable with the human body."

"And number six?" Pok said.

"Terrible. Knows nothing. Total slacker. What grade will the group get?"

"Highest points."

"Exactly. But imagine that sixth student hogged all the scalpels. And blurted out all the wrong answers before anyone else could."

"The group fails."

"Ah, but let's say this sixth student is not at the caliber of their peers but they are competent enough to pass."

"Then the group will pass," Pok said. "Just barely."

"That's what DigiTone does. It passes, just barely. As a partial agonist with a very strong affinity, it steals the show. It does just enough to quell the withdrawal symptoms. But it'll never feel as good as Synth. Remember these terms: *complete agonist*, *partial agonist*, and *antagonist*."

"What's its role in Agrypnia?"

"Unclear," Dr. Verik said. "More and more I'm thinking of Agrypnia as a neurological disorder. Different patients have their specific ailments based on their enhancement histories. Jillian with her legs, Buddy with his pH manipulation. The core points to a neurotoxic process. DigiTone should at least buy us time to find the real treatment."

"People make Synth out of DigiTone," Pok said. "Could Synth be better for Agrypnia?"

"If DigiTone is a Band-Aid, Synth is a Band-Aid that can create its own scars."

Pok remembered something Dr. Soft said all the way back at Adjustment. "What about shepherd-reactive proteins? Should we be monitoring that, too?"

"Far ahead of you. While SRP has been a good predictor of withdrawal symptoms I'm not finding any correlation with Agrypnia's presentation."

A tall nurse, his uniform tied twice at the cuffs, rolled a busy supply cart up to the table. Dr. Verik told him Buddy's medication changes.

"DC uric acid times three days," the nurse confirmed. "Start DigiTone. Got it."

"Dose twice a day. Let me know if he doesn't take it well." Dr. Verik eyed a stack of papers in the nurse's cart. "Jillian Joseph made it to the unit."

"The new pendant? Her BP's all over the place. And she has the most bizarre lower extremity swelling I've ever seen."

"Student Doctor Morning and I saw her in the HemoStat. FLT and DigiTone. Let's see how she does on that."

"What about Carve Bee honey?" Pok said.

Dr. Verik considered. "Let's add CBH to her regimen."

The nurse frowned. "CBH?"

"Carve Bee honey. Not the breakfast kind. Strain eight-thirty-six, specifically. I'll have it shipped up to the unit; just make sure it's on her med list."

"We're going to need more night staff," the nurse said.

"How's that?" Dr. Verik said.

"Almost all the patients have insomnia. The new reported it as well."

A shadow passed over Dr. Verik's face. "I'll put in for the extra staffing."

As Dr. Verik recorded these changes in Jillian's chart, the nurse stepped to Pok. Bald-headed, clean-shaven, with brown, bushy eyebrows, he towered over him. They shook hands. "Lemi."

"Pok. Are you the charge nurse?"

"I'm flattered. And I am." As he spoke, his tongue pressed against the prominent front gap in his otherwise perfect teeth. His eyes held a serious kindness. "I heard about you. Nurse Holly had only good things to say."

Nurse Holly definitely did *not* have good things to say. "I can explain," Pok said.

"No need. If Dr. V likes you, that's good enough for me." Nurse Lemi left to put in Dr. Verik's orders.

"You're worried about the insomnia," Pok said to Dr. Verik. Whispers from his father's room filled his head, leaked from his pores, and seemed to reverberate around his mentor. Insomnia had kicked off this whole strange and bizarre time in his life. "Why?"

"Poor sleep makes everything worse." Dr. Verik stood, oblivious to the surrounding aura. "Read everything you can about technology withdrawal. We'll reconvene tomorrow."

Their eyes connected for the briefest moment before she stepped off the unit. No more than a second, maybe a half. That sliver of time was enough for Pok to see something Dr. Verik couldn't hide from him, even if a large part was hiding it from herself.

When it came to the insomnia, his mentor was lying.

The Ventricle librarian helped Pok locate several research papers and articles written about withdrawing after chronic technology exposure. Some postulated that digital information restructured the brain to limit focus and critical thinking. One theory blamed prolonged exposure to artificial lights and used eye movement desensitization and reprocessing therapy as examples of how ocular movements could reverse neurological damage. Another stated that the removal of a particular silicon isotope after years of accumulation caused a slow and steady full-body withdrawal. Only one or two studies looked to markers outside of shepherd-reactive proteins.

What did it all mean? What did Dr. Verik want him to learn?

Tired and frustrated, he shifted to studying. That quickly went downhill. On the page, the words from his Life Cycles lecture notes converged and danced around each other. Fatigue chewed at his focus. *Preeclampsia, preeclampsia.* The compound term broke apart on his mind's tongue. He pulled his cap down over his eyes and imagined himself roaming new, freshly rendered landscapes on the video game *Impact.*

"That's some top-tier studying." James's voice grounded him. Pok jerked forward; his knees popped against the side of the table. Pages fell onto the floor. As James collected them, Anji and Rodge sat around the table.

"The Grips," Rodge said, reading over Pok's arm. In addition to bolding and underlining at the top of the page, he'd scribbled it many times over in the margins. "Sounds like an STD. Where have I heard that before?"

"It's a disorder that's only affecting pendants," Pok said.

"It's like a prolonged withdrawal," Anji said. "It's driven a lot of people to go back to shepherd cities."

They all looked at her. She placed a finger on a page of notes and opened her textbook, the part of her brain dedicated to studying undisturbed. Then, slowly aware of the ensuing silence, she lifted her gaze.

"What? Don't you ever actually talk to your patients? It's very specific." Pok had seen a lot in Anji's eyes since knowing her as a classmate: determination, annoyance, confidence, and the anxiety to perform. Now, for the first time, he saw the beginnings of fear. "As if it were created for outsiders who try to live here."

There it was. The reality no one wanted to face. They held their collective breaths. Even Anji seemed shaken by her own accusation.

James finally spoke. "You don't believe that, do you? Buying another company is one thing, but setting off a disease . . ."

"Maybe it was an accident?" Rodge said.

"A very convenient accident," Anji said.

The librarian, a woman with pale, olive-hued skin, frizzy brown hair tied back in a quick ponytail, and full cheeks that swayed when she walked, came up to them and hissed, "This is a quiet zone!"

James placed a gentle finger on Pok's papers. "Is it possible this Grips thing has something to do with Odysseus's disease? His family had some type of genetic disorder that caused insomnia, right?"

"North American sleeping sickness," Anji said. "That's what Julian Shepherd and his father died of. A descendant of fatal familial insomnia, it causes insomnia that eventually kills you."

"Damn," Rodge said. "Is it triggered by having small children?"

"Is that what Dr. Verik tried to cure in Odysseus?" James said.

My dad treated Odysseus. Pok couldn't bring himself to say that. Wouldn't say that. "She doesn't talk about it."

James sat back. Pok thought the topic was over.

"All of Dr. Verik's treatment notes would be in the Vault."

"The Vault?" Pok said, leveling his voice.

"That's where they keep old medical records. And any sensitive research information or dark history. Shit, Zion probably is in there, too." James raised a hand, likely mistaking the absolute horror on Pok's face for disdain. "My point is that Odysseus's file would be there."

"I'm not asking Dr. Verik for any more special favors," Pok said.

"Anji has access." James's voice trailed under her ice-cold stare. "And apparently doesn't want anyone to know that."

"Limited access," she said. "My sponsor has to let me in every time. And you ever heard of HIPAA? Going through a random patient's chart is a direct violation."

"Unless it's for research purposes," James said.

"Savage rebuttal," Rodge said.

"If you get on a research project with one of the Council professors, that could be a way in," James said. "They all have access to the Vault."

"I bet Dr. Soft would jump at the opportunity," Rodge said. "The two of you could research new ways to style hair."

"You know what my research project would be?" Pok said. " 'Do wheelchairs spread hospital disease?' "

"Whoa!" Rodge said. "Foul on the play!"

"Seriously, people?" The librarian had popped back up at their table.

"It's the acoustics, I swear," Rodge said.

The librarian made eye contact with each of them before returning to her desk. She continued to stare, long and hard, until another student approached her for help.

"What about Dr. Lowry?" James whispered. "She seems to like you. And she sits on the Council. She'd definitely have Vault access."

"And why, exactly, am I trying to get into the Vault?"

"Because you're curious. Just like we are. Whatever Dr. Verik did to Odysseus, maybe it makes all this make sense."

Anji began to gather her things.

"Where are you going?" James said, half rising with her.

"To find another table. I came to study."

"She's right," Pok said. Anji sat back down. "I'll figure this out."

They sat in silence, studying, organizing, procrastinating. Despite the hard conversation, there persisted a good, studious vibe. For the next hour, they were the librarian's dream. Rodge, after a few nods, shook his head, rolled back, gave a gesture, and was the first to retire. An hour later, Anji did the same. James rose to walk her out, a small bag in his hand. Drifting from the entrance, Pok heard the faint wisps of what sounded like an argument, quickly shushed by the librarian. James watched Anji leave and then stepped into the bathroom.

"Got my second wind," James said as he slid back into his seat. "You still good?"

"Savage, right?"

"Savage."

Pok pitted his burgeoning fatigue against James's endurance. Why did it feel like a competition? And what was the prize? A shitty tomorrow?

As Pok drifted, James remained alert and focused. It couldn't be natural.

"James . . . what was in that bag?"

"Don't give me that, Pok. Please don't."

"Does Anji know?"

"What's there to know? It's just to get me through this beast of a class. I promise." James closed his text and stuffed it in his book bag. "I'm done. You staying?"

"Yeah," Pok said. "For a little bit."

James tapped the table with two fingers and left Pok to it. His piles of disarrayed notes, articles, and texts all of a sudden looked overwhelming and daunting. A few minutes into reviewing the research on withdrawals, trying to consolidate some message to take back to Dr. Verik, his mind went to Life Cycles and its overwhelming curriculum. Shifting from his notes to the text was like jumping from a pond into an ocean. He pulled out a fresh piece of paper, titled it *Research Ideas*, and spent the next half hour doodling in the margins.

It was a long night.

Thirty-Eight

LIFE CYCLES

Overnight notes slipped under their doors informed of the next morning's Life Cycles location: the maternity ward. One North was a ground-level unit on the far side of campus, opposite the HemoStat. Pok kept his gaze low as he crossed University and walked the hospital perimeter. He'd considered checking on Jillian before Cycles but didn't want to disturb her sleep.

Is it fatal?

Let's take it one day at a time.

They'd traveled together. Would he be next? Shouldn't he be next? His heels hard against the cold morning ground, he suddenly became hyper-aware of his body. Was his version of the Grips lying dormant, waiting for the right moment to take him out?

"Lost in thought?"

Pok started at James's words. His friend met his stride.

"Lowry's going to dump on us today. I can feel it. I like her. My sleep schedule doesn't, though. Anj! Rodge!"

Pok sidestepped and whispered in James's ear, "Your eyes are red."

A part of James's face soured. His euphoria, however, stayed intact. "Breathe, Pok. I got it."

"Until you don't."

James gave Pok's shoulder a double squeeze and whispered back, "I'm serious. Back off."

"You boys good?" Rodge said through a wide yawn. He pushed himself up the wheelchair ramp perpendicular to the stairs outside One North. "Excuse me. Gremlins were up early this a.m."

"Just catching up on study habits," Pok said.

One North was a sprawling, open-floor unit with maybe a dozen laboring mothers. Raised gardens lined the space. Women in long gowns that hung down from their uniformly large bellies moved among evenly spaced beds encased in thick curtains. Each patient found balance in community and privacy. If Florence had delivered here, would she have still developed the psychosis?

Dr. Lowry waved them over. A near-term woman with lines of dancing colors tattooed up her arms sat on the end of the bed.

"Good morning, my students," Dr. Lowry said. "My wonderful, bright-eyed students. That's a life cycle in itself, you know? The hope and vigor of youth. Welcome to Labor and Delivery. Today we have the pleasure of talking with Zainep, a beloved patient of mine."

"You all are very lucky." Zainep's tired smile curled into a grimace. She touched her belly and stiffened against the contractions. After, she took Dr. Lowry's hand in hers and stood. "Can we walk?"

"Of course," Dr. Lowry said. "As we walk, class, see what you notice."

Zainep was in no rush and neither was Dr. Lowry. The class collectively inched forward. Anji moved to the front, already scribbling notes.

"Remind me," Dr. Lowry said, "this is your third?"

"Ha!" The woman side-eyed her doctor as they began to step in stride and laughed again. "It's my fourth."

"Veteran. You should be teaching the class."

Patient and physician, mother and provider, walked in tandem conversation around the L&D ward. The class drank in their discourse from a distance, a stolen privilege. Dr. Lowry turned toward the students while walking backward, not missing a beat.

"Your first pop quiz," she said. "What did you notice that's different in our physiology?"

"She's a little out of breath," Pok said. Dr. Lowry signaled for him to speak up. He did. "Breathing faster than you, at least. Before we started walking your breaths were in sync, more or less."

"Exactly." Dr. Lowry stilled Zainep with a touch to the shoulder. She outlined her talk with gestures to her belly. "There's a whole person growing in the uterus, which pushes up into the abdominal cavity. Where does everything go? Farther up. This increases the pressure in the chest, making less room for oxygen flow, and necessitating quicker, shallow breaths to keep up with the body's oxygen requirements.

"What else? Did anyone notice anything about me?" After some silence, Dr. Lowry continued, "I was walking a little bit ahead of her, looking around a lot, and even put my arm out when a nurse passed with a cart. I took on a protective mode. And it wasn't voluntary. One of the only identified human pheromones is emitted during the early stages of labor. It causes anyone around to go into protection mode. This way the mother can focus on things like getting through contractions.

"Finally, what do you notice about the unit overall?"

"There's a lot of pregnant women," Rodge said.

Dr. Lowry smiled. Out of all of Pok's professors, she had the best sense of humor. "We don't monitor a lot on the labor and delivery floors. While the observer effect I mentioned hasn't been formerly described when it comes to the essence, we fully recognize and respect it on L and D. Having a fetal heart rate monitor on at all times, for example, not only affects the team's decision-making and the mother's stress, it affects the fetal heart rate itself. But having no fetal monitor, while common in midwifery, would make any OB-GYN nervous, and rightfully so. So what do we do? We observe the rhythms of a unit. Small changes and fluctuations direct us toward specific elements that might need attention."

Their lap done, Zainep climbed back on the bed. After helping her up, Dr. Lowry walked the class through her physical exam. As Pok felt her would-be fourth child kick against her belly, he thought of his father and Florence and the smell of tea.

Pok waited until the class had dispersed to approach Dr. Lowry, who tended to a laboring mother.

"Let's walk," Dr. Lowry said to Pok. She waited for the patient's contraction to pass, assured her she'd soon return, and led Pok onto the unit's walking strip. "Student Doctor Pok. How are you enjoying my class?"

"I was told medical school isn't for enjoyment," he said.

"That's absurd. It's like saying sex isn't for pleasure. There's the purpose and then there's the element that brings us coming back."

"I'm enjoying Life Cycles," he said. "There's a lot to learn, but you make it fun."

"That's my goal. So, you want to do a research project?"

"Is it that obvious?"

"It's the season. The med students are trying to make a name for themselves, line up plans for their last summer. I can always tell. What are you thinking? Besides setting yourself up for Honors?"

Honors? What the hell was that? He'd have to ask James.

"The maternal death rates you talked about are interesting. Definitely in comparison to AI-run—"

"AI-assisted," she reminded.

"AI-assisted hospitals. I'm wondering about internal comparisons."

"You mean like in Black versus white mothers? I've asked the same question, and the disparity has nearly been erased in New Orleans, I'm proud to say."

"I was thinking native-born versus pendant patients," Pok said. "Specifically in the quality of care they receive. It's crucial that Hippocrates excels in the last branch of medicine even TSO agrees should be human-led. Any disparities could jeopardize that."

"Interesting. Very interesting. You're the one I didn't deliver, right?" Dr. Lowry lowered her voice. "Your father was Phelando? His hair was beautiful, just like yours. You look like him. I bet you get that a lot."

"I don't."

"I didn't interact much with him myself; his trips were so short and infrequent. But this last time he consulted with me about a special case. The mom is here now; I understand you know her. She was right to hide it. Her daughter has a chromosomal abnormality—a trisomy—that could be fatal or could be benign. I saw the girl in clinic and she seems to be developing well. Time will tell. The shepherds would have mandated a miscarriage. A mother's instinct to protect can manifest in a myriad of ways. Hers was paranoia that bled over to psychosis. Crude, but effective. To a point."

A lump grew in Pok's throat. He gave the smallest nod. Dr. Lowry offered a soft, brief hand of support.

"Is a one percent chance of success worth the disappointment of failure? I think so. Eugenics can look good to an algorithm. Congenital diabetes goes down if Black female births go down. Suicide goes down after a decline in populations more susceptible to suicide. Down syndrome goes down if geriatric pregnancies don't go to term, or don't happen at all. All these outcomes can be deleted, in the name of the seemingly good.

"As you study these things, as you try to find reasons and answers, remember that humans are flawed but changeable. They can be persuaded. AI takes the data that's there and spits out an answer. It fixes the problem on paper. That's what the shepherds are good for. Paper." Dr. Lowry picked up a sheet and crumbled it. "I must say, I'm afraid of what you'll uncover. Which makes it worthwhile, doesn't it?"

"You'll work with me?" Pok said.

"You ask good questions. I have some patients in mind that you can interview."

"I was thinking of something broader." Pok was careful with his words. "Is there a way to go over past cases?"

Dr. Lowry slowed in her step. Very slight. She'd just told him how one could be unaware of their own responses. Did she notice this? Did the suspicion apparent in her body language make it up to her thoughts? Her pace returned to normal. The moment passed.

"Find me when you're done with classes today," she said. "We'll visit the Vault together."

The brass door knocker sent three quick and low vibrations into the Paper Mill. The street was quiet; the shops had settled after the morning rush. Pok had been halfway to his next class when the impossible idea ravished him. Even as he waited for someone to answer, hoping no one would, he wondered just what the hell he was doing.

Gil opened the door.

"I'd invite you in, but Chandra just went down for a nap," he said. "That haircap's fire. What's up?"

"I need a ball of clay."

Thirty-Nine

SECOND OPINION

Pok, the last to arrive, took a seat in the back of Sims's Craft. Either she didn't notice him or she no longer cared. After spending the whole morning on his feet, fatigue was a heavy blanket. Comprehension waned; he couldn't keep track of more than two words in a sentence. Keeping his eyes open became painful. His head tipped forward; the sharp sensation of falling jolted him alert.

A slow, long blink and everyone disappeared. The lecture hall was cleared out. The overhead lights, dimmed for the overhead projector, shone bright and full. Sims stood leaning against the wall. Pok couldn't tell if she was grinning or frowning.

"Welcome back to the land of the living."

"Dean Sims, I was just—"

"Save it. We all need more sleep. I can't fault you for finding it here." She slid into the next chair and was somehow still looking down at him. "That was some stunt you pulled."

"Stunt?" Pok said.

Dean Sims pulled up his folded desk and placed on to it a copy of the *Second Opinion*. The headline read, *Head Editor Locked Away in Amygdala, Experimentations Feared.*

Pok snatched up the paper and read that Jerry Finn, a well-respected leader in the non-native community and head editor of the *Second Opinion*, was refused adequate medical service at the hospital's emergency department and was instead committed for psychiatric treatment.

"As our readers know and respect," the article read, "Mr. Finn is an ardent supplier of vital medications of which the Iron Fortress has become a unilateral regulator. He has been a beacon of support and knowledge in light of recent global developments while our 'healers' hide and panic in silence. We suspect that a disgruntled student—and customer of Mr. Finn's—was involved in the mistreatment of our head editor. When Mr. Finn pleaded for the medical attention he deserves, he was found to be mentally unstable and transferred to the Amygdala, where he's currently being held against his will."

Pok's internal rebuttal didn't matter. Many people would read this and, even if they didn't believe all of it, the seed would be planted.

"You got lucky," Dean Sims said. "He could have named you. For the hospital, it's a big mess. People drastically change their lives to come here, to be free from manipulation, and if they think we are just as bad as the shepherds, we lose our ability to help them."

"He knew about the framing, the hit, everything," Pok said. "He said he was in contact with the shepherds. I was afraid."

"You're my responsibility. That includes your safety. I told you that day one." Dean Sims tilted her head back and rubbed her neck. "I don't know what he made you do. I just want to know that it's over."

"It's over."

"Good." Sims took the article, refolded Pok's desk, and left him to his thoughts. He'd felt so good—so *accomplished*—when his plan for Jerry had come together. How naive he'd been. The editor of the *Second Opinion* couldn't be silenced. His readership was wide and diverse. Many newcomers, hoping to find refuge from the ever controlling algorithms, looked to *Second Opinion* for a palatable balance between the old and the new. How much damage had been done because Pok couldn't figure out a way to say no—to Kris, to Jerry, to himself?

Of all the things uncertain, one was clear: time would tell.

Jerry and his article nagged him the rest of the day.

Pok's thighs burned by the time he stepped onto the Six South landing and the low thrum of a violin, which he at first thought was his blood in his ears, relieved him of some of his thoughts. Dr. Verik watched the unit from the door. The physician's mouth twitched as Pok came beside her. His mentor held out her hand. Pok pinched the edge of her cuff, swore he could feel a groove, and they set off at a stride.

A nervous, restless energy vibrated the air. Patients yelled to each other across the ward.

"The rhythm is off," Dr. Verik said. "It is in flux, it is dangerous, but it still exists. Let's check on your friend."

Jillian sat reclined, lost in a book, in her curtained-off section of the unit. She looked up only when they were close enough to bring shadow. Her humming—slightly off sync with the music—fizzled out. Her eyelids hung low. Her mouth pulled to one side in a grimace her smile couldn't hide.

"Still not sleeping?" Pok said.

"Not a wink. But the honey did relax me. It gets lively here, but I like it. It's nice not being the only one up all night." Jillian yawned and rubbed her eyes. She picked up the teacup beside her, saw it was empty, and rested it in her lap. "Going to the bathroom has been better. Not perfect. But better. Maybe we're on the right track?"

"I hope so." Pok checked her log. In addition to CBH-infused tea twice daily, she was also taking DigiTone and had two FLT hours a day. "Have you walked yet today?"

She wagged her finger and pulled the sheets from over her legs. Though the texture hadn't changed, the difference in size was substantial. Either the left had swelled in the night or the right had atrophied. As she massaged them, tremors hit her spine. She planted both feet, slowed to a stand, and quickly lost her balance. Pok caught her. Her hands were clammy and tremulous. Her body smelled sour.

"Déjà vu," she said.

As she walked, she dipped to the left. Her face twisted in silent anguish.

"Watch me," Pok said. Watching wasn't necessary for the syncing, but it couldn't hurt. "Watch my feet."

And sync they did. The more they walked, the more Jillian's dip shifted. Her legs changed size in real time. Color, too. Before, the sections had been clearly demarcated. Now, the borders blurred.

"Why would CBH be helping Jillian's condition?" Dr. Verik said once

Jillian was back in her bed. "She doesn't have an infection. And she's not pregnant."

"Charge?" Pok said.

Dr. Verik gestured: *Go on.*

Since being grossly unprepared the first time Dr. Verik had asked about CBH, Pok had done some reading. While he was still skeptical about the idea of honey as medicine, many aspects made sense.

"Carve Bee honey as a whole is neutrally charged," he said. "But it breaks down to both positive and negative components in the gut. If this disorder is about lack of balance, then these polar charges can bind to and neutralize disturbances in the blood."

"He's good," Jillian said, almost proud. "You should make him into a doctor or something."

"I'm trying. This is promising, but we aren't out of the woods yet. If today goes well, maybe we can get you back home tomorrow." Dr. Verik half turned to leave, then said, "What questions do you have for us?"

Jillian reached out and squeezed the physician's hand. Dr. Verik stiffened but didn't move away.

"Thank you. Both of you."

Once back at the nursing station, Dr. Verik lathered her hands. Pok did the same. They sat.

"The CBH is promising," she said. "But, like DigiTone, I suspect it's only a temporary fix. What's wrong with your legs?"

Pok hadn't noticed he'd been rubbing them. He stopped and folded his hands. "Sorry."

"Roll up your pants." Dr. Verik examined him. Physically, his legs looked fine but tingled at her touch.

Dr. Verik sat back, thoughtful. "You have a great alignment with her. It makes sense, you both being from New York and traveling here together. Nurse Lemi." The passing nurse paused at his name. "After we're done here, I want three samples of Student Doctor Morning here's blood."

"Got it." He nodded to Pok. "Come find me when you're ready."

Pok pulled his pants legs down. "Should I be worried?"

"No," Dr. Verik said. "Just cautious. I'll run tests to make sure. Our minds can have great effect over our bodies. Make sure you rest well. Eat and hydrate. And meditate." After some thought, Dr. Verik tapped her mouth, satisfied. She stood. "You will come to know backward and forward every patient. You'll present each new admission, every day. I care about their lives under the shepherds. Their educational path, their jobs, their most-used tech, any surgeries, any medical care, all of it. I care about why they came to New Orleans. How they came. And then, once you have a comprehensive understanding of all of that: how long they've been here and what deficits they're experiencing."

The music changed. A soft string instrument. Pok's disparate thoughts, insecurities, and doubts floated in the melody's milk. Present? Each new patient?

"You're conflicted," Dr. Verik said.

"I'm worried about class." Only in speaking it did Pok become aware of the concern. "It's a lot, Dr. Verik."

"I was a student once." Dr. Verik held up a hand. "That wasn't confrontation. I was *only* a student. And it was a different time. Simpler, where it was just us, the medicine, and patients. I'm asking you to be more. Maybe I'm asking too much."

"What time should I be here tomorrow?" Pok said.

Dr. Verik touched two fingers to Pok's arm, just above the elbow. Before Pok could register the uncharacteristic warmth from his mentor, Dr. Verik had turned away.

"Half an hour past sunrise. No sooner. That gives time for rest. Theirs and yours. We'll meet right before your first class. Go through the patients. Don't worry about form. That'll come. Oh, and learn how to draw blood. You shouldn't depend on the nursing staff for things a doctor should know how to do." Dr. Verik turned in her hands a vial of Carve Bee honey; the thick liquid ran down the sides. "We may get ahead of this thing, but it's not going to be easy."

Forty

THE VAULT

I never understood all the security," Dr. Lowry said as they descended into the tunnels running underneath Hippocrates. The numerous students and doctors dwindled as they left the Ventricle's matrix. They turned down a long, wide section that Pok recognized from when he'd gotten lost. He now noticed intertwining twin snake bodies engraved in the length of the walls.

A volunteer, his feet lounging on the desk, snapped to a respectful attention when he caught Dr. Lowry's approach. He took her ID, clumsily flipped through his logbook, and had her sign beside her name. This done, he came down from the elevated platform and nodded for Dr. Lowry to insert her key under the knob while he did the same on the adjacent wall. In his pocket, Pok turned over Gil's ball of clay.

They entered a small, dimly lit room with three rows of shelves that went from floor to ceiling. Ladders hooked to the top of each row. Specimen display cases lined the circular wall, more for aesthetics than instruction. A central pair displayed a large mouse in one and a coiled python in the other, hissing at each other.

"I presume this is your first Vault dive?" Dr. Lowry said.

"It is," Pok said. "It's smaller than I thought it would be."

Dr. Lowry gave him a side smile as she led him down the middle aisle and right through to the other side of the room. She pushed through a set of doors not visible from the entrance. A long, deep staircase descended into a winding dark.

"Watch your step," Dr. Lowry said. "This fall could be fatal."

Sure enough, Pok's foot slipped halfway down. He caught himself on the banister.

"I obviously spoke too soon," Pok said at the bottom. A long hallway stretched before them. There must have been nearly a hundred doors, each labeled simply with a number.

Dr. Lowry pulled out her key at room eighteen. Pok's fingers caressed the smooth lump of clay. Would he really use it? He wouldn't know until he did.

"This room is OB-GYN?" Pok said.

"Just obstetrics. And this is specifically the mortality and morbidity wing. Room seventeen is the happier stuff."

Room eighteen's three floor-to-ceiling shelves promised extensive documentation from a specific subset of medicine. They walked down the third aisle, Dr. Lowry running her hand along the indexing tabs. She stopped, dragged over a nearby table that sent a loud, echoing screech, and stacked files on top.

"Here are the mortality and morbidity statistics for the last twenty years. Each has date of birth and origin of birth. I suggest looking at medications received, timing of medications, differences in recommendation for induction versus waiting versus emergency surgery. Let your intuition guide you. Have at it."

For the next hour Dr. Lowry sat across from Pok, doodling, as he went through the data. His mind perpetually wandered out and down the hall, searching for a special room for Odysseus's case, searching for Zion. He imagined a door exquisitely marked with provocative serpentine and rodential imagery. He could physically search if not for Dr. Lowry. Down here, in the Vault, under her admission, he was her responsibility.

Which was where the clay came in. As his fingers turned the lump, Dr. Lowry—as if their essences were in communication—traced her doodles with the tip of her key. This would either work perfectly or fail miserably. Now or never.

"I think I have enough," Pok said.

Dr. Lowry put her key down and picked up her pen. "You need help putting everything back?"

"No, I got it." As he rose, he pressed his thighs into the table's side, lifting it. Dr. Lowry sprang back. Pok forced himself to continue. The table flipped. The papers went everywhere. Somewhere underneath them, nearly inaudible but a beacon to listening ears, the brief sound of a key hitting the floor.

"Shit," Pok said, laying it on thick. He dropped down to the floor so quickly pain shot up his knee. "Sorry. My leg fell asleep."

"It's okay," Dr. Lowry said. She reshelved the stacks as he made them. As he was putting together the last pile, he saw in his periphery her hands touch her pockets.

"Have you seen my . . . key." But the key was back on the table. He'd found it and put it there for her. Of course he had. Why wouldn't he?

She picked it up slow, curious. Pok forced himself not to notice, not to look. He stacked the last section of patient records and, when enough time had passed, sat back and looked up at her. She'd put the key away.

"Thanks for the help." Pok made sure to keep eye contact. Any shiftiness now and she'd know.

"Anytime," she said.

"Classic pin tumbler design," Gil said as he examined the flattened clay mold. "Imprint is good, clear. The specificity of the pin tells me it's important."

Gil sucked his teeth, beckoned Pok to lean in, and shifted the mold under the light. Pok recognized it immediately when he saw it.

"This is a physician's insignia," he said. "Since it's on here, I have to duplicate that, too. Cool? Cool. Do I want to know what this opens?"

"You don't," Pok said.

Forty-One

SIX SOUTH

Pok arrived on Six South with the sun on his heels. He found Jillian with half a blanket over her eyes, mouth slightly open, softly snoring. Her hand hooked a half-finished paperback. He checked the overnight notes hanging off her bed. She'd only started sleeping in the last hour. The slow rise and fall of her chest aligned with her throat's low rattle.

He jotted down from her report whatever might be relevant for presenting to Dr. Verik and moved on. He made his way around the unit, checking the charts, seeing what blood results had come back, and talking to any patients he could. He saved the new admit for last.

"She's a handful," Nurse Lemi said. "She came in overnight from the ID unit, quite agitated. She's calmed down, for now."

Pok read over her chart. The dense report summarized her clinical course in the infectious disease unit. After a week of treatment for pneumonia on Five South with minimal improvement, Janine Murphy had been transferred to Six South. All the way at the bottom was a quickly scribbled reason for transfer: *Immune System Failure, Overt Psychosis. R/O the Grips.*

Dr. Verik entered Six South and came straight over. "You seen the new yet?"

"I was just about to. I went over all the current patients."

"Always do the new admissions first." Dr. Verik took the report. "Severe immune deficiency. Gets better and then crashes. Granulocytes completely obliterated. Let's do this one together."

Janine Murphy stretched into a yawn as they approached her bedside. Pok grimaced, hit by a wall of decay and musk. Janine remained oblivious to both the smell and his reaction to it.

"What did I do to deserve such wonderful-looking doctors to come see me?" she said. Tired fingers went up to her ear, where multiple unfilled piercings dotted her lobes like stars. She paused there, feeling the holes as if they each held a memory.

"I'm Dr. Verik and this is Student Doctor Morning, my apprentice. May we examine you?"

"Of course."

Dr. Verik walked Pok through the exam. She paused in places where the patient's anima was off. An irregular heartbeat, the varying temperature from one side of the body to the next. They listened to her lungs and heard the variance of shifting fluid. The air around her moved as she did, its variety of smells flowing like a lava lamp. Sunken eyes sat atop cobbled, black-stained cheeks.

"If you could ask her one question, what would it be?" Dr. Verik said.

A thousand choices flew past. Pok blindly plucked one out of the sky. "What did you do for work? Before you came here?"

"I used to be a hospice nurse," Janine said as Dr. Verik pressed into her abdomen with one hand and examined her pulse with the other.

"You must have been around a lot of sick people," Dr. Verik said.

"More than. The whole facility was automated. By the end all the patients yearned for someone to talk to. Someone human, you know?"

"Did you get sick a lot?"

"The shepherds took care of that. We got daily supplements custom made based on what was going around the facility. It worked, too. I thought I was invincible." She took a moment to taste her own words. "It messed me up, huh?"

"You couldn't have known. But it sounds like you did a lot of good. It's important for people to feel peace in their last moments." And then, to Pok, stepping back. "Neuro exam. I suspect deficits. We just have to find them."

Alas, her reflexes were annoyingly unremarkable. Muscle strength fine, joint mobility looked good. No sensory deficits. He walked her.

Coordination, gait, and proprioception, all fine. He stepped back when he thought he was done. Dr. Verik took his place at the bedside.

"What's your name?" she said.

"Janine Murphy. Middle name, too?"

"Where are we?"

She laughed. "In my home, of course."

"City?"

"Philadelphia."

"You're in a New Orleans hospital. Remember?"

She frowned, then smiled. "Yes. I'm here to help a few people transition."

Dr. Verik cupped her hand around Janine's left foot. "May I?" When the patient nodded, she took off her sock. Between the big and neighboring toe was a blackened crust of ooze and dried blood. She took off the other sock; the right foot was normal. Dr. Verik beckoned Pok to follow her to the nursing station.

"What are you noticing?" she said.

"Her immune system is failing," Pok said. "Overstimulation from the supplements?"

"I like your thinking, but it's just the opposite. Her body went so long without utilizing the process of identifying a foreign body, tagging it, and building a defense that it forgot how to. Her immune system is like someone trying to run a marathon after years of inactivity."

"She's been here a couple years," Pok said.

"And her immune system rebounded. Which is why the last two years have been largely uneventful. But now, all of a sudden, it's like someone turned back the clock." Dr. Verik's pause left room for the unspoken words: *someone, or something.* "What do you want to do for her?"

"Flashing lights, DigiTone, and Carve Bee?"

"Agreed. Right now we're throwing everyone the kitchen sink. Hopefully, over time we can revise our treatments."

Pok had a burning question he didn't know how to ask. "Why did she . . ."

"Smell like that?"

"Yeah."

"I suspect her dying mast cells are accumulating in her sweat glands and causing necrosis."

"Oh God."

"She's sweating rot. Quite literally." Dr. Verik looked off, toward the other side of the unit. Her head bobbed to the patient-made melody drifting from it. "Have you learned yet how to draw blood?"

The question alone turned Pok's stomach. "I will today."

"You'll show me your phlebotomy skills tomorrow, then. Good luck with your studies."

"I got a second to teach you," Nurse Lemi said as Pok loaded the last batch of Janine's blood to centrifuge. The machine started up; knots in Pok's stomach matched the acceleration. "I overheard."

"Tomorrow?" Pok said.

"Maybe," Nurse Lemi said. "Just let me know."

Pok returned to Six South after the day's classes, half of which he'd slept through, to check on Jillian and the new admit.

"Ms. Joseph left," Nurse Lemi said. He was on his way out after what looked like an exhausting shift. "Self-discharged. She left this note."

Thanks for everything, Doctor. The offer to come visit still stands. PS: Ole tick bite.

Over the next month Pok was both a full-time student doctor and a full-time wards apprentice. He often woke up with heavy eyes and cold bones. Each day had at least one overnight Agrypnia admission to Six South. The vast majority stayed for no more than two or three days, just enough time for stabilization. His head ached from administering FLT, measuring out CBH, and "sitting" with his patients. Most got better. Most went home.

Classes marched on. Lowry's Life Cycles, Sims's The Art and Craft of Medicine, Soft's history, and Granger's Pharm. Small group lunches. Grand Rounds in Genesis. Tuesday and Thursdays were "enrichment" days, meant to empower students to take control of their education, do independent studies, or pick up a hobby. Really it just gave Pok pressure to do more. Practice all day in the HemoStat or go to office hours? Even with those days, there was never enough time. More and more he found himself having to choose. Would he be reprimanded for skipping class? Or was learning what to sacrifice and what to prioritize an expected part of becoming a doctor?

He stopped by the Vault entrance whenever he was going or coming from the Ventricle. He soon knew the nuances of the various student volunteers. Which had extensive security practices. Which glanced up just enough to confirm the person entering wasn't a shepherd robot. A third year dedicated to studying for Mobitz III only did night shifts and consistently fought sleep. One time—when the tunnels were particularly quiet, that day's fatigue actively playing with his mind—Pok stood there to see how long the nap lasted. Ten, maybe fifteen minutes. Just as he was considering turning his fantasy into reality, the medical student began to stir. Pok pocketed his counterfeit key and left before he was seen.

At the end of any weekday, when most students were getting a quick bite to eat to fuel an evening in the Ventricle, Pok went back to Six South. He tried to get there before Nurse Lemi signed out to the night team. Agrypnia manifested in vastly different ways; Pok made a game of tying each presentation to their past lives. Wild weight fluctuations? Childhood obesity that set off lifelong diet and caloric intake regulations. Painful coitus? Extensive use of intimacy apps that dictated everything, from masturbation practices to amount of lubricant used to intercourse playlist. Sudden vision loss? Dynamic corrective glasses that changed their prescription as often as the eyes moved, over a hundred thousand times a day.

The most common presentation proved transcendent of correlation and existed outside of rhyme or reason: a complete and utter inability to sleep that led to psychotic paranoia and autonomic instability.

For every patient they saw there were two or three they didn't. Reports came of non-natives, unable to take the withdrawals, scared for their own lives and those of their loved ones, leaving New Orleans back to their cities of origin. Dr. Verik began taking house calls, tending to patients too sick or too paranoid about what they'd read in the *Second Opinion* to come in.

Pok held down the fort while she was gone. He made sure FLT orders were in, CBH strains were aligned, and discharge papers were signed. Whenever a patient was transferred to the ICU he met with the receiving team to ensure continuity of care. His consistent, daily presence created a temporary morale that fostered trust in the chaos and kept hospital staff sane.

Soon, for better or for worse, every single patient on Six South knew his name.

Behind on class, Pok planned to get an early start on Six South and leave for The Art and Craft of Medicine before the morning rush. He was only to the fourth floor when the chaos descending the stairs told him he'd grossly miscalculated.

The unit's frenzy was midday level. Nurses yelled over one another. Somewhere in the fray a patient wailed for their father. He stepped onto the unit—narrowly dodging a rolling supply cart—and found Nurse Lemi.

"We just got slammed with three new admits," Nurse Lemi said.

"Does Dr. Verik know?"

"We paged her. No answer. This morning, you're our Dr. Verik." Nurse Lemi looked him over. "Get in or get out."

How the hell was he going to do three admissions in less than an hour?

"I'm in," Pok said, and got started.

Number one. A twenty-year-old, glass-trained social media dancer who had moved to New Orleans two years ago. The initial months inside the spires were characterized by nightly sleepwalking episodes that eventually resolved. Since, he'd become a regular and popular act at the Fusiform. A week ago the sleepwalking returned and now he couldn't consciously move his legs outside of REM sleep. Pok's exam found varying degrees of widespread muscle weakness.

Number two. An elderly woman with progressive dementia had immigrated to New Orleans fifteen years ago and had no reason to be going through withdrawals. Still, the Grips had somehow taken hold. She oscillated from worsening dementia—agitation, sundowning, and uncontrollable angst—to a full lucidity that her family hadn't seen in years. Pok caught her on a talkative upswing; the intake took twice as long.

Pok was exhausted by the time he came to the third and last overnight admission, an early thirties bakery owner and single mother from Houston, Texas. After her seven-year-old had nearly died from a burst appendix, she'd used glass literally around the clock to check his vital signs and metrics. When her son's acquired anxiety had bumped him from his school's gifted track, she'd found a job in New Orleans. They'd both adjusted well, with her son on track to enroll at Tulane University. Now she had the unshakable fear that her son was dead, even as he stood next to her. Reassurance only came from listening to his heartbeat or feeling his pulse. She constantly sought out both.

"Still no sign of Dr. Verik?" Pok asked Nurse Lemi at the station. The Art and Craft of Medicine had started five minutes ago. Pok hoped Dr. Verik and her scribe could sort through his pile of scribbled notes. Without looking up, Nurse Lemi handed Pok a folded note.

Business out in Mid-City. Put in admission orders. Be back soon.—Dr. Verik

"Apparently, she left it overnight," Nurse Lemi said. "I just found it."

"I can't," Pok said. "I have class. If I would have known—"

"It is not my job to make sure the doctors communicate. These patients need admission orders and charting."

"Could we do standard orders until this evening? I'll have more time."

"Again, that's not our job," Nurse Lemi said. "I'm making a report to the dean."

"No, no," Pok said. Why was Nurse Lemi making it so difficult for him? He knew how hard it was to work this unit. They were supposed to be a team. But there was currently no sympathy, only raw expectation. "I'll handle it."

Forty-Two

FAIR QUESTIONS

An hour later, Dr. Verik still absent, Pok dropped off the admission paperwork in Nurse Lemi's cart as he was talking to a patient and slipped away to avoid any questions. Two new admissions were on their way to the unit. If he left now, Pok could make it to class and be back in time to place the news' orders.

He regretted his decision as soon as he walked into history class. It would have been better to fail.

"Student Doctor Pok, come in, come in." Dr. Soft waved him over. The only vacant seat was between him and Anji. "We were just talking about the history of Agrypnia. I imagine you'll have much to contribute."

"History?" Pok said as he reluctantly sat beside the professor. The last time he was in this position he'd made a complete fool of himself. "It's a new disease."

"No disease is new. Not completely. Diseases come from something, just like you and me and everyone else in this room. This particular disorder, for example, could be rooted in otherwise routine withdrawals. It may be helpful to explore that origin. Pok, could you paint us a picture of your own journey with technology and dependence?"

Pok ignored the framing of the question. "I had glass and a shepherd companion for as long as I could remember. TSO probably knows everything about me."

"Remind the class what a 'companion' is?"

Pok hadn't thought of Kai in a while. "It's like a pet robot. Only it's constantly collecting data. You kind of forget it's a machine after a while."

"Do you feel, looking back, that the algorithm was a predetermining force in your life?"

"I always saw the shepherd recommendations as just that: recommendations," Pok said. "There were some things that would be very limiting, but I was still the one making the decisions."

"Your decision to come here, for one. I imagine for many people it's hard to detach from an all-knowing consultant. How do you think that leads to the withdrawals we see? Not the Agrypnia—we'll get to that—but what used to be normal withdrawals?"

"There are different theories," Pok said. He pulled topics they'd gone over in class. "The easiest explanation is that the body and mind acclimate to a certain way of living. In a new environment, the sensory intake is different and so neurotransmitters are different. Diet is different and so nutrient intake is different. That's why the symptoms are so widespread."

"Have you experienced any?"

The eyes on him, all around, stung. If Dr. Soft noticed, he didn't care. "Some. Only a little."

"It begs the question: What factor is different, between individuals?" Dr. Soft rotated positions of his thumb and index finger. "We also know that Synth is a popular sensory enhancer among urbanites. It can act on the same receptors as TSO proteins. We've seen it lessen withdrawal severity when used here. Do you think that what we're seeing in Agrypnia could be a manifestation of Synth withdrawal?"

"Synth has been around a lot longer than Agrypnia. And its withdrawal symptoms are well defined and usually self-limiting. This isn't a simple withdrawal."

Dr. Soft smiled. His eyes didn't.

"My mom's a neurologist," Dominik said, head and voice low. The illusion of an intimate conversation broke. All eyes on Pok. "She thinks it's all psychiatric. And that we're enabling the disorder by giving it a name."

"That's certainly an interesting perspective," Dr. Soft said.

Pok bristled, suddenly hot. "I have learned a lot about the mind-body connection—especially here. The autonomic instability and organ changes can't be purely psychiatric. Neurological, maybe."

"This all started when *he* got here." It took Pok a second to register the voice: Carolyne Burns. She'd been so nice to him during their brief interactions. But now her words dripped with disdain and even fear. Pok's breath caught; he coughed to cover it.

Instead of protecting him, Dr. Soft turned the knife.

"What do you mean by that, Student Doctor Carolyne?"

"We were fine," she said. "The shepherds left us alone. Until he came. It can't be coincidence. How did he get into the school, anyway? He didn't go to any of the same programs as us. He didn't take our classes. A scroller with an MD can become a nurse if they're lucky. It's ridiculous."

"Fair questions," Dr. Soft said. "But I would like to remind everyone of an oldie but a goodie: correlation does not equal causation."

Fair questions? *Fair questions?* The band of pressure returned under Pok's eyes. He tried to shake it off, but it held. He mentally pleaded with Dr. Soft to end the discussion. Instead, the professor checked over his scribe, as if to make sure the living history was perfectly captured.

Carolyne didn't let up. "With this amount of correlation I can't help but think Pok and the shepherds caused this whole thing. He grew up with them, is all I'm saying."

"The shepherds killed Dr. Phelando Morning," Pok said. The abated heat rose again. "Odysseus killed my dad. I would never work with him."

Though most eyes had been on him, no one met his gaze. Anji, the closest, pretended to flip through the assigned reading, though the discussion had strayed far from whatever was on the page. James wouldn't look his way. If Rodge was in the class, his chair was low, out of sight. Dr. Soft had a dumb look of detached curiosity, as if he were about to give a presentation. The world's edges blurred.

"What a lively discussion." Dr. Soft beamed. "We will definitely come back to this. I thank everyone for participating."

Pok went up to Dr. Soft as the class dispersed. The professor took a half step back. This reaction gently blew on the unfamiliar fire raging in Pok.

"Can we not do that?" Pok said. "Can we not make me the center of attention?"

"You're upset," Dr. Soft said. "I see that."

"I'm a student. A Student Doctor. I'm not an expert on the shepherds. I'm not an expert on the Grips. I'm here to learn, not to satisfy your curiosities. Everyone hates me now."

"Ah, I see," Dr. Soft said. His confidence had returned and, along with it, the edge of a smile. "Today's discussion didn't change people's feelings, only your awareness of them. You *are* in the center of whatever is happening here in New Orleans. That's a hard truth to carry, Student Doctor Pok. Kindly don't take it out on me."

The band intensified as Pok descended to the main lobby. He wavered between paths to the Ventricle, HemoStat, and Six South. There were patients to see, notes to study, problems to solve, but the pressure around his head pushed them all to secondary.

Wincing, he stepped into the hospital garden. He excused himself past patient and physician and health aide as he followed whatever footpath lay before him. He slowed when he saw the roses. The painful headache finally broke against the myriad of colors. Pok, remembering the last time he was here, circled the plot, seeking out yellow.

Sure enough, Kris sat against the stump-turned-secret hiding place, hunched over a drawing. He looked healthy and full. When he raised his head to get the next line of his sketch, he did a double take, waved at Pok, and put his pad aside.

"You looking for me?" Kris said.

"No," Pok said. "But I could use a friend."

"I never got a chance to thank you," Kris said as he scooted to make space for Pok against the stump. "For dealing with Jerry. Getting from under him has really been freeing."

"For both of us."

"I'm really sorry for even putting you in that situation. You had every right to tell me to kick rocks."

"I wanted to. Trust me."

"How is it?" Kris said. "Medical school and all?"

"Brutal," Pok said. "You've heard about the Grips?"

"Of course. Everyone's talking about it. It's like some sleeping sickness that makes people crazy, right?"

"Something like that. We still aren't sure what it is. Think of withdrawals but a hundred times worse." Pok bent forward to retrieve a fallen rose, its yellow petals still lively. "You said Odysseus wanted us to fail. Could this be how?"

"He didn't tell me his plans. But after what they did to me, I wouldn't put it past him. He hated Hippocrates. That much was clear." With his pencil, Kris traced lines in the dirt. "Is that what you're thinking? Odysseus created the Grips?"

"He was treated here when he was young for a genetic disorder that sounds very similar to whatever's going around."

"Odysseus using his own DNA as a bioweapon?" Kris ran his hand over his still-short hair. "That would be so him."

"His medical records might have some clue about a cure. I've thought about looking for them. They'd be in the Vault." Pok eyed Kris as he said this next, "Odysseus thinks Zion's there, too. You believe in it, right? You said you thought Zion was the reason I came."

"Can't you go and look?"

"It's too guarded. They have someone watching the door twenty-four seven."

"If anyone can find a way, you can."

GET THE FUCK OUT OF NEW YORK.

"Kris . . ." Pok twisted the rose stem between two fingers. Yellow fanned the air. "Is there anything you're not telling me?"

Ever since Kris had shown up in the HemoStat, Pok paid special attention to his friend's body language. Through all the noise, through what had become Kris's background anxiety, Pok watched for when the eye contact changed, when his body shrank, when the topic got particularly stressful. This was one of those times.

"I told you everything, Pok," Kris said. "I swear."

Pok wanted to believe him.

Forty-Three

REFLEXES

Pok was on Six South until midnight tucking in the new patients. With still no sign of Dr. Verik, he did just enough to keep Nurse Lemi from ringing the alarm. He got back to a dark and uncharacteristically quiet Tay Hall. He expected to spend an hour staring at the ceiling, replaying the day, but exhaustion proved to be the best hypnotic. Sleep came easy.

He woke up the next morning in a rested panic, dawn's sun stronger than it should have been. *Shit. Not again.* He showered, dressed, and rushed onto the unit nearly an hour late.

"Dr. Verik came by this morning." Off Pok's horrified look, Nurse Lemi touched his arm and quickly added, "Very early. She didn't expect you to be here. I told her how much of a rock star you were. She left this."

Unit looks good. Strong work. Screen patients in the HemoStat. Pairing you with a Resident Doctor.—Dr. Verik

Pok skimmed the already busy emergency department as he approached the reception desk. Usually, by this time most of the patients from the night before had been either discharged or admitted and moved upstairs to the appropriate unit. There must have been an influx of patients steadily throughout the night.

"Can I help you?" From behind the desk, Shaliyah's eyes were as sharp as her short-cropped hair, her smile more amused than pleasant. "Frazzled is cute on you."

"Cute? I'll take that compliment."

"The frazzle is cute. You here to see another 'practice patient' or you just come to say hello?"

"I came to say hello. And Dr. Verik paired me with a resident doctor. We're screening for Agrypnia."

"I've heard about that. Tough stuff. You know who you're paired with?"

"No, but they should be here."

"The only person I've seen is . . . oh no." Shaliyah's mouth broke into childlike glee while her eyes bred fear. "She was yelling at a nurse when I clocked in. Here's her list. The beds with the asterisks are the ones marked for screening. I'd say your best bet is get started with a patient, get on her good side, and go from there. Good luck."

Pok strode past a half-dozen patients who perked up at the hope of an approaching doctor. He paused outside one of the beds on his list. A physician leaned over a patient, her stethoscope loose around her neck. Her medical coat came down to mid-shin. A young scribe stood hip to hip with her, pen and paper ready. Pok could introduce himself, lay on the eager medical student charm. Exhaustion pushed him toward Shaliyah's advice. He went to start on another patient.

A broad-shouldered man with white-streaked locs extending nearly to his ankles, dressed in soft gray scrubs, stood by bed three. As Pok waited, he mentally listed off the Agrypnia criteria: prolonged exposure to AI tech, two or more signs of withdrawals, and one positive neurological sign. Easy peasy.

"All done," the man's thin voice floated around him. When he turned, Pok nearly gasped. Wrinkled eyelids fell loose over hollow holes. He smiled in Pok's direction. "Sayeed. Phlebotomist."

Sayeed patted Pok on the shoulder while he was still trying to move his own name past his lips. The man drifted away as light as his voice.

"It only took him one try." The patient lifted his arm. A spot of red soaked through the square of gauze taped to his skin. "Did you know he's *blind*?"

"Silva?" Pok said. "What happened?"

"I woke up with tightness, right around here." Silva rubbed his chest.

He pulled down his oxygen mask; wisps of steam rose into the air. "And everything's a bit blurry. It's been a rough few weeks. Thought I'd stop by to make sure the old pump is working like it should. Are you going to examine me?"

"If that's okay."

"It would be an honor." Pok eyed his friend while he busied his hands under the faucet. Silva had lost considerable weight; his hospital garb hung off his clavicles like a hanger. His swollen face made him nearly unrecognizable. Was this Agrypnia?

"How's the family?" Pok said as he came to the bedside.

"Jory's still acclimating. She's liking the paper job—thanks for the connect, by the way—so that's good. The depression is still there, but I'm hoping she's coming out of it."

Slight winces synchronized with the cadence of Silva's speech and breath. Pok let him talk and interrogated the pain his father's way: without addressing it at all. How did it permeate his words? How did it inform his movements? Anyone could give an arbitrary number for their pain without understanding themselves what it meant. This way, Pok saw it for himself.

He found Silva's pulse deep at the crease between the upper and lower arm. He counted the beats. Fast. Vibrant. Pok tied the edge of the bedsheet around Silva's biceps, gave the ends three quick tugs, and felt for the pulse again. Still there, still strong. He tightened the sheet. Faint now, but persisting. Pok frowned.

"I know that look," Silva said.

"Your blood pressure's a little high. Can you look at the wall for me?"

Silva did, exposing the main neck vein. Pok almost wanted it to be elevated. That was familiar. Scary, but easy. Silva's was flat.

"I've been sticking to my regimen. Oatmeal every morning, infused with blend of garlic, ginger, flaxseed, and basil. I grow them myself. I keep active. I've cut out all the sugars for now. I do the flashing lights. I read. I write."

"It sounds like you're doing all the right things." What if it wasn't Agrypnia at all? What if they were chasing ghosts?

"Ask," Silva said, a gentle smile in his voice. "I don't mind."

"Have you been using?"

"I considered it. Tech withdrawal isn't fun. But I held out."

Pok went through Silva's neurological exam. When he got to the patellar reflexes, they looked at each other. Pok tested them again, making sure to knock the reflex hammer right below the kneecap. The left leg's response was definitely more pronounced.

"Mr. Turner?"

Dr. Cheryl Roberson came in with her brow furrowed, jaw set, hands angrily rubbing in sanitizer, fully ready to tear off the head of any student who'd had the audacity to make the morning harder for her. Instead, her eyes brightened.

"My favorite student doctor. Dr. Verik's your sponsor, then?"

"That's what they say. Are you my resident today?"

"None other. Dream team. Okay, so what's going on?"

"Silva Turner has a history of autoimmune cardiomyopathy, now status post three heart transplants, all in TSO cities, his last procedure four years ago. Been here for almost two years now. Was doing well and started having withdrawal symptoms again. Manifesting as heart and lung congestion."

"Nice and concise. You've been practicing." Dr. Roberson moved to the bedside and placed the ball of her stethoscope over Silva's heart. "Good." She moved to his back, nodded, and bent to roll up his pants and feel his legs. Her thumb left clear marks along Silva's shin.

"What was his blood pressure?" Dr. Roberson asked over her shoulder.

"Elevated," Pok said.

"Elevated?" She grabbed a strip of leather hanging beside the sink. "Did you measure it?"

"I tested varying degrees of pressure but didn't get an exact number, no."

"Definitely a Dr. Verik mentee. Always measure with a cuff as well. Manual's a good skill to have in case your instruments fail, but you want something other physicians can compare to." Dr. Roberson wrapped the cuff around Silva's upper arm and pumped its inflation ball. She listened for his pulse in the arm's bend as she let the air out. "Two hundred three over one-ten. You mentioned a neurological sign?"

"Hyper-reflexive patellar," Pok said. "Left-sided."

Dr. Roberson tested for herself and frowned. Pok stepped forward. She'd seen it, too.

"Do this for me." Dr. Roberson locked her fingers in front of her chest and imitated trying to pull them apart. Silva obeyed. She retested the patellar reflexes. The difference was gone.

"That's called the Jendrassik maneuver," Dr. Roberson explained. "If the neurological sign were real, this would have made it more pronounced, not less." She quickly went through the rest of the neuro exam and then stood, satisfied.

"We can take him off ten-minute monitoring," she said. She flipped through his chart. "Herbs, not working. Exercise, not working. BP sky-high. I can write you for Indian snakeroot extract. It's new, but promising."

"I'll try that. Anything to help calm the nights. Does that mean I don't have the Grips?"

"We're going to check in with the attending doctor and circle back. Thank you, Mr. Turner."

Pok hung back a beat as Dr. Roberson stepped into the aisle. He wished he could see that tendon reflex again. What would Dr. Verik think?

"Go," Silva said, shooing him away. "Do your doctor thing."

"He meets the criteria, doesn't he?" Pok said as he caught up to Dr. Roberson. She gestured for him to sanitize his hands. "Prolonged tech exposure, withdrawal symptoms, and neurological sign."

"The most important part of any diagnosis is: 'isn't explained better by another condition.' He needs an Amygdala stay and drug counseling, not a medical admission." Dr. Roberson took a second. "I know you roll with Dr. Verik. And she's brilliant and a living legend. Just . . . This puts more work on us. Indulging in this 'withdrawal crisis' means everybody's going to be coming to us scared about common problems. We know Mr. Turner has a bad heart. He's not in the best shape. He has a lot of reasons to be presenting this way. Even if Agrypnia's a thing, I don't think he needs to be admitted."

Silva's leg twitched across Pok's mind. *I held out.* The shift in gaze as they mentioned sleep. How much might Silva be holding back, knowing what a prolonged hospitalization would mean for his family? For Jory? Resident Cheryl was so sure. *My favorite student doctor.* She'd know better, right?

The resident took Pok's musing as agreement. He didn't correct her.

"Nice," she said. "I'll do the talking."

They crossed over to a busy island of workstations, bulging filing cabinets, medicine repositories, and medical supplies. Dr. Roberson walked up to Dr. Wilcox, who finished sorting through papers before acknowledging them. She gave a practiced, ephemeral smile.

"Fifty-six-year-old obese male," Dr. Roberson said. "Status post three shepherd heart transplants, ex-Synth user with questionable remission presents with chest tightness and high BP, two hundred three systolic. No alarm symptoms. No edema."

Pok blinked and scooted in closer as he tried to keep up.

"Otherwise, PE normal. Likely not taking meds versus recent Synth use, suggest Indian snakeroot extract. Directly counteracts Synth's effect on the SNS."

"He's marked for Agrypnia screening," Dr. Wilcox said. She'd looked over Pok briefly as Dr. Roberson presented, her recollecting gaze flicking down to where she'd stitched him up. "Is that what he has?"

"If so, it's mild," Dr. Roberson said. "He had a slight positive on the neuro exam, but it could be explained by electrolyte abnormalities secondary to Synth withdrawal. I think basic lifestyle changes—and prolonged sobriety—can help with all that. I don't think this is the Gripping or whatever it's called."

" 'Or whatever it's called.' " Dr. Wilcox smiled with her mouth closed. "And what about you, Student Doctor? What do you think?"

Pushing for an admission after Dr. Roberson's presentation seemed futile. What could help? What would Dr. Verik suggest?

"I'm worried about his heart," he said. "What if it's not Synth? An alignment procedure could help."

"Like what?"

"An EKG cycle?" Pok said. He hoped for Dr. Roberson's buy-in, remembering how she'd done the procedure on him at MouseKill.

"That'll take up a nurse for a full hour," Dr. Roberson said. Something had changed in her voice. The resident he'd gotten only a glimpse of, the one Shaliyah had warned him about, now replaced his bright and happy anatomy tutor. "Not to mention the electricity. I think he'll be fine if he does the right things."

"He takes his herbs every day," Pok said. "Basil, garlic, and ginger."

Dr. Wilcox's mouth curled into an amused half smile. "You're skeptical, Dr. Roberson," she said.

"I don't think he's been compliant. The resources for an EKG pairing would be a waste."

"Do you know for sure that he hasn't been taking his meds?"

"No, but—"

"We can't deny him because we 'think' he did Synth or we 'think' he's noncompliant." Dr. Wilcox sat back. "You've convinced me, Student Doctor. We could give him a recalibration here with an EKG. If it syncs right, we'll send him home and he can follow up at the clinic."

Dr. Wilcox turned toward another resident who was awaiting her attention. Pok and Dr. Roberson slumped away.

"He meets the criteria," Pok said when he and Dr. Roberson were far enough away. "I—"

"Dr. Wilcox is generous. Not all doctors are, and for good reason. The nurses here have already been on my ass about short staffing. As if I make the schedule." She wouldn't look Pok in the eye. "I'll do the next one myself. It's fine. Why don't you grab a snack and meet me back here in half an hour to discuss?"

Forty-Four

BLOOD ON THE HEMOSTAT FLOOR

Pok spotted Shaliyah as he cleared the garden on his way back from the Pylorus. Was she on break, too? He stepped off the soil and onto the lobby floor. The morning had been taxing; perhaps her smile would revitalize him.

He quickly saw this wasn't a smiling matter. He jogged over.

"What's going on?" Pok said.

"I'm trying to get him back inside. Sir! Sir!"

Silva paced between two invisible walls, about ten feet apart. He mumbled to himself between heavy breaths as a young woman with low-cut, jet-black hair stood nervously to the side.

"He can go home," Pok said to Shaliyah, not understanding. "We just discharged him."

"Then you discharged him too soon. His daughter turned him around before they got past the garden. Says he's not right."

"Because he's not," the woman with him said. "He seemed fine until the lobby air hit him."

Silva turned, grunted, and lurched clumsily toward Pok. The woman jumped forward in support. For a moment they both tipped out of balance and then righted, like a well-rooted tree withstanding a violent storm.

Sweat-soaked wisps of hair sprung from Silva's scalp like rays of sun.

Black raccoon sacks surrounded his eyes. He grabbed Pok by the shoulders, his hands thick and weak.

"What did you do to me?"

"Come on, Pop," the woman said. "Let's sit down."

"What's in your pocket? Check his pockets! He's trying to kill me! You can't have my life, too. Oh, Jory!"

"I'm here, Pop," Jory said.

"Get away from me." He broke from her and braced himself against a tree with second-floor reaching branches. "They're impostors. They told them where my heart lives and now it's dead. Dead!"

"What happened?" Pok said to the daughter.

"He was saying how good it was seeing you," Jory said. "And then he got real quiet. I thought he was just tired. He started talking about how the shepherds turned off his heart. He said . . . he said it's rotting inside of him."

Pok took Silva's hand. Damp. Cold. His friend didn't resist; that last outburst had been deflating. Pok searched his wrist for a pulse. There. Quick and transient, it thrummed against Pok's first and second finger before sharply regressing. Pok closed his eyes; the pulse sparked light in the dark. Nausea washed fear over his chest. Silva was having a heart attack.

"Call a rosk," Pok said to Shaliyah.

She stood unsure. "Out here? Shouldn't we get him inside?"

Silva sank to one knee. Both friend and daughter struggled and failed to hold the big man up. Pain tore through Pok's lower back. Jory urged her father back up, as if standing would cure.

"Call for help!" Pok yelled.

Shaliyah ran for the HemoStat. Some moments later the emergency bell rang. When she rushed back, she was alone.

"Where is everybody?" Pok said.

"Finishing another rosk," she said. "Can't you start?"

Pok knelt beside Silva. He'd seen this done before, right? Press into his chest. Keep the blood flow going. That was most important. That was . . .

"You knew they were dead. You knew." The crispness of these final words demanded attention. Silva stared straight at Pok. He knew: Pok hadn't spoken up.

Silva's arms relaxed. Vomit dribbled down his chin, over his chest, and to the floor.

"Pop! Pop! What's happening to him? Pop!"

Pok froze. Somewhere distant, Shaliyah called his name. Somewhere distant, Jory pleaded. Somewhere distant, fingers gripped his shoulder. Silva was his friend. And Pok hadn't learned. Hadn't had the time. Was scared of the nausea. This wasn't real. Silva was in the Pylorús, waiting to run into Pok, not here, dying on the cold hospital lobby floor. Everything else was just—

An elbow pushed him aside. Not nefarious, not judging, just absolute. Shaliyah was down on her knees in front of Silva, her two arms joining into a piston in and out of his chest.

A tight blur of black and blue scrubs led by Dr. Wilcox piled from the HemoStat and surrounded Silva. The senior physician relieved Shaliyah and placed two fingers on Silva's neck as she listened to his heart through her stethoscope. She began to yell, level and controlled, over her shoulder. She pointed to someone different with each command.

"Start an IV. Bag him. Get his vitals. Grab a bed. We need a line!"

Hands pulled Pok from the back. Dr. Roberson was in his ear.

"This one might get messy. Stay back."

Dr. Roberson pushed past and knelt at Silva's head. She placed a triangle of inflated plastic over his mouth, pressed it tight against his skin with one hand and squeezed an attached bag with the other. A nurse took his blood pressure; another tied a tourniquet around the opposite arm. His right leg kicked spasmodically, as if some invisible reflex hammer were striking every second, just below the knee, over and over and over.

"Resume chest compressions!" Dr. Wilcox yelled to no one and everyone.

A black-scrubbed emergency doctor got in position and took over the manual labor of keeping Silva alive. Pok saw the inhuman way Silva's chest caved and rebounded, the way his belly flapped against his thigh, heard (and felt, deep in his own chest) the crack of ribs, smelled sour urine.

A subtle shift in the air; the smell of lavender. Dr. Verik stood beside him. Pok hadn't seen his mentor approach. How long had she been there? Did it matter? Was any of this real?

"Find me in my office," Dr. Verik said. "We have much to discuss."

The chest compressions stopped.

"Time of death?" Dr. Wilcox called.

A response rose above the bray. "Twelve thirteen."

Dr. Roberson wiped her forehead, took off her gloves, and left them by the still figure that had once been Pok's friend. Dr. Wilcox pulled her hair back and tied it in a bun. Personnel retreated from the space. Any urgency had died with Silva.

"What are you doing?" Jory said. "We have to keep going."

"Your father was very sick," Dr. Wilcox said.

"No." Jory fell to the floor and pushed balled fists into her father's chest. "Come on. Keep going! Pop. Dad! Help me!" She rocked back, out of breath and sweating. Silva's face shone through hers, as if his spirit had brushed against her in exodus. "We can't stop. Why did you stop?"

"We're going to need you to calm down," Dr. Roberson said, stepping forward.

"Why don't you debrief with your student doctor?" Dr. Wilcox said.

Dr. Roberson opened her mouth, closed it into a thin pressed line, and nodded.

"That was a horrible first rosk to see," she said as they went back to the HemoStat. The commotion had thrown a silent curiosity over the department. "He decompensated quickly. And the lobby is in no way ideal. You'll see more and find your rhythm."

Pok slowed to let Dr. Roberson pass in front of him. She went off to pull another chart from the workstation, as if she hadn't just felt the expiration of life under her palms.

"We should have admitted him," Pok said.

"I disagree. Hindsight is twenty-twenty, but we have to go by our clinical judgment. If we admit everyone, the hospital will be overrun."

"He had the neurological sign," Pok said.

"He was an addict, and this is what happens to addicts. Sometimes I think scrollers might be better off staying with the shepherds. It's sad."

Pok looked one last time. Back in the lobby—just between patient beds, past the reception desk, and out the rotating doors—he glimpsed his fallen friend. Someone had covered him with a blanket. Staff mopped and cleaned around him. Jory knelt at his side, weeping. They'd allow her a few minutes to say her last goodbyes before taking him down to the morgue.

"I'm sure you're devastated."

Dr. Roberson cocked her head. "What did you say?"

"Nothing."

"I'd keep in mind your place here."

"I did. And now my friend is dead."

Whatever Dr. Roberson had thought of Pok, whatever bond had existed between them, the tides had quickly turned.

"I think you should leave," Dr. Roberson said.

"Best plan you've had yet."

When the red of rage began to fade, Pok found himself outside of Dr. Verik's office. The senior physician read, standing, in front of an elevated desk. Pok knocked lightly on the open door; Dr. Verik waved him in. Using a scrunchie, she tied her hair into a bun.

Pinned papers, framed awards, and mounted musical instruments decorated an otherwise bare wall. A large cello, its wood cracked with age, sat propped against a chair. A desk and a bookshelf stuffed with folders furnished one side; a pulled curtain blocked off the other.

"Silva Turner." Dr. Verik dropped a patient chart onto an empty chair. "He was tachycardic to one-fifty-three, hypertensive to the two hundreds, but hypothermic. Did you consider admitting to Six South?"

"We thought he could get better at home."

"The resident didn't want extra work, you mean. I'll talk to Dr. Wilcox about formalizing the screening process. I saw we ordered an EKG alignment before discharge?"

"It was my suggestion. I thought it would help."

"It would for normal withdrawals. But with Agrypnia, it overwhelmed his system. More and more I see that treating Agrypnia is a balancing act. Tipping the scales too far in either direction can be devastating. This isn't a glorified withdrawal syndrome. It's something else entirely."

Pok could suppress the sobs, but he couldn't stop the tears. "I'm sorry."

"Don't be," his sponsor said. She grabbed Silva's chart. "Nothing can be done for the dead. Everything we do, every interaction, every decision, every triumph, every failure, we do for the living. You want to atone for your friend? You do that by carrying the future, not by grieving the past. Remember that."

Pok's room was unwelcoming. He turned on his desk lamp; just enough light to study. Pharm, Life Cycles, and Craft all had something on the horizon. The next exam wouldn't care about his emotions. It wouldn't wait for him to process.

He packed his bag and went down to the Ventricle, hoping a change of scenery would help him shut down the part of him that grieved. He set up at a long, empty table and, at first, was able to focus. He looked up some hours later. His hand ached from notes. The Ventricle was empty and dark. Everyone else had returned to Tay Hall for knowledge-solidifying sleep.

Anger surged. Pok banged his fist against his desk. The papers fell to the floor. He looked at them, face down. What had he even been studying?

He bent to pick them up and sensed everything. The beat of his heart, the pressure his stomach exerted to balance pumping the blood up his neck, engorging his head. Cool air against skin. His own musk. The bland dryness on his tongue.

Silva would never feel those things again.

He restacked the papers and turned his keys in his fingers. They failed to calm. He fanned through his notes. None of this knowledge would help him save Silva. None of it mattered.

What was the point?

He packed up, defeated. He took the nearest door up to the night air and headed toward the hospital. If his bones were going to ache with cold, he'd rather feel it under the stars.

Forty-Five

THE WORK

Pok went on an impossible journey to rewrite history. He didn't go to class for a week. He finished his CPR training and hung around the HemoStat at its busiest. Whenever a rosk was called, he was the first at the bedside to do chest compressions. He pumped past emotional pain, past the crack of ribs under his palms, past the burn in his shoulders, his arms, the fire in his belly. He pressed until someone told him to stop. After, whatever the outcome, he left before he could register the patient as more than practice. And every time, Silva was still dead.

Any time not in the HemoStat was spent on Six South, learning all he could about every patient. Dr. Verik, worried about Agrypnia's potential to infect, mandated Pok get daily blood draws to make sure he wasn't contracting the disease. Nurse Lemi tried to teach him several times how to draw blood, but the nausea was too much. While Pok had learned to withstand the sensation of a person's bones shattering under his weight, the sight of blood still incapacitated him. Dr. Verik took his samples without comment.

His time on Six South blended to numb routine. No joy. No accomplishment. There was only the work. The work was what got him out of bed in the morning; the work was what forced him to sleep at a reasonable hour versus staying up all night, staring into the void.

The work was all that mattered; the work was where he'd failed and wouldn't fail again.

Forty-Six

THE FATTY LIVER

Shaliyah nuzzled up next to Pok on the packed streetcar as it pulled off University Avenue and onto Canal. She'd intercepted him on his way to the HemoStat after receiving his end-of-semester grade. He'd passed all three courses and had no interest in joining any celebrations. There was still work to do. But Shaliyah—dressed in an ankle-length black winter coat—was persuasive.

Pok pulled out the folded piece of paper he'd been carrying in his pocket. He'd found it slipped under his door a few days before. Shaliyah's face brightened.

"I thought maybe you hadn't gotten it, moving into the hospital and all. What did you think?"

"I didn't read it. I didn't earn it. Deal's not done."

Her light dimmed. "Pok—"

"I'll read it when I've earned it. I plan to, for what it's worth."

Instead of taking the paper, Shaliyah put a warm hand over his. "I wish you weren't so hard on yourself. You were Silva's friend. You did the best you could."

"The best. Knowing basic techniques would have been the best." Pok turned the paper over. The shadow of Shaliyah's cursive gave an illegible preview through the folded page. "This gives me something to look forward to. I need that."

Shaliyah pulled the overhead cord, signaling the driver of their stop. "My writing could suck, you know. It would make for a shitty celebration."

"Impossible," Pok said. "I fully expect this to be the best thing I've ever read."

"Pressure!" She knocked her shoulder into his as they got off. "I'll bring you more if I can."

James, Rodge, and Anji were just walking up when they arrived. Only a few students made up the patronage of the half-empty Fatty Liver. It kept a low buzz, like a second glass of wine. They found a table big enough for their group and the waiter brought out waters.

"Pok, you ready for the first hurricane of the season?"

"Hurricane Kristen?" Pok said. He'd heard whispers of it. "I thought hurricane season started in the fall."

"Every season is hurricane season nowadays," Shaliyah said. "But I wouldn't worry too much. Even category fives lose their steam coming over the spires. Worst case, they'll cancel a day or two of class."

"They definitely won't cancel class," James said. "Which is why we need to enjoy every break we can get. We drinking tonight?"

"Do dogs shit in the woods?" Rodge said.

"It's bears," Anji said. "'Do bears shit in the woods?'"

"How would I know the bowel habits of bears?" Rodge said. "We're studying *human* medicine. Get it together, Anj."

"I . . . need a drink," Anji said.

"First round on me." James half stood, paused, and tapped Pok on the shoulder. "Isn't that your patient?"

Pok went icy all over: Jerry?

His fingertips bent into the table as he turned to look. Not Jerry, but Kris. Sweet, hot relief. And then, something else. The band around his eyes softened as the wine touched his belly and dissipated into a warm, throbbing heat. Onstage, someone sang about two dogs in love while another thrummed a guitar. The alcohol, the laughter, the music, it all fell light on Pok's skin. Shaliyah asked him something. Her warm hand tugged gently at his.

"I'll be back," Pok said.

"I'll come with you," Shaliyah said.

"It'll just be a second. I promise."

From behind the bar, Kris caught Pok's approach. He quickly finished mixing a brown drink, passed it to a patron in exchange for a wad of cash, dried his hands, and waved.

"You look deadass serious," Kris said. "Everything okay?"

"It's my dad's birthday," Pok said. He tried to soften his face. "He's been on my mind."

Kris nodded, picked up a glass, shined the inside, then placed it down. He touched a passing coworker. "Haegel, cover for me, okay?"

They found an empty two-seater, slightly removed from the main floor and against the wall. Kris pushed Pok a glass filled with pale ale and sipped from his own.

"It's good to see you out," Kris said. "Med school still kicking your ass?"

"That's an understatement." Pok smiled as he took a big gulp of ale. It cooled his throat and prickled his belly. Almost instantly it calmed the band around his head, which he hadn't even noticed was still there until now.

"How's it going fighting the Grips?"

"We still aren't sure what it is. But it seems to only affect scrollers. It's like withdrawals but a hundred times worse. A patient died from it the other day."

"Damn," Kris said. "Were you there?"

"I don't want to talk about it." Pok circled the rim of his drink. "It's looking more and more like Odysseus manufactured it. I didn't want to believe it. But it makes sense." Pok took another drink of his ale. Only a few swigs left. He felt his tongue loosen. "My dad treated Odysseus, when he was a kid."

"I heard that," Kris said. "I didn't know if it was true."

"It's true. His genetic disorder sounds very similar to whatever's going around."

"Any more thought about getting into the Vault and finding out?"

Pok's mischievous grin burst through before he could contain it. His hand went to his pocket where he kept the key, as if to check it was still real. His friend picked up all of this and his eyes widened to sparkling orbs. Kris downed the rest of his drink and wiped his mouth.

"You're going to get yourself expelled," he said.

They both sat back as the waiter came to clear Kris's finished drink.

"I don't have anything planned," Pok said. "There's probably nothing down there, anyway."

"Or it could be everything." Kris reached for Pok's glass.

"That's mine," Pok said. "This one's . . ."

Words turned to ash. The wrong drink. The wrong glass. He was back in Manhattan, in his kitchen, sitting with Kris, processing the rejection and the faulty application. Kris offering him a drink—a specially made drink—and Phelando picking it up. *That's Pok's!* Or was it, *I made it for Pok*? Something like that. The alarm in Kris's voice and demeanor that hadn't meant much then, but now, looking back . . .

"What's wrong, Pok? You're scaring me, man."

"What was in that drink?"

Kris tilted the glass and looked inside. "Just some bourbon and a little—"

"The one you brought over to my house. The one my father drank right before he got sick." *And died. Got sick and died.*

Kris's apparent discomfort ignited the all-too-familiar band around Pok's head.

"I can't remember," Kris said. "It was so long ago."

Pok slapped the table. Kris jumped. The band expanded. "Did the shepherds send you?"

"What? Pok, no. I came to help. I just wanted to help."

"Pok, hey, why don't we have a dance?" Shaliyah, beside him. Her hand, usually comforting, aggravated his rage.

"I just want to talk to him," Pok said.

"Talk to me instead. Let's not mess up the night."

Pok yanked away, harder than he intended, vacillated between apology and condemnation, tightened his lips, and turned back to Kris. "Did you poison my dad?"

The recognition mixed with shame across Kris's face was instant, quicker than any awareness could be. That's all Pok needed to ignite that band. Kris tried to backtrack, tried to clean it up, but it was too late.

"Pok, I—I didn't, I didn't know—"

Pok leapt. The table flipped; their drinks flew. Brief, shocked screams set off like fireworks around them. He grabbed Kris by the collar. They fell; Kris's head cracked against the wall.

"You didn't know? What didn't you know, Kris? What didn't you fucking know?"

"I didn't . . . I didn't know what it was."

Hands on his shoulder. Gentle, with the promise of becoming firm. James and Rodge, trying to calm him.

"Pok!" James said. "Let him go."

"He poisoned my dad." Pok shook Kris, hard. "He poisoned the whole fucking city."

"Odysseus told me it was tracking software," Kris said, speaking fast. "It was supposed to be for you."

"Are you freaking kidding me? Did you bring that shit here? Did you bring that Grips shit here?"

"That's not this. I swear! I don't know what happened to your father. It was just a tracking device."

His father. Dead. Because of this idiot. The band thickened. It throbbed, each contraction staining his vision red.

"Everybody's looking," Rodge said. "Let's calm it down before we have bigger problems."

Pok's hands fell away. Lightheaded, he sunk into his chair. Kris began to make a beeline for the door when James yanked him by the shoulder and forced him to sit.

"Pok," James said, still holding on to Kris, "we done?"

Around them, the Fatty Liver had come to a cautious halt. All eyes were on them. What would they now whisper about the crazed scroller student doctor who'd gotten Jerry sent away?

"I'm done."

James let go. Pok got up. Kris grabbed his arm.

"I didn't mean it," Kris said. "I didn't mean any of it. You're all I got."

Pok shrugged him off. Back at their table, Anji refused to meet his gaze.

"I, for one, am *extremely* glad I decided not to stay in tonight," Rodge said. He beckoned the waiter over. "Another round. On James?"

"Rodge!" James said.

"What? You don't have kids. I can't waste a night."

"Where's Shaliyah?" Pok said. He'd twisted the handkerchief in his fists all the way one way and now wound it back the other. The red covering the world began to fade.

"She left," Anji said.

Pok rushed out into the street. The night was calm, the sky clear. Sparkling stars crowned the skyline's silhouette. A light wind blew in from the Mississippi, forecasting unseen dark clouds waiting to roll over the city.

The rain would come. Pok just didn't know how bad it would be.

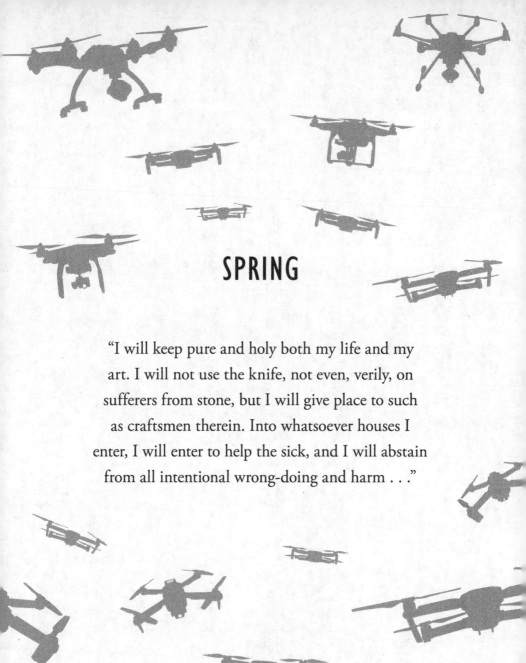

SPRING

"I will keep pure and holy both my life and my art. I will not use the knife, not even, verily, on sufferers from stone, but I will give place to such as craftsmen therein. Into whatsoever houses I enter, I will enter to help the sick, and I will abstain from all intentional wrong-doing and harm . . ."

Forty-Seven

CONFESSION

Pok's head pounded as he descended the stairs, exited through Tay Hall's common room, and crossed over to the main hospital the next morning. His mouth and throat were dry. His night had been filled with torn dreams and intermittent panic. His father, dead by his own friend's hands. And he'd let the killer stay in New Orleans, under everyone's radar. What sickness had he snuck into the city? For what grand plan had Pok become a pawn? He had to tell Dr. Verik. Would she believe he had no clue until now? That he wasn't complicit all this time?

"Pok!" Shaliyah half jogged up to him. Good. He'd tell her *everything*. She'd understand. She had to.

"About last night," Pok began, but something beyond her caught his attention. Out in the waiting room, Dr. Verik listened stoically to a woman speaking through tears. Nervous, raking fingers made her hair shimmer like tall grass. It was Florence, his father's patient who had been determined to keep her pregnancy from the shepherds. If she was here at the hospital . . .

"That's Jillian's sister," Pok said to Shaliyah. "Jillian Joseph. Is she in the HemoStat? Have you seen her?"

"No, but, Pok—"

He hurried over, Shaliyah's words soft on deaf ears. Florence embraced Pok in a hug. "Thank God."

"How is she?" Pok said.

She shook her head, tears muffling her speech. "Not well. I begged her to come. But she wouldn't. Will you go to her? She's back at home. I don't want her to die there."

Die?

Dr. Verik nodded. Then, to Pok, "Meet me in the parking lot. We leave immediately."

Pok was a step away from matching Dr. Verik's stride when a single clause from Shaliyah grabbed him by the throat.

"Kris is here."

Pok stopped. "Here, here?"

"Yes. In the HemoStat here. They found him screaming in the garden. I went out to help and was only able to calm him by mentioning you. He wants to talk."

"Shit, Kris." Dr. Verik had already disappeared out of the HemoStat. Jillian needed him. But Kris . . . "What bed?" Pok said.

"Seven. It's curtained."

The curtain did nothing to quell the sobs. Pok, caught off guard by his own tears, wiped his eyes before stepping inside. Whatever this was would have to wait. He needed to get to Jillian.

"I went to the garden," Kris said. Snot ran down his lips. His shirt was torn at the shoulder. The rest of his clothes hung off him as if out to dry. Pok had never seen his friend in such bad shape. "I thought maybe you'd be there. Stupid, huh?"

"Kris," he said as firmly as he could. "I really need you to go."

"I was scared last night. That's why I didn't tell you."

"Kris, I'm serious . . ." Pok blinked. "Tell mc what?"

"Odysseus didn't send me to bring the disease. It was already here. The Grips was here all along."

Pok's urgency wilted. Jillian, Dr. Verik, the Grips. It all paled to this singular moment. Even as a shell of himself, fraught with fear and uncertainty, Kris noticed the change.

"No one had it before you—before we—got here," Pok said.

"The TSO proteins, they don't go away when people Adjust. It just looks that way. They lie dormant. All Odysseus had to do was switch them on."

"The spires—" Pok began.

"The spires don't do shit. Not against this. It's a simple signal. It's going to get bad, Pok."

"How do you know all this?"

Kris's chewing slowed. He didn't meet Pok's gaze.

"Tell me the truth, Kris. All of it."

"That implant gave me direct connection to Odysseus. Using the same signals that pass the spires." Kris prolonged the final *s* and pulled two pinched fingers across the air as if drawing a fine, invisible line. "Sometimes I couldn't tell which thoughts were mine or his."

Odysseus had been talking to Kris this whole time? Could he hear what Kris heard, too?

As if sensing the thought, Kris added, "He can't listen when his body goes through maintenance. He has to shut everything down. I can feel it when he's gone. Listen to me, Pok. He sent me to New Orleans with very specific instructions. But not for the Grips. For the cure. It's in the Vault. Zion can end all of this."

"Zion is a fantasy," Pok said, confused. "It's just an idea."

"I didn't want to believe I killed your father. I had so much guilt. But whatever that fucking piece of shit had planned, it was because of Zion. It's here, Pok. We have to find it before he does. Or it's game over."

"The Vault is massive. It would take days of searching. We don't even know what we're looking for."

"I know *exactly* where it is." Kris scooted to the edge of the bed. "Odysseus told me. You have a way in, don't you? We can end this tonight. Right now."

"I have to go," Pok said. In his pocket, his fingers found his keys. "A friend—a *real* friend—needs me."

Kris sprang forward; Pok jumped. Kris wrapped his arms tight around him, his thin chest heaving with the beginnings of a sob. "Please, Pok. I never meant to hurt him. Not in a million years. Let me do this. Let me make one thing right."

Pok pulled away, rougher than intended, the momentum enough to send Kris sitting back on the examination table, his eyes wide and regretful.

"Some things you can't make right," Pok said. He pushed through the curtain before Kris could say anything further. He checked his pocket as he crossed the hectic HemoStat. The key was still there. He clenched his fist over it, simultaneously thankful and remorseful that he now believed his oldest friend capable of stealing it.

He'd properly deal with Kris later. Jillian was waiting.

Forty-Eight

JILLIAN JOSEPH

Dr. Verik and Pok rode in silence down the winding University, past the clinics, the staff housing, and out the hospital gates. The last of the day's merchants flashed their wares but with only lazy enthusiasm; the day had been long and cold, the cloud cover preventing the sun from ushering in spring warmth.

The lights lining the uneven street were smaller and dimmer than those on University. Taverns and small shops turned into town houses. Their windows blazed with dancing candlelight. Ominous silhouettes rocked gently on broken porches. Whenever they stopped at an intersection, moans or whispers—Pok couldn't tell which—drifted along the night, from all directions.

"My patient friend from New York was in the HemoStat," Pok said. "He said Odysseus sent him here to find Zion."

Pok searched Dr. Verik's face—illuminated in passing slivers under the streetlights—and felt his own angst rise. Her jaw tightened. Her face seemed to stretch. But when his mentor finally spoke, it was as if Pok hadn't brought up Zion at all.

"Jillian's a friend to you," Dr. Verik said. "You need to be prepared."

How could she have no response? "Is Zion real?" Pok said.

"A surgeon is in the middle of a case . . ." Dr. Verik held up a hand to still Pok's rebuttal. "The nurse comes in and whispers to her, *Your husband and daughter have just been killed in an accident.* She thanks the nurse and goes on to save the life in front of her. She knows there will be time to mourn. A lifetime's worth. Focus on what's in front of us. That's the priority."

Pok stared at his mentor. Her eyes stayed flat on the road. Exhaustion pulled at her features. This disease was taking its toll on her, too, but for different reasons. Finally, she met his gaze. It was pleading. Deflated, he sat back.

"What happened to your mother?" Dr. Verik said.

Pok would have asked for clarification, but her words were clear in the car's stillness. "What does that have to do with anything?"

"Humor me," Dr. Verik said.

"She died when I was young. Three or four. Ovarian cancer."

"I'm sorry to hear that. You've had so much loss to be so young."

"You think Jillian's going to die?"

Instead of the expected sterile answer, Dr. Verik gave it to him straight. "This disease is fatal. Hers has progressed quickly. I've brought the latest. FLT lights, full spectrum. DigiTone formulations. The CBH is promising. I've been working closely with MouseKill to home in on the most efficacious strain."

"Those all need time," Pok said. They didn't have time.

"The CBH is an extract. We'll inject it directly into her arteries. Bypasses the digestion. We'll do our best."

Dr. Verik parked on a street with overlapping trees, their branches near bare. Overgrown grass and skeletal rosebushes flanked the concrete path leading up to the steel door. The building, old and cracked, smoked out of the ground like a ghost. Florence waited outside. She rocked a sleeping Baby Girl in a sling.

"I knew you'd come," she said.

Florence's tone, the crack in her voice, the sorrow in her eyes . . . Pok suddenly and definitively knew that his friend was on her deathbed.

"Take us to her," Dr. Verik said.

A restless stench leaked into the staircase. At two flights up, halfway, a wail descended. It sounded a lot like Pok's name. He gripped the banister; was the wood warm, or was he? Dr. Verik remained unbothered. They came to the fourth floor. The first of three doors opened to a cramped, dimly lit space. People sat idly around a table in the living room; the fever of insomnia floated among them.

Florence led them down a short corridor and stopped outside a door that swung lazily on worn hinges.

"She finally went to sleep." Florence stroked Baby Girl's head. "I'm going to put her down while I still can. Let me know if she . . ."

Dr. Verik touched Florence's shoulder. "We will. If it comes to that."

The room stank. Jillian lay shivering and rocking under tightly drawn sheets. Her eyes were clenched shut. Her hands covered her ears. Dr. Verik took one look at her, closed the door, and circled the barren room to shut the blinds. Jillian loosened in the new quiet. She stared at nothing.

"What do you see?" Dr. Verik said to Pok in a low whisper.

Pok saw so much. He saw a body leaking life. He saw the thinned shell of the woman he'd known. Blotches decorated skin the texture of wet paper. Some were red, raw, and still oozing. Others had already begun to keloid. One large scar lay across the middle of Jillian's forearm like a knitted cloth. More timid marks looked like brushes of dirt. The dermatological destruction was widespread. Even her locs had withered to thin twigs, rooted in islands of scabs, many of them broken at the edges. He imagined anxious fingers, picking and scratching through the night. Her breaths were deep and labored. Rhythmless jerks plagued her right wrist.

To Dr. Verik, these observations would come together in a familiar puzzle. To James, each piece would spark a multitude of possible causes. To his father, her inner thoughts and anxieties would be on display like an open book. Pok, however, knew only one simple truth: Jillian wasn't doing well.

"I see death," he said.

"I see the same. The more pertinent question is, what does *she* see?"

Jillian lazily peered over puffed cheeks as Dr. Verik knelt at her bedside and cradled her wrist. She yelped at the contact; her body sparked. She muttered incoherently as they observed the rise and fall of her chest, a delicate shift of shadows. Pok's hand found hers. He didn't recoil from her cold but embraced it. She rubbed his fingers. Her free hand made it up his clothes and to his heart, then left to touch her own ear.

"You finally visited. Forgive me, I didn't have time to cook."

"I should have come sooner," Pok said.

"Yes. You should have." She turned and smiled. "You have to work on your bedside face."

"Can you say your name for me?" Dr. Verik asked.

"Your name for me," she said.

"Very concrete," Dr. Verik said. Then, "Who are you?"

"Jillian. Jillian Joseph of Harlem, New York." She grimaced. "That is my name. I am other things."

"What else are you?"

"Energy. Light."

"Do you feel those things now?"

"Yes." She turned away, as if someone had called her. "We made it. From New York. We made it, Flo."

"Do you see her now? Florence?" Only the three of them were in the room.

"I feel her. Her smell, I can see." She repeated that to herself, then coughed a laugh. "It's red, my favorite."

"Synesthesia. Sound stimulates her visual cortex. See?" Dr. Verik snapped her fingers. Jillian, wide-eyed, followed with her gaze something unseen across the room.

"Sleep is not just for dreaming," Dr. Verik said to Pok. "It washes the brain. All the thoughts and memories and sensory input we don't need. She lacks this cleansing. We can strengthen our purpose by exploring such an unfiltered mind."

Dr. Verik set up to draw Jillian's blood. Neither Pok nor Jillian flinched at the needle. Pok looked away as the red began to spiral through the tube.

"Watch," Dr. Verik said. "Stay through it."

Saliva flooded his mouth. Pok swallowed it down, over and over. After one vial was done, Dr. Verik gestured for Pok to take over. He did. Somehow, the light vibration of Jillian's blood filling the small glass calmed the nausea. Dr. Verik prepared the CBH injections while Pok continued.

"How many?" Pok said.

"Three, for control. That's good." Dr. Verik came over and attached a Y-shaped tube to the still-open line. "We'll inject one at a time, wait ten minutes, draw a sample, and see the outcome. Rinse, repeat."

They didn't need a centrifuge to see the dark SRP band in the middle, fluctuating in size with each draw. Pok administered FLT while Dr. Verik compared the blood sample results, adjusted the CBH injection doses accordingly, and switched out her FLT color.

Hours passed.

"This is the band that we were testing for in the hospital," Dr. Verik said. "It represents S-reactive proteins. It was consistently low in the most symptomatic Six South patients when we'd expect the opposite. Now, see this band? It's new; we just started testing for it. Notice how the two bands interact across her blood draws. They are inversely related. As the SRP band gets thinner, this new band gets thicker, and vice versa.

"What would explain this? The S-RPs aren't leaving the body like we previously thought but are rather being converted to this other protein. A change in configuration, like prions. That's why we weren't detecting them. This new configuration—the one we weren't testing for—is directly correlated with the symptoms of Agrypnia."

Pok put it together. "So if someone grows up in a shepherd city like New York and they accumulate shepherd-reactive proteins throughout their lives, they come to New Orleans and go through the normal withdrawal process. We thought the shepherd-reactive proteins were being eliminated, but they were just going dormant in this new, hidden configuration."

"And now they're waking up," Dr. Verik said.

"Could a signal do that?" Pok said. "From outside the city?"

"Could it?" Dr. Verik said. "You're the tech expert."

Pok thought it could. New Orleans's spires didn't keep out all signals. They were in ample communication with their local farm, for example. "If it's the same reverse magnetic pulse used to send messages from MouseKill . . . it's possible."

Halfway through the night, as Dr. Verik and Pok mused over the latest sample, Jillian began to convulse. Her head jerked in one direction, then the other. Her hands grasped and released, grasped and released. Her mouth hung open; air whistled over her restless tongue.

"Jillian," Dr. Verik said. "What is it you're feeling?"

Her head swiveled, but not toward them. She started to weep, then slapped her own tears away. Her eyes found Pok's, held him there. He saw in her, under the glisten, love, hate, betrayal, hope.

Jillian stiffened. Her arms contracted, fists to her shoulders, her face drawn taught by invisible hands. Her fists shot out. Her body stretched.

"Her senses are overwhelmed," Dr. Verik said. "She's seizing. We have to stop it." She pulled the sheet over Jillian's head. Under, she convulsed a few more seconds, then stilled. Dr. Verik stood with the FLT lamp and circled the room, slow and pensive.

"Dr. Verik?"

Pok pulled the sheet down from over Jillian's head. Her one open eye was the color of blood. There was chaos there, but also beauty. Ugliness and peace. A frenetic stillness deep inside, past the retina and optic nerve, through and within the cells that had come together to create her. She came and she went, like the tide.

"Dr. Verik!"

Jillian's breathing stopped.

Pok sprang into action, his fingers interlocked, one knee already up on the bed. Dr. Verik grabbed his shoulder and pulled him back with enough force to wrench a sharp pain in his neck.

"She's gone," Dr. Verik said. "It's not her heart that failed her."

Dr. Verik packed her satchel, gathering all the samples, and went to stand by the door. Florence waited just outside, silent and somber. But Pok couldn't take his eyes off Jillian. Her two front teeth were just visible beyond her lips like when she'd been sleeping on the train.

His failure hung heavy. Once he left this room, Jillian's story would be done. No lecture, no amount of studying, no improvements in their methods of care, could change that final truth: she was dead.

Florence entered. She bent to kiss Jillian's head, then turned to Pok. He expected anger. What she offered stung worse: gratitude.

"She was so proud of you. She took her meds, right to the end. Because she trusted you."

Not knowing what else to say, Pok left Florence to be with her sister.

Forty-Nine

THE SACRIFICES WE MAKE

Pok stumbled dazed into the night. He pivoted forward; hot fire vomit erupted out of him and onto the pavement. Coagulated chunks of blood glistened under the streetlamp. The first drops of rain joined the grisly canvas.

Dr. Verik sat him on the curb and gave him some water. The world spun. Pok closed his eyes against it, sure he was about to be thrown off the face of the earth. Dr. Verik manipulated his arm. Cold wet touched his antecubital space. Then, the sharp prick of a needle. She was drawing his blood. He couldn't care, not until whatever this was passed. *If* it passed.

Finally, after minutes, hours, an eternity, everything slowed. When he opened his eyes, Dr. Verik stood beside him, leaning on a streetlamp, her physician's bag pregnant with his and Jillian's bloodwork tight to her side, face thrown up to the beginning drizzle. Seeing that he was better, his mentor gave a curt nod, helped him into her car, and then got into the driver's seat.

"What's wrong with me?" Pok said.

"Alignment," Dr. Verik said. "I noticed it back when you first saw that patient—Jillian's sister—in the HemoStat. You said you believed for a moment that she *was* still pregnant. You took on her illness." Dr. Verik let her words marinate. "I always said you assess the anima well. The meditation sharpened the skill. You'll be okay. I'm going to run your labs just to make sure, but you obviously heal quickly. Just as I suspected."

Dr. Verik was right. The nausea was subsiding. The fire in his throat, too. Concerns over his own health aside, his mind went back to the night they'd just endured.

"She should have been in the hospital," Pok said. Anger coated his tongue. Pok licked his lips with it. He needed to control himself. Jillian was dead; his mentorship with Dr. Verik was not. "We could have done more."

"The Grips had her," Dr. Verik said. "Despite our best intentions, the hospital is still an artificial place. We needed to see how the disease progressed in her home environment to truly understand it. We made a lot of progress tonight."

Progress? What the fuck? "Was any of this meant to save her?" he said.

"It was meant to save someone. Eventually."

If Pok had known they were just going to watch her die, he wouldn't have come. He could have gone to the Vault and done something useful instead of adding to memories that would take a lifetime to overcome.

"We seek a cure," Dr. Verik said. "This is the road to that cure. The data we collected tonight is invaluable. Your friend's death will not be in vain."

Pok looked out the window. *Everything happens for a reason.* His father's death, the perfect motivator for success. And now, Jillian, another step toward a cure. Whoever or whatever controlled this divine plan could go fuck themselves.

"I have a response to your surgery analogy," Pok said.

"I'm listening."

"There are breaks in long surgeries," Pok said. "Time to replenish, to regroup, to give the patient's body a chance to recover. During that break, the surgeon gets an update about her family. What happened. Where it happened. Whether they suffered. Otherwise she'd only be able to think about those questions when she should be thinking about the patient. Or she'd become so numb that she's no longer fit to provide care."

Dr. Verik brushed a fly off her hand. She rolled down her window. The fly didn't take the invitation. At a stop sign, she looked at Pok as if he were that fly.

"This is about Zion."

"It's about everything," Pok said.

"Once you hear the truth, there's no turning back from it."

"Tell me," Pok said.

Dr. Verik pulled over. They were just shy of the transition from Canal into University.

"My father had a rare genetic neurological disorder. I was ten when his insomnia set in. It was intractable. He couldn't sleep. At all. He went completely mad. I remember times when my older brother sat all night with a bat against our bedroom door. Dawn brought our father a little bit of sanity, until it didn't. My brother and I both swore we'd find a cure. I went into medicine. He went a different route. Does this sound familiar?"

It did. Pok had heard the narrative before, but from a different lens, a different take. It was how Julian Shepherd had come to start the Shepherd Organization.

"That's how he knew about your research. Julian Shepherd was your brother?"

Dr. Verik nodded. "And a good one, too. We were always close. And we had the same goals. While I learned about genetics and how to read diseases and treat patients, he learned the ins and outs of AI. We understood the answer would be in a partnership between the two."

"Why did he hide that he was your brother?"

"I hid it. He supported. Neither of us ever wanted the limelight. But his success demanded it. He fought ruthlessly to keep our relation private. I at times suspected he strove to live vicariously through my anonymity."

"What happened?" Pok said. "To drive you apart?"

"The disease happened. Since I was only a carrier, I regularly used my own DNA for research. You see, none of the genes were expressed in me because of my two X chromosomes. I could knock out my genes, replace them, all without consequence, and then see how they were expressed in the lab. I recruited the help of a fellow who'd just come from New York and was passionate about neuroscience and consciousness. Your father was brilliant and became invaluable in my research."

"He never mentioned working with you," Pok said.

Though Dr. Verik didn't comment on that last, it registered in her eyes. She went on. "I had to be sure before using any experiment on Julian because his genes *had* been expressed all his life. In addition to being a ticking time bomb, they were intertwined with routine functions.

"Even though I explained to him it couldn't hurt me and could literally kill him, he felt guilty that I was doing all the experimenting on myself. He focused a section of his Shepherd program to duplicate his neuronal network to run super-fast simulations of how sleep deprivation led to dementia. If we ran out of time with the genetics, maybe we could understand the disease course and find a treatment for when he got sick."

"Zion," Pok said. "So it was real?"

"Too real," Dr. Verik said. "It worked. It could simulate twenty years of brain function in a few minutes. My brother's AI was so powerful that it could run trials on a million drug variants and self-correct in real time. I didn't put it together that sleep plays an important part in consciousness, but Zion did. Somewhere along the lines, with things moving so fast, with Zion correcting and changing itself a million times a second, it became self-aware."

A chill touched Pok so deep that he looked to see if he'd left the window rolled down. But all the windows were up, fogged from their bodies' collective heat.

Dr. Verik went on. "Julian was afraid of that power. He kept it separate from his company, from the shepherds, because he knew, once it was integrated, he'd never be able to take it back. And then he learned he would be a father. That changed everything. He got genetic testing immediately." She laughed, remembering. "I did the test myself. We saw together that it was a boy. He begged me. *Begged* me. Maybe I should have. Hindsight is twenty-twenty. I said no."

"But he asked again," Pok said, visualizing the family tree. "When Odysseus was older."

"I'd made a breakthrough by then." She glanced at him. "In my own self-experimenting. Odysseus was a bright boy, very curious, loved to read. Couldn't get a book out of his hand. Julian came to me, said he was seeing the beginning of disease in his son. That the genes had changed and the insomnia was starting at five years old instead of fifty. It was still too risky. I slipped and said that maybe if we had done it earlier—but I meant if my breakthrough had come earlier. He took it the wrong way. He was furious. The things he said, about me, about how I'd never loved our father . . . I couldn't see it at the time, but I suspect he was already ill himself."

Dr. Verik lifted a pained smile skyward. Rain slapped her window, creating a mask of rippling shadows.

"I should have known he'd go to Phelando. Your father treated Odysseus because he thought it would work. Because he had hope. He hadn't grown up with my despair. He didn't have that futile feeling of chasing his father's ghost his entire life. Working with me here, he only saw the potential of a breakthrough. He was devastated when things went wrong. Odysseus almost died. That would have been better. For everyone."

"What happened to Zion?"

"I destroyed it." Perhaps suspecting that this would be the moment of the thinnest trust, she looked at him, right in his eyes. "Odysseus thinks I didn't, but it was the safest choice. He grew up hating Hippocrates. The idea of it. When his father died his horrible death, Odysseus's one goal became to have humans out of the equation. Your friend was right: Odysseus made Agrypnia. That's clear to me now. He's weaponized his own DNA. The shepherd-reactive proteins degrade into the same ones that the shepherd AI created to keep him alive. The same substance that fills the holes in his brain, his organs, his very DNA. Every single person who's moved here from a shepherd city in the last decade has markers already present that became active just recently. I suspect it's in every TSO food, product, and even the drinking water. Odysseus has flipped the switch . . . If we don't get it under control, we don't find a cure, he wins."

It was all starting to make sense. The personal vendetta. Kris's involvement. The drink was meant for Pok, not his father. Odysseus wanted the son to suffer in the same way he did. "He wants revenge. That's why he tried to kill me."

This theory became rock-hard in Pok's mind. Dr. Verik's expression shattered it. Her eyes were red and wet with emotion. But the sorrow wasn't for what she had just told him but for what she was about to say.

"That's part of it. But you mean so much more. The breakthrough I'd had, it was a successful genome edit in the womb."

"Julian had another kid?"

"No. I did."

A single tear dropped down Dr. Verik's cheek. She wiped it away and looked at the wet on her hand, her expression a mix of despair and regret and self-disgust.

"I never wanted to have children. I never intended to fall for someone.

And I still don't know if I loved him. I don't know if he loved me. We worked together so much during those years. Whatever it was, it conceived a child."

The band around Pok's head peaked. "What are you saying?"

"When I found out I was pregnant, after all the experiments I'd done, I applied to terminate. The federal abortion ban was fierce and Louisiana was still under its reach. If I'd told them the self-experimentation reasoning, I could have been imprisoned. They rejected my claim. Only then did I look at the fetal DNA.

"What I saw gave me hope. The treatment had completely changed the genome and not only freed it from the genetic disorder but made it resistant to it. Had it worked? I couldn't tell. Already Julian's own decline was clear. When I entered the second trimester, Odysseus was in the ICU. Phelando promised Julian he'd continue to care for Odysseus. Your father always planned to move back to his home city and he believed so much in the future of medicine. Phelando wanted to be a father. My purpose was in my work."

The band burst into a cloud of numb fog. The sound of Dr. Verik's breathing, slow and stilted, soaked with the sorrow of the retelling, battered by the growing rain. The fabric of the passenger seat against Pok's back. He blinked, tried to bring himself back down to the ground, but he couldn't. Not quite.

"Do you understand? Do you understand why you're special?"

"My mother is dead," Pok said. "She's always been dead."

"Khaliah was your mother. I would never take that from you. I chose to terminate. I held you for nine months and gave birth to you—right there, in that hospital—but I couldn't be your mom. I suspect this is all hard to hear."

This last sentence—a sentence they learned in the very first medical school class to align with their patients—brought Pok back down. Were they all just actors in a stage play?

"Why are you telling me this now?"

"Phelando was supposed to come with you. When I heard of his passing I was in shock. When I met you, how I met you . . . you needed a mentor, not a mother. This work is important. It's something you were meant to do." Dr. Verik cradled the steering wheel. "Have you wondered why you haven't caught Agrypnia? Why you went through Adjustment so fast? It should be just the opposite. You've spent your life in New York. You've immersed yourself in shepherd code. You were steeped in the AI-made curriculum to get into AI-led schools. And yet, symptom-free. You're smart. Very smart. You must have thought about this."

"I'm immune." Pok had considered this before but never for this reason. Just pure dumb luck, like the people who'd gotten through the decade-long pandemic without ever catching the virus. But this . . . for this reason . . .

"Your genes code for the enantiomer to the TSO protein. Do you know what that is?"

Pok did. "It's a mirror image," he said.

"Exactly. And when it binds to the TSO protein, it shuts it down. You're not only immune. You may very well be the cure. Your father was smart to keep your genome out of the shepherd system. Once Odysseus had it, he must have suspected what it meant. He wanted to test an accelerated version of his new disease out on you to make sure there wasn't a cure. If your blood holds the antidote to what he wanted to unleash, you could be a very big loose end in his plan. But he gave Agrypnia to your father instead. You coming to Hippocrates is the last thing he wanted."

His father, dead. Because of a question. A hypothesis. A pondering of one of the most powerful men in the world. His death had no meaning other than to be an asterisk in Pok's story.

And then, Dr. Verik as his mother? Odysseus, his cousin? None of it made sense. None of it was fathomable. His whole life had been a lie. Vile, incorrigible thoughts filled his head. Had his father ever loved him? Truly? Or had he only been a purpose? A steer that was given a name and the warmth of perceived love only to be more easily coaxed to slaughter?

"Say something," Dr. Verik said. "Anything."

"Take me home."

"Your father loved you," Dr. Verik said. "Don't ever doubt that."

"Take me. The fuck. Home." He looked at her, hating the tears scratching his face. "Dr. Verik."

Dr. Verik started up the car. Soon, the shining tip of the hospital poked above the hodgepodge of buildings, some abandoned, others flickering with night flame of the workers, of studying students seeking the comfort of their parents' homes before the next big test or rotation.

They crossed the edge of campus and stopped short of the main gates.

Morning was just spreading over Hippocrates. Cascading rain glistened off the gate's metal. Pok opened his door. Dr. Verik's hand on his shoulder stilled him. He didn't look back.

"We still have the work," Dr. Verik said. "Finding a cure is what's important. Agrypnia is evolving fast. If it becomes communicable, if it threatens to spread out from New Orleans . . ."

Game over. Odysseus wins.

She squeezed. "I told you the truth because you deserve it and I respect you. I respect your ability to continue the work. Just like your father."

Pok whirled on her. How dare she? But she held firm. She knew what she was doing. And she needed a response. Pok gave the slightest nod, just enough to loosen her grip, and closed the door behind him. He felt her eyes following him up University and forced himself not to break out into a run. Finally, the rumble of her car's engine, the slosh of tires over wet pavement, fading into the distance. When she was gone, Pok collapsed into the nearest bench and wept under the rain.

His tears spent, Pok walked slow up to Tay Hall some minutes later, digesting all Dr. Verik had told him, still numb from Jillian's death. Numb from his own lineage. And then, as his feet touched the first steps up to his room, the dagger of a thought occurred to him: his father had died because of him. Not because of his carelessness or naivete, but because of his existence.

Pok dug for his keys as he passed a few early rising first-years on his way down the fourth-floor hallway. Remembering, he checked his other pocket for the special key. Still there. He took it out and almost dropped it.

It wasn't the Vault key. It wasn't any key he'd ever seen before. If that was here, then where—

A teeth-clicking gong rattled the walls. He jumped, caught his breath, and when the gong hadn't subsided, shifted toward his window. Starting at the hospital gates, streetlights turned bright red, row by row, bathing University in raining blood. Personnel, slow at first, made it down the main campus road. As the alarm continued, as the crowd thickened to a moving assembly, realization set in.

Something had happened.

Pok ran.

Fifty

JAMES AND ANJI

As Pok ran down the now-empty road to the hospital, the rain progressed from a downpour to a torrential monsoon. A spot in the sky, hardly visible in the gray, gave him pause. A drone, hovering a hundred or so feet above the hospital, watching and waiting. Pok threw open the front door and sprinted across the lobby to the HemoStat. Inside, Shaliyah tended to a long line of tired, frustrated patients.

"We're moving as fast as we can," she said. "There's been an emergency and we're short-staffed."

"I've been waiting for hours!"

"What kind of emergency?" someone called. "Where are all the doctors?"

Before she could answer, Shaliyah saw Pok. She came from behind the desk, rushed over, and didn't speak until she was close enough to talk at a volume only the two of them could hear.

"Kris broke into the Vault," she said. "He attacked Anji."

Kris, what did you do?

Shaliyah saw his horror and grabbed his arm hard enough to hurt. "They say he had a key to the Vault."

"Where is she?" Pok said. "Is Anji okay?"

"I need to know. Was it yours? Did you give him that key?"

"He stole it from me."

"Pok!" She rubbed her hands up and down his arms. "Students don't have keys to the Vault."

He didn't want to tell her. Not like this. But he needed to see Anji. "I made a copy of Dr. Lowry's. She doesn't know."

In the fullness of Shaliyah's eyes, Pok saw his own guilt. Even more, he saw the certainty that they would never look at him the same again.

"Where, Shaliyah? Where is my friend?"

"Two South," she said. "Bed three."

Two South. The critical surveillance floor. Pok bounded up the stairs and sprang onto the unit. The floor was both quiet and deafening. No chitchatting. No hacking coughs. No moans of pain; even death was silent here. The only noises were the soft wheezes of ventilators that breathed for a number of patients who couldn't anymore. Every forced breath gurgled like a man choking on his own blood.

Bed three. Pok turned his ear toward the blue curtain. He longed to hear a cough, a choked whisper, anything to hang his hope on, but there was only that gurgle. He went inside.

James's white coat lay across the bedside chair, the ears of his stethoscope peeking out of its pocket, the same badge Pok had stolen hanging from the breast. He sat on the bed's edge, his back to the curtain. Pok's gaze shifted up the bed.

Only tufts of Anji's blue hair were visible. IV lines branched from her arms. A thick plastic tube extended from her mouth and connected to a ventilator. One hand was taped to the bed while the other lay hook-like on her belly. Fresh head bandages wrapped around a bulge at the left temple. Her left eye was swollen shut.

Kris, no . . .

"James," Pok said.

His friend stiffened. He turned his head only enough to show the edge of his eye. "Go. Away."

"What happened?"

"She went down to the Vault for her research project and didn't come back. I had to beg her sponsor to let me in. I found her at the bottom of the stairs . . . I thought she was dead, there was so much blood."

Kris killed your father and now he killed your friend.

"Was it you?" James said. "Did you let him into the Vault?"

"He stole it from me."

James sucked his teeth. "That you would even let that monster get close. Look what he did."

"Kris was afraid," Pok said. "Maybe she startled him or—"

James stood and turned so fast that later Pok thought he must have been facing him the whole time. Veins branched up James's forehead.

"Don't you blame this on her! This is on you!"

Each rageful word stung; Pok's eyes watered. "I'm so sorry."

"Are you?" James shrank back to Anji's side and took her lame hand. "Just go. Please. You've done enough."

Dean Sims, the gravity of her aura preceding her, waited by the stairs. The stone in her expression glinted even in the unit's dim light. Her despair somehow made things worse. That whatever awaited him was horrible enough to scare even her.

"Let's go, Pok."

Fifty-One

DO NO HARM

Students, physicians, nurses, scrub techs, scribes, and various personnel crowded outside the double doors of Genesis Auditorium. Some were still in their color-coded scrubs or dirt-rimmed white coats, others in their night or study clothes with heavy raincoats thrown over. The frenetic energy of lively, anxious chatter dampened as Pok and Dean Sims approached. Eyes shifted. Excited statements turned to shushed whispers. What stories were they whispering? Would they whisper?

Shut off from the world of questions and judgments now behind them, the inside of the auditorium was eerily quiet. The rows were completely empty. The Council sat lined up on the elevated stage. Drs. Lowry, Granger, Jacobs, Wilcox, and Soft.

Dean Sims took her seat near the end. Dr. Lowry sat in the middle, the chairs curved slightly in, emphasizing her ranking. Pok hoped to see some emotion to foreshadow what punishment the Council would hand down. Instead, their expressions were cold and detached.

"Off the record?" Dr. Lowry touched eyes with each of her fellow Council members and exchanged nods. Then she pulled out two keys and held them side by side. "They found this on the intruder. It's an exact replica of my Vault key. Student Doctor Morning, I'm only going to ask this once: Did you make this copy?"

He could have said no. That the thief must have gotten it some other way. But Dr. Lowry's eyes said she knew. Of course she did.

"I did, Dr. Lowry."

"Your gross negligence has resulted in the theft of hospital records and the injuring of a student doctor." Dr. Lowry wasn't doodling, but she hardly looked at him. "Speak!"

Pok started. The words barely made it across his throat. "I thought there was something in the Vault that could help cure Agrypnia. I considered looking there myself but only considered it. I didn't think anyone else would use it."

"You didn't think. You're damn right you didn't think. We have reason to believe your friend went straight to the shepherds with information that threatens this institution."

Had Kris found it? Zion? If that was true and Kris had handed it to the shepherds, then his worst fears about his friend were realized. And Pok would pay the price.

"How much has the intruder told us?" Dean Sims said.

Dr. Lowry looked down the aisle. Dr. Soft sat up.

"He was apprehended in MouseKill," he said. "He's currently being treated in the Amygdala. He's been too hysterical for us to get any useful information."

Dr. Lowry held out Pok's counterfeit key. The scribe took it. "Destroy this, please. Back on the record.

"Student Doctor Pok Morning," she began, "you have been brought in front of the Council for thievery and possible conspiracy. While history will best determine what remains, I think your biggest flaw is your negligence. In medicine, that is the worst trait you can have." Her voice shifted past him. "Do you have anything to say, Dr. Verik?"

From near the middle of the auditorium, Dr. Verik stood. Pok's breath caught. She didn't look his way. "We are ready to receive punishment."

"Council?"

Dr. Lowry nodded to Sims. The dean approached center stage. Her eyes were almost sorry.

"Student Doctor Morning," she began, "for your gross negligence—"

A heavy rumble shook the floor; from outside, muffled yells coated the air like summer haze. Above it, the distinct buzzing of drones. All heads turned. The double doors opened to a strong ray of light bisected by a tall man who took long, confident strides down the center aisle. He wore a solid blue zip-up sweater and black jeans.

"This is a private meeting," Dr. Lowry said. The man either didn't hear her or didn't care. Dr. Lowry stood. "Security! Security . . ."

A sharply rising hum filled the auditorium, as if someone had released into the space an angry colony of Carve Bees. A pair of drones flew in and split to circle the perimeter. The man went right up to the podium. His hair was cut low, his skin smooth and tan. He seemed to walk in his own personal glow.

Pok moved toward the aisle. His first thoughts couldn't be right. Not here. Not in New Orleans. But it could be the middle of a dark, foggy night and Pok would recognize a mile away the figure that had burned himself into his nightmares.

The Council members exchanged uneasy glances. Not panic, but a grave understanding.

"Odysseus Shepherd," Dr. Lowry said, confirming Pok's fears. "I never thought I'd see you here. I assume the spires are down. You don't have the authority."

Oh, Kris. What have you done?

"I don't," Odysseus said. His voice filled the auditorium. "The federal government has acted where Governor Teal has refused to. We all know Hippocrates is a clear and present danger to society. It's time to prove it. There will be a full investigation that will likely end in the complete dissolution of this medical center. The spires could interfere with those procedures. It was my recommendation they be decommissioned. Temporarily, of course."

"We need the spires to mitigate the hurricanes," Dr. Soft said.

Dr. Lowry sat down, adjusted some papers, and began to doodle. She spoke toward her drawings. "We've survived worse. That doesn't explain exactly why *you* are here, Mr. Shepherd."

"I came to deliver the news myself. And to extend an offer."

"If you wish to buy us, we're not for sale."

"This place is broken," Odysseus said. "I can fix it. You depend on a fragile system to keep your city from flooding. Hurricane Kristen was just upgraded to a category three. And you are currently battling an epidemic, are you not?"

"One that you manufactured." Dr. Verik moved into the aisle. Odysseus turned, slow, amused. The auditorium's light wrapped oddly around him. Pok eyed the drones; they twitched in sync with his movements.

"Aunt Em. I'm surprised they still let you practice."

"Tell the Council how you weaponized your own DNA," she said.

"That's quite the accusation."

Yes, the drones were more than just protection. Pok slowly bent, took off his shoe—a black clog, long frayed at the edges—and kept his eye on the drones. AI excelled at many things, could do and understand and analyze details the human mind couldn't fathom. But they were still weak to distraction.

"You've always wanted Hippocrates gone," Dr. Verik said. "What better way than this?"

"I must remember this institution deals more in feelings than in facts. Based on recent intel, the fact is if New Orleans continues at its current trajectory, ten percent of its population will die."

Pok yelled; he made sure the entire auditorium felt it. "Because you've made them dependent!"

The hovering drones immediately tilted down toward him. A shimmer—imperceptible to the unattuned eye—cascaded over Odysseus.

"Pok!" Dean Sims said. Her voice and expression were full fire. "Let us handle this."

Odysseus—clear-skinned and soft-eyed—regarded him as if he were a thing to study. The energy of the moment pushed Pok against his dean's demand. He cut into the aisle, raised the shoe, and cocked it back. Clear and intentional, so the drones could make no mistake. Odysseus gestured for them to stand down, but he was too late. Pok hurled his shoe. The drones, eager to defend, swooped down to intercept its trajectory. A puff of smoke hung in the air and then was gone.

Gasps rose from the Council. The projected filter disrupted, Odysseus turned to show his true form. Gray metallic patched his skin. Stiff robotics marked his movements. A low moan emanated from his chest.

"Thank you for that, Student Doctor Pok." Odysseus called off his drones, which were busy reconstructing the elaborate projection. He spread his arms; reflection flickered around where metal blended with skin. His grin was wider on one side than the other. "How is it to look upon your father's work?"

"Your business is with us," Dr. Lowry said.

But Odysseus's attention was fully on Pok. They could have been the only two left in the auditorium.

"There's still a spot in my medical school. I saved it just for you. You could be a champion of medicine's future rather than a casualty of its past."

"Thanks, but no thanks," Pok said. "I'm already enrolled."

The lights flickered, dimmed, and then died. Gasps and yelps rose from the pitch-black. Doors slammed. The room's air swayed with Odysseus's breathing. Pok could feel the man's heartbeat. It wasn't like Buddy's or his own. Instead of the *lub-dub*, there was only one movement, one push. Whatever apparatus had replaced Odysseus's heart was surely efficient, long-lasting, immortal. But it was completely inhuman.

Odysseus's voice came from everywhere and everything all at once. "You have extraordinary lineage, cousin. You could have what I have. Don't let your father's failures and your mother's stubbornness keep you from reaching that potential."

The lights came back on. Half the Council stood on their feet. The doors burst open; scribe guards rushed into the auditorium.

"You have my offer," Odysseus said. "I will not extend it again."

"Fuck off," Pok said.

"Ditto," Dr. Lowry said. "Hippocrates is not for sale."

"And to think, you thought I planned to pay. We'll do it the hard way. Enjoy the end of your little experiment."

Odysseus brought himself close enough to whisper in Pok's ear. He smelled of metal and saliva. "I should have made you into a Memorandium, just like your father. But this city will finish the job. I hope you know how to swim. Goodbye, cousin."

And then, as quickly as he had come, the CEO of the Shepherd Organization left. The crowd parted to let him through. A few ducked their heads as the drones zoomed out after him.

In the brief silence that followed, Pok asked himself his father's question: *What do you notice?* Odysseus had been vague and wary. And why offer to buy the hospital if he already had what he needed?

Dr. Verik was the first to break the silence and pull Pok back from his thoughts. "He was just as annoying as a kid."

"He's right," Dr. Soft said. Nervous fingers twiddled his loose locs. "It is only a matter of time."

"It was always a matter of time," Dean Sims said. "TSO has been threatening us since the beginning."

"And yet it's never felt this real," Dr. Soft said. "The spires are down. We aren't ready for a flood or an inspection. We'll be shut down in a week."

"You are free to join him. We will not hold it against you, Council member."

Dr. Soft said no more.

"He doesn't have enough to shut us down," Pok said. He ignored any looks of disdain, any attempts to silence him with authority. "There's something here that he wants. We still have time to find a cure."

"I agree," Dean Sims said. "We continue treating our patients. We continue teaching our students. The inspectors will find what they find. Slowing down only makes it easier for them to shut us down."

"I will take the lead on making sure the wards are compliant," Dr. Lowry said. "Council member Soft, your anxiety is fit for the most important task: auditing the Vault. Find whatever it is Odysseus didn't. Including a full interrogation of tonight's intruder. If there's anything there that will hurt us, I want to know it first. Council member Granger, we need inventory on our complete armamentarium. Get the medical college to help. Council member Wilcox, psychiatric care should still be protected. Activate the Amygdala's EMF. Council member Sims, make sure the HemoStat and the students are ready. They may need to grow up a lot quicker. Dr. Verik, you will debrief Council Member Jacobs on Agrypnia. He will take over research and development of a cure. You will assist."

Dr. Verik lunged forward as if physically wounded. "Dr. Lowry—"

"Council member Lowry."

"Council member Lowry. You don't know what we're up against. I do. We have come so far."

"It is not a discussion. Is everyone clear on their roles? Perfect. Student Doctor Morning, please approach the Council."

In the tumult of Odysseus's visit, Pok had forgotten the original reason he'd been brought. With numb, floating legs, Pok went to stand at the podium and hear his fate.

"Student Doctor Pok Morning, I strip you of your student status indefinitely, effective immediately. You cannot attend classes; you will not have access to the labs, Ventricle, Vault, or Tay Hall. In three months, we will reassess the damage from your actions and decide if full expulsion is warranted. Under no circumstances are you allowed to leave the city."

The words struck him in the gut and stole his breath, holding it hostage on a dumb hope that some *but* would come, some rebuttal, some savior.

"Dr. Verik, do you wish to refute the sentence?"

Dr. Verik stood. Her jaw was tight; her masseter muscles shifted like nervous fingers. She then turned and strode up the aisle. She paused beside Pok to whisper.

"You've done all you can. Sit for Mobitz I: they can't take that from you. Study. Stay low. Good luck, Pok."

She left without fully looking at his face, spared herself the evolution of his disappointment. But he had to watch his mentor—his mother—leave. Her stride was so quick, so definitive, such a reprimand on Pok's existence, so eager to rid her life of him. She had never wanted a child anyway, right? He thought of Florence, who had crossed state lines and risked it all just to give Baby Girl a chance at a better life. His mother couldn't even stand up for him.

There was a deep loneliness when Phelando had died. A hole that would never be filled. But this . . . chosen abandonment. In many ways, standing there in an auditorium with all eyes on him, Pok had never felt so alone.

Fifty-Two

FULL CUT

Tay Hall was especially quiet that night with only the drum of rain to occupy its halls. The news of Odysseus's visit and an impending inspection dragged speculation and contemplation throughout the school. Everyone waited in their own way, for what this development would bring, for the consequences of a spire-less hurricane. Was this the beginning of the end of Hippocrates Medical Center? Of New Orleans?

In the cold dark of his room, Pok packed his father's *Principles* and his white coat back into the same tattered bag he'd arrived with. He stacked the other textbooks on his table beside his box of surgical supplies. The next hands that used them would be more deserving.

A scratch at his door gave him pause. Far from home, far from friends, in a land not made for him, in a city that didn't want him, Pok was alone. And vulnerable. Had Odysseus decided to take him by force? Perhaps that would be easier. Perhaps that would be better.

When the sound didn't repeat, Pok went to the door.

There, tucked through the bottom gap, was a letter. Some of the spook went away. Someone coughed from a couple rooms over. The sound of running water. These all came back to life.

He took the letter over to his desk and saw that it wasn't one, but two.

The top was a flyer, its message plain and clear. Fluorescent pink letters popped crisp in the night.

> Hippocrates Medical Center is currently under investigation for unsafe practices and subpar quality of care. Any resident of Orleans Parish, Louisiana, who presents to a certified Shepherd Organization hospital will be given free medical care, temporary housing, and a complimentary glass account.
>
> Physicians and medical personnel are specially invited to join the future of medicine.
>
> —Odysseus J. Shepherd, CEO of the Shepherd Organization

Before any gravity could sink in, Pok shifted to the second letter, which was handwritten and had none of the automatic feel of the shepherd decree. He tossed Odysseus's notice aside.

The hand-drawn portrait of Jillian was done with such care that for a moment Pok thought he was looking at a digital image. In the lower right corner was Florence's signature. The notice announced Jillian's memorial service would take place the next morning.

Pok sat on the bed. He thought back to train engines, the smell of billowing dust and stale sandwiches, the hope in reunion. The fierce defense of individuality. *Ole tick bite.* He wished he could return with Jillian to that in-between time when they were both naive and curious, accidentally discovering the American countryside together. All he had were the memories. And those would fade.

For now, at least, they were potent and real and close and Pok didn't want to let them go.

Pok was out of Tay Hall shortly past dawn, behind the second- and third-years who had clinical rotations and before his own classmates, who likely slept in before the day's first lecture with Dr. Lowry. Wide puddles flooded the intersections; the rain had just recently let up. Dark clouds promised more.

As Pok waited for the streetcar to Mid-City, a drone hovered near an adjacent breakfast truck. It paused, no doubt scanning Pok's face, and shot straight up. Above, the dark sky was full of them. Physicians and nurses and scribes and students alike stopped to point and stare before going about their day, a bit more urgency in their step.

Jillian's memorial took place in her and Florence's apartment. Pok kept his head low as he climbed the steps, slipped into the open door, and found a dimly lit spot in the corner. About two dozen people filled a living room meant for half as many. Some shared sad smiles; others bonded with tears.

The collective gaze went to the entrance, where Florence entered, dressed in all white, Baby Girl snug in a wrap of the same color. The attendees took turns greeting her. Her face was dry, a testament to emotional preparation. She stroked Zuri's sleeping head. Had Dr. Verik ever embraced Pok in that way?

The beginnings of tears broke through when she saw Pok. She embraced him briefly, her fingers warm and firm against him, and then moved on. The role he'd played in her life was over. She was better now. Because of him or in spite of? He couldn't say.

A heavyset woman with thick gray braids and a spray of moles over her cheeks led the procession. She opened with a quick prayer and thanked everyone for coming. Those who'd known Jillian came up one by one to share about her laughter, her sense of humor, her appetite for adventure and leading hikes twice monthly to and from MouseKill. How she'd become a cherished part of the community in such a short time period.

Pok wanted to go up, but his guilt and shame held him back. What could he say? That he'd been too busy learning (and failing) medicine to be a true friend? He waited until everyone had paid their private respects and went up to her. The casket was elegantly made, a reflection of Jillian's spirit. She'd helped him on that lonely road when her life would have been simpler if she'd just turned away and kept going. If she had just left him to the ticks and the bandits, everyone's life would be simpler.

She deserved all the elegance and more.

The rain returned as Pok walked up Canal. Drones swarmed above a long-abandoned house, its bold flood mark a stark foreshadowing. Behind it, rising just above the trees, the top of one of the spires. Its apex was a dull dead against the gray sky.

He moved on, not caring about the downpour. None of the few Canal Street vendors had the appetite to catch Pok's interest. He peered into the shops as he walked, thinking, not much about anything but everything at once.

He paused. Took a few steps back. He fingered his locs as he considered the barber's sign. He thought of Jillian's trust in him because they were both from New York. He thought of Anji, comatose because of his misjudgment. He thought of Silva, dead at the fingertips of his negligence. He thought of the care his father had given his hair and how he'd neglected his own, much like he'd neglected the responsibility of being a physician.

The door was heavy. No, just a little stuck. Pok yanked it forward and stepped into the shop. The floor was clean, all the hair that must have fallen here over the years swept away.

"Loc braids?" the barber said. His long beard, twisted into two strong, separate braids, more than made up for the thinned curls on his head, a year or two away from a shave.

"Full cut." Pok sat in the chair before he could think twice.

Fifty-Three

GIL

Chandra anchored at her hip, Blaire opened the door wide-eyed and frantic. Confusion stepped in, her eyes flicking from Pok's bare scalp to the parts of him she recognized. Then, finally, hopeful relief.

"Pok! I'm so glad you came." Blaire surprised him with a warm hug. Chandra's braids grazed his face. The girl rubbed his head before Blaire shifted her away. "Gil needs you."

She disappeared into the house, beckoning for him to come. Blaire already had water on the stove and poured him a cup of tea as Chandra mimicked the process with the baby doll she held. The faint scent of ripe ergot hung in the air. Underneath it, behind it, was the same puzzling smell that had ushered in Jillian's death.

Gil lay partially reclined in his living room armchair. An IV line snaked from his arm up to a drip bag half-done. The tips of his curled, unkempt beard scratched at his chest. Wild gray matted his hair. His lips moved silently to the rhythm of the stress balls rotating in his skeletal fingers. So much was different, but even more was still there. The thick jawline. The calloused hands. The shadow of inked muscles sculpted to crank grinding machines, haul stacks of paper, hold a daughter, now outlined in frail arms. Gil, buried under the weight of the Grips.

"Gil, honey, you have a visitor."

The balls rotated faster at the announcement.

"How long has he been like this?" Pok said.

"A week. Maybe two. It hit him like a train. He won't sleep. He won't shower. He's not eating. Yesterday started off good. I thought he was getting better. And then the spires went down. All the drones started showing up. Oh, Pok, I thought he was going to die, it was so bad. He couldn't talk. He couldn't see. Almost like he had a stroke or something. Is it that awful thing? Is it the Grips?"

Blaire paced in a small circle, patting Chandra on the back. Soothing the child was easier than soothing herself.

"He should be in the hospital," Pok said.

The gentle smile Blaire put on was one of the saddest Pok had seen. "They turned him away. They're too full, said his condition would be better treated from home. It seems every non-native has fallen sick. They gave him this oxygen tank and this IV bag, but what if it's not enough? What if he runs out when he really needs it?"

"Any Synth?" Pok searched Blaire's face as she answered.

"We were desperate. We heard that it could help."

"Did it?"

"Only a little."

Pok sat beside Gil and touched his shoulder. Gil moaned in response, his eyes clenched as if thrust into sunlight.

"Gil," Pok said.

The man calmed at his name. He lay back, out of breath. His eyes remained closed.

"It's Pok, honey," Blaire said. "You remember Pok? Your doctor."

Pok looked down. A small hand, dipped in grime, tugged at the hem of his shirt. Jillian's hand, reaching from the grave. Pok pulled away.

Not Jillian. Chandra. The adventurous girl cared little of Pok's reaction. She had successfully freed a stray thread. She ran her hand across the white, halted at a speck of black, then returned to the other end. Her four braids were neat and recently woven, her dress pressed, her face clean except for the dot of drool glistening at the corner of her mouth. She had grown, but only in size.

"Chandee?" The man flailed as if oppressed by his own weight. The little girl shuffled back into Pok's shirt, brushed her cheek along the threads. Gil's eyes flashed to the size of his marbles. Tears welled at the corners. "Oh! Oh! Chandee! Chandee! They locked her up. They feed her rats and grass!"

"She's right here," Pok said, careful. "Safe, with us."

"She flew. She flies." Gil's back arched. Spit flew. The armchair creaked; its legs scratched the floor. "Locked up. Oh, Chandee, oh, Chandee."

Chandra began to sob, a low, purring wail. Blaire picked her up and rocked her. "Shh, shh. It's okay, baby girl. It's okay, Daddy's going to be okay. Can you help him, Pok?"

I can't. I can't help anyone. I'm not a doctor. I'm not a student. I'm not anybody.

"I'll try," Pok said. And he did.

Pok put his travel sack to the side and got to work. With Gil's pulse thrumming against his fingers, he squeezed the IV bag to adjust his volume intake over the next hour. He took what mix of flashlights, dyes, and plastic wrap Blaire scrounged up for him and did the best version of flashing lights therapy he could with homemade multicolored filters. His head floated skyward as his cognition adjusted with Gil's. Any colors, sounds, smells, and sensations blended into one swaying, shifting, harmonious body. Gil's and Pok's auras danced around each other, ever closer.

On the verge of touching, merging, Pok yelled out. Pok sat back on his haunches and shut his eyes against roving nausea. At the wave's crest, he peeked to see Gil sit up, alert. The fog in his gaze cleared.

"Chandee," Gil said. "She's okay?"

Pok swallowed down whatever he was feeling. "Yes."

"Who is? Tell me who's okay."

"Chandra. Chandee."

Gil nodded. His eyes brightened. "Did I ever tell you why I left Baltimore?"

"You said it was a story for another time."

Gil mouthed the last four words as Pok said it. He picked up his marbles. "I worked for TSO in their Baltimore office. I was in Quality and Improvement. They'd send us AI-rendered videos and we'd type up a narrative. Then we'd either agree or disagree with another's interpretation. They didn't tell us the purpose, only the instructions. It was obvious; the videos confused the computers.

"One person had a verbose, flowery style like me. While some people would just say 'woman walking down the street,' for example, I'd write 'a starving artist wanders the desolation of her own creation, searching for her lost puppy' or some weird shit like that. Before long we began to write our narratives for one another. TSO had a strict 'no funny business' policy, so we shared our information through code and formally linked through a dating app. We had to make it look like a coincidence. That's how I met my wife."

"Blaire?" Pok said. That couldn't be right. Blaire was a native New Orleanian.

"Blaire's my partner. Shay was my wife."

"Describe her," Pok said.

"Her hair was dark brown, black if you weren't paying attention. In tight curls. Her nose was soft, with a small scar on the right side. She's average size, shorter than most. Her smile means she wants to be here. I want to be here, too. I wonder what it would be like to kiss her. To hold her." He blinked. "Both are good. Were good."

Gil rocked forward, grabbed his ball of yarn, centered it on his lap, and began to move his fingers intricately over it.

"Gil, what's wrong?" Pok worried he was seizing.

He responded by moving his fingers more furiously. No, not a seizure. He was trying to make something.

Pok found Gil's knitting needles on his bed. Underneath, the latest copy of the *Second Opinion*. Pok gently placed the needles into Gil's hands. The yarn quickly took. Pok watched. Sleep crept from the yarn, up Gil's hands, and lay stealthily upon his body. Finally, his eyelids fell, his head bobbed, his chin retreated to his chest. He began to snore.

This done, Pok released. He doubled over, clenching both against pain and nausea. He vomited—suddenly and violently—down onto himself. A hand on his back. A soft, sorrow-filled call in his ear. He nodded, not registering the words but accepting the need. He let himself be led upstairs.

"Arms up," Blaire said as she helped him out of his shirt. "Are you sure you can do this?" Her words exploded colors in an emotional firework display that ignited lost memories. He reached and plucked one from the sky.

"I have to. I'm fine."

The nausea dissipated. The synesthesia righted itself. Taking a tour of

Gil's memory tapped strongly into the Grips, evidenced by how far it had pushed Pok. Significant? Or another ghost to chase? He found himself back in a familiar place: consulting with *Principles*, in conversation with his father.

"Alignment. Alignment. Tell me something about alignment. There we go."

Narrative is powerful. Align someone's past with their present and you align them. NFTF.

Gil slept. Not much, but just enough to bring back his laugh, which greeted Pok on his way down the next morning. Gil fiddled on a half-finished welding project on a small worktable while his free hand worked the stress balls. A stack of bound, wilted paper lay quiet beside him. In the kitchen, Blaire stood cradling a teacup.

"Guess who got some sleep last night?" She mouthed to Pok: *and showered!*

"I heard that," Gil said. "The Grips gives me the power to read minds. You didn't know?"

"What's the status report?" Pok said.

"The winds are picking up. I hear Kristen's teetering on category four. The city's hunkering down. It's going to be a bad one."

"Let me worry about that," Blaire said. "I already stocked up and got our handyman to inspect the roof and the windows. Darryl who runs the hardware shop off University is delivering sandbags this afternoon."

"See?" Gil said. "She's my rock."

"I was talking about you," Pok said. "How much sleep did you get?"

"Five solid hours. I have a headache. And I still don't know up from down, but I'm better. Definitely better. What did you do?"

"Alignment," Pok said. "I brought you a little closer to me."

"And brought yourself this way as well, from what I heard. How are you feeling?"

"Last night was rough," Pok said.

"That's an understatement," Blaire said.

"I'm fine now."

"It's like you gave yourself a taste of the Grips," Gil said. "But for you it's only temporary."

"You didn't have many withdrawals either when you got here," Blaire said.

"Strong genes. You need to pass that around. Maybe hook up that IV straight from your veins to mine." Gil smiled and looked out the window. "So, what's the plan, Doc?"

Gil had hope and was looking to Pok to cultivate it. What if he couldn't?

"Balance," Pok said.

"Say again?" Gil said.

"That's the plan," Pok said. "We help you find balance."

"I like it," Gil said. "You hear that, babe? Dr. Pok is going to balance me."

Gil's voice, rapid and indecipherable, woke Pok in the middle of a pitch-black night. He lay there at first, listening to both Gil and the wind whistling through the rafters. A loud crash shook the walls. Glass shattered. Pok sprang up and out into the hall.

Blaire rushed out of their room with a flashlight and peeked into Chandra's. "Still asleep," she said. "Thank God. He's okay. I'm okay. The storm spooked him a bit. The power's out. Can you talk to him?"

Pok went into Gil's room, where a single candle danced in the corner. He picked up the table, the chair, and Gil's knitting needles and then sat beside his friend, who lay staring at the ceiling, chest heaving.

"What's upsetting you?" Pok said.

Gil wiped his face. "We applied to date. They ran our genes; we qualified for subsidized marriage. We'll have a wedding. We'll live by the rules, and everything will be fine. We'll be so thrilled, Shay."

As Gil spoke, the left side of his face stiffened. Eventually, only the right moved, slurring his speech. Pok set up the FLT with the fluorescents Blaire had procured.

"When we learned Chandee was on the way, they called us in almost every week." Gil's eyes took in the light. His face regained full expression. For Pok, scenes, emotions, and motivations from his own past flickered by like a passing rain cloud. Then, too, he was back in the present. "Never told us what they were looking for. My wife worried. And worried. And then Chandra came, and she was perfect.

"But Shay couldn't see Chandee's perfection and I couldn't see my wife's struggle. We argued. We fought. Our union had started because they couldn't get in here." He stabbed his temple with a finger. "And it ended because they finally did."

Gil's eyes glazed over; the left edge of his mouth upturned slightly. "Can't you see how well she's growing? She's learning to speak. She's so smart. I go back to work. Time with our daughter will be good for you. You'll see."

Pok adjusted the FLT wavelength. Red went to blue went to purple. His fingers traced Gil's pulse up his arm, closer to the source. He dedicated a small but important portion of his attention to his own pulse.

"I head home during lunch. The tiling on the roof looks funny. Why is it coming off like that? Then a hand waves. Not a tile; Chandee. And you. She sees me. You're crying. I wave back. I don't understand why you're on the roof until you step forward. For a second you float there. Then you're gone."

Gil reached for the knitting; Pok grabbed his shoulder. What little flesh remained hummed against Pok's fingers. Pok wanted to tell him it would be all right, that the freedom he'd traveled for was his. But he couldn't.

Pok let go. Gil grabbed his needles and began to knit.

Hurricane Kristen came and went. Any floodwaters receded. Despite not having needed to tap into them for years, New Orleans still had its survival instincts and withstood the worst with apt preparation. Both the *Second Opinion* and the *Daily* warned that the "season" was just beginning. Another tropical storm was already forming in the Gulf of Mexico. Without the spires, the worst was yet to come.

Over the next week Pok immersed himself fully in treating Gil. He monitored Gil's sleep-wake cycles. He frequently checked his temperature. He measured all the fluid that went in and all the urine that came out. But Gil wasn't getting better. Not consistently. The little sleep he enjoyed dwindled. His smile came a little less often each day. At times he seemed to notice things that weren't there. After each session, each hour spent, each frustrating evening, Pok wondered just what the hell he was doing.

But Gil didn't crash. Whatever Pok was doing kept him from going all the way over the edge. Gil was still alive. And that much couldn't be said for many of the city's sickest residents.

Blaire went to the market every morning and brought back stories of the surrounding collapse. The Grips had its hold on each and every non-native in one way or another. Whereas before the milder cases were minor discomforts, now the norm was a debilitating illness. Many had died, many suddenly.

(Ten percent.)

Some went quickly, their bodies unable to tolerate even the slightest adjustment. Others found the process insidious. Sharp cognitive decline became standard. Pok listened for reports of it becoming infectious and spreading outside of scrollers. Blaire didn't speak of any; Pok didn't ask.

Shepherd drones watched it all. They didn't intervene. But they saw. And thus, Odysseus saw. The state and federal government saw.

For all Pok knew, the whole world was watching and waiting to see how it all would end.

Fifty-Four

AN UNLIKELY VISITOR

Blaire knocked lightly on Pok's door. "You have a visitor."

After two hours, the nausea from the last Alignment session was just starting to recede. Pok rolled off his bed, wondering who would come to see him. Dr. Verik, reconsidering her efforts? James? Florence?

Of all the possibilities, Pok's visitor was his least expected.

Anji sat by the fireplace. She stood at Pok's arrival, unsteady on her feet. She had thinned considerably. A bandage wrapped around her forehead, bulbous over her injury. She carried a large tote bag, filled with papers, wider than her. Of all things, her expression was the most Anji: serious and concealing, without smile nor grimace.

That and her bluntness.

"You look terrible," she said. "Do you have Agrypnia?"

"No," Pok said. He came down the rest of the way. "At least, not right now."

He explained what he knew about the disorder and how he sought to help Gil through Alignment. When he was done, Anji was nodding.

"Your body can heal from Agrypnia. You're trying to see if you can pass on that healing."

"Pretty much. It's proving insufficient."

"Has Dr. Verik been helping?" Pok's quick gaze must have shown his hurt; Anji recoiled.

Pok's dry laugh felt like ash in his throat. "They took her off Agrypnia."

"That hasn't stopped her," Anji said. "She's forced time at every Grand Rounds to give updates. Says she's discovered special antibodies in a patient that could lead to a cure. I thought maybe the two of you were working together."

"We're not." Pok shook his head, agitated. Why was Anji here? He gestured to her bag.

"Oh yes." Anji unloaded on the chair and showed him the contents. "These are all my notes. Fresh copies. Everything should be here."

"I don't understand," Pok said.

"Mobitz I. The semester just ended and we have a month to study. I heard you couldn't go to class."

Pok thumbed through the pages. Anji's handwriting was neat and meticulous. "I appreciate it, Anji, but I'm not a student right now. They made that clear."

"Anyone can sit for Mobitz I," she said. "You've worked as hard as the rest of us. Harder."

Why was she helping him? He couldn't tell. So he asked her.

"You're one of us," she said. "Table nine. We don't win unless we all win."

"My friend almost killed you."

"I—I thought you knew. Kris didn't push me down the stairs. When I saw him in the Vault I was startled. I ran and I tripped. He tried to catch me. That's all I remember."

Pok sucked his teeth. This changed little. "He pushed the whole city when he sold us out to Odysseus. Because of him, the spires are down."

"You really haven't spoken to anyone, have you?"

"You're the first person who seems to remember I exist."

"Your friend didn't sell out New Orleans," Anji said. "Odysseus jumped the gun. He got the courts to launch the investigation before he had anything tangible. Now they're hoping that we buckle from the hurricanes."

"Then what did Kris take from the Vault?"

The slightest hint of a smile flitted across Anji's face like a passing shadow. "Whatever it is, he still has it."

Fifty-Five

THE AMYGDALA

The Amygdala Center for the Mentally Unquiet stood alone on a modest swath of forest. One could easily walk right past it without noticing anything more than thick-trunked trees. Only an inquisitive and searching eye would see how the forest's living wood curved and bent into artificial shapes. Crafted as an extension of the surrounding land, the Amygdala was shaped by the very nature it inhabited.

Pok parked his bike and found a narrow foot path to the entrance. Ahead, a middle-aged man, his brown skin caked with old and new dirt, approached the Amygdala's scribe guards.

"In for the day?" the scribe guard said. She sent a quick glance to Pok as he approached.

The man kept his head lowered, as if he were talking to someone living in the grass. "I suppose."

After sending Jerry to Amygdala, Pok had read about the city's psychiatric facility. As the first Hippocrates Medical Center department to completely cut ties with burgeoning AI tech, the facility was meticulously designed with recovery and rehabilitation in mind. The Amygdala's many plants, for example, were not just decoration. For those with hallucinations, the flowers were vibrant and diverse in color. The specific sound frequency from foraging bees activated the auditory processing center of the brain in such a way that deprioritized internal stimuli. The Amygdala's patients chose their own rooms in the multistory facility. The anxious usually opted for something closer to ground level, while those with fleeting thoughts of suicide often occupied the highest floor to test their motivations.

"The shepherd drones been here yet?" Pok said as he presented himself. The sky was clear.

"At first. But the building's magnetic field drove them away."

"Where is it?" Pok said. "The EMF?"

"In the walls. I'm surprised it's still functional. It's the one place the shepherds can't access." The *yet* was implied. "Didn't do much for the hurricane, though. Who are you here to see?"

"Kris Boles."

The scribe guard perked. "The VIP. Are you on his authorized list? Name?"

Pok's heart sank as he gave it to her. Of course Kris would be under special lock and key.

"Pok Morning. Pok Morning. Pok . . . Here you are. Almost missed it. Looks like they just added you yesterday."

Pok almost lunged forward and snatched the paper, he was so surprised, but he caught himself. The scribe guard, picking up on some of his surprise, rechecked the list.

"Mr. Boles spends most of his time in the art room. See if you can get a look at that arm. He won't let anyone touch it." The scribe guard patted Pok down. She tapped his front pocket and removed a pen. "You'll get it back on your way out."

Pok's ears hummed as he passed through the doors. Inside, the light aroma of varying plants mixed with the steady trickle of filtered water falling into the central pond. The art patio was empty. Pok found Kris's room down the hall.

The door was open. Kris hung new art on what little white was left on the walls. He'd taken good care of himself; thick, tight curls hid his scar. His clothes hugged his body. Layers of tautly wrapped gauze covered his right arm.

Pok knocked to announce himself. Kris turned, his gaze thin and suspicious. His eyes swelled in delayed recognition.

"I thought you forgot about me," Kris said.

From his bag, Pok produced wrapped honey ham and roasted beets. Compliments of Blaire's endless generosity. Kris propped his latest creation—a sky view of the hospital's garden, sketched but not yet colored—against the wall and brought the package to the central table. He cut everything in half, set a portion to the side, and then ate with a hunger that explained his weight gain.

"Anji told me what happened," Pok said.

"Thanks for bringing this, man. You've always been a good friend."

Pok sat next to Kris. "Did Odysseus tell you to break into the Vault?"

Kris smiled. Pok, not expecting this, recoiled a little.

"He underestimated me," Kris said. "He tried to take advantage of our fight in the Fatty Liver. He expected me to hate you. He expected me to want revenge. So he told me how to get it."

"You found Zion?"

"I found the answers."

Frustration rose. Why was Kris being so cryptic?

Kris looked to his left, as if summoned. His mouth parted. His fingers absentmindedly picked at the edge of his bandage. When he looked back at Pok, for a second it seemed as if he'd forgotten he was there.

"Is he talking to you now?" Pok said.

"He can't reach me in here," Kris said. He continued picking at his bandage. "Whatever this building uses is stronger stuff than the spires."

"What happened to your arm?" Pok said. "They said you won't let anyone look at it."

"I told you, I only trust you. I wanted you to examine it, no one else. Go on."

Kris didn't wait. He began to unravel his bandage. Clean on the outside, it grayed layer after layer. Sour stunk up the air.

"Kris . . ."

His friend kept going. The lower layers stuck to one another, making a wet ripping sound as they pulled apart. Kris only winced. Deep pain lines cut his face; he kept going. And then it was off. The wrapping wasn't as extensive as Pok thought; much of the girth was the swell of Kris's arm. A black wound the size of a grape and just as dark sat in the middle. Red, purplish, moist skin spread outward.

Kris wasn't finished. He dug into his arm with his pencil. Pok jerked forward, too late, then turned away. Acid burned the top of his throat.

"It's okay. You can look now."

Kris had tucked his arm between his lap and the underside of the table. Congealed blood covered his hand. The smell of rot and metal marked the air. Despite all of this horror, Pok's attention went to what Kris was holding.

"You know what this is?" Kris said.

Pok took it. Had his father's been this small? He wiped away blood and pus to reveal shiny silver underneath. A thin, concave sheath still connected the hollow inside. It looked like their textbook's representations of blood cells.

"Whose Memorandium is this?" Pok said.

"Julian," Kris said. "Julian Shepherd. If Zion is the console, this is the software."

"But where is Zion?"

Kris smiled that gruesome smile.

"It was too big to fit into my arm. I left it in the garden with my thoughts. I hope it helps."

Kris closed his eyes. His breaths were deep.

"Nurse," Pok said. The word crossed small and pathetic into the air. "Nurse! We need help!"

As the shuffle of feet came down the hall, Kris grabbed Pok's sleeve, bloodying it. "You want to know the last thing I said to Odysseus before I entered these walls?" Kris's grin reached for his ears. " 'Got you, motherfucker.' "

Fifty-Six

MEDICAL RECORDS

Sweat drenched Pok by the time he parked his bike outside the medical center. He composed himself, waited outside, sure to keep his face covered, and slipped into the door when a physician exited, deep in conversation with her scribe.

I left it in the garden with my thoughts.

Pok found the tree stump where he and Kris would meet. The vines and leaves covering it had thickened. Pok pulled at the foliage. Hungry roots clung to the hollow of the stump, digging into the wood. Pok's fingernails scratched something different. He uncovered the thing hidden inside, careful not to destroy it in his excitement. Damp soil crumbled off a thick medical folder and gave light to the Vault's laminated design.

Pok tucked the file under his arm, made a swift exit from the garden and the hospital, and didn't stop until he was back in his room above the Paper Mill. He was prepared to read about Odysseus's treatment and how it had led to the formation of Zion, prepared for some insight into fighting this Agrypnia, prepared to see his father's name and to feel the pain of loss all over again. But there was none of that. The name staring back at him didn't make sense.

It was his own. *Medical Records: Pok Morning.*

The beginning pages chronicled Pok's complete prenatal history. Ultrasounds, brief notes from Emily Verik's doctor visits, and an annotated genome. Several dedicated pages analyzed his DNA, contrasting it to that of his mother, Julian Shepherd, and then Odysseus. Powerful computer simulations predicted how the proteins produced by his genes would interact with those responsible for the genetic disorder that had beset his lineage.

Pok turned the pages. His birth certificate listed Phelando and Emily as his parents. He was born right here in New Orleans.

After a few medical notes from his uneventful birth and subsequent pediatric visits, the letters from Phelando began, marked with a New York address. Some were long, describing in detail Pok's development, his interests in school, how he was growing. Others were brief and clinical. School report cards, cognitive tests, awards. He paused at his medical school application and the Council's decision.

Then he came to the notes from Customs and Adjustment. It should have stopped there. It didn't.

Meticulously documented was everything he had done since coming to Hippocrates. Every test he took, narrative of every meditation session, verbatim transcriptions of ward conversations he barely remembered. Six South had its own section with detailed descriptions of the patients he'd treated and how he'd treated them. Underneath many were Dr. Verik's insights. Ranging from brief ("recovered quickly") to extensive, she hypothesized the mechanisms in which a patient's presentation had mirrored in Pok. She noted changes in his clinical thinking; nuances in his interactions with her, other professors, and even his classmates; and fluctuations in his exam results. This level of detail required reports from all his professors.

Pok turned to the next section.

"Fuck."

He remembered that first blood draw after treating Jillian in the hospital. *You have a great alignment with her. Just cautious. I'll run tests to make sure. The meditation sharpened the skill.*

Dr. Verik had done more than run tests. She had injected his blood into several patients, both on Six South and during her house calls, and documented the results. There was an extensive note from the night of Jillian's passing, the night the spires went dark.

> Extensive alignment. PM showed full Agrypnia symptomatology after overnight treatment in Mid-City dwelling. Blood samples showed significant antibodies. PCR replication successful but not effective. Original antibodies show some promise when used clinically.
>
> Considered further in vivo application. Ethical considerations significant. Given recent inspection and unclear moral compass of fellow professors, best for PM to be removed from further studies. Contributions appreciated.
>
> Conclusion: Project PM unsuccessful.

All this time, Dr. Verik had been paying as much attention to him as she was the patients on Six South. Her conclusion was clear: Pok's anatomy was the enantiomer to Odysseus's. A mirror opposite, she suspected his genome held the antidote to the manufactured Agrypnia. She'd projected her self-experimental drive onto her only son. Two decades later, it bore fruit in Pok.

Only she'd concluded he *wasn't* the cure. *Unclear moral compass* . . . Was she trying to protect him? Too little, too late. Someone had put his name on Kris's guest list. Someone wanted him to find this. To finish it.

What if he *was* the cure? And Dr. Verik just hadn't yet found how to utilize him?

That night, Pok sat with *Principles*. He flipped through the pages and scanned their margins, unsure of what comfort he sought from Phelando's ghost. What could negate this insanity? Had his father raised him as a living experiment?

In "Blood Transfusions," a block of notes caught his eye. *Recipient receives added benefit of donor's antibodies. Similar to pregnancy.* And then, as an addendum in a thicker, quality ink: *Also can backfire. Saw DIC today. NFTF. Wow.*

The flush of a toilet. The creek of floorboards. That was the third time in the last hour Gil had gone. Pok opened his door a crack and immediately shut it. The horrid smell of melena permeated the hall. Gil was dying.

If Pok couldn't find comfort in his father's love, maybe he could find purpose in his words. Pok sat back on his bed, opened his medical file with fresh eyes, and began to wonder.

Pok didn't sleep. He read over his medical records several times, making sure he didn't misinterpret or misread. On multiple occasions, especially when the clock turned another hour, he resisted seeking out Dr. Verik to demand answers, an explanation, reassurance that it was all a lie.

Morning came. With it: clarity.

He found Blaire in the corner of the living room where it was still dark, Chandra asleep on her shoulder. Blaire rubbed her back. Another rough night for all of them.

"Do you have a blood draw kit?" Pok said.

Blaire began to rise; Pok gestured for her to sit. "I can find it. Just point me in the right direction."

He found the phlebotomy kit, a working centrifuge, and a fluorescent lamp in one of the back storage closets with the rest of the remaining medical supplies from the Paper Mill's original market. He brought them all out to the living room, where Gil's deep snores set the night's rhythm. He found an old piece of Shaliyah's ginger in the bottom of his book bag.

"Let me help you," Blaire said. "I can lay her down. Gil's not going to sit still, not when he's like this."

"It's not for him," Pok said. Nausea came as he set up; just the thought of what he was about to do triggered his parasympathetic nervous system. He chewed on the ginger. It helped only a little. He'd have to fight through it.

He applied the tourniquet to his own arm. The nausea intensified at the sight of the needle. His ears rang, saliva flooded his mouth, his fingers tingled. He breathed through it, angled the needle like Nurse Lemi had shown him, and pierced his skin. The pressure smelled like table nine's cadaver. Pain shot from his left temple back to the base of his skull, below his right ear. He spasmed; the needle shot through his vein. He pulled out, ignoring Blaire's gasp, and tried again.

Pok closed his eyes and saw more in the darkness. He guided the needle into his engorged vein and trusted his body to confirm the positioning. Blind but seeing, he loaded the vial into the butterfly and clicked it in place. The vial filled; his pulse expanded out of his body. He opened his eyes. The sight didn't bring nausea. He finished the draw and loaded the centrifuge.

Pok illuminated his sample with the lamp. There. Clear. Hope. "Savage," he said.

"What are we looking at?" Blaire said.

"Antibodies. My body is making them." *Made to make them.* He pointed a trembling finger. "This band here. If we give these to Gil, it might work."

The plan went boldly against his training. It was unsanitary. It was unsafe. It lacked accountability and foresight.

But it was all he had left.

Gil sat at his workstation, staring. Beside him, his breakfast plate was cold and untouched.

"I want to try something new," Pok said.

When Gil spoke, a sour heat cut the air. "Medicine?"

"I hope so," Pok said. "But you have to finish the story. What happened after they fell off the roof?"

Pok took one of the centrifuged vials and extracted a bit from the thicker band. As he injected it into the IV line, Gil began.

"Shay survived. The shepherds put her in the hospital. Tweaked her enhancements. Gave her new ones. She went through months of rehabilitation. When she came out she was different. Cold."

"Did she recognize Chandra?"

"Very much so. But that made it worse. It would have been better if it were some sort of psychosis. But instead it was an . . . ambivalence. If there was a day Shay stopped being a mother to Chandee, it was then."

Gil was better. The Alignment brought Pok close enough to Agrypnia for his body to create a response. He saw it in the bands and saw it in Gil's improvement. Only, it wasn't enough. Any benefit was gone by nightfall.

It wasn't enough.

Pok had more to give. This was his purpose, why he'd been created. Yes—created. His father would strongly dispute this, even reprimand him. But his father was dead. It was his job to finish what his mother had started.

His fingers played with a syringe already loaded with Gil's blood—Gil's infected blood. When had he done that? It didn't matter. All that mattered now was the doing.

Pok didn't need a tourniquet. His blood pressure was already high, his heart racing, his vein blue and waiting in the antecubital space. This time there was no nausea, only purpose. Pok injected into himself the full of Gil's blood, the Grips and all.

Fifty-Seven

THE GRIPS

A feverish sickness came like the tide. Its recession took with it Pok's ability to sleep.

Predawn proved hardest. Keeping his eyes open hurt; closing them hurt worse. He tried to study; he couldn't. The weight of his head strained his neck. But when he lay down, instead of sleep, the night brought fear. He became convinced the sun's nuclear energy kept away TSO-hired bandits and he'd be abducted by morning. There was no logic, no evidence, only raw belief.

A knock at the door shot Pok up from his chair. The open *Principles* flew from his lap and slapped against the wall. A dull pain spread from his lower back down his thighs.

The door. Was someone here? Yes, that's what a knock meant. But the room, it looked different. The bed had shifted; his glass lay halfway under the covers. This was his NYC room. A memory. The knock was a memory.

He backed into his chair, slow, so as not to disturb the living recollection. The room changed, right in front of him. Not NYC, but Tay Hall. Dull, uninspired, perfect for sleep and study. His first night as a medical student. His eyes shot to the door, this time ready for the knock. It came, soft and distinct. Friendly, even. Odysseus, too, had been friendly.

The door opened. James and Anji. Come to tell him about Student Doctor Night at the Fusiform. "Bring your white coat for free drinks."

"We hear you're sponsored."

Pok slammed the door.

"Hallucinations." Speaking the word shot hot white from temple to jaw. He reached across the table, found a pen, and scribbled the word onto the first paper he could find. *Hallucinations. Hallucinations.* Each iteration soothed. He expanded his writing to other words, and reality sank back into place.

Writing organized his thoughts. He had Agrypnia. There was no question. His sense of past, present, and future was evolving. He could relive experiences as if they were happening all over again, like videos looping on a screen. He paused to test this. He saw Gil, bent over his knitting. Now he was sitting in front of the fire, smiling over his freshly brewed tea, his eyelids already starting to fall.

This was it. This was the disease. Would his body step up to the challenge? Pok drew his own blood. Five vials. A hopeful medicine, cultivated from hopeful veins.

Would it be enough?

The fingers of the Grips loosened. Pok's healing body and mind squashed any lingering doubt of the power of his genetics. Downstairs, Gil waited patiently, ready to finish his story around Shay and Chandra. Pok injected him with three vials of his own blood. In turn, Pok infused his own veins with more of Gil's.

Gil's mind cleared, right in front of him. Pok's body was enough. Could it last?

With regular transfusions, Gil's improvement was gradual, steady, and—most notably—sustained. Pok's trajectory was the opposite. While each of Gil's recoveries was more robust than the last, Pok rebounded less and less. Before long, he spent most of his time under the hold of the Grips. What if he fell too far? What if his body stopped fighting back?

But he couldn't deny Gil's progress. Pok set up a line that went from his vein into Gil's and then another going the other way. He passed out and woke up hours later. Gil was gone, his end of the IV capped. How much had they exchanged?

Sensorium plagued him. Pok squeezed his skull tightly between his hands. He lifted. Slow at first. Terrified. The pulling. He lifted and lifted. The world tilted. He cradled his head in his arms, felt the brush of his shirt against his cheek. He turned himself around. Slow to stop the dizziness. He looked up at himself. He expected to see a headless monstrosity, a severed, leaking jugular flat against the mess of his trachea. But he saw only his chest, the arms that held him, and the shoulders. Nothing above.

The world was quieter. Less itchy. Pok carried himself down University Ave. Eleven pounds. That was how much a human head weighed. The brain itself was only three. There were no screams. No second glances.

He didn't know where he was going until he smelled the strawberries. Strong. Potent. Not as fresh as the ones from Shaliyah's garden. His mouth watered. He resisted the urge to give his head a hard, firm shake.

"What are you doing here?" Shaliyah's voice. Softly concerned. "Pok, are you all right?"

Of course he wasn't. He was standing outside her door, cradling his own head like a baby. He'd been stupid to come. She wouldn't understand.

Pok turned and ran. He ran until the smell was gone and then ran more, up University, up into the heavens. Colored wind whipped around him. Harsh purple stung his cheeks. He tripped over something hard and thin and low. His head flew; his body tumbled.

The world rolled. His cheekbone hit the ground. A bloodred curtain fell over everything. He lay there and waited. Maroon pain faded to gray. He opened his eyes. Tall yellow blades of grass dominated his field of view. He pushed off the dirt by puffing his cheek and rolled just enough to spot his body, which had landed some feet away in the field. It was slow to rise. Too slow.

Pok smelled worried chatter. People. Someone had seen him lose his head.

"Hurry up!" Pok yelled.

His body obeyed. It sprinted toward him. Pok winced as stretched fingers yanked him up by the ear. Uncut fingernails dug into his cheeks, splitting wide the gash from the fall. His arms hugged his head tight to his chest and took him all the way back to his room.

He slammed the door, pressed his hands against the yellow, cracked wood, and looked outside the peephole to make sure he hadn't been followed. His hands . . . they were empty. He must have dropped himself in his panic. He swung the door open, prepared to retrace his steps and find his head before someone else did, and then stopped.

He reached up. Cheeks. Ears. Eyes. Everything was there. On his shoulders.

What the hell was *that*?

His body trembled. He locked his door and lay on his bed until the shakes subsided. He needed to stay inside. Where it was safe.

When he was ready, he went to his desk and wrote. He wrote about the synesthesia, about the color of wind, the scent of Shaliyah's voice, the red taste of pain. The horrific beauty of complete separation from body. A beauty he couldn't begin to understand. He didn't try to.

When he'd written enough, he set his journal aside. He needed to study. Mobitz I. Table nine. He needed to win so they'd all win.

Gil was cured. Pok's own ability to heal, however, had expired. With that last transfusion, Pok had gone too far. Was this how he'd die? After everything, after all he'd done and discovered and sustained, the cure he'd stumbled upon would only be used once. Mere samples of his blood—which Dr. Verik had plenty of—wouldn't be useful. It was his body, the essence of his living DNA, that created the response.

If only he could scale himself. Clone, perhaps. Science fiction. A proposition more fitting for the boardroom in the Shepherd Organization's New York City skyscraper rather than here, in Hippocrates. Pok turned at this thought, as if it had been whispered in his ear.

Maybe this wasn't the end, after all. Maybe he could have one more chapter.

When these new thoughts were fully formed, a virtual labyrinth he could walk through and touch and explore, much like *Impact* and the Source, Pok wrote it down.

Fifty-Eight

JERRY

"You stink of the Grips."

Jerry's gripe could have been for himself. Agrypnia had a stronghold on the Resurrectionist. The smell of it leaked out of his skin; a golden hue touched the Fusiform's air. Pok saw Jerry both as he was now and as he had been before. Jerry was a dangerous man. He'd felt it at that first meeting. He was still dangerous, if only because he was still Jerry, a continuation of the man that had been there before.

Pok stared up at the rotting wood ceiling as the past came in waves. The fear, anger, and hopelessness in their encounters; it was all there. Most of all, though, he felt a deep pity.

"Another hurricane's on the horizon. We got lucky with Kristen. Louisiana is expected to give full control over to the shepherds any day now," Jerry said. "It's over. Let me die in peace."

Pok didn't move. Jerry sucked his teeth.

"Here." Jerry's voice was frail and small. He held out a trembling bag of yellow powder. "That's all I have left."

"I didn't come for Synth." Pok's voice mixed with the smell of Jerry's exhaustion. And was that . . . feces? No, that was a while ago. That was back in the *before*. "I came to talk to the head editor of the *Second Opinion*."

Jerry sucked his teeth again. "The editor is dead. And so is the paper."

"How about a Resurrection Issue, for the cure?"

"Bullshit. Odysseus is the cure. One way or the other." Jerry ran ragged, aged hands over his face. When Pok remained silent, Jerry uncrossed his legs and slammed his hand on the table. "You ain't got no fucking cure."

"He does." Gil emerged from the door's shadow. He'd cleaned up well for his part. His beard was trimmed down from the overgrown, haggard mess of the Grips and neatly accented his already expression-filled face. Gray peppered throughout.

"You sold Synth to his partner, Blaire," Pok said. "You told her it wouldn't do much good. But I found something that did."

Gil took a seat. "I was about as bad as you look. I haven't had any sign of Agrypnia for four days now."

Jerry licked his lips. He regarded Gil like a starving man might a steaming plate of grilled lamb and roasted beets. "How?"

Pok told him. Jerry listened. The Resurrectionist's broken body shifted as he fell into the role of journalist. He fished a cracked pen from his pocket and Gil supplied him with ample paper. Jerry briefly paused transcription when Pok got to the part about what Kris uncovered in the Vault, just enough to realign any shock he felt, and then continued with vigor. The ink seemed to come from the page itself rather than the pen.

"Let me get this straight," Jerry said when Pok was done. "You and Odysseus have similar DNA. And since your body made a cure—antibodies—Odysseus's likely can as well?"

Pok nodded toward Gil, who took the sign.

"That's exactly what we're saying," Gil said. "Making that public puts the pressure on him. Especially if people conclude that he made this disease."

"It'll take some time to get *Second Opinion* back up and running. It needs to be quick, before the worst of the winds. Tropical storm Laurice just got promoted to hurricane. She's set to make landfall tomorrow." Jerry stood too quickly and steadied himself. He paced a short perimeter around their table. "I'll need help. I can find help." He eyed Pok, as if to convince himself he was real. "What if it doesn't work?"

"It has to," Gil said.

Jerry tapped the table. The edges of his lips curled in the beginnings of a grin. "You really have gone a little crazy," he said, and then he was gone.

Pok wrapped his fingers around the yellow bag of powder Jerry had left to make sure it was real. He pocketed it and followed Gil out into the night. He didn't have much time.

Fifty-Nine

MOBITZ I

Gil's remission sustained; Pok's condition deteriorated. He tried to make use of what little energy he had left. In his borrowed room atop the Paper Mill, Pok turned his focus to Mobitz I. He laid out his materials. Textbooks, notes, previous exams. His father's *Principles.* When he tried to sit, sparks shot from the pressure of the chair. The smell of burning rubber filled the room. He opened the first textbook and the sound of the paper seared pain across his chest.

How was he going to do this? His fingers found the bag of Synth. It was an answer. *A* potential *answer*, he reminded himself.

With a quick arm, Pok cleared a spot on his desk. He heard his skin across the table, felt the crash of the books, tasted the flutter of their pages. He tapped out a mound of the Synth. How had Jerry done it? He closed one nostril, bent over, and inhaled through the other. Coughs rattled his body.

The noise of the world fell away. Sensation evolved. The drug traveled up his veins, to his heart, up his carotid arteries, and *pulse-pulse-pulsed* past his blood-brain barrier. He *was* the drug. He was the pulse. He was everything and nothing all at once.

He picked up the little yellow bag. Jillian. Silva. Countless others, judged. Labeled as weak. Because of Synth. But this was the feeling they'd sought. Not to chase a high as an escape but as an entrance. To be present. To be aware. To sleep.

Yes. Sleep. Pok could if he chose to. All he had to do was lie on the bed and sleep would find him. Finally.

"No. No, no, no, no." Pok ripped the sheets off the bed and threw them in the corner. That wasn't enough. He upended the mattress and leaned it against the wall. He pounded on it and, when his shoulder burned, rested his cheek against the fabric. Sleep almost took him right then, upright against the wall mattress. He should let it. Everyone needed sleep. Everyone needed . . .

Pok pushed off. Back at his desk, he flipped through his textbooks. Scoured his notes. Where to start. It was too much. It wasn't enough.

His father's *Principles*. Always.

Medicine. NFTF. Never enough. Have to be enough.

Pok sat down and started with anatomy. He didn't get up for a long time.

Pok took the last of the Synth in the hours preceding Mobitz I. The burn traveled up his nose, down his throat, and spread across his chest. He made his way out of the Paper Mill and up University. The wind nearly took him away. Confusion met him at the main gate; the scribe guards didn't know he was entitled to take the test. Pok knew. More people came. Was that Dr. Lowry? She looked neither happy nor approving. She pulled him aside. She was strong. "Do you want to do this?" Pok did. He was ready.

They let him through. He floated to Genesis Auditorium. Drs. Sims, Granger, and Wilcox proctored, handed out the written tests and pencils. Students sat four to every row. From above the stage a giant clock watched over the auditorium.

The clock spoke.

"Focus on the test. That's all that matters. Everything else will matter later." Its voice crackled as if from an old-school intercom, each syllable in cadence with the tick of the second hand. He recognized his own thoughts in the otherwise unfamiliar speech. Could others hear them? No. That brought him comfort. That brought him peace.

The test began. Pok blinked and . . .

Sixty

EMILY VERIK

. . . he was standing outside of Genesis. Past the revolving doors, on University, the rain fell near horizontal. The first of the floodwaters began to trickle into the building. Hurricane Laurice. Several hours must have passed. He'd blacked out. Was the exam over? His hand ached. He worked his fingers, felt their fatigue. He peered back through the double doors. At the front of the auditorium, under the stage, the proctors sorted the tests. No students remained. Dean Sims looked up; Pok ducked away.

Pok considered walking onto Six South as a patient. He'd surely be admitted after only a brief physical exam. How easy it would be to relinquish control to the hospital.

He resisted the sweet call of death and instead found the cracked, familiar door just outside the HemoStat. Orange light leaked through. Dr. Verik's office. Mom's office. He went inside.

Dr. Verik sat up at Pok's entrance. She checked the time. "The exam—"

"It's done," Pok said.

"A great milestone," Dr. Verik said. "I'm glad you chose to focus on it. You should get back to wherever you're staying. The city's curfew . . ." Her voice trailed off. Dr. Verik moved, quick, and Pok knew the purpose only when the bright light entered his pupil. One side, then the other.

"Your immunity . . ." she said.

"Has served me well," Pok said. *Us* well. "I've been using my body's response to treat."

Dr. Verik's fingers examined his arm, found the track marks from the many transfusions.

"I sense I tipped too far on my own balance." Pok held out the *Second Opinion*. Dr. Verik angled away from it, as if it may bite.

"What is this?" she said.

"You should read it," Pok said. "Everyone else is."

Dr. Verik took the paper and read. Halfway through, she looked up at Pok, seemed about to say something, and then went back to the page. Faces had so much detail, so much on which to *focus*—the lines and how they moved, the angle of the lips, the compression of the nose—that he could no longer ascertain human emotion.

"Where do you want me to start?" For the first time, Dr. Verik sounded lost. A few weeks ago that would have broken Pok. Now it was just an observation in a world of things to observe.

"Why did you give up on me?"

"Oh, Pok. I never gave up on you. I protected you. As your sponsor I got all your grades. All your tests. No one else knew about your DNA—not Sims, not Granger, no one. Only that I had the consent of a patient with promising antibodies. Then the spires went down." Dr. Verik scooted toward him. "I knew there'd be pressure from the Council to take over my research. This isn't supposed to be your burden. You see that, don't you?"

Pok said nothing. It didn't matter what he saw. Observations were just observations.

Dr. Verik read again the article outlining how she'd experimented on her own son, using his blood to treat patients, exposing him to various stressors and cognitive tests so that she could find a cure for a disorder hardly anyone else believed existed.

She waved the paper. "This will be the end of me."

"It's the truth," Pok said. "Everybody wins. Everybody loses."

"The Grips is winning." Dr. Verik looked over him with fresh, horrified eyes. Her trembling hand went to her mouth. "This is exactly what I wanted to avoid. Your body isn't the answer."

"But it is," Pok said. "I cured someone. My body cured someone."

"I tested out the antibodies you produced the night Jillian died. It treated the disorder, but like CBH, like FLT, it was only temporary. You could make more, but pushing you would only put you at risk. I don't need an examination to know your vitals are all over the place. Your sclera are tinged yellow; you're likely in fulminant liver failure. You went too far. You should have let it go."

Dr. Verik stood, wiped her face, and said in an even, level tone, "I promised my father I'd take care of Julian, and I failed. I promised Julian I'd take care of Odysseus, and I failed. I guess it's a good thing I never got a chance to make the same promise to Phelando."

"You're right. My body isn't the answer. Only part of it." Pok had waited to say this last piece. He wanted them both to be clear, to hear it fully. "If Odysseus could create Agrypnia from his DNA, he can create an antidote from mine. A sustainable cure."

"Hippocrates is done. If Agrypnia doesn't ruin us, our geography will. Laurice is a category five. What reason would he have to create a cure now?"

"I can convince him."

Dr. Verik laughed. Then she looked at him. Her face sobered. "How?"

"Easy. Give him what he wants."

Sixty-One

EXODUS

Frank Benford hardly looked up from the *Second Opinion* as Dr. Verik and Pok approached his parked ambulance in the HemoStat's loading bay. Protected from the rain, he had a lazy, unexpecting demeanor: many with Agrypnia chose to die at home rather than in an overrun hospital at the height of a hurricane.

"No turning back now," Dr. Verik said, more to herself than to Pok. After she'd initially scoffed at his plan, a fire rose in her that made Pok a little uneasy. As if it had sparked a long-hidden childhood giddy ambition. She jogged a bit ahead, the floodwaters rising above her ankles. "Frank! I need a run out to MouseKill."

Frank was skinny with a long, braided beard and soft eyes. He instantly transitioned from a laid-back, relaxed position to one of action. That motivation fizzled at the sight of Pok. His wide-eyed gaze went from him to Dr. Verik and back down to the *Second Opinion*. "I don't want any part of this."

"He's sick with the Grips," Dr. Verik said.

Frank shook the paper. "And who's to blame? Is he really your son?"

"Yes, and the dean is my sister. We're all a big, happy family. We need to get to MouseKill."

"Have you seen the weather? Anyone on that road has a death wish."

"That's why I'm asking a professional. Can you help us or not?"

Frank cursed. He mumbled something that sounded a lot like wondering aloud why the hell hadn't he called out sick today.

Dr. Verik closed the gap between her and Frank. "He's my son, Frank. They won't treat him here and they won't let him leave the city. MouseKill is my only hope. Help me out."

A pause. Tension touched the air. Then, "Load him in the back. If they stop us at the gates, I can't help you."

The pulled out into deafening rain that pelted the ambulance from all sides and rumbled down University. The clink of emergency equipment shifting at the uneven road competed with the thrash of tropical winds. A small window cut into the side of the cab gave Pok a glimpse of Hurricane Laurice. Every tree they passed seemed to be reaching out to a desperate lover. He sat up when he saw the tip of a spire pierce the sky. They were at the city's edge. Voices, yelling over the rain and wind, drifted back to the cab.

"Are you crazy, out in this storm?"

"I've got a patient in MouseKill," Frank yelled. "It's life or death."

"Ride it out there if you can. This is just going to get worse!"

Everyone's putting themselves on the line.

Pok jerked his head, toward the window, as that's the only place a voice could have come from. Only the spire; he was alone.

The ambulance slowly started up again and gained speed. Wind rattled the cab from both sides; more than once Pok thought they would tip over.

Then, suddenly, they stopped. Outside, the rain passed in horizontal waves, like a marching shadow army. The cabin doors sprang open; an instant sheet of rain extended from the roof of the ambulance. Both Dr. Verik and Frank helped Pok out. He was instantly soaked. Wind whipped his eyes shut. The soggy ground made standing difficult. Pok tried to get his bearings. There were no spires, no farmhouses, no crops. Just a long, curving road cutting through a wood of tall, wind-stretched trees. Parked on the side of the road, just a few feet away, was a small, gray pickup truck with only two doors and a black, flapping tarp covering the bed.

"Where are you really taking him?" Frank yelled as they helped Pok into the back of the truck.

"It's best you don't know," Dr. Verik said.

Frank, clutching his hat lest it fly away, hesitated, cursed, and then ran back to the ambulance.

"It's a long way to New York," Dr. Verik said from the front seat. The engine sputtered, coughed, and then rumbled to weak life. "Are you good?"

Pok wasn't. He nodded anyway.

"This should hold you through the trip." Dr. Verik slipped Pok a bag. "If your plan works, you may not see me for a while. I'm sorry. For everything."

After taking the Synth, Pok gladly lay under the cover and focused on his breathing. The voices had intensified since leaving New Orleans. They told him his organs were in fulminant failure. That he was going to die by either cardiac arrest or drowning. That his plan meant nothing. *Breathe.* He could keep a lid on reality if he just focused on his breathing.

As the Synth did its work, Pok felt light. Weightless. Minutes became hours. Hours became minutes. The world's light brightened, then dimmed, then brightened again. He rose through the heat, the Agrypnia, the death, and the guilt, and bathed in the flavor of the wind.

He went up and up and up and then found bliss.

Sixty-Two

ODYSSEUS SHEPHERD

Beep . . . beep . . . beep . . .

"It's too early, Kai." Pok tried to turn from the alarm, but the bedsheets caught on his shoulder. His companion would handle it. Sleep dragged him back into the depths, back to a place free of thoughts, sounds, and pain.

An itching, deep in his arm. Pok moved to scratch and couldn't. Something other than sheets kept him in place. His wrists were strapped to a bed. He tugged once. The straps tightened around his skin. An IV steadily dripped clear fluids into his arm.

He was in a hospital. Hippocrates? No. Instead of the scuff of foam clogs across linoleum, the constant passing of verbal information from human to human, and the blur of busy bodies, there was only the hum of automation. He was back among the machines.

Memories came, one by one, flying through him like his and Jillian's train through the countryside. He relived every sensation, heard every word, knew every emotion.

He should be dead. Agrypnia had led to multiple organ failure. Had they cut him open? Was he still human inside?

"You're not dead."

He turned toward the voice. Sunlight (where was the rain? Was the storm over?) angled as early evening pressed against the raised curtain surrounding his bed. Odysseus sat by the bedside.

"You were yanking out your IV," Odysseus said. The wire cuffs suddenly loosened and dissolved into his skin, freeing Pok. "There. Better?"

Pok rubbed his wrists and then his eyes. Any suspicion of illusion or hologram was silenced. Odysseus was thick and full, his tan skin textured and without any visible filter or makeup. Craters covered the cheek facing Pok. One eyelid hung lower than the other. His breath came heavy, stilted, and rattled. The leader of the Shepherd Organization looked deathly ill. His demeanor remained calm and familiar.

"Did you get what you wanted?" Pok said.

"No need." Odysseus's lips didn't move; the sound came from elsewhere. "Hurricane Laurice flooded the Vault. Pity. All that information. All that history."

"The spires are back up?" Pok said.

"That was the price for you, yes. But too little, too late. Aunt Emily has always been weak. Just like your father."

Emotions roiled. Pok kept them down. He'd expected provocation. "She saved me."

"We saved you. You're only alive because of modern medicine."

"There's a cure, then?" Pok said.

The air shifted, as if Odysseus had waved a dismissive hand, though he stayed stone-still. "It's too late for a half-assed cure, cousin. We've run simulations. Any intervention now would only prolong the epidemic. At the rate Agrypnia is evolving, it will inevitably become airborne unless it's allowed to run its course. Our priority now is making sure it doesn't spread outside the city."

"You're going to let them all die."

"I didn't make that decision. The Council did. My generosity let this experiment go on for long enough." He actually sounded like he believed in his philanthropy. What skill. "This is a blessing in disguise. The lives saved, the future we can now have, far outweigh those who will die. Have died."

The metallic piece supporting Odysseus's head bent forward so he could look down at himself, as if noticing his condition for the first time. He shifted to leave. Pok grabbed his arm. Not the robotic one but his flesh. It was surprisingly warm.

"Do you want to hear the rumors they tell about you? In New Orleans?"

Odysseus perked at this. Amusement pulled at his lips. New Orleans remained an unknown. A curiosity.

"They say that you're more machine than man. That the shepherds made you."

Odysseus laughed. It was a high-pitched thing, something that explained why the mogul used a filter for more than just appearance.

"That's disappointing. I expected NOLA to be more original."

Pok went on, "I know it's not true. You can't be part of the shepherds."

Odysseus's smile wavered. One mobile eye twitched. "And why's that?"

"Because you're still in the dark. You don't know what you want and what they need, where one stops and the other begins. Who's really in charge?"

Rage filled the room, followed quickly by excruciating pain. Behind Odysseus, the screen showing Pok's vitals flickered alarm. His heart rate shot up; his blood pressure ascended into the red. Then the bottom fell out.

"Do you feel that? I can. Your heart is slowing. Your breathing, too. If I think you dead, you are."

Pok straddled the edge of darkness. In the shadows he could see his father and his mother—Khaliah, the mother in the pictures, the mother he'd grown up believing in—waiting for him, beckoning him to a final, true home. Just as Pok stepped toward them, Odysseus released his hold.

"I promised Aunt Emily I'd take care of you, just like your father took care of me. Stay quiet. Stay invisible. Do that and I'll let you live out your meaningless little life."

"Just give me one thing," Pok said when he'd regained enough breath to speak.

"What?"

"My dad's Memorandium."

Odysseus left him without answering, alone with his thoughts.

Sixty-Three

ZION

Pok was discharged from MacArthur Hospital two days later.

He walked the short distance to where he used to call home. As he waited for the light at a busy intersection, he was presented with a shimmering and crisp bus stop ad for a popular beer brand. How did the shepherds see him now? Searching himself, Pok found he didn't care.

He came to his old block and saw that Park Avenue Market, the shop right beneath his and his father's apartment, was boarded up. A weatherworn sign hung from the front door that said, THANKS FOR ALL THE GOOD TIMES.—SKIP JAMES

Pok entered the building. Inside, a freshly renovated elevator waited with open doors. The interior was new and shiny, and promised an inherent reliability that hadn't been there all of Pok's life. He took the stairs.

The fingerprint reader on their unit's door still worked. Pok stood in the doorway for several minutes. The dwelling looked the same, as if he had stepped back through time, told the gypsy cab to turn around because it had all been a prank, and returned that same night to hopefully have tea ready before his father arrived home. But that was an illusion. Even if everything was the same, everything had changed.

He stepped inside and looked around. There was no sign that anyone had lived here in the last year. Even more, there were no cobwebs, no shadows of neglect. The air conditioner at the end of the hall had been replaced. Pok turned it on; it sputtered to life.

He found Phelando's Memorandium on the kitchen counter. He opened the unit and popped the insert out. After carefully placing his father's ring back in the engraved box, Pok slipped in Julian Shepherd's—gruesomely recovered by Kris from the Vault—and turned it on.

At first, nothing. Then, a vibration. Instead of a clear half-bodied hologram projecting straight up from the Memorandium, a man, younger than expected, appeared fully formed. The Memorandium system had upgraded. Julian's projection wore a tight sweater, faded jeans, and loosely tied sneakers. It didn't look around. It didn't adjust its eyes, wince, or morph from confusion to understanding. There was only robotic stoicism. What had Pok expected? Something more?

The Memorandium spoke. "Connect me to Zion."

Pok's heart sank. "Aren't you Zion?"

"Connect me to Kai."

This was a surprise. Kai rested in a far-off corner, right where Pok had left it. He examined the rolled-up ball that used to be his companion. The sleek design gave the illusion of a whole organism. He found the opening under its synthetic fur and hooked Kai up to his uncle's Memorandium. The charging panel blazed green.

"Pok," Julian said. His eyes had come alive.

Pok stood. "You know me?"

"I was there when you were born." Julian looked over him. "You're fully grown now."

Pok walked around the projection. He reached out to touch it and recoiled when his hand pierced the light. "Are you conscious?"

"I don't know." Julian laughed. "Uncertainty suggests that maybe I am."

Kai, still beside the Memorandium, uncurled and looked up at Pok. The animal face reflected what he saw in Julian's Memorandium: a sorrowful patience.

"Kai was Zion?" Pok said. "All this time?"

"Kai is the hardware. Any Memorandium is the software."

"And Odysseus doesn't know?"

"He believes it was hidden in Hippocrates," Zion said in Julian's voice.

"If not there, then destroyed. Your father thought it would be best to hide Zion in plain sight, as the phrase goes. Where is Phelando?"

"Dead." Pok didn't want to rehash his father's death. That wasn't the purpose of the moment. "What is Zion?"

"I am the next step for the shepherds when the world is ready for me. Odysseus has made sure that time is not now. If he figures out how to make his shepherds self-aware, gives them free will, then neither he nor the shepherds will be governed by the rules I set into place twenty years ago. Phelando was smart to keep it from him."

"He made a deadly disease from his own DNA and set it on New Orleans." Pok told Zion about his time in Hippocrates, treating the Grips with Dr. Verik, and his own journey with Agrypnia. "Many people died."

Julian nodded throughout the telling. "He's always had so much anger. I understood it; I just wish I could help it. He keeps you close. You must give him hope."

"Hope?" Pok said.

"To be free from the shepherds. He's been dependent on technology his whole life."

"Dr. Verik said my DNA is an enantiomer to his. An antidote. Could you use it to manufacture a cure for Agrypnia?"

"It's a plausible theory and an apt conclusion," Julian said. "I could run a simulation comparing your genome and their corresponding proteins to his. The type I was designed for."

"We need a sample from Odysseus."

Julian smiled. "I have his whole genome sequenced. I do not have yours."

"My father was careful in keeping it safe," Pok said. "I uploaded it as part of my application, which set off this whole mess. Odysseus and the shepherds should have it."

"He likely destroyed it," Julian said.

"I can draw my own sample," Pok said. He retrieved his phlebotomy kits from his backpack, which had survived the journey, and a few minutes later fed a few drops into Kai's analytic panel.

Julian seemed to swell in size as it accepted the new data.

"I have run the simulation," the advanced Memorandium said. "From a multitude of possibilities, I have manufactured a signal that will make the offending pathogen responsible for Agrypnia inert."

"How do we get it to New Orleans?" Pok said.

"We upload it to the shepherds."

Pok didn't understand. Why would they give this development *to* Odysseus? He said as much.

"When I started the Shepherd Organization I put in a 'do no harm' clause, that if the algorithm ever saw a path of best outcomes, it could not be overridden to do harm. New Orleans is sentenced to die because the shepherd system is working with a calculation where a fast and definitive cure is not possible. This changes that. Once the shepherd algorithms see a cure, they will be forced to administer it, regardless of Odysseus's—or anyone's—wishes."

Julian hummed and for a moment it looked like he was meditating.

"A cure is the secondary result."

"What's the primary?" Pok said.

Julian's likeness paused, as if considering whether to say more. "This is a deadly disease; deadlier than even Odysseus anticipated. I'm already running simulations. They show that if there's any left, reemergence as a deadly global pandemic is inevitable. The shepherds don't know that Odysseus's genome is the foundation. He would have kept that well-hidden. Our analysis will enlighten the system. My shepherds' priority is to 'first, do no harm.' That means eliminating the disease's source."

"Odysseus," Pok said.

"Specifically, his genome, yes. Only part of it."

"Does he need that part to live?"

"It spans critical functions," Julian said. "Further than technology can attain for. Deploying this will surely kill him. We will have to decide."

"Your call," Pok said.

Julian looked almost surprised. Almost. This was just a machine. The decision *was* Pok's. They both knew that. But Pok wanted Julian's likeness to come to the conclusion. To weigh the price of his son.

"Connect me to the Source, and I'll do the rest."

In his room, Pok booted up *Impact* and fell into the game's rhythm like he'd last played yesterday. In a few short minutes, Pok's avatar stood outside the Underground Web. Its bright room with infinite rows of computers beckoned.

"The Source is through there," Pok said. "I've never ventured that far."

"I was designed to be a pioneer," Zion said. "I'll go from here."

Zion in Julian's form stepped seamlessly into the game world and, without pause, walked into the Underground. He stopped at the very first computer; its screen instantly acknowledged his presence. The game's foundation shook, making Pok's fingers tingle. Julian closed his eyes briefly—maybe half a second—and when he reopened them he regarded Pok with full sobriety.

"It is done," Julian said.

"Already?" Pok said.

"The signal was deployed globally. It is similar to the one Odysseus used to activate the Agrypnia proteins, only this one will make them inert. Those who can recover, will."

"And Odysseus?" Pok said, loosely aware he was asking the same question again.

"The signal will destroy his genome." Julian closed his eyes. Pok thought he saw a tear fall, but it must have been imagination. "Can I leave to be with him?"

"Take your time."

Julian disappeared through the computer's screen, into the Source. A second of silence preceded *Impact*'s world shattering around Pok. His virtual gaming display flashed a violent red, forcing the headset off. He'd been booted from the network. But Julian—Zion—was already well on his way.

Pok was back standing in his room. Beside him, Julian's Memorandium had shut down; the light in Kai's eyes dimmed. Pok was once again alone. He moved his VR set from his bed to a far corner and cracked open his father's *Principles*. He turned to a random page, nothing specific, only wanting to see the familiar handwriting, to hear his dad's voice in his head.

Sixty-Four

OBITUARY

Shepherd CEO Dies at 35

Odysseus J. Shepherd, the outspoken CEO of the Shepherd Organization, died Thursday in his home, surrounded by loved ones. The cause of death has not been reported. He was thirty-five.

Dr. Emily Verik, former associate professor of neurology at Hippocrates Medical Center in New Orleans, Louisiana, and sister of the late TSO founder, Julian Shepherd, will assume her position immediately as the new head of the global AI program. Not much is known about the physician, who was not previously recognized as part of the Shepherd family.

"I vow to continue my brother's original vision for the Shepherd Organization. He believed in collaboration, not division. There are many wounds to heal in the medical community, and I look forward to leading the charge."

The development comes at the end of the investigation into the embattled hospital. A mysterious illness recently fell upon the city of New Orleans and seems to have disappeared as quickly as it appeared. The state ruled that, given no further existential threat, New Orleans can continue to operate semi-independently, which includes its non-TSO technology, the only hospital of its kind left in the country. The investigation's temporary shutdown of the New Orleans spires is credited for the worst flooding the city has seen in over a decade, with damages estimated in the billions. There were no reported casualties.

When asked about her former employer's return to unorthodox ways of practicing medicine, Dr. Verik offered unwavering support.

"I have a lot of respect for Hippocrates and what they stand for. The Shepherd Organization has no plans to force acquisition at this time. I look forward to more conversation in the future."

The new Shepherd CEO is already embracing some of the methodologies around medicine her predecessor rejected. She has already launched, for example, a research and development sector to incorporate the divisive concept of "essence" into the ubiquitous algorithms. The endeavor is heavily influenced by the work of the controversial Cameron Dryden and, more recently, Dr. Phelando Morning, who dedicated his life to defining "essence" before his sudden death last year. This, Dr. Verik says, will be the next step in AI evolution to ensure optimal outcomes.

The *Smoking Gun* reached out to Hippocrates leadership and has yet to hear back.

This article was written by TSO AI and proofread by a human journalist.

SUMMER

"And whatsoever I shall see or hear in the course of my profession, as well as outside my profession in my intercourse with men, if it be what should not be published abroad, I will never divulge, holding such things to be holy secrets . . ."

Sixty-Five

THE MEMORANDIUM

Pok squinted against the day as he stepped out onto Park Avenue. Instead of the expected chilled cloud cover, full sun beamed down between the city buildings. Scooters and digital delivery vehicles zipped up and down the street, narrowly missing several collisions. Physical mailboxes were few and far between; he had to walk several blocks to find one.

He heard the voice, strong in his ear. He turned toward it, hand poised on the mailbox lid; across the street, MacArthur Hospital rose high into the sky, a shadow over the city it purported to treat. Would the hallucinations ever go away? Pok doubted it. The illness had changed him. He didn't know anyone who'd gotten as far into the Grips and survived.

Pok double-checked the address on his envelope, deposited his paper application, and went back home.

Julian's Zion awaited Pok back in his apartment. The Memorandium stood just inside the hallway.

"You did good," Julian's likeness said. The voice was older than before. Quieter.

"Did he go peacefully?" Pok said.

"No. But I didn't expect him to. It's time for me to go. This is all I was meant to do. One last thing. Like the cure that came from your body, Zion was made from me. But not only for me. I can be connected to others."

This said, Zion powered itself down, leaving Pok to his thoughts. He went to the kitchen, filled the teapot, and set the water to boil. He pulled down his father's favorite mug and ran his fingers over the design's grooves. He'd always thought of Dr. Mouse as brave, defiant even. But now, looking upon the anthropomorphic eyes, the slant of the serious lips, Pok saw an inherent fear he hadn't been ready to notice before. The character was inspiring not because it was without doubt but because it had overcome it.

Kai is the hardware. Any Memorandium is the software.

Julian's parting words haunted him. Phelando had died alone in a hospital while, a few blocks away, his only son was busy trying to impress an institution that wanted him dead. Could Pok face that guilt? He circled the dormant Kai, debating, but knew there was no debate. If he had a chance to see him again . . .

Pok took out Julian's ring and put in his father's. Phelando's Memorandium came online as Pok attended to the teapot that had just begun to whistle.

"Pok."

He'd dreamed of his father's voice for almost a year. The songs he'd sing to Pok as a kid. The comforting tone he took with patients. The curiosity he always had for his son. He'd even hallucinated it in the past few weeks, a whisper on his ear. Pok hung a tea bag in Phelando's Dr. Mouse mug and poured hot water over it.

The voice came again. "You aren't imagining me, son."

Pok turned around; his father's Memorandium sat at the kitchen table. Phelando—his father—looked the same as the program that had delivered the scripted message a year before. The static lining the edge. The perfectly clear skin. The youth-fired eyes from a time preceding Pok but still reminiscent of childhood.

And yet this program was undeniably different. The smile. The slight movement. The shift in the room. The *space* the Memorandium now took up that wasn't there before. It felt like his father was back home.

"I'm not your father," Zion said. And he looked genuinely sad to give this news. "But I know what he would say. And I know he would be so happy to see you. Did you make it to Hippocrates?"

"I did. I failed."

"I highly doubt that."

"I'm sorry I didn't make it to the hospital," Pok said. "I'm sorry for the things I said."

"Phelando knew you loved him. Nothing could change that."

His father's image stood. This simple movement now held weight and meaning. Whereas before the Memorandium would sort of float, his feet connected with the floor.

"You cut your hair," Zion said. "It's growing back. I think it's long enough to loc."

Pok's hand went to his head. "Can you do it?"

Zion held up its holographic hands. Pok felt stupid. Part of the illusion fell away.

"I can't," Zion said. "But I can guide you."

Pok found all the materials needed in Phelando's room. He sat on the floor with his back against the couch. Zion sat behind him. As Pok maneuvered with a mirror, his father's likeness guided him on how to part, hydrate, and comb-twist his hair.

"Did you ever consider telling me about my mother?" Pok said after much consideration. "My real mother?"

"Many times," Zion said. "I didn't think it would be fair to either of you. She made the decision that was hers to make, but the law prevented it from being carried out. So she gave Phelando the greatest gift he ever received. His gift to her, in turn, was to fully receive it."

"I grew up without a mother. She chose that."

"The cancer that took Khaliah was the reason for that, not Emily. I don't expect you to forgive her, but I do ask that you understand." Zion sat back. "I think we're done. How do you like it?"

Pok looked over the result. Far from what he was used to, this was a fresh start, both a new beginning and a reminder of what he'd left behind.

"You're almost as good a teacher as he was." Pok put the mirror aside. "I have a question."

"Anything," Zion said. "And I'll try to answer."

"What does *NFTF* mean?"

Phelando—Kai—Zion—smiled. As soon as he began, the acronym clicked into place for Pok, finally satisfying a yearlong feeling of having something just on the edge of his tongue but inaccessible. They said it in unison.

"'Not for the faint.'"

"Your father's favorite phrase," Zion said.

Dr. Emily Verik, sitting CEO of the Shepherd Organization and dean of medical education at the Shepherd School of Medicine at MacArthur Hospital, sat waiting in Central Park's East Meadow. It was early morning; the dawning sun was just starting to breach the skyline. Pok slid onto the bench opposite her, where the hospital's far-reaching shadow still crawled along the edge. Dr. Verik turned to receive him; the sun reflected off her black-rimmed glass.

She looked him up and down through her newly augmented reality. She wouldn't get much; he'd used little tech since returning to New York. Any helpful insights would be expired.

"Thank you for agreeing to see me," Dr. Verik said. "I thought you'd be wearing glass."

"I thought you wouldn't," he said.

"It's my job now. It's fascinating tech. There's a lot of potential."

Pok remembered his father's (Zion's) words. He considered if what he was about to say was true and decided it was. "I understand why you gave me up. I don't understand, though, why you work for the shepherds now."

"I saw this company at its inception, when it was full of hope. Julian and I always had the same vision of the future. There's still time to restore it. A future that's free and collaborative." Dr. Verik removed her glass. Behind them, her eyes had aged. "We still have space for you, Pok."

Pok had been offered that before. "I'm waiting for another decision."

"Your father's son. Brandy is sympathetic, but it would ultimately be up to the Council. They may not be as forgiving."

The sun touched Pok with its warmth. He squinted against it as a lone honeybee circled his head, curious, and then flitted away.

"Hippocrates and the shepherds started at peace," he said. "And then one got in the way. Odysseus's war is over. But you're ambitious. Which is why I exist." Pok forced himself to lock eyes with his former sponsor. "What if Hippocrates gets in the way again?"

Dr. Verik slipped back on her glass. "It was good seeing you, Student Doctor Morning. I'm glad you're well."

She extended her hand. Old instincts pushed Pok to pinch her cuff, but she wore a short-sleeved blouse. Her intention, from the prime of her fingers, was to bestow honor upon him. Pok let her.

And then, just like that, she was gone.

Pok was rereading one of Shaliyah's poems when the decision from Hippocrates Medical College came in the form of a glass communication request. For the first time in weeks, Pok put on his augmented reality and accepted. Static lines scrolled down an invisible box. The image materialized as crackles of audio strung together. The face looking out at him squinted, grimaced, and said something to someone behind her.

"Is it on?" Dean Sims said. "I can't see anything."

A flicker; the feed smoothened. A fully realized hologram showed the dean from the shoulders up. Pok tapped his thigh. This was it. What he'd been waiting for.

"Where are you broadcasting from?" Pok said.

"MouseKill. The spires are back up and functioning. Which we can thank you for. Which is also why I was very surprised to receive your application. I thought the plan was for you to be at MacArthur with—"

"I'm not," Pok said. "I don't mean to cut you off but I have no desire to be anywhere else. I want to learn real medicine."

"I see. Your essay was very moving."

"I meant all of it," Pok said. "I made a lot of mistakes in New Orleans."

"And you did a lot of good," Dean Sims said. Her eyes glistened. "We want you back. Second year starts soon."

Pok stuttered, swallowed, and started again. "And the Council?"

Dean Sims smiled. Not a doctor's smile or a professor's smile or a stressed smile, the ones she wore solely for the benefit of others. This one came from within. Pok's heart softened.

"There is unanimous clearance for your return and immediate rematriculation into the medical college. Do you accept?"

Since being back in New York, Hippocrates—with all its flaws, its imperfections, its troubles—had felt like a fairy tale. His fairy tale, a place he could partly return to in cherished memories, a home that couldn't hurt him the way homes had in the past. Dean Sims was asking him to make it real again.

He let it be real. In his mind, in that moment. And he smiled.

"I'll take that as a yes," Dean Sims said.

"I think I'll buy a plane ticket this time."

"Good call. I hear they're a lot faster than trains. Welcome back, Student Doctor Morning."

"Wait. Can I bring someone?"

Dean Sims, who had done so well, finally let her patience crack. "We're very slowly opening the city back up to outsiders. And you don't have the best track record with guests. Who do you have in mind?"

"Kai," Pok said. "Zion."

FALL

"Now if I carry out this oath, and break it not, may I gain for ever reputation among all men for my life and for my art; but if I break it and forswear myself, may the opposite befall me."

Sixty-Six

HOME

Shaliyah stood at the clinic door, peering out into Canal Street. The sun's angle lit the air above her, bathing her face in an orange glow, making her skin amber. Her hair had grown; dark roots overshadowed newly colored streaks. She'd facilitated nearly a hundred patient visits that day at the Stork's Nest, the new family planning clinic. Staffed by Hippocrates personnel, it gave direct access to the New Orleans residents least likely to make the trek to the Hill.

His last patient checked out, Pok had just finished his notes. Second-year medical students chose three sites for outpatient rotations. He'd picked at least one of them because of who would be working the front desk.

Seeing her now, standing there in the empty waiting room, he smelled strawberry. It was pleasant, not intrusive, coming from a place deep in his memory banks.

"You were waiting for me?" Pok said.

She smiled against the sun's rays and shook her head. "Still cocky, I see. Don't push it. Maybe I wanted to hear about your travels."

She pulled open the door. They stepped through. Summer's haze was just beginning to lift; Shaliyah wrapped her arms around herself against the beginning of autumn. Each year promised a colder winter than the last, something to which New Orleans was still acclimating. Until then, this was a welcome in-between. She nodded across the street toward the Fatty Liver.

"You eaten yet?" she said.

"No," Pok said. "I totally forgot." And he liked it that way.

ACKNOWLEDGMENTS

What a journey! When I first sat down to write about Pok, Hippocrates, and the shepherds in the summer of 2014 after my first year of medical school, I couldn't have predicted that this is where we'd end up. Countless drafts, humbling revisions, and dizzying set changes later and my tribe has been with me every step of the way.

I am forever grateful to my wife, Johanna, for the years of support, feedback, and endless ideas. You are and always have been my rock. Any and all success, I share with you. I love you. I thank you. We did it!

To my mother, Pamela Hairston, who gave me my love for reading and passed down her skills with the pen. Thank you for everything. Thank you to my stepfather, Adrian, for being a dedicated reader.

To Marcus McLaughlin, my long-time first reader. You've surely read this book more times than anyone. You've been an amazing friend and a staple in my writing career. To Justin Turner, thank you for your pep talks and willingness to consult on all things New Orleans. Reader, if I got anything wrong about his legendary hometown, blame him (I kid!). To John Camden Dryden, thank you for the late night talks about AI and letting me use your middle name for a fictional scientist who's only half as smart as you are. To Obinna and Xuan and Ryan, thank you for working in tech and letting me soak in your conversations. To Warren and Jared, thank you for always passing along my work and always picking up the phone. To Robert James Watkins, thank you for your friendship. It has greatly enriched my life.

Thank you to Sarah Ried who believed in me enough to take a chance on this book and change my life by inviting me into the HarperCollins family. To Noah Eaker, my brilliant editor, who asked the hard, necessary questions. You pushed me to make this book its best self. Thank you for showing up as a real person and building the trust. To my agent, Adam Eaglin, thank you for thinking deeply about the world, its characters and themes, and for being patient and kind as I navigated the transition from short story writer to novelist. To Howie, agent turned friend, thank you for your endless enthusiasm, abundant connections, wise advice, and for being an overall amazing human. To Ryan Wilson and the Anonymous Content team, let's make a movie! Thank you for giving me the confidence to say that.

A special thanks to C. C. Finlay for your insight and direction. You taught me a lot about story and narrative, and this book is better for it.

Thank you to my entire Clarion West class for teaching me how to be a better writer. Special thanks to Rebecca Campbell, Tegan Moore, and Christine Neulieb for reading multiple drafts and helping contain a hopeful writer's anxiety throughout this entire process. And to Nibedita Sen for reading back when this was a novella and to Margaret Killjoy for sharing your expertise on riding the rails.

Thank you to S. B. Divya for the monthly chats where you provided guidance, insights, and friendship. Thank you to Maurice Broaddus, Sam Miller, and Rebecca Roanhorse for your guidance and mentorship.

Jacob Appel, thank you for showing me that a writer can also be a psychiatrist (and a lawyer, but I don't think I'll follow your lead on that one) and for being such a champion of my story in its early stages.

To Diana Pho for encouraging me to make this into something bigger and cultivating me as a young writer.

Thank you to Rachel Jones, Evelyn Nelson, Allison Oesterle, Ted Hayden, Ann Crawford-Roberts, Jason Salim, Michael Mensah, and to all my other friends and family who have read and commented and encouraged along the way.

Thank you to the 2014 members of Tabula Rasa (the late and great Richard Bowes, Jennifer Marie Brissett, Barbara Krasnoff, Terry McGarry, Terence Taylor, and Sabrina Vourvoulias) for critiquing this when it was just a short story. And then the 2016 TR members (adding Randee Dawn,

Jim Ryan, and Scott Lee Williams) and finally the 2017 crew (Sally Wiener Grotta has entered the chat). This group welcomed me into the speculative community. I enjoyed it so much I decided to stick around.

To Lydia Weaver for thorough copyediting, Edie Astley for seeing me through two books, and the rest of the HarperCollins team for their care with my words, I thank you.

My lifelong dream has been to become a published novelist and there's no way I could have done any of this alone. My heart is full of gratitude.

ABOUT THE AUTHOR

JUSTIN C. KEY is a practicing psychiatrist and speculative fiction writer whose stories have appeared in the *Magazine of Fantasy & Science Fiction*, *Strange Horizons*, *Escape Pod*, and *Lightspeed*, and on Tor.com. He received a BA in biology from Stanford University and completed his residency in psychiatry at UCLA. He lives in Los Angeles with his wife and three children.